The Advent of the King

The Selkie Trilogy, Book 3

Mara Li

The Voice of the Sea

published by

Dutch Venture Publishing

Copyright © 2024 Dutch Venture Publishing

Author: Mara Li (pseudonym of Marieke Veringa)

Cover design: Marieke Veringa

Text editor: Genta Tanjung

All rights reserved. No part of this publication may be reproduced and/or published by means of print, photocopy, microfilm or any other method, whether electronic, mechanical, by way of photocopying, recording or any other means, without the prior written consent of the publisher.

PROLOGUE

*"**Y**ou know the story of the White Prophet. There is another one you need to hear.*
Do not run away from me.
I know you can hear me."

1

DEPARTURE

One of the shutters is ajar to allow some air into the musty bedroom. I look through the window and see the sun, gradually smothered by clouds. A strand of shells strung together, taps quietly against the glass. The deep and even sound of Arthur's breathing has not changed in the past several days.

Every day, I sit by his bedside and nothing ever changes, except the sunlight that enters the room. Today, I have averted my gaze away from him and I'm standing in front of the window.

I can see the island. The horizon seems very near, just beyond the edge of the village. Nearby, I can see the apple trees swaying in the rough winds. I hear my mother and Ana talking to each other downstairs, and a moment later I hear shutters being closed forcefully.

A storm is coming. The signs have become quite familiar to me. My skin starts to tingle and the smell of iron drifts on the wind. The entire village braces for impact as huge thunderclouds gradually gather over Avalon.

Yet my thoughts do not linger on the increasing winds or on the sea fiercely trashing its waves against the cliffs. I'm thinking about the ambiguous dream I had last night and the voice that was calling me. The moment I opened my eyes, I could still hear the sound echoing in my ears and I felt shivers running down my spine. Now I cannot remember whose voice it was.

I turn to Arthur and look at him. *"Was it you?"*

No reaction – he only gives me silence.

I let out a deep sigh and put my hand on his. It feels cold. Not as cold as the hand of a corpse, but also nearly not as warm as the hand of a healthy boy.

"I want you to come back, Arthur," I say to him. "I want the spirits to let you go."

2

"He's not our prisoner."

The voice is neither Rona's nor Ana's. I jump out of my chair with my heart pounding as I catch a glimpse of a creature by Arthur's bed.

The wolf's fur is as white as snow and her eyes are like ice. Her paws make no sound as she moves.

"Your brother has willingly gone to the other side. He's carrying out his duties, as commanded by the Fisher King."

It is not my first encounter with a creature from the Other World. Still, I'm struggling to keep my nerves under control. "Why are you here? Is something wrong with Arthur?"

"I'm here to talk to you. Do you have any idea who I am?"

I shake my head.

"You have heard of me, Nimue. I am the White Wolf from ancient times long gone by. I raised the first White Prophet, when the world was just a vast wasteland. I called him my son and he called me his mother."

I remember that story, just like the voice in my dream told me I would. Many weeks ago, on a dark winter afternoon in the Ark, Will told us the story of the White Prophet: a baby who was left by his parents to die in the forest. His parents took care of his healthy twin brother, but believed the pale and ill child would die within a day. Instead, a white she-wolf had crept out from among the trees to take the child under her wing. When the boy had grown up, he returned to the human world and begged his family to stop destroying the forest. He was cast out and exiled once again. According to Will, that was how the White Prophet came to be: a mortal man living on the edge, that boundary between the human world and the wilderness. Not a spirit, but not fully human either. A vengeful creature of the wilderness, or a bridge builder... Will wasn't entirely clear about that.

My hands are sweaty. I look at the wolf. "I thought that was just a legend."

"The truth is often disguised as a legend."

"So it was you," I whisper, almost relieved that I solved the riddle. "*You* were the voice in my dream about the White Prophet."

"In your dream?" the wolf repeats. The ears on her large head move backwards and forwards. "If I had the power to visit you in your dreams, I would."

"But I heard a voice," I insist. "Someone spoke of the White Prophet and told me that there's another story I need to hear. If it wasn't you, then who was it?"

"I don't know. Maybe there's another spirit trying to give you the same message. We need the White Prophet again."

"Why have you come to me?" I ask. "I'm not the White Prophet."

"Because, when we let your mother go, you promised us your child. You possess the gift of the selkies and your lover is a shaman. The child that grows within you is a Holy Child. And so we must have it and raise it as I once raised the first prophet. Your child will be the next White Prophet…"

"How can you be so sure of that?" I snarl and wrap my arms protectively around my belly. "Those are just fairy tales and memories from a long time ago. This is just a baby. *My* baby!"

"Did you not hear me? It's a Holy Child. You and your brother have a strong influence on the world, Nimue. Wherever you go, reality changes. As it's the nature of the magic in your blood, and it's the nature of the selkies. And now the White Prophet will return to protect us against the madness and destruction of human works."

"It is the Hunter! He's the one destroying our world! You must know that!"

"I do know that," she says. She sounds sad. "How did you think the curse came to be? All your gases and toxins seeped through the roots of the tree until it became sick. The Hunter didn't always exist, Nimue."

I let out a deep sigh. "I didn't know what I was saying that day on the beach. I was… I was distracted and confused. Please, I'll give you something else. *Anything* else…"

"We don't want anything else, Nimue, daughter of Rona. Only the child. We will come for the baby as soon as it is born, that's why I'm here, to tell you. Alongside the Fisher King, the child will herald in a new era. An era for the spirits. We have suffered long enough at the hands of men."

"But the Fisher King is dying…"

"Thus he must be cured, and your brother must save him. I will see you again, Nimue, at the birth of our prophet." She turns away from me and when she casts me one last glance, her eyes shine like starlight. "Be warned, child of the sea: the Hunter craves your magic. We sense that he's searching for you, in both your world and ours. Never let him steal the secret of the sea. Die for it, if you must. And always be vigilant."

I inhale sharply. Before I can ask another question, she's gone.

"Nimue?"

I whip around. My mother is standing in the doorway, holding a linen basket. "I heard you talking. Is Arthur...?"

I shake my head. Arthur is still asleep.

The spark of hope in her eyes vanishes, but she quickly recovers. She puts the basket down and starts to take Arthur's sheets off. "Are you alright, dear?"

"I had a visitor," I say hoarsely. "A white wolf. She reminded me of the promise I made at the beach."

My mother halts in her movements for a moment. "We won't let that happen."

"What if she's right?' I ask. "What if it's the right thing to do?"

"Sweetheart. Do you really believe that?"

"I don't know what to believe anymore!" I sit down on a stool by the window. "What can I do to keep the baby?"

My mother remains silent for a long time. When I look up, she slowly takes a clean sheet, her lips pressed into a thin line. Her dark eyes are locked on my brother's face.

"Mum?"

"You could run away." My mother drapes the clean sheet over Arthur's body and carefully tucks him in. "This island is a haven for the spirits, it always has been. The Whispering Pool by the beach is one of the rarest crossroads between our worlds. If you stay here, they can easily find you. If you were to flee, they would have to use all their powers to track you down."

"Are you serious?" I ask. "Leaving Avalon? Leaving you and Arthur?"

"We have talked about this before. You promised me you would find the father of your child."

"Yes... When the time is right! Not so soon, not when I just got you back!"

"I believe the spirits are getting weaker every day," Rona says. "The farther you travel from Avalon, the harder it is for them to find you."

"They are desperate! The spirits want to survive, but we need the Other World too."

"Maybe so. But isn't it cruel to take a newborn child away from their mother?" Rona walks up to me and tilts up my face by the chin. "I love you so much. Once, I had to flee just so I could give you and Arthur a chance. Now I think it's best for you to leave this island."

"Mum," I whisper. My throat seems to be shut tight. "I don't want to go."

She kisses me on the forehead. "I know."

Suddenly the rain starts to clatter against the window. I jump up to close the shutter. A moment later, my view of the apple trees is obscured by an immense amount of water pouring down. The sky opens its maw and roars with a furious clap of thunder.

For seven days, Avalon is being lashed by the storm. It feels like a giant is shaking the island. Foaming seawater reaches over the cliffs. A howling wind persistently seeks to find a way through the cracks of Ana's round house. The days are long and dark, almost impossible to distinguish from the nights. The clattering of the rain mingles with the roars of thunder. Sometimes I sit by the flickering fire for hours and listen to the creaking of the shutters and the walls. My heart pounds with every jarring sound. It brings me back to that other stormy night. Arthur is so fast asleep that he doesn't hear a thing.

After the seventh day, we wake up to an unexpected silence. The wind has forced itself to sleep like an angry child. Now a slight mist has settled on the hills and valleys of Avalon, on the beaches and even on the vastness of the sea. Mum's words keep going through my head. I become restless. Every movement in the corner of my eye startles me, afraid that a spirit has come to claim my child.

One morning, I wake up early, with butterflies in my stomach but my head surprisingly clear. I know it's time to make a decision. The sky and the sea have calmed down, but the mist remains still. I slip out of bed and wake up my mother.

"Nimue?" she whispers sleepily.

"I'm leaving today," I whisper back.

Instantly, she is wide awake. She doesn't oppose or try to change my mind. She just wraps her arms around me and holds me for a while. Her warmth and smell, still unfamiliar to me, are like precious discoveries I never thought I'd find again.

"I don't want to leave," I say again, hoarsely.

"But you have to." Rona lets go of me and brushes my curls aside. "Get dressed. We have a lot of preparations to do."

After the sun has past the highest hill of Avalon and slowly begins its journey down towards the bottom of the sea, I quietly enter Arthur's room. I sit down on the edge of his bed and touch his stubbly cheek. For a while I watch his eyelids, with their golden lashes, blinking restlessly a few times. Is he experiencing something on the other side of reality? Or can he somehow feel that I'm saying goodbye to him?

"I won't be gone forever," I promise him softly. "Wait for me, Arthur. I'll wait for you."

He sighs deeply and blinks rapidly again. Then he seems to calm down, as if sinking into a deeper sleep.

"I will come back," I say. "With the father of my child. And once I'm back, we will never be separated again."

I take the leather cord from my neck and lean in. Arthur allows me to slightly lift his head, as if he were a doll. I arrange the necklace neatly around his neck and place the seal pendant on his chest. "Keep this for me. I hope you know we will always be with you, wherever you are."

My mother appears in the doorway, together with Ana. Struggling, I get up from the bed and walk away from Arthur. Mum takes my hand. "The boat is ready."

"I'm scared," I whisper.

"Don't be," my mother tells me. "Be brave and have faith."

"I'll be back," I promise for the third time, clinging to the thought.

Mum squeezes my hand gently. Then she takes me outside, to the small port where *The Herring Gull* is waiting for me.

On the verge of a hazy dawn, I moor *The Herring Gull* in the harbour of Camlann. The mist has settled here too, like a transparent veil that seems to muffle all sounds.

I recall this harbour to be a busy place. I remember teeming docks and crowded warehouses, freighters and hundreds of fishing boats. Now there are fewer boats, and many of them seem to be in a degraded state. The few people I see move differently. They walk hurriedly, without talking to each other, and some of them are boarding up one of the department stores. I just stand there and watch for a while, until someone notices me. I turn around quickly. I don't know whether the owner of *The Herring Gull* is still around, but I don't want to take the risk of being recognised as a thief. Or even worse: to be recognised as myself. Those men from Detection could be anywhere.

I pull the large hood of my new anorak over my head, sling my bags over my shoulder and leave the harbour behind me as I go through narrow, winding alleyways that lead up to the city centre. I notice how many houses are deserted. For a while, I follow a group of people who, like me, trudge on with luggage on their backs. Past the centre, they take a turn in a different direction and suddenly I'm alone again. I pass the last few houses and finally, the street turns into a lonely, little road through barren fields.

It's obvious that something has changed in Central Europe. You can tell from people's faces. You can feel a heavy presence in the misty air. Filled with foreboding, I head off.

2

THE WALLS OF BREVALAER

"Nimue, you can hear me. You can see me. Stay and listen to what I have to say to you. Listen: the sea was silent and unable to move..."

I'm standing in front of a huge creature. It has the body of a man and the antlers of a deer. His voice rumbles against my eardrums. What he has to tell me is vital, but I'm frustrated because I can't find Arthur. After all, Sela promised me that I would see my little brother if I drank from the Whispering Pool...

The man with the antlers extends his arm. He is still talking, but I notice that he's slowly starting to disappear. A moment later, I wake up from my dream.

There is a chilly mist when I wake up.

I haven't been able to properly dry my clothes for days. At the end of each night, I wake up in a world shrouded in wisps of mist.

With a shudder, I sit up straight. No matter how well my clothes protect me from this sharp north-easterly wind, the cold humidity has found a way to my skin. Time to get up. Time to warm up my sore muscles and get moving.

First, I wait for the nausea to fade away.

I comb my hair with my fingers. A few hours before I left, I asked my mother to cut it shorter. She protested, but I insisted. She sighed in defeat as I watched locks of hair fall onto the floor.

My breakfast consists of a piece of stale bread, salty fish, an apple, and a few sips from my water bottle. I eat it while walking. My backpack feels much lighter than a few days ago. I must be getting closer to Brevalaer.

It also means that I'm getting closer to the marshes. I think of Wolf, the father of my child. The last time I saw him, I left him with Will. Will must have returned to the Ark, so that is the first place I want to look.

When Wolf comes to mind, I feel a familiar combination of longing and uncertainty. Is he thinking about me as often as I'm thinking about him? Or was it easy for him to let me go? I'm afraid of how he's going to react when I tell him about our child. He might hug me. He might shake his head. I could not be more nervous.

At noon, the fog has changed into a fine haze. It will probably not fade completely today, but I have gotten used to it. Even with the sun at its peak, the mist sticks to my arms, my face and my legs. It should give me aches, like pins and needles. The falling rain is toxic enough to cause blisters. But this mist does nothing more than block my view and make me uncomfortably clammy. It must be an other-worldly phenomenon, I can feel it in my bones.

Now that my vision is clearer, I look ahead. The road is a straight, long black line running through a hilly landscape, where there are no other settlements: a clear sign that I'm approaching the Periphery.

When I reach the top of a hill, I take a second to catch my breath. I put my hands on my belly, as if to protect the life inside me. I wonder if I will have a son or a daughter. I wonder if it will have red hair, or jet black.

Suddenly, I ask myself why there is a barricade running through the deserted, hilly landscape, from north to south. It looks like the backbone of a gigantic beast, breaking through the horizon. I stare at it with narrowed eyes. A few kilometres further on, there's a railway. I can see the tracks from the hilltop. So far, I haven't seen a single train passing by, even though I have been watching the tracks for days. Now I'm beginning to understand why: the tracks are cut off by a barricade of stone. I expected to be looking at the first houses of Brevalaer by now, but I see a large wall instead.

I rearrange my backpack and descend from the hill. The sun has moved further west by the time I finally find myself facing the city barrier. I stare at it with an open mouth. It is a construction of iron plates and wooden pillars, built on a foundation of stone. Barbed wire and electric cords are meant to deter anyone from attempting to scale it. I don't quite understand what I'm seeing, but it is clear that I won't be able to get into Brevalaer this way. With a sense of foreboding, I start walking along the length of the wall. There must be an entrance somewhere. If only for the transportation of goods. Or has the storm destroyed so much of Central Europe that there is no traffic between Brevalaer and the rest of the continent anymore?

I'm in luck. After about half an hour's walk I reach the train track, and there is a gate with iron doors, large enough for a freight train to pass through. The tracks are flanked by two watchtowers, and I'm being watched from the roof by guards on the parapet.

Or maybe they are just looking at the people gathered at the gate. There might be fifty people, maybe even more. I don't bother to count. They are dressed like me, in anoraks and with protective headgear to protect them against the rain. They seem to be carrying all their household goods with them. I hope they're wearing sturdy footwear for their own sake.

I have noticed more and more people wandering the roads between Camlann and the Periphery. Vagrants. Refugees? I recognise the expression on their faces. I see emptiness in the eyes of people who were somehow spared from a terrible fate, but have lost almost everything.

Carefully, I approach them. The gate is closed and these people are obviously hoping that someone will open it. I wonder how long they've been standing there.

My question is answered by a young woman with broad hips and tousled hair. She wears it even shorter than I do – her brown locks barely cover her ears. There is a three-year-old girl by her side, holding her hand. They share the same brown eyes and the same snub nose. I notice how exhausted they look.

"Would you like some water?" I offer her my bottle, which is almost empty.

The young woman looks at me in despair. "You don't have enough left."

"I have two more bottles in my bag and I can refill them in Brevalaer."

"I don't think we'll be able to get into Brevalaer."

I glance at the wall, tracing its length from left to right, then slowly shift my gaze back to the armed men in front of the entrance. "You mean the gate won't open?"

"We have been waiting here since sunrise."

"I don't understand," I say, confused. "Why won't they let us in?"

"Go ahead and ask them yourself."

I look at her and hesitate. Is it wise to make myself known to those strange, suspicious people in front of the gate? I'd assumed that in Brevalaer I could replenish my provisions and find some shelter in the Ark. I'm exhausted from the long walk. I look at the young woman and her daughter and offer the girl my water bottle again. She eagerly pulls it out of my hand, her little fingers denting the plastic. She reminds me of Katell; hungry, Undreamed Katell.

"I am Nimue," I say.

"Anouel. This is my daughter Marie."

"How long have you been travelling?"

Anouel seems to be counting the days in her head. "Nine, ten... Every day is the same if you walk long enough."

I nod. "And where are you from?"

"Guer. I can't recommend it." She softly adds: "There is nothing to see... Nothing left to return to."

"The storm?" I whisper back. "Or was it the plague?"

"The Black Influenza came first." Anouel runs her fingers through Marie's tangled hair. "It killed both my husband and my mother. When the storm came, the district officials left us behind in quarantine. A few people managed to break free. We set off with a group of twenty people. My brother and I believed we would all be able to make it to Brevalaer." She shakes her head. "Now there's just five of us left."

"I'm so sorry," I mumble.

"Me too. And what about you? Who did you lose?"

"How do you know I have lost someone?" I ask.

She smiles sadly. "You have that same look on your face."

She is probably right. I nervously pick at a fray on my anorak. "I'm looking for someone." I stare at the gate again. One thing seems certain: if I do nothing, I will never get past the gate. I make up my mind and say: "Anouel, will you come with me?"

Anouel says nothing, but she follows me as I slowly shuffle through a crowd of people, my hands wrapped around the straps of my heavy backpack.

The two men guarding the gate look at me suspiciously, and I mirror their attitude. The man on the left has short, grey hair and equally grey eyes, the other looks younger and seems slightly more curious. They are both wearing dark green jackets and flat, red caps. If this is their uniform, it bears no resemblance to the camouflage clothing from Detection. Neither of them are displaying the logo of the Asclepius Congregation. What are they – soldiers of Brevalaer? City guards? Volunteers?

Whatever their duties might be, it is clear that they do not see it as their task to speak first. I glance around and notice that several people are looking at us. I gesture at them. "There are a lot of people wanting to go in."

"You are supposed to clear the gate before sunset," the older man says.

"It would help if you opened the gate,' I say. "Since when has Brevalaer been closed?"

The man clenches his jaw, as if chewing on his answer before spitting it out. "We do not welcome refugees. Please turn around."

"I'm not a refugee," I protest.

"Do you have any relatives in Brevalaer?"

"No, I'm from Gwennec. I'm on my way home."

"Gwennec." The eldest seems annoyed and lets out a sigh. The youngest points to my backpack. "Do you have any identification with you?"

I look at him, apparently in a very ignorant way, because he speaks to me as if I were a child: "The passport that proves you live in Free Breizh?"

I laugh out loud, because for a moment I think he is joking. But his serious look puts an end to my amusement. "When I lived in Gwennec, nobody had a passport like that!"

The man makes an impatient gesture. "You need a passport to get into Brevalaer. Please identify yourself."

"I'm from Breizh," I say again. "Born and raised in Gwennec. I am a fisherwoman."

"Where have you been all this time, not knowing you would run into a wall on your return?"

"I have visited my family," I tell them. It's not even a lie. "First my cousin near Cami. Then my mother and..." I press my lips together. Suddenly I remember the border post between Brevalaer and the rest of Central Europe. I knew there was a quarantine station at District 15, but I had not expected that so much could have changed within one winter.

"You have crossed Central Europe without noticing there's an epidemic terrorising us?" It is clear that he does not believe me.

I shake my head. "I call it the Black Influenza," I say softly.

"I call it Stay-the-fuck-out-of-my-town. Breizh needs to protect itself."

I strongly doubt that a wall could stop the Black Influenza from entering the city. I probably have more experience with the disease than anyone here. I have personally experienced every broken molecule of it, and I still wake up at night with trembling hands, my mind filled with suffocating thoughts, and haunted by a whispering voice. But I keep it to myself, deciding not to divulge that information. "So you won't let us in?"

The young man seems to feel a little sorry for me. "You can apply for asylum with the district officer of Brevalaer. He takes care of all the applications."

I sigh. One way or another, I'll have to enter this gate if I want to track down Wolf. Not to mention the other people here, who don't even seem to have a home or hut to return to. Once again, I feel overwhelmed by the trail of destruction that is left by the great storm and the Black Influenza, which is still spreading despite all the efforts of the Asclepius Congregation. In Avalon, everything seemed so far away, like a distant memory... Now, the truth hits me like a tsunami. "How do I apply for asylum?"

The young man enters a guardhouse built against one of the towers and comes back with a form. I look at it as if he is handing me a can of worms.

"Surely you can read...?"

"Gwenhael's grave, of course I can read!" I take his pen and pull the paper out of his hands. Using my real name is too risky, even if the district official of Brevalaer has no connection with Cormack.

When I hand him back the completed form, he gives me an intense look. "Good luck, Nicole. If you can prove that you are indeed from Gwennec, I'm sure you'll be fine."

"What about all the other people?"

"Can't help you with that."

I let out another sigh. "Where can we wait until you can?"

"Not here." My question seems to surprise him. "We are not allowed to have refugees camped outside the gate."

"Then where should we go?"

He doesn't answer. I look over my shoulder, at the deserted tracks and the vast hills.

"Stinging jellyfish," I mutter.

"I'm sorry," he says, and I think he really means it. "Every Monday, the district official organises a meeting. We'll have more information then."

I'm about to turn away from him, until I change my mind and ask: "What day is it today?"

"Tuesday."

He looks at me as if I were a poor stray dog, and I feel embarrassed. The long journey from Avalon to Brevalaer has made me lose track of the days completely. All that mattered so far was the sun's arc through the sky and the long nights that followed; a darkness in which the stars were my compass.

Anouel joins me as I find a spot at the edge of the messy, makeshift camp. Like most of the others, I let the backpack slide off my shoulders and use it as a seat. It is just a little more comfortable than the ground that is thawing from the late frost.

"Thanks for the water," Anouel says. Marie has already finished it. "I'm afraid I have very little food left to share."

"Don't worry about me," I say, still thinking about the closed gate. "This is going to be tougher than I thought. But we'll get in."

Anouel looks pensive. "I've heard that there is another way to cross."

"How?"

"They say there is a group that... helps people." The little girl puts her head against her shoulder and she gently rocks her.

"Who is willing to help us with this? The people of Brevalaer certainly aren't, that's for sure."

Anouel shrugs her other shoulder. "Who? No idea. My cousin left for Brevalaer about a month ago... Maybe longer. She never came back, so who knows? She might have made it across."

She makes it sound as if the wall of Brevalaer is a giant rift.

"But it's supposed to be a secret," Anouel continues. "They say that if you want their help, you have to know the position of the moon. But it was cloudy last night."

"It is the third day of the crescent moon," I say. "Is that a code?"

"Then you should be able to find them three hills north from the main gate. That's how it works, see? For every day of a crescent moon you count one hill to the north. For every day of a waning moon you count back. It's a way for them not to get caught, I guess."

"Very clever," I say. "But how do you know it's true?"

"I don't," Anouel admits. "It could be just a rumour, but if it's true, it would be our best shot." She goes quiet for a moment, and I understand her silence immediately, realizing that the chances for them to be admitted by Brevalaer were small. Suddenly I notice she is holding three coins in her hand. "This is all I have left. And I'm willing to bet one of them that the Marsh Birds really exist."

"The Marsh Birds?" I repeat. "Is that what they are called?"

Anouel nods.

"Wrap me in fishing nets and throw me to the bottom," I chuckle. "Three hills north, you said?" I scramble up with stiff joints and swing my backpack onto my aching shoulders. "Put your coins away, Anouel. You're going to need them on the other side."

***

The valley is surrounded by rocks and berry trees – a suitable place to take shelter. Up ahead, against the ridge of a hill, are a few unfamiliar tents. They blend in with the colour of the grass surrounding them. I wonder how much effort it took to get them past Detection.

The tents are like villas in a slum, because the rest of the valley looks like it's littered with makeshift shelters covering the luggage on the ground. Shelters made of plastic bags, wooden planks, sticks and rags. Anouel turns a bit pale as we take in the camp. We find barrels everywhere – medium-high barrels that may once have contained oil. They form small havens of light, small fireplaces that burn against the rising dusk, and keep groups and individuals warm. But most people have gathered in the middle of the valley around a wooden cart. Someone is sitting on top of the cart... someone who, despite the approaching chill of the evening, is not wearing a coat.

I recognise him by the way he sits, with his legs crossed and his fingers restless as ever. One hand is holding a cigarette, the other hand is drumming against his thigh. Finola's blonde braid is shorter now. When I last saw Will, he prominently wore his sister's mark to his shoulder. Now it's just a single blonde strand, woven into his own dark brown hair. Someone, perhaps Mirna, has taken care of his hair as well. It always used to be a little too long and now he is wearing it short, particularly at the nape of his neck.

He looks a lot tougher. Tougher and older.

But his smile remains the same. His crooked little smirk always gives me the feeling that he knows more than he is letting on. I couldn't hear what made him smile, but when Anouel and I come closer, I can finally make out what he's saying.

"... I swear on my grave, they will turn you away at the gate of Brevalaer. But you are more than welcome here. We provide clean water, rainproof clothing, soup. Blankets will be given to children and women first. It's best to share..."

People are handing out bowls and water bottles, rain ponchos and blankets. It doesn't surprise me at all that Will is able to provide all these things. It is also clear that this is not the first time they have taken in the ragged travellers for Brevalaer, as everything goes orderly and fast.

"Go on," I say to Anouel, giving her a gentle push forward. "He said children get a blanket first."

Will has jumped off the cart and disappeared into one of the tents. I don't want to let him out of my sight, so I squeeze through the crowd and run after him.

One of the tent flaps is half open, but when I step inside, Will isn't there. I look around. There is a cot in the corner – no more than a straw mattress with a couple of blankets carelessly thrown over it. On the blankets is a packet of cigarettes. A thick, hooded jumper is laid out in a messy bundle and looks like it's being used as a pillow. The rest of the tent is mainly used as a storage area: I see a few wooden crates and some plastic baskets. I lift up one of the lids and discover more oiled rags, provisions and bottles of clean drinking water. Survival items in an empty wasteland. In a crate next to it I find different kind of items: three rifles, neatly stacked, hopefully unloaded. I shake my head and my curiosity is replaced with aversion.

"You lost, girl?"

Will's suspicious voice tells me that he has not yet recognised me. I hear him take a step closer.

"Everything you need is outside. You are not supposed to steal from us."

I suppress a grin. "You never really trusted me, did you?" I turn around. "Hello, Will."

"Nimue!" Will looks at me as if I just appeared out of thin air. "What are you...?"

"Looking for trouble, Will?"

"I can't believe you're here. What are you doing here?"

"I've come back."

"So I see." His face shows a range of emotions going from shock and bewilderment to relief. "I have often thought about you. Anything could have happened to you. You and Arthur on that boat... I didn't know..." He surprises me as he pulls me towards him and presses a kiss to my lips. Then his hands slide through my cropped hair. "What is this? Where's your long hair?"

"Inconvenient when travelling."

He exhales; a sigh and a laugh at the same time. He lets go of me and takes me in from head to toe. "Nimue of the sea."

I smile. "Do you have room for an old acquaintance?"

"Where is Arthur?" He looks behind me, as if he expects my little brother to be hiding somewhere.

"He's still on Avalon. On the island," I clarify. "With my mother."

"So she's alive? And Arthur, he's alright too?"

"Later," I say softly. I'm too tired to tell the whole story now. I'm not even sure if Will would believe me. "Do you know where I can find Wolf?"

"Wolf? Did you come back for him?"

"I need to speak to him urgently."

"Oh, you need to speak to him, do you?" He looks at me rather probingly and I'm under the impression that something amuses him. "Well, he didn't come along on this ride. But you don't have to look so worried, he'll be back. And in the meantime, I'll help you get to the other side of this damned wall."

3

THE WAY HOME

"Are we going to the Ark?" I ask.

"I'm afraid that's no longer possible."

"Did something happen?" I imagine the underground bunker as I remember it: suffocating, claustrophobic, but safe. "Please tell me Mirna and Conn are alright."

Will reassures me. "We haven't lost anyone else, Nim. Everyone is in good shape, healthy even." He grins for a moment. "It's just that our carts are not very useful in the marshes. Both front and back wheels keep getting stuck in the ground."

"You didn't build decent roads while we were away?"

"We like it the way it is."

"Soggy and smelly?" I tease him.

"Soggy and smelly."

We both laugh. Then Will tells me to get some rest. "We get up before sunrise."

I nod. "What about you, Will? Do you still wait for Finola every night?"

He touches the blonde lock in his hair. The sudden sadness in his eyes breaks my heart. "I don't think I will ever get my sister back."

"Will..." I'm not sure what to say. I take his hands and hold them tightly. A bit too tightly, I guess, because he flinches somewhat. I understand how he feels, because I don't know if I will ever get my little brother back either. Finally, I let go of him. "I'm exhausted."

"Then I'll just have to be a gentleman." He gestured to the makeshift bed. "You can sleep here tonight. Out of the wind, away of that damned fog."

"Will, I can't do. It's *your* tent, *your* secret mission."

"Have you looked at yourself in the mirror lately? You look extremely pale."

I rub my face. "Well, I've been walking a lot. And the weather isn't helping either."

"Please, Nim, sleep here tonight. There are enough fires to keep me warm."

I decide to give in and as I lower myself onto the cot, I feel relieved. My ankles are swollen and sore, despite the sturdy boots Mum and Ana gave me. "What about Mirna? Why isn't she here?"

"Ah, if Mirna were here, I wouldn't need a fire to keep me warm," Will grins. "She's working, like me. She'll be so happy to see you."

With these words, he exits the tent, leaving me alone to get some sleep. I cross my legs and rest my hands on the slight curve of my belly. There are days when I think I can feel the baby growing inside me.

"We are lucky, little one," I say softly. "According to Will, your father is close by. It won't be long now, I promise."

I take off my boots and wiggle my toes a bit to get the blood flowing. Then I lie down and curl up under the covers. All this time I have been stuck in that awful fog. I have watched the moon wax and wane as I was using the chilly earth to sleep on. This tent is a blessing for both me and my baby.

"One day, we will all be together again... Wolf and I, your Grandmother and your Uncle Arthur..."

I fall silent. I embrace myself and the child that grows with every heartbeat, and I try not to think about Arthur, who I left behind in Ana's house. I try not to think about his missing leg, his chapped lips and his sunken cheeks.

He seems to be able to survive without water, without food. He's breathing, but he is barely alive. The old Arthur died that day, on *The Herring Gull*, delirious and restless on the hard, rocking floor of a cabin...

Stop! I squeeze my eyes tightly shut. I will not remember him like that.

I exhale slowly and try to relax. The real Arthur isn't chained to a bed in Avalon. He is somewhere out there, travelling, free and in good health, with two arms and two legs, as he should be. And one day, I will see him again. I promise myself that every night. And I promise that to him, too, whispering in the dark, hoping he can somehow hear me.

I am not completely awake yet when Will enters the tent in the morning. He has an apologetic look on his face when he addresses me. "I'd let you sleep longer, but we've got a long journey ahead of us."

"It's alright." I sit up straight and comb the snags out of my hair.

Will helps me up. He frowns. "You seem different."

"Different how?" I know from experience that I shouldn't get up too quickly, so I slowly put on my boots. "Oh, yes, my hair is shorter."

"That's not what I meant." Will lets out a sigh. "I know that look on your face. You're keeping something from me."

I stay silent.

"Here." He throws an apple at me and I manage to catch it just in time. "At least make sure you eat."

"Do we have to take everything with us?" I gesture to the bags.

"We'll take those three bags, and these crates." With some effort, Will lifts up the wooden crate I checked out earlier. I know there's ammunition in it.

"Are there people you don't trust?" I ask.

"I have enough reasons not to. Can you carry those for me, please?"

I lift up a bag, but my back feels sore and weak. "What's in it?"

"Apples." He raises an eyebrow. "Too heavy?"

"It's alright. Have you ever had to use a gun, Will?"

We leave the tent and walk towards the cart that is waiting for us. The horse is harnessed and made ready. I look up, where the moon is slowly fading and the sun is already rising, its morning glow blocked by hilltops surrounding us. Smoke from last night's campfires mingles with the mist spreading through the valley.

"The fog seems to get denser every day," Will mutters. He puts the crate into the back of the cart and I throw in the bag of apples. He looks at me. "There are times when I have to, you know. When we go through customs, for instance. We usually manage to avoid the guards, but when we stick to the same routes, they will catch on quite easily."

"And are they firing at you too?"

"Sometimes." He frowns. "My purpose is clear, Nimue. I'm bringing these people to safety. I'm not ashamed of it."

He puts the rest of the necessary items into the cart. A group of people is eagerly waiting in the morning chill. He smiles at them and helps them with their heavy bags. Among them are Anouel and her little daughter. I walk towards them and lean against the back of the wooden cart.

In front of me I see a young couple with their twelve-year-old son. They introduce themselves as Nanicka, Cezar and Hannus. Two younger children shyly lower their gaze as Will lifts them into the cart. The girl squeezes the boy's hand. They are both wearing worn-out shirts and shoes, and overalls that seem a bit too big for them.

"Where are your parents?" I ask.

The boy looks up. He shakes his head. Dead? Or lost? I wonder.

"Come sit next to me," I suggest. "What's your name?"

"Pedre," he says softly, after he hesitantly lowers himself into a spot to my right. I notice that he protectively keeps the girl on his other side.

"Is that your sister?"

"Yes. Alma."

"My name is Nimue."

Will climbs onto the cart. It creaks and judders before departing the valley at a snail's pace. I can feel the wheels struggling in the soft earth beneath.

I ask: "Is anyone waiting for you on the other side of the wall, Pedre?"

His silence is telling.

We are heading west and I'm sure we have left Brevalaer far behind. I wonder if there are any villages nearby. We follow a paved road, which must have been built for a destination beyond Brevalaer. But judging from its lack of maintenance, nobody cares about this route. There are cracks everywhere, and grass, wild clover and thistles are forcing their way up through the tarmac.

I move to the front of the cart and climb onto the seat next to Will. I think I see a hint of green up north, a thick forest... It must be a marsh. A little further behind us is Brevalaer, like a walled fortress. The barbed wire fence is a sharp dividing line from north to west.

Will points ahead. "Look. Those are the customs posts."

From afar, they look like small, wooden towers manned by ants. Up close, they would probably be a lot more intimidating.

"Anything for Free Breizh," Will says.

"What in the name of Gwenhael's grave is Free Breizh?"

"It's Breizh, without Central Europe. You've been on the road a while, surely you've noticed things. People leaving their districts, fleeing from the Black Influenza. Cities are begging Rome for help, but Rome has collapsed like a sandcastle. Their water treatment works are heavily damaged by the storm, hospitals are sending patients away. They just don't have the capacity to deal with the storm victims while half the population has to be quarantined." He looks at me sullenly. "Can you guess what happened next?"

It's easy to guess. "The Asclepius Congregation?"

"They came out of the shadows; became the heroes and the shepherds of the people."

"What they do is like giving people rat poison for a cold." A horrifying idea crosses my mind. "Please don't say they took over Breizh."

"On the contrary. The Asclepius Congregation controls Central Europe, and Breizh is closing them off. It started with Brevalaer and Saint-Thonan. They noticed that something strange was going on with their patients, who were declared healthy after treatment."

"Apathetic, sleepless, as if the most important part of them is missing?"

"Exactly. And their distrust increases every day, as you can see from the measures they're taking. As long as Central Europe is at loggerheads and the Asclepius Congregation doesn't achieve a satisfactory result, the whole Periphery keeps its borders closed. And Brevalaer is a watchdog with bared teeth."

"How does Free Breizh treat the infected people?" I ask softly. "How do they fight the Black Influenza?"

"The wall. Why do you think the refugees are so eager to pass it, and why do you think Breizh refuses to take them in?"

"But it spreads via air," I object. "A wall can't protect people from airborne contamination."

"Well, they are doing the best they can. And they are doing better than the rest of Central Europe, for that matter." Will shrugs his shoulders. "They are lucky Breizh is so sparsely populated."

"But I refuse to believe that there is not one sick person in the whole of Breizh," I say incredulously.

"Oh, there are sick people alright. And it's not just the Black Influenza... Because they have closed their borders, there is no transportation for medicine and food supplies..."

"Oh, Gwenhael..."

"But a large area has been designated for shelter. A wide, sparsely populated piece of land on the coast..." He looks at me for a moment, with a crooked smile. "You'd feel right at home there."

"Gwennec?" My mouth drops open. It's outrageous. "They've taken Gwennec for quarantine purposes? But there are people there! *My* people!"

"It's not as bad as you think. And it's not just for quarantine. Orphans, homeless people, refugees who have managed to cross, even the handful of refugees who are granted asylum; they are all relocated to Gwennec, or have ended up there themselves."

"But why Gwennec?" I ask. "There is no fertile land, there are no orchards, there's nothing to live on except the sea. What are those people doing there?"

"Where else can they go? Think, Nimue. Where would you go if you are sent away from every town or village you pass? To Gwennec, the end of the world."

After a short silence, I say: "So we're not just going past Brevalaer. We are going home."

"I thought you'd be happy." Will's smile is fading. "I wanted to surprise you. But... you look like you'd rather go the opposite way."

"I don't." I stare at the horizon. We're getting closer and closer to my old village. "It's just strange to be here... It feels wrong without Arthur."

"Nimue." When I don't respond, he puts his hands on my shoulders and gently turns me towards him. "What happened to Arthur? What are you not telling me?"

I hesitate, but he keeps looking at me and won't let go of me. I finally give in. "Shortly after we boarded *The Herring Gull*, harbour patrol was alerted. Arthur got shot and his leg was injured. There was nothing on board to get the bullet out, so it got infected... He became very ill. "

"Weren't you able to cure him?"

"I tried, Will. But a bullet is not the same as the Black Influenza. And the Hunter..." I shake my head. Will doesn't know anything about the Hunter and I don't want to give him nightmares. I have enough of those myself. "I'm very tired."

"Of course." He puts a hand on my shoulder. "But you said he's still alive. That he's on Avalon."

"It was a close call, but the islanders saved his life. However, we couldn't save his leg."

Will looks at me in horror.

"It was awful. At first I couldn't stand looking at it without getting nauseous. But I have gotten used to it by now."

"I'm sorry." He embraces me briefly and firmly. "We have to move on."

Whether he means continuing the journey or getting on with our lives, I don't know. I just know he is right on both accounts.

A few hours before nightfall, we exchange the paved road for a sandy track that takes us to the fence. Will shows us where the barbed wire has been cut.

I help him push aside the iron cables. "Is there a chance we could be electrocuted?"

"The electricity has been cut off. Sometimes they repair the fence – in that case we have to find a new place to cross. Are you in pain?"

I feel caught as I rub my tired lower back. "It's nothing. Is this passageway big enough?'"

"It just about fits."

We let Anouel go first, with Marie, Alma and Pedre under her care. Nanicka, Cezar and Hannus follow suit. Will unhitches the horse and carefully leads him through. We silently watch as Will guides him past the cut barbed wire. His withers touch the top cable, and his manes get stuck in the vicious iron. Will stays calm, cuts off a piece of the mane with a knife and a few moments later we find ourselves in Free Breizh.

"Welcome," Will says. He grins. "You're halfway to the promised land."

I shake my head as we follow him. From the marshes and woods of Brevalaer to the secluded island of Avalon, there is no place where I ever felt like I truly belonged. Once, I believed Gwennec was that place. But I no longer trust the sea, and with those rocky shores and sharp winds, it is certainly not our promised land.

To my surprise, Will reveals a second cart that's waiting for us – hidden behind trees, covered with branches and leaves.

I look at him a bit stupidly. Will laughs and says: "We have our ways."

"If the guards come, they'll take the other cart."

"True. I'll have to think of something. Meanwhile..." He pats the horse's neck, then lifts the children to the ground. "Forward march."

"Hm," I say, not being very helpful.

"A bit more excitement would be nice." He puts the horse in front of the cart with the harness that was in the cart. "Or a smile, maybe. Come on, Nimue. What's the matter?"

"I miss Arthur."

"And you feel bad that you left him behind." Will guesses without looking at me. I suspect he's standing with his back to me on purpose while he buckles the harness. "And you're wondering if Wolf is worth making this whole journey for." When I don't answer, Will sighs and turns around. "You haven't asked me anything about him. You're making this whole journey to find a man you barely know. I'd be terrified."

"I'm not terrified."

"I can see it's tearing you up inside. It must be very important." He grabs my shoulders, so I can't turn away and escape confrontation. "He reminds me of you, you know? Evasive, knows more than he's letting on, and full of secrets."

"Sounds more like you."

Will starts laughing. He lets go of me and I help him prepare the horse. Then we hop onto the cart. My backside feels sore from sitting on these wooden planks for so long.

Will clicks his tongue and the horse flexes its muscles to pull us all forward. Forward march, to the sea. To Wolf. Will knows me very well, that's for sure. What if Wolf turns out to be a waste of time? I will have left Arthur for nothing.

The next morning, I wake up with the familiar feeling of nausea. With a groan I roll over onto my back and stare at the sky. It starts to transition into a soft, pink hue. Maybe today will finally be a clear day. I put my hands on my stomach and slowly breathe in and out. Close to the ground, patches of fog are floating like damp veils. As soon as I stretch out my hand, it is surrounded by fine droplets that do not harm my skin.

"Odd, isn't it?"

I hadn't noticed that Nanicka is awake and looking at me from her bed. She stretches her arm and slowly moves it through the mist. "You'd think we would all be covered in blisters by now. Maybe the world has changed. What do you think?"

I shrug my shoulders. To me, it's one of the many mysteries of the Other World. If only I could put all those puzzle pieces together, I would have an answer. Has the mist descended to cover the world for the rest of our lives? It's as if we are slowly disappearing, a little more each day. Even if it's a clear day, soon we may not be able to see the sky anymore.

That evening, we find the first sign of human life since the wired fence: a large farm surrounded by orchards. The family takes us in without too many prying questions. We are all relieved that, on this third night, we are not at the mercy of the open air. We are given a warm meal and a cozy bed. When we leave the next morning, everyone is in a cheerful mood. I put my arm around Pedre and Alma, and when Anouel starts singing, I finally get Pedre to join in. Encouraged by her brother, even Alma tries to sing along. She has a sweet voice, but nothing is as sweet as the image I see before me when I look up. The road descends into a valley and up ahead, the land is flat. I can smell it before I see it: the smell of salt, carried by the wind. The smell of algae and seaweed.

And there, far to the north, against the horizon, I see that grey line I haven't seen for such a long time.

My body responds to it like a magnet. The voice of the sea stirs something in my blood. It sings my name – I can feel it in my bones. For a brief moment, I experience this insane desire to dive into the water and swim for miles and miles. My instinct tells me that air and light are not as important as the shadows that can be discovered down there.

But then I shake my head and smile at the thought. This is not my own instinct, but an echo of Sela's selkie blood, and I refuse to give in to it. What happened to my mother was enough warning.

Will leans into me from aside. "I think you're home."

I nod, with a lump in my throat.

He casts a glance at my face. "Are you happy or sad?"
"I don't know," I say. I laugh and feel tears rolling down my cheeks.
Will smiles too. "Welcome back, Nimue of the Sea."

4

The Village at the End of the World

There are places that are so deeply engrained in your memory that they seem impervious to change. For me, Gwennec is that place. As we drive through town, everything seems exactly like how I remember it: the market square, the zigzagging streets and the once-imposing buildings; the smells of tar, smoke, paint, and donkey droppings. There are many familiar sounds too: the loud clattering of carts, the murmuring and shouting of people trying to get through while passing each other... I look around with a smile plastered on my face which probably makes me look like a fool.

Everything is still the same.

But when we leave town and drive along the paved road that leads to the fishing village, I'm confronted with a sobering reality. I was expecting empty spaces. I was expecting small houses with gardens, fishing boats bobbing on the waves. I search the horizon for the windmill with its slow, rotating wings, but all I see are the many tents and makeshift shelters on the once empty beach.

My face must have gone white with terror. Will says: "This is the end of the world. This is where they all end up."

"Sweet Gwenhael," I whisper. I raise my gaze unwillingly to the home of the saint I have just invoked. There is nothing on the hill – no old church that defies time, storm and adversity. I can only make out a few stones left from the foundation.

For some reason, that touches me deeply.

"Are you alright?" Anouel asks.

"Everything is gone," I murmur plaintively.

Fortunately, I don't have time to feel too sentimental. We reach the encampment, and someone hurries out of the tent to greet us. I let out a cry of excitement and jump off the cart before Will brings the horse to a halt.

This young woman is Yannick, my best friend, whom I left in the ruined village when Arthur and I set out on our journey. It takes a few seconds for her to recognise me, but then we run into each other's arms, laughing and crying.

When she lets go of me, she looks at the cart behind me. "Where is Arthur? Is he not with you?"

"It's a long story."

"But... where is he?"

"Later," I promise her. "He's safe. But it's complicated."

Yannick knows exactly when I'm ready to talk and when it's better to leave me be. She takes my hands and says: "I thought you'd never come back."

"As did I sometimes." I think of Wolf. Is it a coincidence that my search for him brings me back to Gwennec? I smile. "I couldn't stay away, even if I wanted to."

"But why have you come back? Will made it sound like you were finally able to track down your mother..."

"Will? The two of you know each other?"

"Of course," she laughs. "I know a lot of your new friends. They all told me the same thing: how persistent you were, how dangerous it is out there. Gwenhael's blood, I had no idea, otherwise I would never have let you go!"

"I have seen things I never thought possible," I sigh. "And I have learned a lot too."

She looks at me with a serious look. "Are you happy?"

Happy? Every time I turn around to catch Arthur's gaze, I remember he's not here with me.

"Excuse me," Will interrupts. "We've all had a long journey."

"Of course," Yannick replies, as I watch her transform to become the capable and confident leader she must be by now. "Everything is ready. Come with me."

"Where are we going?" I ask.

"Because the city and the beach are fully occupied, we had to improvise," she says.

We pass many tents as she leads the way. I'm not sure if it was intended or not, but there are lots of narrow streets separating the tents from each other.

"These buildings are not so safe anymore after that heavy storm. Did you see them? From wherever you were coming?"

"Oh yes," I assure her. "So which building is still fully intact?"

"That one over there. Made out of stone and cement. Our own little hospital."

"That used to be the school," I say in surprise. "You've turned the school into a hospital."

"We had to. It's chock full, but it offers shelter and we are able to keep it reasonably clean."

She opens the door for us and we wade through a puddle of water and detergent that disinfects our boots. For a moment, it feels like stepping into a memory: the hall, the notice board on the wall where they once pinned up a list of vocational courses, the three doors to the classrooms. The corridor leads to an annex that used to be a dusty library, but now I see a stranger coming out in a hurry, carrying a roll of bandages.

"It took some fitting and measuring," Yannick says. "We keep our stocks in the library. Everything has to be stored and numbered." She points to a room that used to be an old classroom. The door is ajar. "That's the dormitory for those who have to stay overnight for observation. And here we have first aid and medical check-ups."

"That's our classroom," I say.

"That *used to be* our classroom. Education had to make way for fixing nosebleeds and broken arms."

"And what's over there?" I point to the room at the end of the hallway, where the youngest children used to learn to how write and count.

"Quarantine. No one goes in or out without permission." She turns to the others. "Please be mindful of that. The door should always be closed. If you see anything out of the ordinary, alert the Medical Officers immediately, or a doctor. Alright?"

Anouel, Nanicka and Cezar nod.

Yannick bends down to address Alma and Pedre. "Did you understand what I just said?"

"No entry," Pedre says. "I'm hungry."

"I have to pee," Alma adds.

"Then we'll have to take care of that. You can use the toilet after we've checked you. It won't take long." She leads us into the old classroom. I'm taken aback by seeing such a large number of people inside. The window is open, but it doesn't help clear out the musty smell. Our old chairs and desks have been rearranged and supplemented with pillows, blankets, and straw mattresses. The old teacher desk is now a hospital table. There is a straw mattress on top, covered with blue paper.

"I thought we'd be the only ones in today," I say, dumbfounded.

Yannick looks at me and starts laughing. "Not everyone is brought here by Will."

"I'm just a guy with a cart," Will grins.

"How did they get in?"

"The wall is long," he says. "Those who want to risk their lives can feel with their hands when the power is switched off. Sometimes they do it out of thrift, even. Or if they have the money, they'll bribe someone. Groups who have heavy weapons join forces."

"Plus, there are other smugglers," Yannick says in a sullen tone. She puts Alma on a stool in front of her and gently touches the joints in her arms and knees, then her back and stomach, then the glands at her throat. "They are exploiters. Sometimes they're customs officers from Free Breizh who take bribes and promise residence permits. But what can you do? If you don't have any weapons and you don't know your way around, it's the only way to get in. Some smugglers are clever and they make a lot of money now." She lets Alma take a deep breath, a stethoscope against her chest. After a moment, Yannick seems satisfied. "Just a slight cold. Well done, sweetheart. Is that your brother?"

"This is Pedre," I say. "They were on their own." It terrifies me to think that these two children were at risk of being victims of exploiters and smugglers.

Yannick doesn't seem surprised. How many orphans has she seen already? How many of them are able to survive in a camp on the beach?

"Is everyone who arrives in such bad shape?" I ask.

"Most of them, yes. They will all have travelled for weeks and immediately rushed to Gwennec. The district officials decided that it is compulsory for everyone to get a medical check-up. It only takes one person for a bad case of diarrhoea to spread...'

"Has it happened before?"

"Don't get me started. We've survived that crisis, but the hospital in the city was at full capacity after just three weeks."

"Brevalaer has a bigger hospital," I say. "Don't they do anything at all?"

Yannick rolls her eyes. "Brevalaer refuses to take in refugees without residence permits."

"I have to go," Will suddenly interrupts. "Please tell Doctor Merric I'll be in the town hall."

"Hold on." Yannick quickly grabs him by the sleeve. "You know the rules."

For the next few minutes, I watch with pleasure as Will reluctantly undergoes a physical examination. When Yannick gives him a satisfied look, he pulls down his jumper and hurries away with his remaining dignity. I chuckle.

"Your turn," Yannick says.

She checks the back of my throat, presses a stick to my tongue and says: "You haven't brushed your teeth properly."

"How cah I ush my eeth?"

"You have any cavities?"

"Ho wah?"

She takes the stick out of my mouth.

"I said, so what? My cavities are *my* business."

She laughs when I make a face and push her off me. I allow her to listen to my lungs and heart and check my joints. "You're covered in bruises too," she says.

"You should see my backside. Done yet?"

"Hm-hm." Her hands slide over my belly. "You're a bit fatter than you used to be, aren't you? What have you been eating lately?"

"Apples, salted meat, some bread," I list.

"And before that?"

"Lots of fish."

"How's your bowel movement?"

"Divine," I say.

"When was your last period?"

"Seriously?"

"Hey, I have to ask. I used to know exactly when it was your time. You wouldn't stop cursing," she laughs.

"Alright then." I lean forward and whisper in her ear: "It must have been about thirteen weeks ago."

"What?"

"Shh." I wink.

"But…"

"I haven't told anyone yet."

"Nimue!" She glances down to my belly, then back up at me. I can almost hear her thoughts: *am I making fun of her, should she pity me, am I beaming with joy…?*

"Later," I promise. "Not here."

Finally, Yannick lets out a deep sigh. My smile seems to reassure her. "Just wait over there until I've finished," she says. Her look tells me that she doesn't intend to keep me here any longer than necessary, and that I'm about to have a very different kind of interrogation.

I go outside and walk down the street, taking in the familiar yet strange surroundings. A jeep passes by me and stops at the entrance of the building. Once, this would have been a rare sight; now I am the only one staring at it. *Keep walking.* People scurry from tent to tent. They are standing in groups. They talk, fiddle with pans and keep low fires burning in front of the entrances to their tents. The light colour of their skin tells me that they're not from the coast. Their hands lack the calluses that you get from fishing, hauling in catch and casting out nets every day.

I look at them as I walk past, but nobody pays any attention to me.

When I reach the point where the paved road turns into a sandy track, I stop. This used to be a barren area. A plain beach where the tide gets trapped in gullies and ruts, full of crabs and shellfish. And behind it, I used to be able to see the tide, either retreating or throwing itself onto the sand.

But the beach has now been taken over by refugees from all over Central Europe, and the sea has been swallowed up by dense fog.

I hear someone approaching me and suddenly Yannick stands beside me. For a while we just stare at the misty landscape, the end of the world. I have the feeling that we are thinking the same thing: *the world we once knew is gone.*

"It started slowly," Yannick says finally. "Groups started to arrive when Brevalaer's borders were still open. Not everyone came directly to Gwennec. Most of them stayed in Brevalaer, others wandered off to Saint-Thonan and Kerzaoz and even Daouloc. Nobody cared about the few people who ended up in Gwennec. We thought we had plenty of room."

"But then more people came," I guessed.

She nods. "Brevalaer got selective. They got scared. Especially when they noticed that their doctors didn't know what to do about the epidemic. To protect their own residents, they threw all refugees out, hoping to be able to contain the risk of infection."

"And now they won't let anyone in."

"By law, anyone can apply for asylum within four days, as long as they don't camp near the border gates. But now they only grant asylum to refugees from Rome. They still have money, I think. But they end up here too." She smiles, but without joy. "We also take care of them, of course."

"So Will has told me."

"Will has dedicated his life to helping as many people as possible," Yannick says thoughtfully. "Along with Mirna, Conn and Wolf... They see it as some kind of personal mission."

The moment she mentions Wolf's name, my body tightens like a bowstring. I let out a deep sigh and Yannick looks up.

"Wolf," I whisper. "Have you met him? Is he here?"

"He doesn't come here often. I saw him once..." Slowly, understanding dawns in her gaze. "Are you telling me... He's the father?"

"Yes, he is." My hands rest on my belly again.

"Wolf! By Gwenhael. I thought it was Will," Yannick confessed.

"Will? Shark blood! I could never be with him. There's too much anger in him."

"And Wolf? What's he like?"

I think for a moment. "He is strong.

"You have a very unusual taste," Yannick says. "That one time I saw him, he seemed... well, a bit strange. He kept in the shadows and looked like he was seeing something from the corner of his eye all the time."

I smile. "Ah. That's just the way he is."

"And you fell for that?"

"I did," I chuckle. "I'd be dead without him."

Yannick doesn't join in. She seems startled by those words. Then suddenly she hugs me until I almost hear my bones crack. "Please don't say that. Don't tell me you almost died."

I put my arms around her. "I'm safe now."

"Safe..." She lets go of me with a sigh. "What happened?"

"Let's go to Saint Gwenhael. We can talk there."

"The church is gone, Nim. The big storm was the final blow to it."

"I've noticed, but I want to go to the hill."

We walk slowly through the encampment staying silent once more. We leave the many refugees behind us as we climb the hill. For some reason, no one has pitched a tent here.

There's debris everywhere: at the top, on the slope, spread over the entire hill by wind and water. Only three walls are still standing strong: a part of the entrance, a wall from the chapel and there's a stone arch which used to hold a window. Something cracks under my feet. When I look down, I find some shards of stained glass.

"The church bell fell down when we wanted to move the sarcophagus," Yannick tells me. "Franseza's husband got hit by it and broke his arm."

"Franseza still lives here?"

"You will probably see her soon."

"And the sarcophagus?" I think about the massive stone statue of the resting saint, Saint Gwenhael, the heart of the church, the place where hundreds of candles were lit each day, dripping wax onto the statue.

"We tried to transport it to the village. But it was too heavy, so it broke. Only the head and chest are still intact."

I let out a deep sigh. "Has nothing from the past remained?"

"There are some things left..." Yannick sits down on a large chunk of stone and brings her knees towards her chest. I take a seat next to her. "But now it's your turn. Tell me what happened."

"Where do I even start?" I look out over the village – where our houses have been replaced by tents, until suddenly I see the muddy rooftops again and I can even see a few sails through the mist. "Do you remember that song my mother taught me?"

Yannick thinks. "Was it a lullaby?"

"Yes, it was. That's how it all started."

When I finally finish my story, Yannick has become really quiet. She holds my hand and her fingers feel limp, as if she needs all her energy to process my story.

"Do you believe me?" I ask nervously.

She stares ahead, across the encampment. "It sounds impossible. Your mother, a selkie? And Arthur, trapped in the Other World… like a spirit…"

"Arthur is not a spirit, Yannick, and neither is the Fisher King."

"Alright." She nods, and breathes deeply in and out. "Alright then. So, they are real. We both know there are too many mythical stories going around in Gwennec for them to not contain a kernel of truth. Right?" She laughs, nervously. "Are there spirits here too?"

I look around me. I haven't seen them since that day on the beach. "The Fisher King made it sound like they were once everywhere, you know. But… they're dying."

"Just like us."

Like my village at the end of the world, groaning under the weight of thousands of dying strangers. I sigh deeply and say: "Just like the rest of the world."

"I know someone who would believe you no matter what. Your grandmother."

A smile appears on my face. "Yes. And she would have been so happy to hear that Mum is still alive."

"You miss her, don't you?"

I pull my knees up to protect myself against a rising, chilly wind. We have but little shelter on top of the hill. "Without her and Arthur, I don't know what my home is anymore."

Yannick firmly puts her arm around me. She feels warm. For a few minutes she just holds me, without me having to talk. Then she pulls me to my feet. "You do have a home, Nim. You are home now. And you are always welcome at my place. Come on, I can't leave you here shivering like this with a baby in your belly."

Yannick's house hasn't changed much. Against the stone wall, a rooster flutters out of the rain barrel as we pass. The mooing of cows reaches us from their pasture behind the yard. Only the roof looks new.

"All the tiles flew off, from the porch all the way to the barn," Yannick says. "I was terrified."

"The storm?" I guess.

She nods. "It peaked at midnight. I thought that this time, there'd really be nothing left of the village. I thought it would be like that tidal wave... That it would be the end of Gwennec."

I look up at the roof in disbelief. "Gwennec is stronger than we thought, don't you think?"

"I think we all are."

She takes me inside and I'm greeted by the familiar smell of her house. In the kitchen, it smells like fresh bread, like it always did. Yannick sits me down on a kitchen chair and prepares a thick porridge for me. I put a large spoon of honey into it and finish the contents of the bowl within ten minutes.

I lick the spoon. Wow. I missed that. "Where are your parents?" I ask.

"Mum is working the fields. Dad is at the town hall with Franseza. Will is there too."

"What's going on there?"

"The district officials are worried about the expansion of the camp. And we don't have enough medicine, we don't have enough clothing... We don't have enough of anything, actually. Brevalaer refuses to open the gates for supplies. They're afraid that we bring in the Asclepius Congregation. If Gwennec has to turn away refugees, or if we can't take care of them anymore, I don't know what will happen to all those poor souls... But Dad said that Gwennec is working on an emergency measure. I don't know what their plan is."

I try to process it all. But the food and the sudden warmth make my eyes sting with fatigue. I rub my face. "I can tell them all about the Asclepius Congregation. If I can do anything..."

"Not now." Yannick gives me a stern look. "You're an idiot, you know that? Going on a trip like that while you're pregnant. It's mandatory bed rest for you, Nim. For twenty-four hours at least."

"But I..."

She holds up a finger. "I'm serious and I won't take no for an answer. Rest. You can take my bed."

Yannick takes me to her bedroom. We climb a ladder and reach a small, square room. It is tidy. Yannick's bed has clean sheets on it.

"We slept here before we left," I say, coming to a stop in the middle of the room.

"We did." She pulls back the sheets. "And every morning after that I cursed myself for letting you go."

I start to undress. "You couldn't have stopped us. We had to make this journey. And I... I'm alright."

As if I were a small child, Yannick waits for me to crawl into bed so she can tuck me in. She shakes her head and has a wistful look in her eyes. "I don't think that's true, Nim. How can you be? I think you're still searching for a home." She kisses me on the cheek. "You'll find that again. I'm sure of it."

When she reaches the doorway, she stops. "I've been praying for you every day, you know? That Saint Gwenhael would watch over you, out there on the wild sea."

"Thank you," I mutter. "Maybe it worked."

"Good night, Nimue."

The door closes softly. Moments later, I fall asleep.

5

REUNION

"*The sea kept still and could not move. Darkness enveloped her. For centuries they were like that, undisturbed...*"

I wake up. The room is dim. Yannick must have closed the shutters while I was asleep. There is a bowl of lukewarm soup next to my bed. I eagerly eat from it until it's empty. Then I let myself fall back onto the bed and before I know it, I'm asleep again.

When I wake up once more, it is as if my head is all fogged up. I wrestle with my pillow to find a better position to lie down and squeeze my eyes shut against the daylight coming through the crack in the shutters. Apparently, my body has had enough rest, because I'm unable to fall back asleep. My stomach growls – I'm hungry again.

With a sigh, I shake off the covers and can instantly smell my own sweat. Shark blood, how long has it been since I had a proper wash? A quick dip in the lake in Breizh, that was the last time, but the water was so cold that it didn't last long.

Yannick has obviously guessed the kinds of situation I've been in. Either that, or she smelled me when she put me to bed. There's a bucket of water in front of me, with a bar of soap and a towel folded up next to it. I make sure to wash myself properly before I put on my fresh clothes and climb down the ladder.

The door to the yard is open and the sea breeze properly wakes me up. I smile and take some food from the kitchen: two eggs and a piece of soft, warm bread.

When I'm halfway through my morning meal, Yannick comes in. She's wearing the white apron of a medical attendant and is holding a basket filled with sheets in her arms. "You're up! Good. How are you feeling?"

"Like I have a hangover," I complain. "How long have I slept?"

40

"A day, a night and another half day," she says cheerfully. "You really needed it, didn't you?"

"Obviously." My hands comb through my hair until I feel like it's no longer all over the place. "Did I miss anything?"

"Ah." She puts down the basket and starts folding the sheets neatly. "Sunrise, sunset. The usual stuff. Here, before I forget." She hands me a tin pillbox. "Take these. With compliments from the hospital..." She throws me a conspiratorial smile. "The brown pill is vitamin D, the other one is folic acid. For your baby."

"Thank you." I wash the pills down with a swig of milk. "They must be incredibly expensive."

"Whenever I'm able to smuggle something in, I will. I just wish we had more..." She pauses, with a frustrated look on her face, then shrugs. "It is what it is. By the way, Will and Mirna have come back. I think you should go with them."

"Where to?" I ask in surprise.

"I don't know. Will said it would cheer you up."

I follow the path along the cliffs, shielding my eyes with my hand and staring at the sunlight reflecting on the water. Not far from the shore, a large ship lies at anchor. I watch it for a long while, but don't notice any movement on deck. The ship looks old. It's a rusty container ship that used to carry barrels of oil when the Oak Field, Gwennec's oil drilling platform, was still active. I wonder what it is doing here, in the shallow waters near the coast.

Will and Mirna are waiting for me at the old school building. Mirna cries out in joy when she sees me. Before I know it, I find myself in her firm embrace. It makes me laugh out loud and I hold her just as tight, until my ribs start to hurt.

"You look great," she says.

"Really?"

"Well, actually, no," she admitted. "You look alive, though, which is more than I dared to hope for. Will told me that you stole a boat."

"It was a close call."

Mirna nods with a serious look on her face. "I'm so sorry about Arthur."

"I've missed you, Mirna." I don't want to talk about Arthur right now, so I look around to find her brother, but he's not here. "Where's Conn?"

"In the Ark. Someone has to look after our home."

"Alright, ladies. No time for chitchat if we want to steer clear of the night." Will wraps an arm around Mirna's shoulders. "Nimue, we could really use your help."

"With what?" I ask. "Where are we going?"

He shows me a piece of red rope, as if that's the answer. I give him a confused look as I shrug.

"We call it Code Red," Will says. "We send pigeons to Gwennec, just in case something goes wrong. I picked up this tape from Greyhead an hour ago."

"Greyhead?"

"That's what he calls the pigeons," Mirna says with an indulgent smile. "Not that it matters, he can't distinguish one from the other, anyhow."

"Nonsense," Will says. "There's Greyhead, Blackhead, Bluehead..."

"And Dumbhead." She darts away from under his arm and picks up a stuffed backpack. "We don't know what's going on, so we're taking everything with us: blankets, medicine, bandages.... Based on our calculations, they can't be very far away, so I think we'll run into them before nightfall."

"That means they must already be on this side of the wall," I conclude. "What could possibly be the problem?"

"Anything." Mirna doesn't sound worried. "A broken wheel axle, crying children, it could just be a minor crisis. Trust me."

There's a smaller cart waiting behind the school. It's the same beige horse as the one we used on our outward journey. I ruffle its mane while Will throws the backpack into the cart and hops on. He takes out a cigarette and starts picking at some tobacco. I notice that his fingers don't move as nervously as they used to. "Come on, you two."

Mirna is already in the cart when I hesitate. "Do you really need me?"

"I'm pretty sure you can be of help," Mirna says. "Come on, Nimue. You could use some distraction."

I turn to Yannick with a questioning look on my face, but she just smiles and shrugs her shoulders.

Mirna is right, actually. I could use some distraction from Gwennec. I want to feel the wind in my hair.

Mirna holds out her hand and I let her pull me into the cart. I sit down and Will clicks his tongue. With the now familiar, laborious sounds and movements, the cart goes forward. Will whistles a tuneless melody around the cigarette in his mouth.

I lean forward to Mirna. "He's changed, hasn't he?"

She smiles. "He has found balance. He no longer needs to be an outlaw to do something good. What he does now is tolerated by Gwennec."

"So what exactly is he now?" I think out loud. "A benevolent people smuggler?"

"Don't let him hear you say that," she chuckles.

"It's humanitarian aid," says Will from the trestle. "And I can hear you just fine, you swamp bugs."

I try to make myself as comfortable as possible. "You're not alone, are you? Conn is in the Ark. You're in Gwennec." I look at Mirna. "Who's helping you?"

"Wolf," she says.

"And who else?"

She hesitates for a long moment. Will glances at us over his shoulder. "Snakes."

"*What*?" I'm confused. "Tell me I heard that wrong."

"No, it's true," Mirna says. She pulls up her legs against her chest and wraps her arms around them, as if to protect herself, which makes me realise that just the thought of the Asclepius Congregation brings back terrible memories. "The world is falling apart. It's not just a division between Breizh and Central Europe or the wealthy and the refugees... The Snakes are divided amongst themselves. Those who have found us at least."

"Who are they?" I want to know. "How did they find you?"

"Will sort of *knew* how to find them."

Will says: "A few days after you left Camlann, we noticed the first signs. They started leaving messages in old places where we used to meet."

"You mean when you handed Katell over to them," I say sharply.

Will looks pained. "Even when you're at war, it's useful to communicate with your enemies. That's how I was able to get you into the Asclepius Congregation."

"But they don't know where the Ark is," Mirna says. "They don't know with how many we are, or what we do exactly."

"I bet you didn't even know Will was able get in touch with them," I say sharply.

"You're right," Mirna admits. She doesn't look very happy about it.

"Does it matter?" Will asks, clearly annoyed. "Everything has changed. Besides, I was curious. They left notes in iron tubes, with a time and a place on them, asking me to meet them. I ignored it at first. Later, camera footage showed up on a... transmitter?"

"A very small computer," Mirna explains. "The quality was very poor, but it's a technology that they are trying to revive in Central Europe."

"What did you see?" I'm becoming more and more intrigued. Which member from the Asclepius Congregation would do this, and for what reason? I try to remember everyone I saw and talked to when I was there. Only Dr Moal and Cormack himself stood out for their intelligence and enthusiasm. The rest of the staff didn't leave a big impression; I doubt anyone would dare act against Cormack Cairn.

"Someone was wearing a mask. The sound was bad. We couldn't hear whether it was a man or a woman. He... or she... insisted that we meet somewhere. Then they showed us pictures of children." Mirna bites her lip. "They showed us their personal files. They were all going to be Undreamed if someone didn't help them escape. The person said they could get them out of the institute and asked if we could collect the sick and bring them to Gwennec."

"We were very skeptical at first," Will says. "But we decided to go. We took Wolf with us to keep an eye out."

He stays silent for a while and I feel more and more tense. "And?"

"That person with the mask kept their word. The children were exactly where they told us they would be. Most of them were healthy. Two were ill... We lost them that same day. The rest made it across the fence. And we never stopped doing it. We help the children who are on the death list – that's what we call it. We also help children who have already been Undreamed. It's inhumane to leave them there."

"And Wolf meets Snakes who help smuggle the children outside, and brings them to us," Mirna explains. "Or as far as he can, at least. Sometimes we have to pick them up somewhere, like now."

"You mean..." I breathe in sharply. "Wolf is with them now?"

She smiles. "That's why you're here, right? To find him?"

I cannot answer right away. All kinds of emotions suddenly crash against me, like waves against a rock. Fear, sharp as that of a fleeing animal. Desire. Hope. Fear again.

"Nimue?"

"Did he ever mention my name?" I ask hoarsely.

"He doesn't talk much. He just does what he does." I think Mirna sees the disappointment on my face, because she squeezes my hand. "Words aren't really important, you know. Rather, ask yourself why he is *here*. He could have gone anywhere; he could have been safe and far away. Instead, he chose to help us. A man like him has a reason for everything he does."

I nod, but I'm not able to smile back. "What about this masked person?"

Mirna shrugs her shoulders. "He's there too sometimes. We still don't know who it is."

The sun disappears behind the edge of the world and a waxing moon rises above the misty hills. We are now several hours away from Gwennec, in a no man's land between the sea and Kerzaoz. I'm so engrossed in my own thoughts that I do not notice the glow of fire at first. Only when Mirna gently nudges me do I become aware of it. It is a very small light in the complete darkness around us. We drive straight towards it, the car creaking and squeaking and finally coming to a halt.

People are sitting around a campfire. Their faces are weakly lit by the flames, their backs are shrouded in shadows, and there is more smoke than fire. Will and Mirna jump off the cart. I slowly follow their lead.

Someone is coming towards us. My heart stutters, because I'm expecting to see Wolf. A moment later I realize that it's not him, but someone dressed in a long, black coat. When I see his face, it feels like it's beating out of my chest, but this time in terror. His head is deformed, non-humanlike. I flinch as nightmarish images of the Hunter flash through my min. Only then do I realise what it is that I'm seeing: just a mask – an oxygen mask like the ones I saw in Cormack's display case. They were used when people first emerged from the Arks and the air was full of poison.

I exhale slowly and watch the masked man shake Will's hand. He says something, but I can't hear them from my secluded spot. Will nods knowingly.

I join them and stare at the masked person. Do I know them? Their gaze seems to rest on me from behind the mask. They tilt their head like a curious dog. I have a feeling that they're staring at me as intensely as I'm staring that them.

Just as I'm about to ask something, I get distracted. Behind them, on the other side of the campfire, a man appears, carrying firewood. It's too dark to see his face, until he bends down to put a log on the fire. The flames hiss, and smoke and sparks leap up. The erratic light reveals his face.

It is as if I just saw him yesterday.

I immediately forget about the person with the mask. I'm vaguely aware that Mirna and Will are watching me, but I don't mind. I approach the fire.

Wolf raises his head. I just stand there, five steps away from him, and with a thump in my chest that he must surely hear. Part of me wants to touch, taste and embrace him, another part wants to turn away and flee. It makes it impossible for me to move.

Wolf seems to be experiencing the same thing, or maybe there is another reason why he remains still. We look like two strangers who forgot how they got to know each other.

One of us has to make a first move, I realise, but he doesn't. I blink to protect my eyes from the smoke and walk up to him. Up close, his face is even more familiar, and I can hardly believe that it has been weeks since I felt those lips against mine. His features still remind me of a wild animal. His eyes are large and black and they scan every inch of my face. His nostrils are wide, as if he is taking in my scent. The way he clenches his fists betrays a slight tremor.

I manage to smile hesitantly. "Is this how you greet me?"

One of his hands relaxes. As if he expects me to walk away at any moment, he slowly puts his rough, warm palm against my cheek. I relax and realise how tense I was. His touch reminds me of that night in Camlann, surrounded by darkness and dimly lit by an oil lamp.

"What happened to you?" His voice sounds hoarse and soft.

"What do you mean?"

He stares at me with a dreamy and slightly confused gaze.

Suddenly I realise why, and I laugh. "This is how I look when I'm clean."

"I see." His fingers slide up, touching the fuzzy ends of my curls. It awakens all the feelings I had for him. I hold my breath and stare back at him. I want him to smile. I want him to kiss me.

Yes, I want him to kiss me now, and when he won't make the first move, I'll do it myself.

I can tell that he is surprised. I can feel it in the tension in his arms, his body close to mine. His fingers claw in my hair. I feel a burning sensation that doesn't come from that sad excuse for a campfire.

Suddenly, he moves away. He takes a hard, deep breath and takes two steps back, leaving a distance between us.

"What's wrong?" I whisper, disconcerted.

"You shouldn't be here." He still has trouble breathing, it seems.

"That's not true," I say. "I'm exactly where I need to be."

"Didn't you find her, then? Your mother?"

"I did. It's such a strange story, full of magic and..."

"Then why are you here now? I don't understand."

"I'm here for *us*, Wolf. I'm here because of what happened between us." I put a hand on my stomach, which has become an automatic gesture for me. His eyes follow the downward movement. Wolf becomes very quiet.

"You can at least listen to what I have to tell you," I say.

Wolf nods. He glances past me and I become aware of the other people present again. Apart from Mirna, Will and the masked person, there are two men about my age, staring into the fire with bored expressions on their faces. Three children are asleep, but one girl keeps her arms clasped around her belly and looks extremely miserable. Mirna is kneeling down beside her, soothingly stroking her hair.

Wolf takes me by the elbow, a touch that startles me. He leads me a little ways away from the others, where we can sit down on a protruding rock.

"Tell me," he says.

And so I do.

He doesn't say anything while he's listening to my story, but I didn't expect him to. Wolf has his gaze fixed on his hands. When he finally looks up, it is to look at my belly again. I feel like he is looking for a sign, a swelling, something that reveals there's a life growing inside me.

I take his hand and press it against mine. "Are you afraid?"

He swallows. His Adam's apple moves up and down.

"Wolf," I say with a tremor in my voice. "I need to know what you think. I've come to ask you what you want. Do you want..." It takes me a moment to gather my courage. "Do you want to have this child?"

Wolf stays quiet. His hand trembles under mine. I can't quite make out if he wants to caress me or push me away. The silence between us becomes unbearable and the longer it lasts, the colder I get inside.

He doesn't want me anymore. Maybe that night meant nothing to him. Maybe I was very wrong about him. I try to suppress a feeling of anxiety. "Wolf. I need an answer."

"Nimue." He sounds even hoarser than before. "I'm so sorry. I shouldn't have done this to you. You are too young and too vulnerable."

"I'm strong enough to hear the truth," I snarl at him.

"I know." He gently caresses my face.

"You are strong. But I wasn't. I've been irresponsible and now you are paying the price for it."

"Nonsense," I say, frustrated. "I don't regret anything."

"I hardly knew my own father," he says, after a moment of brief silence. "I remember my grandmother. Then all of a sudden, all of my people were gone, killed by trappers. I don't know how to be a father. I was raised by the forest, Nimue, by the darkness and the wild beasts and on pure survival instinct. And then a different kind of fear and darkness came when they brought me to the Institute. Do you understand that? Nothing in my life has ever prepared me for this."

I lean into him. "Still. I need you."

He strokes my cheek with a calloused finger. "You should have stayed with your family, where you are safe. Where you will be cared for. How can you be so sure that I have anything to offer you?"

"Because..." I think of how he held me, pressed against the ground, in a ditch. The rancid water from the sewers washed up under me, the men from Detection swarmed above me, but he protected me and kept me safe. I think of how he wrapped me in an embrace during the nights, keeping the cold and the voices in my head at bay. I think of how he sang his lullaby to me and chased away the anxious thoughts of the Hunter. "Because I have seen you in the worst of circumstances. You kept me standing – and I helped you. We're stronger when we are together."

"We were, once."

I don't know what else to say. Maybe he's right... Maybe we only drew strength from each other because there was no one else to cheer us up. Maybe the magic I felt for him was inspired by the bleak reality around us. Nothing more than a dying spark in the night.

"Still I came," I say with difficulty. "I'm at home. And you are here too."

"What's your plan? Do you want to have your child in the middle of a refugee camp? In the middle of a continent that is falling apart?"

"No. That is not what I want. I didn't know how bad it was."

He lets out a deep sigh, as if he is carrying the whole world on his shoulders. "When I sent you off to the sea, it wasn't because I wanted to be away from you. I saw the truth. You are a child of the water, and I am a child of the forest. I hate water and I hate depths. It's too dark for me. It frightens me, like a nightmare."

"What are you telling me?"

"That I never thought we would be together. You went your way and I went mine. I told myself..." He stops and closes his eyes.

"What?"

"I let myself believe that your love for me was just a childish crush. Just one sweet night, and then you would answer the call of the sea. Even I was able to hear that voice."

"You never even thought that there was a possibility I'd come back for you? Or..." This second thought is even more painful. "You never thought about looking for me?"

"No." He slowly shakes his head. It must be obvious how much the truth pains me, because I can no longer hide the agony in my face. He puts his hand against my cheek and immediately pulls back again. "I will take care for you and the child. Even though I fear I haven't much to offer. I will try to give you what you ask for."

"You're not happy with it," I conclude, feeling defeated.

"Are you?"

I protectively wrap my arms around my bulging belly and stare at the smoking fire in front of me. "That's not the point, Wolf. The spirits want to use this child for their survival and we have to protect the baby."

"You shouldn't have made that promise," he says with a sigh.

"You weren't there. You didn't see my mother. She was so gaunt."

"If I had been, I could have warned you not to negotiate with the Others. It might have turned out well in the past, but not with the way they are now."

"You're a little late with that advice," I snap.

He remains silent for a long time, before softly admitting: "It is my fault."

"To hell with that! I wanted to do it, that night. I wanted it with *you*. I don't regret it..." I start poking at the fire with a twig. The smoke thickens and the flames hiss angrily. "I have no intention of giving the child up, Wolf. With or without you, I will fight any spirit that wants to take my child away."

That finally elicits a weak smile from him. "Is that your plan?"

I angrily throw the twig into the fire. "No, by Gwenhael's bones. That is a fact."

I don't get to hear his answer, as we are interrupted by a loud moaning. It sounds like a dying animal, but it's coming from the child I saw squatting down earlier. It looked like she was in pain. The moan ends in a wail and slowly fades. I get up to see what's wrong. Will and Mirna are leaning back. As I get closer, I smell the acrid, sour smell of vomit.

"What's wrong with her?" I ask.

"I'm not sure," Mirna says. She's holding a burning branch in her hands as a light and looks distraught. "She's very cold, her face is swollen..."

"Since when has she been like this?"

Wolf, who has followed me, says: "We were forced to stop because she couldn't continue. She has been showing symptoms since this morning. It's getting worse now."

I look up. The masked person stands motionless at the edge of our circle, bathing in both the darkness and the glow of the fire. "Do you recognise these symptoms?" I ask.

They slowly shake their head. From behind the oxygen mask, the voice sounds muffled and impersonal. Not male, not female. "It's too early to say. The symptoms of the Black Influenza can be very different during the first few hours. The bumps may still be growing or it may have settled in the lungs."

If it is the Black Influenza, they are all in great danger. I dread the thought of Will and Mirna falling victim to the corrupt Hunter inhabiting their bodies. Or Wolf, Gwenhael protect him...

"Move aside," I command. They do as I say. I cautiously move around the pool of vomit and place my hands on either side of the sick child's face. She is not fully unconscious, for her swollen eyelids flicker when my hands touch her red, irritated skin. Mirna is right: she is as cold as ice, as if her blood has stopped running.

I beckon Mirna. "Give me a bit more light."

Mirna does it, obviously reluctant.

I pull down a puffy eyelid, which makes her moan weakly. Her mucous membranes are not soft pink, as they should be, but almost white. Her lips are thick and blood-red. I push her jaw down to check her tongue. It is just as swollen.

"It's not the Black Influenza," I conclude. "What did she eat?"

Nobody seems to know anything. I turn to the two boys who are still sitting down, staring at the fire. "Did you see her eat anything?"

"Don't bother," Wolf says softly. He crouches down beside me. "Those two have lost their souls."

"Ah." I turn back to the girl, furious at the Asclepius Congregation for turning two strong, young boys into such useless shells. "I bet you feel terribly guilty, going to the trouble of smuggling them all the way to Gwennec," I growl at the masked person. "It wouldn't hurt to keep an eye on the kids, you know. Don't let them just put anything in their mouths."

I examine the girl's pockets. "Ah, there." I show the bystanders the red berries. "Baelberries. Doesn't anyone know that you should never eat those?" I don't really expect an answer and I don't get one either. I throw the berries into the fire. "Just give her some Blue Amenity, it grows all over the hills, and she'll be fine tomorrow."

The masked Snake wraps an extra blanket around the child, then lifts her off the ground and puts her in the cart. It takes more effort than I would expect from a man. I follow his movements with narrowed eyes. There's something familiar about the way he moves. As the Snake walks to the front of the cart, he stumbles for a moment. The ground is full of shallow pits, invisible outside the circle of fire.

Behind me, the flames hiss, and the fiery glow fades. Wolf has thrown sand onto the fire. It takes a few moments for my eyes to adjust to the darkness and for the moonlight to be bright enough to take in my surroundings again.

Will and Mirna talk to the Undreamed boys. They obediently allow them-selves to be taken to the back of the cart. Mirna puts a blanket over their legs. Maybe it's my imagination, but I have an inkling. Wolf is avoiding my gaze as he walks past me. It frustrates me, and when I want to climb into the cart and his hand is suddenly on mine, I push him away.

"Let me help you."

"I can climb, Wolf."

He says nothing. His hands disappear. Before climbing onto the cart, I glance at the Snake. He stands a little farther away from us, motionless, waiting. He blends in nicely with the landscape.

"You're not coming?" I ask.

He shakes his head. "I can't be away for too long."

"So you walk the whole way?"

"Not quite." He gives no further explanation, and without a goodbye, he turns around and starts walking into the night. I notice how he stumbles, how his ankle is bothering him with every step.

Suddenly I think I know who it is.

I jump after the Snake and catch up with her. "Wait," I say. "Take off your mask."

"I can't just…"

"Sini!" I interrupt her. "You are Sini, aren't you? I recognise the way you walk."

The Snake becomes very quiet. After a moment of stillness, she slowly lifts her hand and pulls the oxygen mask from her head. Sini's face is white in the moonlight, and dark where it is shrouded in shadows.

I stare at her. "I can't believe it's you."

"Why not?" Sini sounds a little cold. "Did you really think I don't have a heart?"

"I was more under the impression that you didn't have a head." She seems furious, and I press my lips together. "I… I'm surprised, that's all."

"A lot has changed, Nimue."

"I can see that."

"I do have a head. And I have sharp eyes and ears, too."

"I can see that," I repeat.

Sini is silent for a moment. Then she says: "We were wondering what had become of you. Dr Cairn had the country searched, all the way from Cami to Gwennec. You left without trace." There is a hidden question in her words, but I do not answer it. Sini seems annoyed, as she is waiting for me to say something. "Aren't you going to give me any answers?"

"No, but you will."

"Why should I?"

"To prove that you are on our side."

She smiles briefly and points to the cart. "I have already proven my loyalty."

"Then do it for me, Sini."

She lets out a sigh. "When you escaped, things started to change. All those children, running for their lives..." Sini has an uneasy look in her eyes. "I don't think you would believe me when I say we never knew."

"Never knew what?"

"How frightened they were. How much we hurt them."

"Don't be a fool," I say softly.

"I *have* been a fool. We thought that the fate of humanity was in our hands and we wanted to help. It's not unusual for children to cry in strange surroundings, you know. It's not unusual for them to be afraid of machines and unfamiliar people... We were saving their lives, right? We cured one patient after another and tried to rid the world of Black Influenza. Dr Cormack and Dr Moal knew exactly what they were doing."

I give her my sharpest look, and Sini falls silent for a moment. Then she lowers her gaze. "Everyone knew that Dr Moal had a dark side. Nobody liked him, not even Doctor Cairn. But we needed him... He was indispensable, that's what we told each other. After you disappeared, a few of us weren't so keen to join the search. I think most of us were relieved you got away. And Pierrick started to question Dr Moal's work. He even broke into Cormack Cairn's office to go through his files."

"Who is Pierrick?"

"He works for Detection. Broad-shouldered, doesn't talk much?"

I shrug. In my mind, all the men of Detection look alike.

"He approached me. He talked to me about the patients, about how they were taken, about what he'd read in classified reports about the effects of the Undreaming. He didn't trust Dr Moal anymore. He wanted things to change.

He said that there were a few others who thought the same way and he asked if I believed him. I said yes."

I nod slowly. My admiration for Sini has grown in the past minute. "Cormack doesn't know?"

Sini smiles weakly. "We keep a low profile. It's the only way we can make a difference. God help those children if Cairn were to fire us. I can't imagine what he would do."

That worries me. "Cormack was never deliberately cruel. Not in that way."

"He has changed, Nimue. I don't know if he would be cruel, exactly, but he has become unpredictable. His temper flares up and dies out like a storm. He usually keeps to himself in his office. He seems very gloomy."

I have to process everything she's telling me. "Is he angry with us? Does he want revenge?"

Sini shakes her head and raises her hands. "I can't read his mind. No, I don't think he is vindictive. But if you ask me, you broke his heart."

"He hardly knew us," I say. "We were there for less than ten days!"

"He was thrilled to have a cousin – you noticed that too, didn't you?"

"Enough to break his heart?"

Sini shrugs her shoulders. "He's a loner. The memory of Benji is what drives him, but it has never given him the freedom to live his own life. Winning you over, getting your approval – that meant a lot to him."

I feel a growing sense of guilt. In the weeks following our escape, I barely thought about Cormack. To me, he's an idiot I didn't mind losing, but it wasn't my intention to break his heart. I wonder if that makes him more dangerous. If he's anything like his stepfather, that pain could make him even more bitter than he already was. "What do you think he's going to do?" I ask uneasily.

"Like I said, he is unpredictable."

"Nim!" Mirna calls out from the trestle. "We still have a few hours ahead of us. Will you hurry up?"

"I'm coming." I look at Sini again and offer her my hand.

A smile appears at the corner of her mouth. She takes my hand and her grip is stronger than I had expected. "Good luck," she says.

"Will I see you again?"

"Who knows?"

As she utters those words, she turns around and leaves us. I watch her walk away until Mirna calls me again, then join the rest in the cart. Wolf holds up a woollen blanket. Without asking me for permission, he wraps it around my shoulders. I hold his gaze for a moment. He doesn't smile, but this time he doesn't avoid my gaze. His warmth is more important to me than the blanket and I decide to sit very still, so as to not frighten him away.

6

LANCE OF THE LAKE

Finally, and as unexpectedly as a lightning strike, he reappears in my dreams. Arthur is not alone; the blonde girl is still with him. Will he have recognised her by now? Does he know that her name is not Goldilocks, but Katell? I'm standing near him, but he looks right through me.

Katell says: "My king, why have we stopped? This way we will never reach the Fisher King's tower."

Arthur throws her an annoyed look. "There's a river up ahead, and maybe even a road too."

Katell shakes her head. "This is the right way, I'm sure of it. You must trust me, for this is why I was sent to you. We have to go *that* way." She points downwards, to a large lake that shimmers like glass. "Beyond the water there's a plain. And beyond that plain we'll find the tower."

"What happens when we reach the lake?" my brother asks. "Are we going to swim?"

"There is a boat, my king."

"I have a name, Goldilocks."

"Indeed you do. Arthur, the Coming King."

"Just Arthur."

So he does remember his own name, but not Katell's, it would seem. And Katell... I can't tell if she remembers anything of her old life.

"Arthur," I say, even though I know I shouldn't. "Arthur, I'm here!"

"Did you say something?" Arthur asks, but he doesn't look at me.

"Only that we can't stay here," Katell replies. "We have to find shelter before it gets dark. Stop thinking and start walking."

"As you command," Arthur grins while he takes a theatrical bow.

I follow them on my invisible feet. Arthur and Katell struggle to keep their balance on the steep slope, but I slide down easily, like a gust of wind.

"Wait." Katell freezes, then whispers. "There, in the valley..."

"Shadow People," Arthur whispers back.

I can see them move: dark figures slowly moving past thorny bushes, unhindered by those sharp, grasping branches. They are as silent as shadows. They appear and disappear unpredictably. Can they see Arthur and Goldilocks? Or even me?

We silently wait for the dark shapes to move on.

"Come on," Goldilocks whispers.

"Do we really have to go that way?"

"This is the only way I know. They are gone now. Just... just keep your eyes open."

When we finally reach the valley, the air has become colder. Am I simply imagining it or is there truly a scent of frost in the air? The trees I have seen so far are bare, but I can't tell whether it's because of the changing season, the drought or whether it's from disease.

Just like the ridge, stones are scattered throughout the valley. The soil has a reddish colour, as if the blood of giants has seeped into it. To my relief, there is no trace of the Shadow People we saw earlier. The only sign of life are the bushes pushing their way through rocks. They have no leaves, only thorns.

"The light is fading," Katell says warningly.

So soon already? I look up to the sky and see a palette of brassy colours.

Arthur and Katell build a shelter of stones against the slope and I feel useless. I can tell that they have done this many times before.

Arthur gathers thorny branches to build a fire. The flames glow warmly on my Dream body. Just in time, for the daylight around us is fading away.

"Here we go again," Arthur murmurs. "No moon, no stars. Only darkness."

The girl shivers. I can only see Katell's face, lit by the flames. Her hair looks like a halo.

"Are you afraid?" Arthur asks.

"Of course I'm afraid. And those Shadow People..." As if it's a sign, she falls silent and Arthur sits up straight.

The surrounding sounds suddenly seem louder: the crackling of the burning wood, the wind that blows through the dry valley, the pounding of my own heart. What have they noticed that I haven't?

A heartbeat later, I hear the sound of clattering teeth: a few steps away from the fire, just out of the light. When the sound stops for a moment, I hear a hissing breath.

Katell has become even paler han she already was. She presses her back against the rock face.

I hear slow footsteps and breaths that sound as if the creature is eagerly taking in their scent, the sound of teeth clenched together... It would only take one leap for the creature to...

I don't know how to help them. Still, I let out a soft warning when I see Arthur crawl forward. He pulls a branch from the fire. Everything hisses and crackles and sparks jump up like bright lights until they are swallowed by the darkness. Then, I can see the size of the beast approaching them: it's not much bigger than a dog, but it's broad and muscular like a bull.

The beast lets out a low growl. Arthur swings the torch, and the flames are fed with air, growing larger.

"Go away!" he shouts. "Go away or I'll set you on fire!"

The growling of the beast becomes louder, hungrier.

"Arthur!" Goldilocks squeaks.

Yellow, lamp-like eyes stare at Katell and my brother. I stand beside the beast, frozen with fear. He doesn't see me, he looks right through me, just like the humans do; his eyes remain fixed on the torch.

Then, as if by miracle, he retreats.

Katell and Arthur remain motionless for a long while before Arthur wedges the torch between two boulders, ready to grab it again if necessary.

"They are afraid of fire," he says softly. "Good."

"For now."

"What do you mean?"

Katell hesitates for a moment. "Like new-born animals, they are afraid of things they don't know. What if they lose that fear, Sire?"

"Fire burns, whether they are afraid of it or not." Despite those resolute words, I see Arthur's hesitant look. "From now on, we'll always keep a torch with us. We'll fight them with stones and flames, if necessary."

Katell – no, in this world she is called Goldilocks – doesn't protest, although I can still see cold sweat glistening on her forehead. My little brother stays upright, his eyes fixed on what lies beyond the fire. If something moves in the darkness, would he see it in time? I wish I could stand guard for them all night – Gwenhael's grave, why am I so useless here?

"Sire?" Goldilocks suddenly whispers. "I see fire. There, by the lake."

I squint my eyes and see it too: a distant glow, small like a candle flame. The light is very clear, even though the lake is at the other side of the valley and at least an hour's walk from here. It looks like someone set up camp there.

"Who could it be?" Arthur asks.

"Whoever it is, he can see our fire too."

"The space between us is full of thorns," Arthur says. "I'll keep an eye on it. Try and get some sleep."

"Just a few hours," Goldilocks says. She sounds tired. "Then I'll take over, Sire."

"Arthur."

"Make sure to wake me up."

"Why do you keep calling me Sire when you're ordering me around?" he chuckles. "If I am a king, then I'm a king without a country. Have some sleep. I promise to wake you in a few hours."

I lose track of how long I've been watching over them. Suddenly, the sky lights up like a lamp. I don't see the sun; the sky is just a dull plain colour.

"You said you would wake me up!" Goldilocks shoves Arthur reproachfully. "You fell asleep and no one kept was on watch duty." Her blonde curls stand out in all directions. The daylight shines on them and glows on her skin.

"Sorry," my little brother mumbles.

"We could have been killed, do you realize that?"

He stands up and brushes the red gravel off his trousers. "I'm sorry. Fortunately, nothing happened. Do you know what that means?"

"What, Sire?" Goldilocks folds her arms.

"That we can rely on fire." He picks up the burnt-out torch and weighs it in his hand. "A bigger branch would be better. An old rag and some oil…"

"Oil?"

"You know what oil is, don't you?"

I'm also surprised. Katell grew up next to the oil rigs of Gwennec… has she really forgotten everything? That thought drives a stake through my heart.

Arthur and Goldilocks follow an unclear track to the valley, trying to avoid the grasping branches of thorny bushes.

After a while, she says: "What's oil?"

Arthur's deep frown makes me realise that even he has trouble remembering. "It's like water, only thicker. It doesn't sink when it leaks into the sea and birds and fish die from it. They make oil lamps out of it, which produce light for hours."

"How does it smell?"

"Like… I can't remember."

"Oh, Arthur," I whisper.

"I know how you feel," Goldilocks says. She clearly didn't hear my voice. "When I first came here, I had all these strange thoughts and dreams that I couldn't place. They disappear after a while."

Arthur frowns. "What *do* you remember?"

The path narrows rapidly. Goldilocks bends down under a low-hanging bush. Arthur has to lower himself on his knees to cross the rocky ground. Meanwhile, I slip easily past the tangle of branches.

"By Gwenhael," Arthur growls.

"Who is Gwenhael?"

Arthur shrugs his shoulders.

"I remember a nest," Goldilocks says. "I think it belonged to a huge bird. It was high up on a mountain. It was cold and dark. It stank. And it was full of fear."

"Were you alone?"

She shakes her head. "There were others too, but he came to me… The Hunter. I ran as fast as I could and hid. I discovered that the Hunter moves more slowly in daylight. Still, I wouldn't have made it if I hadn't found the tower."

"The Fisher King's tower? Is that why you know where we have to go?"

She nods. "The Fisher King told me I was safe with him. He was not as weak then as he later became. He told me what was going to happen to him and that you would come, Sire. A young king to assist the old king. He was waiting for you. He is still waiting."

Arthur sighs. "I didn't know anything about this."

***

No matter how much time passes, the sky remains a nondescript colour. I wonder if I should wake up. Maybe this is one of those dreams where time seems to fly, but not a minute has passed in reality?

Up close, the lake is much larger than it seemed as viewed from the mountain. A beach full of pebbles leads to the surface. A thick mist rises from the water, obscuring our view of the other side.

"Do you think the person from last night is still around?"

Arthur nods towards something that is emerging from the mist a few steps away: the fire is still smouldering, and next to it are a wooden bowl, a pair of leather shoes, and two flints. "He must be somewhere nearby, unless he saw us coming and fled."

"Or he ran away from something else."

"Perhaps. Give me the torch." Goldilocks hands him the stick and Arthur lights it up. "Do you see those footsteps?"

They lead away from the fire, towards the lake shrouded in mist.

"At least those are human tracks," Goldilocks murmurs.

"Aren't you curious?"

"I'd rather be careful. Besides, it's time to cross the water... The lake is much bigger than I thought."

From the edge of the water looms the tall figure of a man. "Arthur," I say warningly. "Katell, watch out!"

"You said we didn't have to swim," I hear Arthur say. "I hope you were telling the truth, because it's impossible to swim that far without drowning."

The girl bites her lip, her worried gaze fixed on the invisible other side. "There was a boat. Last time I was here..."

"Who are you?" The stranger approaches them. He is holding a burning torch in one hand, in the other a lance. The shaft is made of thick wood, the huge blade is cut out of stone. He threateningly swings the burning torch in their direction. "What are you doing here? I know monsters like you can't stand fire!"

"We are not monsters," Arthur says. "Can't you see that?"

"Monsters come in all shapes and sizes."

"If we were monsters, why would we carry fire with us?" Goldilocks asks. "We just want to cross the lake, that's all."

The man with the lance squints his eyes suspiciously. "What business do you have on the other side of the lake?"

"Do you know what it's like on the other side?" Arthur asks.

The man stays silent.

Arthur tries another method: "What is your name?"

"I don't give my name out to strangers," the lance carrier replies. "All you need to know about me can be seen with the naked eye: my fire, my lance."

Goldilocks moves the torch away from him.

"We don't want anything from you," Arthur says. "Let us find a way to cross the water so we can part ways peacefully."

The man whistles between his teeth. In the ensuing silence, he takes them in from head to toe, as if silently contemplating something. Goldilocks nervously looks at the lance in his hand. If he decides to use it, they would have to make a run for it... I see Arthur putting a hand on her shoulder.

Finally, the man lowers his weapons. "I believe you. But I cannot let you cross the water just like that. Incarnated nightmares wander the other side. It's not safe out there, except in the tower..."

"We *are* going to the tower, you fool! Who are you to stop us?"

"Who are you to want to enter the tower?"

"Our intentions are good," my little brother reassures him. "This is Goldilocks. My name is..."

"He is Arthur, the Coming King. You should be helping him instead of getting in our way!" Goldilocks takes a step forward. She looks so small next to the much taller and broader lance carrier. He looks down at her in amazement. "Every creature in this land who remains loyal to the Fisher King should assist him!"

"The Fisher King is in the tower," Lance says. "Why does your friend call himself king? Is he a traitor?"

Goldilocks gives him a puzzled look. She gestures around her, indicating the barren, misty landscape. "Can't you see that the Fisher King is dying? The land is poisoned because he is weakening. And because of his weakness, the Hunter is able to prowl freely through the Two Worlds! He destroys everything he touches. The hills under our feet, the water we drink, the trees, all of the Fisher King's subjects. And the people in the Second World. But it is not too late."

To my surprise, she grabs Arthur's hand and pulls him forward as if he were a gold-winning cow in the market to be admired. "The Fisher King begged for him to come! The Fisher King is waiting for him. He is late, but at last he came. We have to go this way if we want to reach the Fisher King before his final hour. These are dark times and if you care about the Two Worlds, you must help your new king!"

The man's astonished look shifts from Goldilocks to Arthur.

Arthur lets go of her hand. "Goldilocks, you're making too much of this."

"You are rather young for a king," the man with the lance says.

"What the Fisher King says is true." Goldilock sounds confident. "So don't try to stop us."

"It is not pleasant on the other side," the lancer says. "I won't let you go alone. If I have to, I will use my lance in your name. Sire."

At first, Arthur looks uncomfortable, as if he wants to protest, but after a moment of hesitation, he says: "Thank you. Now can you tell me your name?"

"I would like to, but ..." The lancer bows his head and only now do I realise that he can't be more than a few years older than my brother. The hard lines around his mouth and the dust covering his face make him look older. "I mean... I know I had a name, not long ago. No matter how hard I try to remember it, however, I can't recall it."

"Me neither," Goldilocks says softly. "The Fisher King has given me a new name."

"And you, new king? Can you remember your name?"

Arthur nods. "My name is Arthur."

"Then at least you have a piece of yourself in this cursed land," he says. "You may call me Lance."

I take in the young man from head to toe. He has ash-blond hair and light blue eyes, the colour of a misty morning sky. His clothes are simple and dirty from mud splashes, his hands are large and strong. He is taller than Arthur, and his weapon towers above him. A fitting name, *Lance*.

"Is it really that bad on the other side?" Goldilocks asks.

Lance shows them his smile again. "If you're careful, you might be able to survive. And now that I'm with you, your chances will increase even more."

"Have you crossed the water?" Arthur asks. "Where is the boat?"

"Come with me."

The pebble beach makes a slight turn as Lance leads them away from his camp. The mist meets us from across the lake. All I can hear is the splashing of their boots through the shallow water. I don't make a sound at all.

"That fog never seems to clear up," Lance says. "And it's even thicker on the other side."

"Is that normal?"

He shrugs. "It's coming from the tower, I think."

"It's the dying breath of the Fisher King," Goldilocks says softly.

They wade further along the shore in silence, until a boat with four oars comes into view.

"It's not very big," Lance says. "Goldilocks, you take the helm. The king and I will flex our muscles for a change."

Together, they push the boat out into the lake. I watch how Lance climbs in first. He holds out a hand and helps Goldilocks get in too. I wonder how I will travel as a spirit – will I glide across the water or will I nestle between their legs in the dinghy, staying invisible?

A sudden jolt in my belly startles me. For a moment it fades away, just like my brother, and I feel my real body calling to me.

"Arthur," I say quickly, "Arthur, I'm waking up. Wait for me!"

To my surprise, Arthur jumps up. He turns around, his eyes squinting as he peers through the mist.

"Arthur! Can you hear me now?" I want to shake him to make him remember who I am – who *he* is. "I'm coming back, Arthur, I..."

As if through a veil, I see Goldilocks turn around in the sloop. "Arthur? What are you waiting for?"

"I thought... Didn't you hear anything?"

"Hear what?'

"Someone was calling my name."

"That was me," she says. "Just now."

My little brother blinks a few times. He shakes his head before striding through the water and quickly climbing aboard. The last thing I hear is his voice: "You're right. Let's go."

7

THE DESTINATION OF THE STARRY WIND

I wake up with a fright, jumping back from the Other World into my own body. I stare up at the dark ceiling, my heartbeat fast and my breathing heavy. I get up and glance at the bed next to me. Yannick hasn't stirred. She didn't wake up because of my restlessness. And I was right: in my world, no more than a few hours seem to have passed. I quietly put on my clothes and leave the room. It's not even dawn yet. I step outside with a chunk of bread in my hand as I'm instantly greeted by the chill of the late night.

These days, the old beach road has more car tracks than carriage tracks on it. Automatically, I head for the beach, until I realise that I won't find the emptiness of the past there anymore. I step off the road and climb up a much narrower, neglected path towards the cliffs. By the time I reach the top, I'm out of breath. With two hands on my belly, I sit down in a pit, my back nestled against a rock. From this cliff, Arthur and I used to watch our yellow kite escape, until it was just a yellow dot in the sky, slowly fading away. Our only problem back then was us bickering about the future... I wish I could turn back time.

His absence makes me feel angry. What good will it do to chase him as a ghost, when he ventures deeper and deeper into a strange and dangerous land? If I could protect him, I would. But I couldn't protect him from that bullet. I wasn't able to protect him when he needed me on *The Herring Gull*. And now he can't even hear me. Frustrated, I clench my fists in my lap. Arthur and I are like two ships drifting apart.

At least he has Katell with him. This Katell, who calls herself Goldilocks, is brighter than the shell I left behind in Mum's care on Avalon. So that's what the girl meant when she told me she was somewhere else. Her Undreamed spirit has been hurled into the Other World, with no recollection of who she is, where she came from. Without explanation or protection against the thousands of dangers and the Hunter. Now that I know this happened to her, I have no doubt that all the other prisoners of the Asclepius Congregation have suffered the same fate. The boy, Lance, must also be walking around somewhere on our side of reality, as empty and broken as Katell.

"Oh, Cormack," I growl. Does he even know what he has done?

Very slowly and silently, the sky begins to clear. I stay where I am and watch the impressive colour palette of daybreak. The sunlight tries to penetrate the haze, but I know that it will be hard for the sun to succeed. I'm starting to get cold and I can no longer sit still, so I decide to head back. This time, I take the beach road, and I notice a woman I recognize making her way towards me.

I call out to her: "Franseza!"

My old schoolteacher sees me and her tired face lights up for a moment. "Nimue! I heard you were back. It's so good to see you again."

"It's good to see you too, Franseza. Or... should I say Mrs Madoc?"

She lets out a smile. "I think you have graduated by now. Let me take a look at you."

I feel a bit uncomfortable, but I allow her to take me by the shoulders and make me turn in a circle. "You were so skinny the last time I saw you. And you looked so defeated. I see now you have changed. You're staying with Yannick, I presume?"

I nod.

"Thank Gwenhael we have enough space," Franseza sighs. "To be able to build the emergency shelters, we had to collect all the materials from the old and ruined houses, and still it's not enough."

"I have seen it."

"I'm sure you would rather rebuild your own home."

"Eventually," I mumble. The future is still nothing but a blur to me. But decisions will have to be made soon. Will I stay and give birth here? Will I be able to cope with leaving my homeland for the second time? Do I return to Avalon? Is Wolf going to be part of my future or will he flee into the forest as soon as he can?

"Has Arthur come too?"

I shake my head and look up at her. "He is with our mother. Safe." I notice that I say that last word with so much emphasis that Franseza shoots me a questioning look. I quickly change the subject. "You're up early."

"I started work two hours ago. Brevalaer slightly opened the gate yesterday morning. Apparently, the refugees were crowding around the gate in the rain. Now we are expecting hundreds of new people and I don't know where to shelter them. Most of the tents are occupied, and the medics are working over time..."

"I thought Brevalaer doesn't allow refugees for any reason," I say in surprise.

"The residents are unhappy. They are pressuring the district officials. I expect that with the bad weather coming, there will be more resistance to their policy. Nobody likes to see children sleeping in the rain and mud." She stays silent for a moment and her face becomes drawn. "Even the most compassionate amongst them aren't charitable enough to share their city with people who are ill. They don't want to get their hands dirty, so Brevalaer puts the refugees on the train and quickly sends them off to Saint-Thonan." She snaps her fingers. "The gate opens, the gate closes. And Saint-Thonan won't even let them in. They hand out food and water and chase them on to Gwennec."

We remain silent as we walk through the camp. It's already starting to look like a small village, with muddy streets intersecting and washing lines with children's clothes on it. Perhaps the sea breeze will have a chance to blow them dry before the next downpour, but with this thick mist I have my doubts.

"Gwennec has open fields," I say finally. "We can build new houses. We can teach them new crafts."

Franseza sighs. "We do have the space, but we don't have enough facilities. Purified water, protective capes, waterproof shelters, and vitamin supplements are limited... and what will happen in two years? Or in three? Will children grow up here, will people build new lives here? Can we send more fishermen out to sea when the city market is already faltering? The fish prices are dropping, many boats have been damaged by the Great Storm. I don't know if Gwennec would be able to take such a burden on her shoulders."

We are still passing many tents. It certainly is overcrowded here. Even the sea air doesn't completely blow away the stench.

"I really want to help all these people, but it's just not possible," Franseza says.

I'm trying to understand what that means for Gwennec. For the people who have always lived here: surrounded by emptiness and scarcity, held up by their own calloused hands. By Gwenhael, what will happen to us?

"You may be right, but these people are here now," I say. "And many more will come. In Gwennec, we survive by solving problems. If a boat is sinking, we close up the leak."

Franseza smiles. "That's exactly what we have to do. Have you seen that ship?" She points to the sea, to the old oil tanker behind the shallows.

"I have. What is it?"

"That's *The Starry Wind*, one of the first cargo ships to sail from the inland to the coast. She was built fifty years ago and has been damaged considerably over time."

Confused, I look at the unwieldy iron monster. "So?"

"The city council ordered her repair months ago. They couldn't get funding for it, but Yannick's father has donated some money. She is finally seaworthy again, although the interior still needs a lot of work." She smiles suddenly, a little mysteriously. "Tomorrow night, they will announce her destination. Here, on the beach. Make sure you're there for it."

She leaves me on the beach and I wonder where in Gwenhael's name the ship could be sent off to. My thoughts are interrupted by the sound of running footsteps behind me, and three refugee children splash mud as they run past me, heading for the sea. I hope that one day, my own child will be able to do the same. I want to teach them how to swim and I want to see them run, I want to teach them the names of the shells and fish. Until now, I've just been busy worrying: about Wolf's reaction, about what the spirits would want with my baby after they're born. Now, for the first time, I long to hold my baby in my arms.

It feels a bit like magic. When I turn around, I see Wolf. He keeps his distance, but I'm sure it's him. No one else I know stands like that; expectant, motionless, at a safe distance from the sea.

Again, I realise that he has chosen his name well. Like a real wolf, he stands at the edge of my habitat, too shy to approach on his own accord, ready to walk away when I fend him off. How long has he been standing there?

I shout against the wind and stretch out my arms. He keeps standing there for a moment. Then finally, he walks over to me. When he reaches me, he takes my hand. I feel a brief sensation of pleasure.

Wolf keeps his gaze on the sea. "I do think she's beautiful."

"She is beautiful today," I say thoughtfully. "Tomorrow, she will be destructive."

"Have you become fearful of the sea now?"

I think for a moment, then shake my head. "No more than I sometimes fear myself. I know how destructive she can be, but she remains a part of me." I look at my free hand, spread my fingers and close them again. "You once told me that I'm not fully human."

He grins. "You thought that was nonsense."

"I know now that you were right. Wolf... are you afraid of me?"

Wolf lets go of my hand. He gently takes me by the shoulders and turns me around so he can look me in the eyes. "You have a connection with the Others. I saw it in your eyes the moment you opened my cell door. But you are human in your heart and in your mind. I would be a fool to be afraid of you."

"I'm a bit afraid of it myself," I admit. "Even now. It makes everything so complicated."

Wolf brushes a strand of hair from my face. "It's a gift, Nimue. And a weapon. The more you embrace it, the stronger it will make you."

"Do you really believe that?"

"I do."

Carefully, I put my head against his shoulder. Part of me expects him to move away. To my relief, he doesn't. He feels much stronger than he was when we escaped the Asclepius Congregation. Perhaps he had forgotten how it was to be together... how it could be again. I allow a little hope to enter my heart.

"How long will you stay in Gwennec?" I ask.

"At least until tomorrow evening."

"For that meeting? Franseza was talking about it."

"They have a plan." Wolf puts his arm around my waist and points his gaze back to the sea. He gives no further explanation, or perhaps he doesn't know yet what the Gwennec district official has come up with. Together, we watch the sea and the children until I get cold.

A large part of the beach has been cleared. Tents have been moved to the back, a platform of wooden scaffoldings has been set up. A large fire drives away the early darkness and keeps us warm as we gather around the platform. I take in the people around me. There are villagers, townspeople and refugees; even though we are not one people, we still stand together, shoulder to shoulder.

I'm standing next to Yannick and her mother. Alma and Pedre are nearby and I keep a watchful eye on them, afraid they might get lost in the crowd. After spending the afternoon flying kites on the beach, they are no longer afraid of me. On the contrary: Alma has decided to follow me like a puppy, and Pedre is never far behind either. Not that it bothers me. I know Anouel was willing to take them under her wing, but she has her hands full with her own small daughter. Marie has developed a nasty cough. I see her in the distance and we wave at each other. I'm glad to see that she has Nanicka, Cezar and their son with her. At least they have each other as friends, now that they're making this unfamiliar place their new home. The relentless fog, the eternal wind by the shore and the tents on the beach are not how I would have liked to introduce Gwennec to them. I rather would have taken the whole group to Yannick's house, but with Alma and Pedre there, the bedroom that the four of us are sharing is too small. And even if I gave up my bed for a refugee, even if we filled the shed with sniffly, coughing children, there would still be hundreds left on the exposed beach. The tents are a weak barrier against the elements. Yannick thinks an influenza outbreak is bound to happen that way. Once that happens...

I sigh and pull Alma away from two long legs that almost run her over. To keep her with me, I put a hand on her shoulder. She is fine with it and leans against me. My belly is barely showing, and I already have a five-year-old to look after now, I think with a chuckle.

Someone pushes himself forward through the crowd. It's Will. His gaze wanders in every direction until he sees us. He smiles then and comes over to join us. Mirna arrives right after him, followed by Wolf. It's strange to see him like this, surrounded by so many people. Gwenhael spare him, he clearly seems to be getting a bit tired of it. I catch his eye and caress his arm.

"Poor soul," I whisper to him. "Don't worry, they won't hurt you."

"I know." He manages to throw me a confident smile. That's something else I don't see often.

Franseza climbs onto the platform, followed by Yannick's father. Yannick smiles and waves at him. He grins at us a bit sheepishly. They are accompanied by people who are only vaguely familiar to me: that small, balding man is the district official of Gwennec. He rarely left town to visit our fishing community before. The last time I saw him, I was only eleven years old. The other woman next to Franseza is the market master. Then there is the harbour master, a tall, well-dressed man who smiles all the time. I remember him best, because he once gave us a loan when *The Ragdoll* had suffered serious damage after a particularly bad storm season. I remember Dad working hard to repay the debt and when the man noticed our struggle, he let us keep the money. Dad's dignity was never fully recovered, but I was really grateful.

I don't remember seeing those four people together before. They have nothing in common, except for their wealth in a community where money and goods are scarce.

"Do you know what your father has been up to lately?" I ask Yannick.

"Not really. I know it has something to do with that ship, but they all kept it very quiet."

"Gosh." I fold my arms. As soon as the district official raises his hand and asks for silence, I give him my full attention, just like the rest of the crowd.

"Good people of Gwennec," he says. "Brothers and sisters of the city, brothers and sisters of this hospitable fishing community... thank you all for coming here. And a warm welcome to our friends from afar, the weary travellers, those who have lost their homes. You have our deepest sympathy. We welcome you and we work for you, for when we, the people of Gwennec, look at your faces, we see ourselves in you. We too know the fear of having to flee in the night. We too know how it is to lose your house and goods. We too had to get back on our feet and rebuild our lives. We did not leave Gwennec. Instead, we relied on the land and the sea to sustain us. And it has sustained us, if only to the meagre minimum of subsistence. And I fear that this brings us to the first half of our message: you are most welcome, however, we won't be able to survive when our numbers have grown so large. We lack food, water and shelter. We cannot give you what you need."

Oppressive silence ensues. I look around me. The people from Gwennec look uncomfortable. Anouel has gone white in a matter of seconds. She holds Marie tightly.

"It is a simple fact," the district official says. He doesn't seem very happy about it either. "How many nights will you last in a tent? It won't protect you from the wind or from your children getting sick. Storm season seems far away, winter even more so, but there's not enough time to build shelters for all of you. We cannot protect you from something we ourselves have been struggling with for years."

"You have enough land!" someone shouts from the audience. I cannot see who it is, but I can hear the anger in his voice. "And there's nowhere else to go!"

"It's true," someone else adds. "I'm from Lum Urbo and there is nothing left to go back to. No power, no water treatment plants, no police. Everything has come to a grinding halt!"

"My wife died during the epidemic. My parents and my brother were put in quarantine. I never saw them again and I don't think I ever will!"

"I was working in Rome. They have sealed off the city! Every ill person is dumped on an island off the coast to perish."

"People died in every town we passed. We didn't *want* to come here – we were forced."

"My dear people!" The district official raises his hands in the air. "Let us finish speaking first. You haven't heard the second half of the message yet."

It doesn't seem to matter anymore. Panic has seized the people who have gathered. Around us, the refugees begin shouting to drown each other out. Each of their stories is a tangled thread in the tapestry of our new Central Europe. I pull Alma and Pedre close. Yannick looks at the stage in shock, at her father who is standing there in silence. His sheepish smile has vanished.

At last, it is Franseza who loudly claps her hands together and rises above the din with her cry. "We understand your fear!" she assures everyone. "We didn't come here tonight to send you back. We have come to offer you hope!" She takes a deep breath and then continues, not giving the crowd a chance to react again: "It's true that Gwennec is the end of the world. That has been the truth for generations. But we all know that something exists beyond our borders: countries that were abandoned, continents we are cut off from. For decades, the sea was too rough to sail, the storms were too wild, and each of us needed their strength on their own piece of land. For a long time, Gwennec was nothing more than a buffer, a shield for the interior. Central Europe has all but forgotten us, and we eek out an existence on the very fringes of civilisation. Now that Central Europe has broken down, Gwennec cannot unravel any further, because we will all break for real if that happens. But that doesn't mean there is no hope." Another deep breath. I can't tear my eyes away from her. "Gwennec doesn't have factories like Rome. We don't have computers, we don't know what it's like to live in the big cities. But there is something we *have* learned on our own. Something we can do better than the engineers in Lum Urbo, better than the oilmen in Camlann, better than the government in Rome... And that is navigating a ship."

Suddenly, it dawns on me which decision they have made. Why the oil tanker was brought to the coast, why Yannick's father put so much money into it.

"She can't be serious," I mutter to Yannick. My friend looks just as disconcerted as I am. "No-one has ever come back from an expedition!"

On the stage, the harbour master has taken the floor. He smiles as if Franseza has just offered us a wonderful holiday trip. "Our ship is solid, seaworthy and above all, big. *The Starry Wind* is able to guarantee a safe crossing for several hundreds of you."

"Crossing?" shouts Anouel. She has lifted Marie in her arms and is staring desperately at the platform. "We have already been through such a miserable journey, and now you are sending us out to sea? Where to?"

"To the north," says Franseza. "Far north. We know that Great Britain has drowned. There are a few islands left there, but they are not big enough for us to found a new community there."

I bite my lip and think of Avalon. No – if I told anyone about the island, the same problem would arise there as here in Gwennec.

"We also know that the overland journey passes through barren steppe and tundra, far beyond the outer limits of Central Europe. But the north can be reached by boat, perhaps even within a month."

"Think of the possibilities," says the district official. "The north is wide open. There is no epidemic there. The north has room for us, there will be plenty of food and water, the air is not polluted by years of fumes and exhaust. Will it be tough? Yes, it will. But we are not sending you there empty-handed. There will be a medical attendant and a good helmsman. *The Starry Wind* has room for people and supplies. Not just provisions for the road, but everything you will need to build a new life: seeds, livestock, everything from sewing equipment to a small water purification machine. And, as far as Gwennec can spare, building materials. Brevalaer and Saint-Thonan have agreed to contribute. Soon, life will not be harder than it is here in Gwennec."

"This is madness," I whisper. Yannick has no answer yet, but Will thoughtfully licks at the edge of a new cigarette he's rolling.

"It might work," he says.

I turn to Wolf. "You say something! You know what it's like up there. You know we can't send ailing parents and children there."

Wolf puts a warm hand on my shoulder and says nothing. Maybe he wants to wait and see what else is revealed. He doesn't like to speak, especially when it's not necessary. I decide to remain silent and wait too.

On the stage, the district official continues. "We understand what we are asking of you. We are hoping for enough volunteers who have the courage to embark on this expedition. If you are afraid of the journey, let me reassure you: *The Starry Wind* is strong enough to weather storms on the high seas. You can see her from the coast; up close she is even bigger. We have done our best to create space for families with children – cabins have been built, compartments have been created using partitions and curtains. I admit, it sounds primitive, but is it truly worse than what you have to endure here? And bear in mind that a thousand people can easily fit on board, although we are starting with a group of five hundred. No, it is not a temporary journey. Anyone that boards must be prepared to work for a new life, free from Rome, free from the collapse of Central Europe. Nevertheless, the ship will make a return trip to bring news. Messages can be taken and returned. And if some of you manage to find safe refuge, then the others can embank on this journey too. Think about that." The district official smiles at us all. "This is not the end of the world. This is the beginning of a new one."

He gives us some time to let his words sink in. And I have the feeling that it is working. People are talking and whispering to each other all around me, and instead of anger, I sense a hesitant excitement.

"The north is far," someone says. It is a big man wearing a bright red mackintosh, the hood pulled up, even though it is dry. I can tell from his accent that he comes from far inland. "It is dangerous and wild. None of us are prepared for it. Even with food, we don't know what we're getting ourselves into."

"That's why there is a guide." The district official speaks softly, but everyone keeps quiet to be able to hear him. He looks pleased. Perhaps he had expected an argument like that and has saved the best until last. "Someone who knows the landscape. Someone who knows which dangers to avoid and how to make the wilderness our ally."

I'm suddenly aware of the wind penetrating my clothes. The heat from the big fire seems to be losing its strength. I look at Wolf, who has planted his hand firmly on my shoulder.

"Thanks to him, we know what to expect. He is the only one of us who has travelled this path before. You will be safe with him."

I feel my body become petrified all the way to my bones when the district official calls out Wolf's name. And when his hand disappears from my shoulder, the cold wins over my whole body. I can only watch as everyone in our neighbourhood turns to Wolf. Will, Mirna and Yannick seem as surprised by the revelation as I am.

Wolf's eyes briefly meet mine. I shake my head.

On the stage, the district official calls out to him for the second time.

Wolf doesn't run forward. He backs away, further and further, like a frightened animal. And then, with great strides, he flees into the dark.

"Go!" Yannick gives me a push in the back. She pulls Alma and Pedre out of my arms. "Run."

I do not wait. Overwhelmed by painful feelings and fear, I leave the crowd behind.

8

TWILIGHT SONG

I find him in the dark, far away from the camp and the fires. Far from the beach road, which on nights like this is the only safe path for strangers like him. Wolf may be a stranger to Gwennec, with its jagged coastline and treacherously steep cliffs, but he knows how to navigate the rugged terrain without getting injured. I'm reminded of that fact when I finally find him, almost by accident. I barely manage not to bump into him.

He has chosen the hill of Saint Gwenhael as his refuge, standing beside the only crumbling wall that's left. His back is straight, his legs stiff. He could pass for an abandoned statue.

I carefully avoid the few protruding stones of the foundation among the grass. The grass is still short from the long winter, though I suspect it will soon shoot up. I don't think anyone from Gwennec is going to bother protecting the hill from turning into complete wilderness. The days of the old church are no longer.

Even when I have almost reached him, I'm not sure he realises I'm there. "Wolf?"

He startles as if I have just shouted in his ear.

"I'm sorry," I mumble.

He relaxes, if only a little.

Slowly I get closer, until I'm standing next to him. During the day, this stop provides a spectacular view of the village. "Did you think I wouldn't find you here in the dark?"

He does not respond.

"This is Gwennec, Wolf. This is my world. And I wish that, for once, you wouldn't run away from me."

Not even the shadows can hide that my words have stung him.

I sigh. "*You* are the guide for that trip to the north. You haven't mentioned it before."

When he finally answers, his voice is rougher and huskier than usual: "They came up with the plan weeks ago. I agreed to it as soon as Franseza made the offer. I didn't know you were coming back." He seems to be trembling. "I didn't know you would be with child."

"I promised you I would come back."

"A sweet promise." He doesn't say it condescendingly, rather tenderly. "I didn't think you'd have the chance to keep it, even if you wanted to."

"You could have a little more faith in me!"

"Or maybe you should have a little less faith in me." He turns his face towards me. "I'm not a fairy tale hero, Nimue. I'm hardly anything at all. I don't even know what I've become or where I'm going..."

"I know where you are going," I say. "This is your chance to get back home. I get that." I look at his dark face. "When I had to choose between you and Avalon, I chose Avalon."

"It is not the same."

"It's not that different." We stand together in silence. My imagination fills in what my eyes can't see: the houses and sheds, the wharfs and boats, the fishing nets stretching from wall to wall... Even if the sun were to rise now, the village would never look like it did back then.

"Those people down there need you," I say.

"*The Starry Wind* will leave, with or without me."

"How much chance do they have in the north, without you?"

His silence speaks volumes.

I bite one of my fists until it hurts. "I can still travel, though not for long. But, Wolf... I have to make a decision immediately. Should I stay here or return to Avalon? If I choose the latter, I must leave soon... provided Free Breizh allows it."

"I know."

"There is a third option," I say hesitantly. "I can come with you to the north."

"No." He turns halfway towards me and I see tenderness in his eyes. "Brave, foolish Nimue."

I open my mouth to protest, but he puts a finger to my lips to make me shut up.

"Once I was a shaman. Once I saw the paths of people as a tangle of roots and branches, going up and down. Just like then, I no longer see reality, but I... I am shaman enough to know that our paths do not align. Your path leads to Avalon. That's where you need to be, Nimue, with your family."

I choose my words carefully. "I walked all the way down that road. On the island, it made a sharp turn. So I went back, Wolf, until I found you. And as for family..." I shake my head, amazed that he can see so much and yet is so blind at the same time. "That's you. Don't you get it? You're not only a father once our child is born. The child is already here. You are a father now!"

I'm standing close enough to see that these words are deeply affecting him. His mouth drops open a little. Then he swallows, his Adam's apple going up and down. "I hadn't thought of it like that," he says hoarsely.

I let out a laugh, take his hand and put it on my stomach. "Then start thinking about it like that! You only have to want it. So tell me, Wolf: what do you want?" I step closer, until my body presses against his. Our hands are pressed against my belly, with no escape. I feel his breathing falter, then quicken. "Tell me what you want."

I have caught him. He slowly moves one hand from my belly to my face. The fingers of his other hand weave through my curls. His forehead presses against mine. I feel his warmth against my skin and his breath on my lips.

"You. I want you, and the child."

Triumph awakens my body. "Say that again."

"I want you."

"Then prove it."

I don't have to wait long for his kiss. It is neither tender nor shy. This is another version of Wolf claiming my mouth; a predator on the loose, leaping forward. I feel my knees weaken, and as if he senses it too, his hands push me to the ground. He hovers above me, close enough to feel his chest move against mine.

His mouth moves from my lips to my neck. Close to my ear, he breathes a few words: "I'm coming with you to Avalon."

My answer is smothered by another kiss.

He refrains from putting his weight on me for now, mindful of my belly and our child. His breath is quick. My hands cling to his shirt. It's strange how he can still smell exactly the same, I think in all my excitement. Earth and grass and campfire smoke, that's what he smells like. And when I press my face against his shoulder, I also smell a hint of sea salt.

"Ouch!" Pain shoots through my lower back as I lean in for another kiss. Only now do I feel the bumpy ground that I lie on and the sharp edges of the stones in my back. With a groan, I get up.

Wolf takes a little longer to come to his senses. He breathes hard. "Is something wrong?"

"My back. It hurts from the pregnancy." I rub my lower back to get the cramp out.

"Come here," Wolf says. He sits up and pulls me into his embrace. Far away from the lights, far away from the warmth, I lean against him. He tenderly caresses my belly as if he were already touching the head of our unborn child, and he rests his chin on top of my head. "I should take better care of you. A hay bale is the least I should offer."

I chuckle at the memory of the hut and the hay bales.

"They say babies can already hear sounds in the womb," I say. "Wolf, I promised him you would sing for him."

"Him?"

I shrug. "Or her. Would you like to have a son?"

He laughs softly. "I just want him to have five fingers, one head and two legs. A son or a daughter..." He is suddenly silent, as if he only now realises that he is really having a child.

"Sing for him," I urge him.

"What should I sing?"

"You know exactly which song I mean." I clear my throat and make a shy attempt of my own: '*Hush, little brook, the forest slumbers softly, and all the wolves howl, howl in the night...*'

"You sing it better than I do."

"I've forgotten the rest of the words."

He hesitates for a moment, then his hoarse, low voice sounds in the twilight of the hill of Saint Gwenhael:

'*Hush now, little creek,*

the forest slumbers light.
And the wolves cry,
cry out in the night.
Be still, do not be afraid,
for the night so deep dark blue.
In my arms you are protected,
and no animal will harm you.
But mother my,
I am far from weary
I hear the alfen king,
the king calling to me
The darkness won't be long
with its alluring song
Dear mother, can you hear
those wild strings so near?
And mother my,
you will not hear
the alves with their singing
The fiddle with its strings of delight
who says I still have to dance tonight?
and I must follow, for a long, long time
until the morning light.'

In the silence that surrounds us after his hoarse voice has died out, I hear the rustling of the sea. The wind is shifting in our direction, carrying the cold from the water and the smell of the big campfire on the beach. I nestle closer to Wolf's body, pull my legs up and point to the dark hole at the bottom of the hill.

"Once, you could see the lights of the houses twinkling down there. There was a path that went down a few miles. In the summer, the verges were full of clover, and flowering thistles, and blackberry. And at the end of that path, the beach began again. That's where we lived." I close my eyes. The darkness won't let me see what I want anyway, and my memory is so vivid that I can almost touch our house in my mind. "That is where I was born. That's where I played with Arthur. That's where I fished on the sea."

Wolf doesn't answer right away. He gently strokes my hair. "Would you rather have our child grow up here?"

"I would like nothing better." But I gloomily shake my head. "There is nothing left anymore. The houses are gone, our boat is gone. Even Saint Gwenhael is gone. Every time I walk through Gwennec, it is as if I'm walking among ghosts and echoes."

"Ghosts and echoes," he mutters. "That's exactly what the north has to offer me."

"Were you serious then? Do you want to go to Avalon with me?"

He nods slowly. "If that's what you wish."

"And the sea...?" I turn my head so that I can see him. "I can't promise you a ship as strong as *The Starry Wind*. Arthur and I had no more than a fishing boat. That means standing on deck whether it is raining or storming. There's no place to hide on a boat like that."

"Curse the sea," Wolf says softly. "North or west, what does it matter? I have to cross the deep anyway."

"Can you swim?"

He grimaces. "Like a dog in distress."

"That's better than nothing," I reason. He laughs.

"Wolf?"

"Hm?"

"Kiss me again."

He takes my chin in his hand and ends up covering half my face with it. Again I smell the smoke, the grass and that whisper of sea salt – perhaps a promise of what is to come if he ever learns to love the sea.

Wolf may not care about the waves or the darkness below the surface, but I'm a child of the sea and he surrenders to my lips without hesitation.

9

YANNICK'S CHOICE

I find Will next to his cart. It is a misty, grey morning. The mist forms little droplets on his nose and in his hair, and it has made my clothes damp. A few people are loading crates into the back. Will is sitting on the trestle with his legs crossed, cleaning the horse harness with a cigarette between his lips. He has obviously been at it for a while, because the rag he is using is as black as his hands.

When he sees me, he shows me his crooked smile. "Good morning, princess of the night. Stayed up long?"

"You could say that."

His grin widens and he gives me a wink. I chuckle and let him think what he wants. The truth is, Wolf and I haven't tried to make ourselves comfortable again on that uncomfortable hill. For most of the night, he held me in his arms and I talked – about everything I could remember: about Gwennec, about Arthur and my mother, and about my dreams about the Other World. Sometimes he asked some questions. Mostly he just listened. When the night had advanced so far that we were close to dawn, even the last of the refugees had crawled away into their tents. The great fire had gone out. Wolf had kissed me goodnight and I had slipped into Yannick's house, where my best friend was so deeply asleep that she didn't even move an eyelid when I slipped under the covers next to her, with Alma and Pedre being on my straw mattress.

I climb onto the trestle and take a seat beside Will. His annoying cigarette smoke wafts into my face. Pulling a dirty face, I pluck the cigarette from his mouth and throw it on the ground.

"Hey!"

"Has anyone ever told you how disgusting that is?"

83

"Mirna complains about it all the time." He takes me in from top to bottom. "Can I help you?"

I take a deep breath. "I want you to help me cross the border again."

His eyebrows rise almost to the point where they disappear under his dark hair. "Really? Did you lose something?"

"Actually, I've found what I was looking for."

"Wolf," Will guessed immediately. "I'm not following you, Nimue. Wolf will be boarding *The Starry Wind* in a few weeks."

"Wolf and I are going back to Avalon. We've talked about it and we have decided that it's better that way."

"Ah." I know Will well enough to see the disapproval in his eyes. He leans back a little, the cloth forgotten in his lap. "And now you need me to smuggle you back outside the border of Free Breizh. I hope you have a very good reason."

"Will, I'm pregnant."

His mouth drops open a little. I remain silent, partly to give him time to process the news, partly because I don't know what else to add. Finally, he whistles softly between his teeth. "Well. That turns things upside down."

"Quite so."

"Wolf is the father…?"

"Obviously!"

He smiles briefly; a smile that almost immediately gives way to a worried frown. "I know Gwennec is not the best place right now, but the world outside Breizh is worse. Are you sure you want to travel through it, in your current state?"

"My family is on the island, and since it is far away from this chaos, we will be safe there." I embrace myself, and in doing so, I embrace the unborn child within me.

Will nods slowly. "It's wiser to leave now, before things escalate further. It'd be better for at least one child to grow up in a place away from all the chaos."

"Isn't that also the purpose of *The Starry Wind*?"

"Yes, it is. But what will the pioneers find in the far north? Nobody truly knows and yet dozens of refugees have already applied. Including pregnant women and parents with toddlers."

"They are hoping for a chance to start again," I say, without quite convincing myself that they have good prospects.

"They will try. Most of them are not prepared. Well, they'll arrive in the springtime and maybe the summer will be good for them. But after that? What if winter strikes harshly? We're talking about the north, Nimue. Colder and farther than we've ever been. And now you're taking Wolf to your island. For good, I suppose."

I shift uncomfortably on the trestle. If Wolf were to join *The Starry Wind* expedition, he could teach the pioneers where to take shelter, how to cope with the hardships of that wild land. I feel as though I'm taking away their chances.

"Nimue." I look up at Will. He nods at me gravely. "It doesn't matter. If Mirna was carrying my child, I'd abandon the lot too. The whole bloody lot."

"Would you really do that?" I ask softly. "For good?"

He lets out a sigh. I wonder if he can answer that question honestly, because Will is driven by his urge to take up arms against everything he sees as injustice.

"Hypotheses are of no use to us," he concludes. "You and Wolf want to leave and who can blame you? That island sounds like paradise on earth."

A paradise. I think of Fergus, my grandfather. When I left Mum, she hadn't been able to bring herself to visit her father. Ana told him about the miraculous return of his eldest daughter and after that, nobody ever saw the old man wandering around the island anymore. Some said he locked himself up in his home out of fright. Dark rumours even claimed that he had taken his life on the cliffs near Gulls' Island.

I personally refuse to believe that Fergus took his own life. He is too selfish for that.

And then there's Arthur. My dormant brother, with his leg maimed for life. How can I face seeing him every day, lying on that bed in the small bedroom in Ana's house? Every day he has to be washed. His bed is regularly changed. Mum lovingly combs his blond curls. Arthur will grow older, without ever lifting his eyes. We will have to shave him. We will see him turn into a man. And never, never will we hear his voice again. Only in my dreams can I watch him, as a lone observer. At least he is unharmed there, and he remembers too little of the people who love him to let his heart be broken. That is a consolation, though it doesn't make Avalon a paradise.

I feel a surge of despair. If there really is nothing I can do for unconscious Arthur on Avalon, how am I to continue my life on the island? Will I have to introduce my child to her uncle, a man who may as well be dead in almost every respect?

"Nimue?" Will frowns.

I tear myself away from these sudden, gloomy thoughts. "How soon do you think we can leave?"

"Not until next week," he says. "We are about to drive to Saint-Thonan. I also received word this morning that ten refugees are stranded on the farm."

The disappointment on my face must be evident. Will puts a hand on my shoulder. "You need this extra week to get ready. After that I can take you to the border, no problem. I'll smuggle you across without any risk to you. But after that, there's not much I can do for you." He looks pensive. "You can try to arrange a car to Camlann, although many cars are stopped and checked."

"Will, just crossing the border is more than enough..."

"I can map out a route for you that's far from the main roads. But I cannot help you find a boat."

"I saw the ports when I came back from Avalon," I say. "So many people have abandoned everything to go inland. I can pay some money for a boat, and I believe there are plenty of fishermen who want to go elsewhere. They will take anything I offer them."

"There's a good chance," Will mutters. Through the mist, someone calls out his name. He puts down the horse tack. "I have to go soon. Be ready when I return, which could be a week, maybe two. I'll try to hurry."

"Thank you, Will."

For a moment, his serious look is replaced by a gleam in his eyes. "This is the last thing I will ever do for you, Nimue of the Sea."

I get off the cart and laugh softly. "After this, our paths will part, Will of the Ark."

"Some friends come, some friends go." With his arms crossed, he watches me as I walk away from the cart. After only a few metres, he becomes a blurry figure in the mist that's conquering a little more of the world every day.

Yannick is tending to Alma and Pedre. In his sleep, Pedre has drawn the blankets towards himself and Alma is shivering in the cold. Yannick carefully puts an extra blanket over her, without waking her.

I turn the oil lamp down. In the rest of the house, the lights have already been turned off and outside the closed window shutters, night has fallen. A little white light seeps in through the cracks. The moon hangs low in the mist, bright enough to claim her territory in the sky without being completely smothered by the fog. She is round and full, like a woman who could give birth at any moment. I wonder how long it will be before I carry such a belly myself. I can't say I'm looking forward to it.

"I have to tell you something." Yannick sits down on her bed with her legs crossed.

"I have to tell you something too," I confess. I lower myself onto my own straw mattress, pull my legs up and tug the blanket up to cover my knees. "Wolf and I have been discussing something."

Yannick nods. "You talk first."

I hesitate for a moment. "We are going back to Avalon together. For the child, and for ourselves. I don't know for how long." Another hesitation. "At least for a few years."

Yannick bites her lip. She bows her head. "And *The Starry Wind*?"

"Wolf is a father. We understand what he can do for the people of *The Starry Wind*, but we must think of our baby first and foremost."

She nods again. Maybe it's because of the dim light, but she seems to be getting paler. "When?"

"Soon. As soon as Will returns from his mission. He thought it would take about a week, two at most."

"I get it." The silence feels heavy. Yannick looks up. "My turn. Nim, when *The Starry Wind* leaves, I'm joining the expedition as a Medical Caretaker."

Perhaps I should have seen it coming. Yannick, the angel of Gwennec who unceasingly devotes herself to people in need. I had not considered that she would go somewhere else and it jangles me.

"I decided last night, after I recovered from the initial shock. You were no longer there... they spoke at length about their plans... About the possibilities of building a new society."

"What about your family?" I ask hoarsely.

Yannick smiles briefly. "They're worried, of course, but they trust me. And Dad has put a lot of money into the project – he understands what's at stake. He understands that it concerns the lives of hundreds, maybe thousands of people."

I answer her smile, albeit a lot sadder. "And you must help them. You can't just stand by and watch others struggle."

"This is what I want to do," Yannick says softly. "I see what is happening in Gwennec and I know that it cannot go on like this. I believe in the expedition of *The Starry Wind*, Nim. And I can help. That is who I am."

"It's for a good cause." I squeeze the words out with difficulty. "Unless a disaster happens, there's no turning back. Yannick..."

"*The Starry Wind* will sail back one more time."

"Even so."

"I know."

The truth dawns on me. If Yannick goes north and I go to Avalon, that means it's the end for us. There's no way we will be able to send each other messages. We will live the rest of our lives wondering about each other's fates. After Arthur, I'm now going to lose her too. It feels like there's a lump in my throat.

"Of course I thought Wolf would come along as a guide," Yannick says. She tries to sound light-hearted, but she can't quite hide the tremor in her voice. "So we'll have to get by without him. I think we can manage, if we keep working hard. It's just an extra challenge, isn't it?"

"If you're from Gwennec, you can handle it," I mutter. It is a lie. I saw it in Wolf's face last night and I see it in Yannick's eyes right now: the only one who can prepare the pioneers for the far north is the man I want to take to Avalon with me.

"We still have time," Yannick says. "*The Starry Wind* doesn't set sail until all the preparations are done. Will still has to come back. Until then, we'll carry on..."

"We'll keep going," I confirm, without the conviction I would like to feel. "We'll get through the darkness."

I hear Yannick snort. It almost sounds mocking – not something I'm used to, coming from her. "We are *fleeing* the darkness by going north. This is not an act of resistance, Nimue. We are running away. I have no hope of defeating the Black Influenza if we stay here."

"You've given up?" That's not like Yannick either. It hurts, like a vicious stab wound.

"You mean you haven't?"

I wrap my arms around my waist and do not answer immediately. I cannot lie to her, nor can I say that I know everything will be alright.

My silence seems to be enough of an answer for Yannick. She stares ahead and the silence hangs between us like a thick fog, until she unexpectedly says: "Tell me again how the Black Influenza came to be."

"Why?" I ask wearily. "If you're right, it can't be reversed."

"Because I'm not a fool. I know it can chase us as far as the north. If that happens, I at least want to know what it is. What it *really* is."

I nod slowly. "The Impact released poison from our factories into the sea, the rain and the soil. Our world began to bleed, and the wounds we received were felt in the Other World. Just as their wounds were destroying our world. Now, the two worlds are tearing each other apart, and you are right, there is nothing we can do about it. Only the Fisher King can save us."

"It's just that the Fisher King is no longer there," Yannick adds quietly.

I think of the gaunt man in the throne room – a spirit bound by chains. "He *is* still there, but he is disappearing, just like all the other spirits. They are affected by the disease, just like us. Only they don't die, they... they break. They become hunters, led by the greatest Hunter of all." I feel the sickening fear I always experience when I think of the Hunter. "They hunt us, they hunt each other. I don't know where that will end, Yannick. Maybe the worlds die and we take the Hunter with us into our graves." My voice trembles slightly. "Or maybe the Hunter's power will spread to our world and we'll all soon be his prey, until there is nothing left."

Yannick's voice is as constricted as mine. "How do you still have hope?"

I hesitate and heave a deep sigh. "Benji believed that we had to kill the spirits before they could kill us. He believed that killing the spirits would put an end to the corruption."

"That's not a bad idea. Is it possible?"

Again, I hesitate. "I think it is the road of despair. The road we're supposed to take is longer and harder and unclear..."

"Nimue, listen to what you just told me! How can you continue to insist that we must protect the spirits!" Yannick's voice swells with every word. "Look out the window! We are desperate! We've never been so desperate! If your uncle Benji had any idea how we..."

"I have faith in Arthur," I interrupt her softly. "I believe he can resist the Hunter. I believe in the Fisher King. Just one single victory is not enough." I look at Yannick seriously. She has fallen silent, her lips tightly clamped together and a deep frown sitting between her eyebrows. "I think we have to take the long way round. That we should listen to the story of the White Prophet and stop dominating the world. She won't let us control her, we can only try to live by her side. Yannick, do you understand what I mean?"

Her facial expression changes a few times, as if she is struggling to sort out her thoughts. Then she mumbles, almost unwillingly: "Like the sea."

"Yes, like the sea," I agree. "And when we think we have mastered her, and can bend her to our will, the storms and the darkness come to overpower us."

Yannick doesn't seem consoled. "Is there any hope?"

"I still have hope! I know that Arthur's on a journey there, and I will do everything to assist him."

"And yet you flee to Avalon." Yannick shakes her head. "I don't know if we're safer up north. I don't know if you're right. Either way, I'm going with *The Starry Wind*, Nimue. This doesn't change my decision."

Maybe she's right, I think gloomily. Maybe fleeing as far away as possible is the only chance we have left. But she's not right about Avalon... Maybe Wolf and I are fleeing from the problems in Gwennec, but Avalon is also the Island of the Spirits, the Island of the Whispering Pool. I run straight into their arms, with their new prophet in my belly.

I drop down on my mattress and pull the blanket up to my chin. "Let's sleep."

Yannick falls silent. After a while, I can hear the rustling sound of her settling down in her bed. Her breathing and stirring tell me that, like me, she will lie awake for hours. No doubt her mind is also racing with thoughts. Can I accept that I have won Wolf and lost Yannick? Can I let my best friend leave for an unknown country without anyone watching over her? How have I become the linchpin in the wheel that puts the fate of hundreds of people at risk?

I feel like a blind man trying to find his way.

10

The Letter

The weather is starting to clear up, although the fog remains low to the ground. The temperature rises and in the following days, the residual sharpness of winter disappears. Even the rain clouds slowly move away. There is always more to do than can be done in a day and I throw myself into the work a little too enthusiastically. It's a form of distraction and it ensures that I'm dead tired by the time I can finally snuggle up in my bed at night. Or in Wolf's arms, if we can find a dry and warm place together. Sometimes it's an unused barn, with the hay bales he promised me, sometimes it's a tent we have to use, meant for a new family in tatters that will arrive the next day.

As the temperature rises, so does the optimism in the tent camp. Before, I saw people just bumming around, lifeless and depressed, but now, many are full of energy again. People laugh with each other while doing all kinds of chores. The healthy help us care for the sick. The strongest gather at the new harbour outside the village every day. From there, they take row boats to the giant cargo ship. Inside the hold, huts are being built and a kitchen is being furnished. On deck, the railing is strengthened and made higher, so that the future children are not in danger of falling overboard. I don't know who the captain of *The Starry Wind* will be; in any case, it has to be someone who can navigate far beyond the boundaries of any map we have.

Together with Yannick, more villagers of Gwennec will join Yannick on the ship. My old classmate Mart is one of them. Taran, Marci and Judikael, Arthur's old friends, have also signed up. I spoke to them two nights ago. They were very quiet, especially when I didn't tell them anything about Arthur's fate. They wouldn't have believed the whole truth, I think, but they seemed grateful that Katell had at least found a safe refuge. With Will's help, they had made it back to Gwennec, and I don't have to talk to them long to find out that the Asclepius Congregation still haunts them every day. I understand why they choose to sail with *The Starry Wind*, but I fear what awaits them in the new land.

The same goes for Anouel. She tells me that she's making the journey for Marie. After all, her daughter has little future in a place where there is nothing more than the sea and the gifts it has to offer.

"There has to be a safer place," she believes. "Where we can do more than just survive."

"You know nothing about the wilderness. Or about the predators that are used to being at the top of the food chain." I don't know if I'm trying to stop her, or if I'm just trying to ease my own conscience a little by warning her. "Wolf says summers can be wet and winters can be without a single day of thaw."

"We can learn to deal with that. People used to live there, why can't we do it again?"

I will not argue with that. All the pioneers of *The Starry Wind* have a reason to go north, whether they come from Gwennec or from much further away. If they have nothing to stay for, who am I to deny them an uncertain but hopeful future? It is not that different from what Arthur and I did: we too left Gwennec, with only a few words from an old diary to guide us.

And yet... I cannot turn off my worries.

And so the days are strung together. The better weather and the hopeful refugees are in stark contrast to the growing restlessness in my mind.

Before I know it, the first week is over and Will comes back to the village. He's not alone. I'm in the infirmary taking care of a refugee girl, who has an ulcerated wound on her knee. Gwenhael knows how long she has been walking around with it. I try not to hurt her while dabbing the festering edges with disinfectant. That commodity is becoming increasingly rare here.

Will calls my name from the doorway. It hits me – the time has come. Time to pack up our things and leave Gwennec behind for good... That thought is pushed aside when a second person appears behind him. She is wearing her long, black coat, but she has taken off the oxygen mask for the occasion.

"Sini," I say, surprised.

"We need to talk," Sini says by means of greeting. "I have a message for you."

Behind the school building is a quiet place where we can talk. The mist has started making damp patches on the walls. Sini hands me an envelope. There is no writing on the outside, and it is clear that someone else has opened it before.

"It's from Cormack Cairn," she says, before I can ask. My anxiety must be evident because she makes a reassuring gesture. "You are not in danger. He specifically asked for the letter to be given to you."

"Cormack doesn't know where we are." I look from the letter to Sini. "Have you betrayed me?"

"It's not like that." Sini presses her lips into a thin line. "Cormack, too, hears the reports of refugees flocking to Gwennec. And he began to notice that patients are disappearing from the Institute, especially those who have already been Undreamed. And the fact that such soulless people manage to slip past the borders of Brevalaer and find shelter in Gwennec sets tongues wagging. I had not yet returned from my trip, but Pierrick was there. According to him, Cormack spoke of the smugglers as if they were a plague of rats that must be exterminated. His anger was explosive. Two days later, he calmly addressed Detection and the doctors. He said: "I have a letter for my cousins. It will be in the atrium. If anyone knows how to reach them, let that person bring the letter. Until then, I will not ask questions." Pierrick waited three days, then he took the letter and passed it to me. I read what it said." Sini gives me an unapologetic look. "And I decided to give it to you. Do with it what you will."

I silently take the letter out of the envelope. Cormack's handwriting is a little tidier compared to the chicken scratch I've seen from him before, as if he composed this short message with long pauses in between.

To Nimue and Arthur,

My only family

First of all, I hope that this message finds you in good health. Our farewell was not as I had wished, and I partly blame myself for that. Perhaps I should have listened to you better, Nimue, and especially to you, Arthur. In retrospect, that would've been wise. If anything good has come out of it, it is that I have had much time to reconsider myself and the Asclepius Congregation.

However, that is not why I hope to reach you now. I have news from Benji. Old words on old paper; thoughts of his that remained unknown to me until now. I found the documents tucked away deep in his archives.

In all sincerity, I believe I cannot withhold his words. They have kept me awake for nights. Now I want to share them with you, but not via an impersonal telegram.

I do not know where you are, nor who will hand over this letter to you. If you are clever, you will find yourself in what is now the only safe haven in Central Europe: somewhere in the new Free Breizh. Let us meet there. Let us talk. I beg you, not as a blood relative – but as a cousin.

With hope,
Cormack

I slowly blink at the words on the paper. I never even fantasised about meeting our cousin again, and I never expected him to assume such a pleading tone. I need time to sort out my thoughts and I can't tell what Sini is thinking.

I lick my lips. "Is this a trap?"

"Maybe. Do you think he'll gain anything by catching you again?"

I hesitate before saying: "Probably not. He realises that there's a mole in the Asclepius Congregation. At most, I would thwart him in his attempts to Undream even more victims." Especially now that I know what happens to the souls of such 'patients'. My mood grows grimmer. "Sini, Cormack has no idea what he's doing. The Undreaming must stop, the sooner the better. If there is a chance I can convince him of that, I must try."

She nods. "You want to meet with him, then?"

I know that this means Wolf and I will have to postpone our trip. Part of me is relieved to be seizing the opportunity; another, more rational voice in my head warns me of the dangers of waiting too long: my pregnancy is progressing, and I'm not particularly looking forward to a gruelling journey that will see me staggering around Central Europe like a fat goose. And yet... this is about a cause that is bigger than me.

I nod. "I will speak to him before I leave. I just won't let him lure me out of Gwennec. Let him come here. Let him come and see the Undreamed in our camp."

Sini looks at me in amazement. "You want to get Cormack to Gwennec?"

"Do you think you can arrange that?"

"That's going to be complicated, Nimue. My faction is not yet ready to give up anonymity..."

"Can you arrange it?"

Sini licks her lips. There's something in her eyes that I never noticed during my stay at the Asclepius Congregation. Ambition? "I'll see what we can do."

"Tell him not to wait too long," I say. 'The Snakes have cars. Let him use one."

Sini's smile is thin. "You mean *we* should put him in a car."

I shrug my shoulders. "Do what you have to do. As long as he comes here only to talk to me, not to steal our children."

"We wouldn't allow that," Sini says. "I can promise you that, on our lives."

Someone from the infirmary calls my name – Nanicka or Anouel. "Sini, do you have something I can write with?" I ask.

She picks up a pen from her pocket. There is only a little ink left in it and I have to try it on the envelope a few times before it works. In Gwennec, we switched to the much cheaper carbon pencil years ago.

I turn the envelope over and scribble my short message on it:

Cormack, I will wait for you until the moon is half full. No longer. I'll come alone, and so will you.

Nimue.

Sini puts the message in the deep pocket of her coat without comment, along with the pen. "I believe you're making the right decision."

"Do you know what he discovered about Benji?"

"I have no idea. If anyone can get through to him, it's you. Do your best, Nimue, because lives depend on it."

"So... no pressure," I mutter. Again, I hear my name being called. I hold out my hand and Sini grabs it. "Good luck. And Sini? Thank you."

For that expression of gratitude, I get a rare, sincere smile out of her.

Then she turns around and walks away with her typical limp.

At the end of that afternoon, I have a pounding headache. When I meet Wolf in the barn that has become our private room, I slip into his arms like a sleepy kitten and tell him about Cormack's letter. "Sini believes that I might be able to get through to him. Don't you think I should try?"

"Hm," is his short answer.

"You immediately knew what happened to Undreamed Souls. Now I have seen it myself, when I saw Arthur. Katell in the Other World, cut off from her body and her memories... And the other boy, Lance. We could run into him here in the tent camp. If Cormack knows about it, maybe he'll finally stop the madness."

"Do you honestly believe that?"

I chew on my lower lip. "I believe he can be a good man."

"Ability is not always enough."

"I believe he also *wants* to be good man."

"Wanting is not always enough either."

I turn around in his arms to look at him. "What would be enough, then?"

"For him? I don't know if anything will ever be enough." His face is sharp and dark in the dusky light of the barn. "Not according to me."

I understand. The years in Platform Zero have emaciated his body and wounded his mind. "Still, I must try. Not for Cormack, but for Katell. For all the Undreamed."

Wolf lets out a sigh. "I'll come with you."

"I said I would meet him alone."

"Not even if both my arms and legs were injured, Nimue. I *will* come with you."

"I don't know if that will make it any better..."

"It is not a question. My job is to protect you and our child from everything. If Cormack wants to see you, he will have to meet with me too." Wolf kisses my forehead. "I will be as silent as a watchman."

I can't deny that the thought of Wolf by my side makes me feel safer. With a smile, I snuggle closer to him. I feel his fingers run through my hair until I sink into a deep sleep.

'The sea kept still and could not move. Darkness enveloped her. For centuries they were like that, undisturbed... "Oh," sighed the Sea. "Oh, where have all the stars gone that the sailors used to navigate by? Where are the fish and plants in my belly? And where is the moon, which could draw my tides? It used to be different!"

The Darkness heard this, and he rejoiced.'

11

The Stolen Grail

I don't have long to dwell on the unfamiliar voice and its mysterious words. Before I know it, I'm floating next to Arthur, who is walking up one hill, then down another with Goldilocks by his side. They are following Lance, who confidently guides them through the misty landscape. Large, thorny brambles grow around them. Lance gathers dry branches here and there and ties them to his back.

"To make a fire?" Arthur assumes.

Lance nods. "The higher the flames, the safer we are."

The hills start to pop up in quick succession and the ground becomes drier and easier to walk on. I peer into the mist, at the shapes and silhouettes that are visible, and the few details that are being revealed whenever the torches come close to them. When the group also leaves the bushes behind, the landscape seems to become completely bare and open. It would make a good pasture for cattle, I think to myself, if grass could grow here and the fog lifted, at least. Not even a blade of wild grass pushes its way out through the cracks in the earth. Nothing offers shelter from the permanent cold lingering on the plain.

When the darkness unexpectedly reappears, Lance throws the branches on the ground and they start building a fire, as big as possible. The flames cut through the night and chase away the cold mist.

"The light will alert all the creatures in the area that we are here," Arthur murmurs.

"And other souls too," Lance says. "The fire will scare off the monsters, but it might be a beacon for the lost."

"The... lost?"

98

"Like you and me and Goldilocks. I have seen more people like us: hopelessly lost people and frightened children. All on the run, not knowing where to go."

All victims of Cormack, I think sadly.

Goldilocks nods solemnly. When Lance gets up, his limbs creak and he leans on his spear. "I will stand guard. Young king, take over the next watch when I wake you up."

"I can take a watch," Goldilocks protests.

Lance smiles. "You are tired. Sleep when you can."

"Do you think I'm weak?"

Lance laughs out loud. "I think you are tired. I'm trying to do you a favour."

Goldilocks slumps down on the ground again, this time closer to the fire. She looks displeased, but doesn't object to his offer again. She is paler than usual, the corner of her mouth sags a little and her eyes look dull.

"It's my turn to look for food," I hear Arthur say.

"There is no food here," says Goldilocks from her spot by the fire. She doesn't even look at him. "Everything is dead."

"If these monsters can eat, so can we." Arthurs gets up.

"You can't just go wandering around!" protests Goldilocks. "There are monsters, and the Hunter could turn up!"

"If we don't eat, we won't even make it to the tower. I won't and you won't either, Goldilocks. Maybe Lance will – that guy is like a bull."

Lance shoots him a crooked grin.

"Be careful." Goldilocks seems to be too exhausted to protest any more.

Arthur pulls one of the torches out of the ground and holds it up. The flame creates a path of light before his feet, at least for the next four steps.

"King, take this." Lance offers him a knife. I'm standing close enough to see that the blade is made of stone.

Arthur seems to notice it too, because he asks: "Don't you have any real iron?"

I cannot explain Lance's uneasy grimace. "No iron. I assure you it's sharp enough to cut through a bearskin. That's what I did with it, anyway, a few nights before I saw you. Use it if you must. Never hesitate. Any monster that smells hesitation will devour you whole."

"I won't go far." Arthur takes a torch in his other hand.

I silently follow my brother as he walks away from the campfire. The first few steps do not seem so scary, but then the mist swallows us up. I am immediately overwhelmed by a feeling of loneliness, even though Arthur is so close by that I can touch him. I try to put a hand on his shoulder – my fingers go right through him. Arthur visibly shivers. I quickly withdraw my hand; I don't want to frighten him.

The torch cuts small openings in the darkness. In that light, I see his breath vapourise.

After a while, the earth begins to show traces of life: thin blades of grass, which further down slowly make way for sickly-looking plants. Arthur sinks to his heels and starts rooting out the plants and tubers with Lance's knife. I see him taste one and then eat it all the way.

A cry pierces the misty night. Arthur shoots upright. I wildly look around me. Even in my sleep, I can feel my heart pounding heavily. The cry sounded sharp and high. Goldilocks? No, the camp is behind us and the sound came from some place in front of us.

Again that cry, closer and more frightened.

"Go back to the fire," I beg Arthur.

But he raises his knife and torch and stalks stealthily forward. I follow him, frightened and helpless.

Behind the hill, a fire is burning, much smaller than their own. It is smouldering and seems to be struggling to stay alive. By the little light it gives off, I see two tiny figures running away from something. One is coming our way, the other is fleeing into the darkness.

"Stop!" the frightened, insistent hiss of the person closest to us resounds. She comes to a stop halfway up the hill, staring out. "Olwen. Come back! Don't go over there!"

Olwen doesn't want to – or cannot – obey her. She is no more than a shadow against a background of deeper darkness. Are these two Undreamed souls, or are they human imitations – Shadow people, who are staging a play to lure Arthur closer?

The person on the hillside stares at her companion with something in her eyes that seems like frozen horror. She gestures at something, her voice hushed for some reason. Out of fear?

Then I see it too: the creature has been standing there all along, dead still and blending in with the night so well that it's almost invisible. Now it slithers forward, smooth as a hunting cat. Olwen faces him anxiously, like a little bird nailed to the ground, as if she has lost control of all her limbs.

My heart is pounding even harder. I know him, I suddenly realise. I would recognise that rotting smell and those shark-like teeth anywhere. *The Hunter! Run, Arthur, run!* I try to pull him away. Again, he shivers, without moving.

The Hunter leaps forward. His black claws seize the girl.

Olwen screams.

Then she makes a strange, guttural sound.

The screaming stops.

Nearby, the other girl lets out a low, drawn-out wail. She appears to be too scared and overwhelmed with horror to realize that she needs to run.

Arthur creeps forward a little. "Hey! Over here!"

She jumps up. The Hunter also shifts his attention, perhaps because of the sound, or perhaps because he has simply finished with his prey and is now focusing on his next meal. Standing fully erect, he is gigantic: thin and long as a bare tree. Everything about him is sharp and designed to rip apart its prey.

His many eyes focus on Arthur. And then – sweet Gwenhael. I am sure he sees me too. He grins widely and I flinch.

"Quick." Arthur isn't talking to me, but to the girl who is still alive. He drops the torchlight at her feet. "Get behind me!"

She gasps and finds shelter behind his back.

"Can you run?" he whispers.

"If you run, he will jump you," she squeaks.

Arthur turns his gaze upon the Hunter. I realise he doesn't know how dangerous the creature is. He has no idea what he is up against. Or will he guess that this is the monster Katell was talking about?

The Hunter approaches slowly. He circles the dying fire as if weighing the risk of the flames against the chance of making two more victims.

"And if you don't move?" Arthur asks.

"Then I'll dance with you," replies the Hunter.

His voice still sounds like the scraping of nails over stone. Every cell in my invisible body that wasn't already panicking is now screaming for them to get out of here.

"Ah!" The monster has decided to pass by the fire and instantly seems to be a lot closer. "Now I see your face. Can you recognize me as I recognize you?"

Arthur takes a few steps backwards. "I don't know you at all."

"You will know me soon enough, child-king." A red tongue darts out of his mouth and licks his pale lips. It reminds me of a huge, underground reptile. "I have longed to make your acquaintance for a long time."

"Go away!" My brave Arthur raises his stone knife, but that only elicits a hissing laugh from the Hunter.

"A stone knife won't hurt me. Well, what is this? Do you cower before me? Am I not equal to you? A king on the rise, a conquering king? Come, put down your toy sword and your fire. I don't carry weapons either, except my own flesh and teeth. Let's make it an equal fight." He spits the words mockingly, laughing as he says them.

"Run." Arthur thrusts his elbow into the belly of the fear-stricken girl. "Run until you see a fire!"

She turns and runs right through me. It makes me woozy. The world around me disappears for a second, then reappears. Everything has shifted: Arthur is standing next to Lance and Goldilocks, facing the Hunter, their torches like burning swords aimed at the monster.

"How do you know who I am?" I hear Arthur ask.

The Hunter laughs. "I know you better than you know yourself. I know you inside and out. And soon, I will know the taste of your warm blood."

"You don't know me. You are lying."

"Am I?" The monster laughs softly. "You don't believe that, child-king. You don't believe that any more than you believe that your little fire can keep me away from you."

I know that the Hunter is right. Believing that a single flame can put a stop to it is as foolish as thinking that the sea can be stopped by a pebble.

And then his eyes bore straight into mine. "Dear sea witch! Did you think you could help him? Or are you hoping that he might help you?"

"Leave him alone," I whisper, still feeling dizzy from the girl running through me. "Don't you touch him!"

"He's such a brave little child, isn't he?"

"Who are you talking to?" Arthur snarls, before I can reply.

The Hunter lets out another laugh. "I spy, with my little eye... One is blind and the other is stupid!"

"Back off, devil!" Lance barks. "I know who you are!"

The Hunter hisses. "Fire won't hold me back forever!"

"Tonight it will," Lance says. "You've got your prey, Hunter. Take it and leave."

"The sheep think they can take on the wolf!" Despite these mocking words, the Hunter doesn't try to get closer to the fire. He stands motionless for a while, the flames illuminating every bit of dead skin on his body. The flicker of his pointed teeth and his blood-red tongue are unmistakable. "One day, your fire will burn out. Then I will leap from the mist and feast on your flesh and bones." The Hunter slinks backwards. "Soon, your time will come."

When he picks up the fallen girl from the ground, she emits a low, anguished wail, but hangs limply in the Hunter's arms as he grips her tighter and slips away through the mist.

"She was still alive." Arthur seems as distraught as I am. "By Gwenhael! I thought she was dead."

"They are never dead." The unknown girl slowly approaches them, the fear evident on her face. She is carrying a torch as well, so that he can finally see her face clearly. She must be several years older than Arthur. Her skin is dark, kissed by a sun that doesn't shine in this land, her hair is a black mass of tangled strands. With anguish in her eyes, she gazes in the direction where the Hunter vanished with her companion. "It would be better if she were dead. But he carefully keeps them alive."

"Them?" Arthur echoes.

"The souls he hunts. He brings them back to his nest alive. We don't know why. We hardly know anything anymore." The girl shivers so violently that she almost falls to her knees. "We all know who the Hunter is, and that being caught means hell."

Goldilocks nods. "Do you remember your name?"

"I do. I am Morgana."

"I am Goldilocks. These are Lance and Arthur."

And Nimue, I want to say. My words are thinner than the mist surrounding us.

Lance picks up his knife, then takes in Arthur from top to bottom with a frown etched on his face. "We'll put the torches up around the camp tonight."

For the next few hours, Goldilocks stays close to Arthur. I despondently wonder if I should stay. Maybe I should try to wake up. My presence doesn't help my brother one bit.

"Did you hear what he said?" Arthur doesn't ask me. "One is blind and the other is stupid. What was he talking about?"

"I have heard that he lost his mind," says Goldilocks thoughtfully. "After he tried to put a horrible curse on himself."

"Who told you that?"

"The Fisher King."

"The Fisher King sits chained in his tower." Morgana speaks unexpectedly. She is standing with her back to the flames, which intensify the shadows on the plains of her face and light up the rest of her skin as if she were partially made of fire. "And the Hunter scours the land. We didn't know much, but that's what we both remembered when we woke up. It is as if this knowledge had been put into our heads while we were asleep."

"How come you still remember your name?" Goldilocks asks.

Morgana rolls up the sleeve of her red shirt and shows them a piece of dark skin.

"I still remembered my name when I woke up. When I felt like I was starting to forget it, I panicked. And I had a stone, which I used as a weapon. So I did this."

Even from my spot, I can see that the name *Morgana* is carved into her flesh in bloody scratches.

"Whatever happens to me here, I will not forget my name." She rolls down her sleeve again. "He can't take that away from me."

"And... Olwen?" asks Arthur softly.

Her mouth twitches for a moment. "She is on my other arm. I reminded her of her name every day."

"And who was she, besides that? Do you know her from before?"

A pregnant silence ensues and the agony is plain on Morgana's face. "I think she is my sister." Morgana trembles slightly, not only from sorrow but from a white-hot, silent anger. If she were fire, she could melt iron.

"I'm sorry," Arthur continues softly. "I didn't know he was keeping her alive. I saw her fall. I heard… I thought it was quick. If I had known, I would have tried harder."

"And then you would have fallen victim to the Hunter too." It is Lance who comes to stand beside them, wide-legged, with a torch in either hand. "Don't go looking for unnecessary danger. We don't know what the Fisher King wants from you, but he has already given you a name." He sticks one torch into the ground just behind Arthur. The other one he places two steps away. "King in his name. None of us can do anything when the Hunter grabs his prey, you have seen that for yourself. The best way to help is to free the Fisher King."

"King?" Morgana suspiciously looks at Arthur. "King of what?"

"The Coming King," says Goldilocks. "He has come to free the Fisher King from his chains. What Lance says is true – we must travel quickly. Tomorrow, we will cross the plain to the place where the ground cracks. The day after that, we can reach the tower."

"Travel with us, Morgana," Arthur says. "It is dangerous everywhere, but the four of us are stronger together than alone."

"Stronger than when alone," Morgana repeats. "That is true. Alright, I will come with you. I'd like to see how this… *king*… frees the Fisher King."

Arthur and Goldilocks get up to help Lance with his fire-barricade. I stay next to Morgana; that is why I'm the only one who hears her whisper: "If she is alive, I can save her."

For some time, I slip into a deeper sleep and don't perceive what Arthur, Goldilocks or Lance are doing. When I fall back into the dream with a jolt, the travelling companions have already moved far away from their campfire. In front of us, the tower is looming up out of the mist, like a giant that we suddenly bumped into. The fog has grown so thick that only the foundation can be seen, yet I recognise it at once: this is where the Fisher King lives. The gigantic, carved stones were once pearly white when I visited the old king; now they are grey.

I hear Goldilocks say: "No monster dares to come here. I think even the Hunter stays at a distance, so for now we are safe."

"Don't think you're safe anywhere," Lance corrects her. His eyes search the tower. "Where is the entrance?"

"There isn't one, really." Goldilocks takes Arthur's hand and leads him forward, until he is standing right in front of the stones. "He is waiting for you, Coming King. Call and let him know you have come."

"How?" He touches the tower. "No one will hear me through this wall."

Goldilocks remains determined. "It is your right to enter, Sire. You must be the king who demands entry."

"I'm not a king..." He gropes the wall, hoping to find a crack or an alcove that reveals a secret door. "I'm just Arthur, Goldilocks. I don't know where I come from or... where I belong. I don't even know how I got the clothes on my body."

"This way you'll never get in," she says angrily. "Were you called by the Fisher King, yes or no?"

"I don't know! I told you, I don't remember."

Lance's hand lands on Arthur's shoulder. "None of us have the memories we would like to have. But we have not fallen prey to the Hunter and we stand before a safe haven. Try it."

I stare up at the only window in the tower. The only time I was here, it was in a dream, and I found myself in the middle of the great throne room.

My attention returns to Arthur when I see that he is putting his hands flat against the wall. "My name is Arthur! Fisher King, if you've been calling me, maybe it's time to let us in!"

Behind him, Goldilocks makes a disapproving sound and Morgana suppresses a chuckle. Despite everything, Arthur grins briefly. "Hello? Knock, knock!"

Morgana gasps and Lance curses. A deep groan can be heard from within the rock. An opening appears where Arthur was holding his hands. It is a narrow passageway that leads into the darkness.

"Lance," says Arthur, "lend me your knife."

With the weapon in his right hand, Arthur crouches before the opening. Protected by my invisibility, I venture inside. In front of us is a tunnel, or perhaps a staircase – it is too dark to see properly.

"Take the torch," Morgana whispers. "What do you see?"

"A staircase. It's long... I can't see the end of it."

"Then go," Goldilocks urges him on. "Don't be afraid."

I'm quite nervous myself. What if it's a trap? What if the Hunter has ambushed the Fisher King and is now waiting for us in the darkness?

Holding up the torch in front of him, Arthur crawls inside. I'm careful not to let him walk through me again. It smells musty and earthy in here, like a cave. After a few steps, we can stand upright and our feet find the first steps of the stairs. Arthur lets the light shine in front of him, as far as it can reach.

There is no monster on the stairs. But the steps climb out of sight.

The others follow my brother inside. A moment later, the opening disappears, as if there never was a hole in the wall.

"I don't like sealed rooms," Morgana mutters.

The stairs winds up, and as I silently accompany them, their footsteps echo loudly and brusquely on the stone steps. The torches cast erratic spots of light and bring the shadows to life. All the while, we see no sign of the Fisher King or anyone else. When the stairs finally end and lead us to a narrow, dark corridor, they all have to catch their breath, except me. Arthur aims the light of the torch at the door in front of them.

"A lock," Morgana sighs. "And no key."

Lance leans against the wall. "Maybe we don't need a key. The tower obeyed Arthur downstairs too..."

Arthur feels the lock with a frown. He fiddles with it until it falls to the side. With a creak, the door opens a crack. "It was already forced open."

Lance puts a finger to his lips. Feeling anxious, I slip past him into the circular room. It's different than I remember it: the walls are still white, the floor is still made of hard, black stone, and a little daylight pours in through the only arched window. But this time, the glass is broken and lies in shards on the floor.

The massive seat is in the middle of the room. It seems to have been chiselled out of the same black stone as the floor, and the back is as high as a standing man. There are no drapes on it, no cushions, no runner on the ground. Only a few metal rings. Chains that are fixed to the floor, dangling across the wide armrests. I sneak around the throne. And there he is – the old man who once spoke to me.

I take in his lifeless face as Arthur and the rest come after me.

"No one's here," Arthur whispers.

"The Fisher King is here," says Goldilocks. "He cannot leave. The chains are keeping him from leaving."

"Why?" asks Morgana.

"Because he was afraid that the Hunter's curse would turn him into a monster."

"And what if that's exactly what happened?" Morgana looks at the broken lock with suspicion. "He may have done that himself. He could come after us."

Slowly, Arthur approaches the throne and falters as soon as he sees what I have already seen: a white ghost, dressed in clothes that have lost all their lustre. The spirals and circles that run across his face contrast sharply with his translucent skin. The cloak hangs in ragged folds around his body. His crown seems too big for his head. His hands lie motionless in his lap, the wrists bound by shackles.

"Your Majesty!" Goldilocks runs forward to kneel before him. She looks upset as she glances up at Arthur and the rest. "It has become much worse."

"Fisher King?" Arthur approaches hesitantly.

He is dead, I want to say to him. *The poor king has died on his throne.*

Then his eyelids blink and a little later, the Fisher King opens his eyes. They are as light-coloured as frost.

Goldilocks rises to her feet. "Majesty, I have brought the Coming King, as you wished."

"The Coming King." The Fisher King's gaze slowly shifts from me to Arthur. It takes a long time before he speaks again. "Ah, there you are. You have come at last. I have waited so long. I sent messengers and still you did not come."

"I..." Arthur seems to be lost for words. What did he expect to find? A man on his sickbed, perhaps? Or a powerful figure behind bars, whom he should have freed? Certainly not this frail figure, which looks as if one strong gust of wind could make him shatter like the glass in the windows. "I'm here now. Only I don't understand what I can do for you. Goldilocks was with you before, why couldn't she have unlocked your chains? Why does it have to be me?"

The Fisher King shakes his head. One of his hands moves a little away from his lap and he crooks a finger. Goldilocks gives Arthur a meaningful look, as if she wants to shove him forward. Arthur comes closer and leans in. The Fisher King visibly strains as he puts his hand on Arthur's forearm. "It is not for us to wonder why the sun is destined to shine... or why the bird flies... You were born from the power of the sea. The power of change flows through your blood.

Oh, Arthur, young king. You carry so much more power within you than you know."

"Your Majesty, I'm afraid you are mistaken. I wouldn't have stood a chance against the Hunter if my friends hadn't rescued me."

"Good," says the Fisher King with an unexpected smile. "That's good. A crown and sceptre don't mean you have to be alone."

"I have no crown or sceptre, Your Majesty. No one has ever made me king. That title is undeserved..."

He remains silent as the Fisher King raises his hand with effort. "Take the crown off my head."

"What...?"

"The crown, boy. Take it and be king in my name. I don't have the strength to help you."

"Fisher King, I can't just..."

"Arthur, just do it." Lance steps forward. He bows his head before the Fisher King, then takes the dull crown from his head. I stand there as if rooted to the spot. Lance is holding the crown in his hands. A small, pale light from the window reflects off the dull gold. "The Fisher King is too weak to be king. Someone must stand up and fight in his name."

Goldilocks fills the hall with her soft voice: "The Fisher King must be healed and freed. If he believes that this is your task, accept it."

Arthur swallows audibly. I come to stand next to him; an encouraging gesture that is of no use to him. "Do I really have to?" he says.

"Why don't we give it a shot?" Lance's mouth curves into a crooked smile and he puts the crown on Arthur's head. "Long live King Arthur."

I almost start to laugh when the crown immediately sags down his forehead. Arthur himself does not laugh. He seems to shrink under the weight.

"Well, now. Boy. Young king." Without the crown, the Fisher King seems even thinner and smaller, his voice no more than the rustling of a dry leaf in the wind. He sinks deep into his hard throne, the chains grinding against the stone. "Promise me you will fight for the Two Worlds. Be my advocate and be my honour."

"I hardly know what that means." My little brother looks nervously at the dying king and, to my surprise, slowly lowers himself to the ground. He takes the chained hand in his. "I promise I will try to do what you ask of me."

Pride, love and fear flow through me. My brother, my Arthur... Is he aware of what he is getting himself into?

As if he could hear me, Arthur then adds: "I don't know if I am as worthy as you think, Fisher King. I will do my best... But it would help a lot if you told me exactly what I have to do."

The Fisher King looks relieved. "Young king, once there was a Grail by my side. The Grail of water that could quench the thirst of the whole land. The creature now called the Hunter stole it from me. I thought he would never dare come to my tower, but he had become reckless and powerful. And I... I'm too weak to stop him." Self-reproach is evident in his voice. "Now the Grail is in his possession. For the good of the Two Worlds, you must find it." His breaths leave him in huffs and puffs. His voice dies away. "Your Majesty?" Arthur squeezes his hand and bones crunch under his fingers. "That Grail – what do we do with it once we find it?"

The Fisher King seems to get lost in his own thoughts, not hearing the question. "Once, I had a brother... He was radiant like the sun. Oh, brother."

Lance frowns. Goldilocks looks confused. Morgana peers at the Fisher King, her arms tightly crossed in front of her chest.

"Your Majesty... The Grail? You must tell me how I can save you."

"Take back the Grail. The Fisher King must be born again... From beyond death, he reappears... From the depths of the sea, he is reborn."

"He's talking nonsense," Morgana whispers. "He is delirious."

Arthur grabs both the dying king's hands, more roughly than is probably good for him. It works, though, because the Fisher King's eyes refocus on Arthur's face and the distant gaze fades. "There you are again, young king."

"I never left, Your Majesty. You spoke of the Grail."

"Yes, the Grail. Fill the Grail with blood."

"With... blood?"

His head is bobbing up and down. Is it a nod, or a sign that he is losing consciousness? "The blood of the brother. Let it become a Blood Grail, for the sake of the Two Worlds..."

"Fisher King, whose blood?" insists Arthur. "Who is the brother?"

"We are the brothers," murmured the Fisher King. "The Fisher King and the Hunter. Two halves of the same coin, never far apart." He is silent. His breath rattles in his chest. It's a nasty sound that would give me goosebumps if I had a flesh-and-blood body right now. "I suppose... it's time for change... I suppose I waited for too long... out of fear." A deep breath. "There is no other way. To save one, the other must die. Yes, so it is, so it is... That old blood magic. If one can exist, the other must perish."

"You mean... we have to kill the Hunter?"

The eyes of the Fisher King open wide for a moment and bore into Arthur's gaze. "Do as I say! The blood magic, the Grail, my brother..."

And then the voice trails off. The Fisher King reminds me of a wounded butterfly fluttering to the ground, broken. But instead of the ground, it is the throne that catches him. His head slumps forward and comes to rest on his emaciated chest.

Arthur remains kneeled, seemingly in shock. "I think he's dead."

"No..." Goldilocks' voice is a mere exhale. Bewilderment and incomprehension fight for precedence in her expression. She crashes to the throne, almost pushing Arthur aside. "No, he can't be dead! We were supposed to come and free him. Not that he... He never told me... He promised me more time!"

"What will happen to the land when he is dead?"

She approaches the throne cautiously, her arms wrapped protectively around herself.

"Won't the Hunter have free rein then?" Lance inquires.

"Arthur had to free him, that was the plan." Goldilocks begins to tremble. "That was the plan!"

Lance gently pulls her up and leans in to the king. "Listen. He is still breathing."

Goldilocks takes a few deep breaths. "He saved my life. If I can't keep my promise to save him, he might as well have let me die. All of us." She gets up and focuses her red-rimmed eyes on my brother. A fire is burning behind those clear blue pupils. "I knew you would take the crown. So make sure you are worthy of it, Sire. Promise me that."

"I have just promised the Fisher King that I will do my utmost..."

She grips the front of his vest with her hands. "Take an oath. Swear it on something that really matters."

I didn't know Katell could be so fierce. Arthur, too, looks down in amazement at the frail girl in front of him.

"Alright, I swear. Look." He reaches under his vest and pulls out the pendant on the leather cord. I gasp. My seal pendant!

Goldilocks stares at it. "Where did you get that?"

"I have been wearing it since I woke up. I don't know if it is mine or a gift from someone I have forgotten. For all I know, I may even have stolen it. But I want to believe that it means something good. So I swear it on this pendant... and on anything that it may stand for."

12

BENJI'S WILL

If Arthur saves the Fisher King, he might be able to come back. Maybe the Other World will let him return to his own body, sinking back into it seamlessly...

With that thought still lingering, I wake up from my long dream. I turn around and feel Wolf's arm slipping away from my body. He is still asleep. Through the cracks in the barn wall, I see the grey light of the misty dawn. The sea rumbles nearby, making sounds louder than the voices coming from the tent camp.

I sit up straight with a blanket around my shoulders. I'm surprised by how early it is. It feels like I have been away for days.

"You're awake." Wolf's voice sounds hoarse from sleep. When I look back, I see his dark eyes on me.

I smile. "Just barely. It's still early."

He sits up too and pulls the other blanket over my lap. "You'll get cold."

"It's alright." I wait a moment. "I dreamt of Arthur."

"Ah. Nothing bad, I hope?"

"I don't think so."

"Share it with me."

I tell him what I know, what I have seen when I was a kind of silent ghost. He thinks about it in silence, while outside, the sun is rising. "Time in the Other World and time in our world are like two rivers," he says finally. "It may be that your Arthur is caught in a faster current."

"It sure feels like it." I rub my throbbing temples. The dream makes me feel as if my head is already full, before my own day has even started.

113

"There is a way to get rid of your headache," Wolf says. "There are herbs that can clear a shaman's head, like St John's wort. But since you're pregnant, maybe rosemary would be better, and... we call it *huldrevot*."

"I don't know what that is," I mutter. Any remedy for this dull, cramped feeling is more than welcome.

"Be careful with the Hunter," Wolf says softly. "This time he hasn't been able to do anything to you, but he is devious. I worry about his increasing strength."

"Yes, it was frightening indeed," I admit. "And not just for myself. He could have taken Arthur."

Wolf strokes a tangled strand of hair from my face. "It seems that Arthur has found good company. They will keep each other safe."

I nod. "And he will kill the Hunter."

"Maybe. It will not be as easy as it seems, Nimue. The Hunter is not just a normal Other. He is as powerful as the Fisher King ever was, and he keeps getting stronger."

It takes a long time for the next question to take shape in my mind. "How do you know so much about the Hunter?"

"I do not." He averts his gaze and his mouth tightens. "I used to have a friend on the Other Side. A long time ago, before I was disconnected."

I remember him telling me that. I think there is a story behind this that he doesn't like to bring up. I lean in closer. "Who was it?"

"Someone with great power, until he fell prey to corruption." He looks up and the tight lines around his mouth disappears. "I don't want to bring up stories about my painful past, Nimue. We have more important things to worry about."

I'm a bit disappointed. Wolf is a master of secrets. But he is right: today is not the day to add more weight to my already burdened mind with ambiguous stories from the Other World.

"It feels as if a rain cloud is hovering in my brain," I sigh.

"We still have hours to go. I have something that will help you. It's a breathing technique that you can easily make your own." He puts his hands on either side of my head and lets me breathe slowly. I close my eyes. His low voice steers the air in and out of my lungs, following the rhythm he determines. "Now feel the ground beneath you," he says. "Feel how it supports you. It will never let you fall."

I become aware of the stability that carries me. The dizzy feeling in my head is decreasing.

"And feel your body. Your legs. Your belly." His hands move and wrap around my thighs, warm and firm, then lie at my belly button. They slide up my sides. I start to chuckle.

"Don't get distracted," Wolf reprimands me, even though I can hear the laugh in his voice. "Feel how your mind is no longer wandering in the Other World. You are here, anchored in your body. You are right *here*." His hand cups my face and it is his kiss that makes me open my eyes.

"I'm actually feeling better."

He slowly lets go of me. "You will feel better after you have eaten. Go walk along the sea for a while. This is an easy method, Nimue. Those herbs will help you if you really need it."

"This is fine." I get up and stretch all my muscles, from my toes to my fingers. "Do you still want to come with me today?"

"For you, I will look him in the eyes." Wolf says it lightly, but I know how much it costs him.

I take his arm and together we step out of the barn, into the daylight.

His car is moving down the beach road before it stops at the edge of the tent camp. I stare at it from the top of a small dune. The door opens and the familiar man with his dark, bouncy curls gets out, holding a bag in his hand. All his movements betray his hesitation. Someone gets out after him: a figure in a long, black coat and a mask similar to the one Sini wore. Yet it's not Sini. I can tell by the way this person moves, without a limp. Maybe this is that Pierrick fellow she was talking about. It's smart of them not to send Sini along – Cormack would have recognised her as quickly as I did.

The person dressed in black says something to my cousin, then gets back into the car and drives off.

Cormack remains very still, casting a glance around. He looks lost.

I approach him. Wolf is only a few soundless steps behind me.

Cormack doesn't see me coming right away. As soon as he notices me, his face changes. I see hope, despair and a little bit of fear. I come to a stop right in front of him, not quite close enough for him to touch me. A silence follows. He seems afraid to speak first, but I keep quiet.

At last, he understands that it is up to him to break the ice. He clears his throat. "It's so good to see you."

I believe that he is being sincere. I cannot say that I feel the same. "So, you came alone," I say.

"As you can see." He smiles uncomfortably. "My guide refused to speak to me. I wonder how much I'm paying him for his treachery."

"They are doing what you should have done a long time ago," I snarl.

Cormack swallows. He looks past me at Wolf. His face shows no sign of recognition and that fuels my anger. He should be haunted by Wolf's face in his bloody nightmares!

"When you wrote me back, you said you would also come alone," he points out.

"I changed my mind."

"I already suspected you would, although I expected you to bring Arthur along."

I remain silent.

"Where *is* Arthur, Nimue?"

"Safe," I lie.

He doesn't believe me. Cormack takes a step closer. "Something is wrong. I can tell."

"That's none of your business, Cormack."

He opens his mouth and looks worried. I briefly shake my head: a warning for him not to pursue the subject. I don't know if it's because of that, or if it's more because of Wolf, who is towering over the both of us rather menacingly, like a scowling predator.

Cormack spreads his hands in a sign of peace. "You blame me for a lot of things. And you're entitled to your anger, Nimue. But since you've agreed to see me, I hope that means you're also willing to listen."

"I agreed to see you because I have things to tell you."

His eyes light up. "Well then, let's talk." When I don't move, he adds: "I promise I don't want to hurt you. In my letter, I wrote nothing but the truth, word for word. Can we go for a walk?"

I gesture towards the camp. "Do you want to see the refugees?"

"I would like to see Gwennec," he says softly.

I let out a sigh. Fine, if the man wants to visit our village... I see no harm in it. Gwennec is not that impressive.

"I have never seen the sea."

That touches me somehow. "We have plenty of sea. This way."

I take him away from the beach road, via the narrow path to the cliffs and from there, down a rocky track, where the beach is finally without those white tents. Cormack glances at Wolf, but Wolf keeps his promise: he remains a silent watchman.

"So," Cormack says, as we walk across the wide-open expanse of sand towards the sea. The tide is low. "This is where you grew up. With this view."

I look at him for a moment. "It's not much."

"On the contrary. It's impressive." A subtle smile tugs at his mouth. "You know what space is. And emptiness. Freedom."

"You must not have had much freedom under Benji's command," I murmur.

It's meant to be a jab, but if Cormack realises, he doesn't show it. His smile widens slightly. "You're not wrong about that. My father left little room for others."

"Why did you want to come, Cormack? What have you found out about Benji that is so urgent?"

"You really don't want to talk to me about other things, do you?" He sighs deeply.

I hesitate. "It's not that I dislike you. You and I just see things very differently."

"Right." He coughs behind his hand, then clears his throat again. "Well then, let me share my findings with you."

He opens his bag and takes out a large, brown envelope. The paper is thick and it smells musty when he hands it to me.

I turn it over and recognise Benji's square, jerky handwriting. Without saying a word, I pull out the sheets covered in writing. Almost immediately, the strong breeze gives them a tug.

I focus on the words. There are so many of them, carefully penned in line with each other, as I have seen Benji do before. It dawns on me that I'm looking at reports again. The top one is dated far later than the documents I found in Cormack's display case.

Cutting off their spirit has become common practice for patients suffering from the Black Influenza, although the death that quickly follows makes the whole procedure useless. However, I do not feel despair. I'm convinced that I will soon discover a method that will enable the patients to keep on living healthily.

They now stay alive. But what kind of life is it? Sometimes I wonder if I had wanted Esoldi and Finn to keep on living with those dull eyes, those eyes that patients use to stare at me. They have become mere shadows of themselves. I am a doctor, not a priest. Sentimentality has no place in my line of work – not when it enables thousands of people to live on besides their loved ones.

There is another way to eradicate the disease. I'm convinced that it is not our minds that must be killed, but the spirits that destroy us in the first place. The Other World is beginning to become the cancer of our bodies. So how does one stop something that is intangible? How does one kill a spirit?

That last sentence was scratched out, made almost illegible, then scribbled in the side lines again. What kind of struggle did my uncle go through writing down those words? I turn over the paper.

Spirits are not made of the same matter as our bodies, but that does not mean that they have no substance.

The first thing to be determined should be whether they have blood.

Anything that has blood, can bleed.

Anything that can bleed, can be hurt.

Everything that is wounded, will either heal or die.

So the question is: how do you spill their blood?

I crumble up the paper in my fist. Cormack's eyes widen in shock as he looks at me, and that alone fills me with grim satisfaction.

"*This* is why you have come? To feed me more of these lies?"

"I doubt that they are lies."

"I don't care if there is any truth in it." I raise my arm and throw the wad of paper as far away as it will fly. The wind picks it up and plays with it in the air, carries it towards the lapping line of the sea. "It's also poison, Cormack. You need to understand that."

"You say it's the truth."

"Cormack." I rub my head. The cobwebs of this morning begin to wrap their threads around my mind again. "There is so much you don't understand about the Other World. You have been playing with it like a toddler playing with fire. You don't even see how much you have set ablaze already. Benji has controlled you like a puppet on strings and you worshipped him as if he were a god. Open your eyes! He was a bitter man seeking revenge. He wanted a war and the Asclepius Congregation was his gun. Anything else is a lie. I'm sorry." I take a deep breath and feel a stab of guilt when I see his face. "I really *am* sorry. You have to stop the Undreaming. You're destroying everything you touch, just like Benji."

I expect a protest. Perhaps I even expect him to lash out at me. Cormack looks at me and amidst the fog, he slowly loses his usual imposing appearance. He seems pale and uncomfortable instead.

"I have also brought something else." He hands me a second piece of paper from his bag. No envelope this time, just a folded-up letter.

"What is this?" I don't need any more angry words from Benji.

"Check the date," says Cormack softly.

I unfold the paper reluctantly, with half a mind to get rid of it before seeing what's on it.

2130 A.D.

At first I don't understand what's so special about that date, but then it slowly dawns on me: "The year in which Rona disappeared."

"And the year my father died. Nimue, read it. After that you can send me away or lecture me. But read this first, please."

It is not a report. Just a note from Benji's documents, not as carefully written as his observations on the Black Influenza. It's not even a long letter. My eyes skip over it.

I lie awake. Sleep doesn't want me; I don't think I deserve it. Thoughts are forcing their way to the surface. For years I have kept the lock to their dark room closed. Now that door opens to a crack.

Have I gone too far?

For a long time, I believed I had exchanged my love for bitterness, even hatred. Now that I look back, I realise that it was precisely this that led to my darkest hours. I tried so hard to reject someone I have always loved: my sister, who tried to save us from an empty existence on the island. I dare say I managed to cling to the darkness for a long time – far too long. As I brush the rust off my heart, I realise that there is much more love between us than hate. We are bound together by shared memories, a shared homeland, the same pain and hope. By blood, which I cannot replace or undo. Perhaps this is the deepest truth I have yet discovered: that those brought together by blood have no choice but to save each other. Then to redeem each other. Perhaps it is not too late, even for me.

Are these the last words of my uncle, before Mum exchanged his life for her own? "Cormack?"

Cormack coughs again, an abrupt and loud sound.

"What does it mean?" I insist.

"I don't know," he admits. "It may have been no more than a wistful side note, or he may have felt regret. If that's true, it was too late anyway. Rona had already disappeared by then and we both know that he died shortly afterwards."

I keep my eyes on the paper and remain silent, this time not because I'm reluctant, but because there is a lump in my throat.

"Nimue," Cormack says softly. "What my father meant by it is no longer important. He is dead, and with him, the true meaning of his words has died. What matters is what was left behind. *We* are what was left behind; we are the heirs in his will. Perhaps we have the freedom to make it mean whatever we want it to mean."

Now I look up from the sheet of paper, straight into his pale and sunken face. It is not just the mist and his nervousness that make him look bad. Have his worries consumed him? "What do you mean?"

"I mean… I have decided to believe that my father wanted to make peace with your mother. That he wanted to return to the love they once shared. To make peace with himself, if you will."

I find myself staring at him, my confusion growing with every word he speaks. "Do you want to reconcile yourself with me too? Is that what you're saying?"

He shoves his hands into the pockets of his coat and turns his face towards the sea. "I want there to be peace between us, Nimue. We don't need to repeat Rona's and Benji's history. I really wish Arthur were here."

So do I.

"He distrusted me from the beginning." I hear Cormack let out a sigh. "You didn't. I thought we understood each other."

"What exactly do you want, Cormack?" I interrupt him, before he can get overly sentimental. "What kind of peace do you want to achieve?"

A short silence. "The world needs help. I can help."

"You could end the Asclepius Congregation. That would make a difference."

"I think the Asclepius Congregation has a lot to offer." My sharp intake of breath is probably a clear sign to him that I want to protest that statement, and he raises a hand. "I truly believe that, Nimue. But not the way we are now. We have gradually lost our vision."

"There was only ever one *vision*," I say in a low voice. Wolf comes closer. His hand on my shoulder is hard, his fingers digging into my skin betray his own thoughts. "Benji's vision came from revenge. I remember the wording in his documents, Cormack. He called it a war."

"I will make it a vision of peace." He sounds so sure of himself. "The world needs doctors. We have them. The world needs shelter and medicine. We can provide those. The world needs a way forward, a compass that leads out of the darkness of central Europe. We can be that compass."

"Not as long as you cut the victims off from their own souls," I say. "You see their living bodies, but what you don't see are their souls – how lost, confused, and hunted they are. Alone in the Other World, incomplete. I do!" I have to allow myself a moment to calm down. "I saw them," I repeat, a little calmer. "Benji was wrong. He didn't save anyone. *You* didn't save anyone. So get rid of that cursed Asclepius Congregation. To hell with it!"

Cormack turned around halfway through my outburst. He now clenches his jaw. I see the meaning of my words dawn on him, slowly but surely. And maybe, I realise, he has suspected something like this was happening for a while. Maybe even Benji knew already. Maybe that's why Cormack is standing in front of me now, unsure of how to carry himself, no more skip in his stride and no more easy smile on his face.

"Then tell me," he finally says in a hushed tone, "what the hell do we do with all the infected victims of the Black Influenza?"

"Maybe..." I hesitantly look from Wolf to Cormack. 'Maybe I should try to save them, after all. As long as I'm able to."

"You want to save them? *Every* victim? Perhaps you don't realise how big central Europe is, Nimue."

"I've often thought about Benji," I say softly. "Sometimes I wonder if he might have been right about something... that our gift means we have a responsibility that Mum gave up on too easily."

"Nimue," Wolf growls next to me. "Don't make promises that could endanger our child."

"I can still heal people," I protest.

Wolf shakes his head. "Today, yes. But tomorrow you might not. You don't have much time left."

"A child?" Cormack grows paler. He looks from me to Wolf and doesn't take long to solve the puzzle. "Are you... are you expecting?"

"Yes," I simply say.

Cormack opens his mouth. He looks as if he wants to come closer, before he decides it is better to shy away. He shakes his head. "Of course... Then he's right. I can't ask that of you..."

"*What*, Cormack?"

Cormack seems to be pondering his own thoughts. "Nimue, your gift was Central Europe's hope. If you don't do it, how can you ask me to just stand by and watch?"

"You have to," I say. "Undreaming is not a cure, Cormack. Anything is better than that... mutilation."

"Tell me, and this time give it to me straight." He takes a step closer and now there is nothing left of the charismatic man I once met in the Asclepius Congregation. This is an exhausted man who sees his hope fading away. "What do we do with the people who are already infected?"

I lower my gaze. I cannot look at him. There is only one alternative and he is going to make me say it out loud. "If I cannot save them, we must let them die."

"Can we do that? Can you?" He comes closer and I'm surprised he doesn't sound angry. His voice is quiet, almost friendly. "Nimue, look at me. What will you do if the Black Influenza strikes Arthur? Or him?" He nods to Wolf. "Or someone from Gwennec, someone you love?"

I can't look him in the eye. I mutter: "Then I have no choice. If it were about Arthur or Wolf... I would save them."

"You can't save everyone. You will end up hurting yourself… and your baby too. I'm not like Benji – I would never ask something like that of you."

I look up and see he's standing very close to me. Wolf shifts his weight so that his shoulder is subtly between me and my cousin. I don't think he needs to worry, because I take Cormack's word for it: he's not like Benji.

Cormack waits a moment to give me the chance to answer. When I remain silent, he sighs: "You must accept my help. What I have come to bring is not nearly as powerful as Sela's gift, but it is better than nothing. Take this, and be very careful with it. It is still rare." From his bag he takes a glass tube, filled with a dark red liquid. He presses it into my hand.

"Blood?" I ask, slightly disgusted.

"Something much more precious. Do you remember our investigations into the source of the Black Influenza? Once a person is infected, we can see it in their blood and we can extract small amounts in a preparation. We call it *Zh-15*."

"I remember that stuff," I say through clenched jaws. "Moal injected me with it. He wanted me dead."

"Moal is gone. He fell ill and died a week later."

My mouth opens in an animal-like grimace.

"Before he died, he discovered something. A way to isolate the mutated corpuscles. That's what this serum does. Or… tries to do." He hesitates a moment. "It's not medicine, but it inhibits the deterioration of the body caused by the Black Influenza."

"This *stops* the Black Influenza?" This day turns out to be filled with bewildering discoveries. "Why didn't you say so right away?"

"Because it's not perfect, Nimue. Yes, the serum can help control the symptoms. Sometimes even for so long and so well that the symptoms can be treated on their own. But that is rare. And it has to be administered within a day of the first symptoms manifesting. With entire city populations adrift, it's very difficult, if not impossible. Moreover, it is impossible to predict when the serum will be effective. It seems to work slightly better on victims who are infected by the variant that settles in the lungs."

I stare at the tube in my hand. "That doesn't sound like it's doing much good."

"Maybe not, but it could. We have administered it to fifty patients. Ten children and forty adults... Three of them... Three children improved so much that we are able to keep them stable."

"Three," I repeat dully. "And the rest?"

"Twenty of them remained alive for a month; longer than any victim we have seen before."

"And the other twenty-seven? Did they die despite the serum?"

"Not exactly. Ten of them are alive... In a coma, but alive."

"It's not much..." I close my fingers around the glass tube. The stuff inside weighs almost nothing. "How many people can this amount save?"

"Only one person. I'm sorry, Nimue. Perhaps it presents you with an impossible choice. But we are producing more of it and we are trying to improve it. So will you take it?"

"Yes," I say. "Of course I want it."

"Good." He is silent for a moment. Is it my imagination, or is his breathing constricted? A moment later, he speaks again as if nothing has happened. "The Asclepius Congregation will provide you with more. But I do want something in return. I want to see you and Arthur more often."

I should have known that he wouldn't just accept that Arthur is gone. I carefully slip the precious serum into my pocket. What can I say? Is a lie appropriate, now that he has shared that glimmer of hope contained in a tube? I decide that Cormack deserves at least a part of the truth.

"Arthur is gone," I say. "The spirits have taken him."

Cormack looks nonplussed, before he blurts out in shock: "Good God! You mean he's dead?"

"Not dead. In a deep sleep. His body is safe, that's all you need to know. And his soul... He is with others, the Undreamed ones. He wanders the world of the spirits."

Whatever Cormack expected to hear, it wasn't this. I cannot blame him for his baffled silence.

"He doesn't know who he is anymore, he only remembers his own name. But he is not alone. And he has... a plan."

"Why?" my cousin says. "To what purpose?"

"To do what Benji wanted to do, I think. To kill the spirit that makes everything sick and to save the king who keeps the Other World healthy. All this mist... haven't you wondered where it comes from? It doesn't burn us like rain. It's getting thicker every day. I think it's slowly swallowing up our world, just like it did the Other World. I don't think your serum will do any good if the Fisher King isn't cured soon."

I don't know if the meaning of this really gets through to Cormack. "Why Arthur?" he asks.

"Because he belongs in their world," Wolf says unexpectedly. "Just like Nimue. Their blood makes them part of their world and part of ours. Who else would the spirits prefer?"

"You mean the blood of a selkie. From Sela."

I nod.

"You say there's a spirit that causes the disease. So Benji was not wrong!"

"He was partly right," I admit. "There is one spirit in particular... He is called the Hunter, and he destroys everything, in the Other World as well as in ours. So you're right, Cormack. We are not each other's enemies. We don't need to be."

He slowly exhales. "I expected something very different when I drove here this morning."

I don't know what he expected instead. It doesn't matter much.

Cormack says bitterly: "You and I, the best hope to fight the disease... and yet too insignificant."

"We might make a small difference, Cormack." I gently release myself from Wolf's grip so I can put a hand on Cormack's arm. He looks at it in amazement. So does Wolf. "If people die, they die. But there is so much we can do for the living. Did you see the highest hill in the village? There was a church there once – St Gwenhael. After the great flood, someone told me that the saints of St Gwenhael were not there to save us from disaster. They were there to remind us of who we should be when those disasters inevitably come. Back then, I was too angry to understand... But now I do. When it is dark, we must make sure the light keeps shining."

"And dark it is." He shakes his head. "Keeping the lights on? *That's* your plan?"

"I can't make any more of it."

He rubs his face. When he lowers his hands, his eyes have turned red. "I will not lie. You have given me bad news. I had hoped for something better."

"You don't look well." Now that I'm closer to him, I can observe him better. "Is something wrong?"

"This? Just a cold." He turns in the direction of the tent camp in the distance. "Those people have it much worse. Gwennec has too many refugees, doesn't it? Show me the camp, Nimue. After that, I can tell you what I can do for them."

"For the refugees? Brevalaer leaves few resources along the border..."

"I'm not Brevalaer." He shows a smile. "As for the borders of Free Breizh, I think my organisation has already shown that it doesn't care about them. I didn't know they were crossing the border, of course. Consider the possibilities of what we can do when they do have my explicit permission."

"I can imagine," I murmur. I take him to the tent camp and for a while, we keep quiet while Cormack takes in the muddy, narrow streets and the tents that don't properly keep out the wind.

"You would do that?" I ask after a while. "For the refugees in Central Europe?"

"To keep the light on?" For a moment he shows a smile, then his facial expression returns to weary seriousness. "You thought I was a monster, Nimue. But I believe I'm helping people. The serum can be improved. I came here to tell you that. I want to do something meaningful amidst this chaos."

"Me too," I say softly. "And the Undreaming?"

He hesitates visibly. "Are you sure that what you know is true?"

"Don't doubt me."

"I don't," he says. "You are Rona's daughter. I always knew you were deeply connected to the Other World. Ever since Doctor Moal examined you."

"Those theta waves in my head?" I scoff. "They told me I was dreaming while being awake."

"That's what you do. That's how you travel... that's it, isn't it? Go on a journey while your body is still here?"

I glance at Wolf, who is walking behind us. Only when he nods do I say: "I only see Arthur when I'm sleeping, if I'm lucky."

"There are ways to control your mind." Wolf says it softly, as if he doesn't actually want Cormack to hear him. "I can help you with that. But now is not the time."

"The Undreaming must stop," I say to Cormack. "Right now. Today."

"Perhaps." Cormack doesn't look pleased. "You underestimate the attraction of having a living body, Nimue. When death lurks, you long for things you would never dare do otherwise…"

"Undreaming is wrong, it is perverse. If you want peace, if you want to seek reconciliation, that is my demand. Swear it, by Gwenhael!"

He surprises me by laughing out loud. It is a warm, booming laugh. "Gwenhael is not my saint."

"He is ours. Gwennec needs that promise." I look at him. "And we need the serum. Breizh doesn't trust the Snakes, but if we can convince them that you're coming to help…" I suddenly get an idea. "Would you sign an agreement? Would you sign your name under a treaty?"

"Are you Gwennec's spokesperson?"

"No," I say. "Though I'm going to have to be *your* spokesperson. They will trust me if I vouch for you."

At least, I hope they will. I can sense Wolf frowning next to me. I pretend not to notice, because this is finally some sort of plan – something that can give Gwennec and the rest of the world hope.

I hold out my hand to Cormack while pinning him with my gaze. "This is your chance to establish peace. Your father has given you all of his power. Use it as fuel for that light I was talking about."

I can't exactly read the emotions on Cormack's face. It is as if sunlight and shadows are crossing it at the same time. He grabs my hand and holds me tight. I feel a shiver run through him.

"I will sign any treaty with Gwennec that you want. I need time to arrange everything, but I'll do it as soon as I can. And then we can be a light, you and I."

"You and I," I confirm, bewildered by the turn our conversation has taken. Gwenhael's bones, I hope I can make it happen. Can I make Gwennec listen?

THE ADVENT OF THE KING

13

HOPE

Gwennec's town hall is one of the most beautiful buildings in the city. Its stone facades date back to a time before the Impact, and while the rest of Gwennec sank into a haze of mud, brine and dust in the decades that followed, the district administrators have always done their best to keep the white marble pillars and walls clean.

It is the first time I am entering it. We gather in the largest room, a space with high windows overlooking the market square. Outside, stalls and carts are filling the square to the brim. As I made my way through, I noticed that the atmosphere is grim. People want to sell their goods, but they don't want to linger for too long. The buyers need food, but money is becoming scarce.

Last night, five people who showed symptoms of the Black Influenza were brought into the old school building. Their skin was cold and grey, their black lumps bulging obscenely. One girl was constantly coughing up blood. She was dead before I could go into my trance, dead before I could administer the precious serum with trembling hands. I cured the other three. Then it all went black before my eyes. Yannick told me that Wolf carried me outside. When I woke up in her room, I was glad I had not used the serum.

Even now, it is still sitting in my pocket, unused. I know it is selfish and I can feel the guilt gnawing at me. But I have to consider the possibility that Wolf, Yannick, Alma or Pedre might fall ill. And then what? What if I faint again? What if the Hunter attacks my thoughts and Wolf is not there to gently guide me back? Then I will only have this liquid in a tube. So I keep it for myself, as long as this is the only supply I have.

"Welcome," says the district official. "Sit down."

I let myself sink into the chair with a sigh of relief. Perhaps it is more out of fear than rooted in reality, but I still feel my knees buckling gently with every step I take. My head throbs painfully.

I know I'm being watched. The harbour master, the district official – I'm a stranger to them, just a fisher girl with messy hair, clothes in need of a wash, and the shadows of fatigue on my face. Not a remarkable occurrence in Gwennec.

I got Franseza Madoc to convince the district official to let me in. To get her to do that, I had to confess part of the truth to her and show her the serum.

There are other people. Two doctors I don't know. A medical attendant. A couple of people who look as tired as I am – I suspect that they too have had a night's vigil, somewhere near where a crisis was happening in the tent camp. A crisis is always happening somewhere, these days.

The door opens and closes again. A man enters, looking around him with a guilt-stricken face. I know him; his name is Pereg Berthou and he is the owner of several large fishing boats.

"Excuse me for being late. People are trying to leave the city and so the roads are jammed." He lowers himself into a chair opposite me, and curiously lets his gaze trail over me. "The fisher girl from Bertram? I thought your family was lost after the tidal wave."

"Not entirely," I say. "My brother and I survived. We've been away for a while."

"I knew your father. He was a good man."

I smile at him.

"For those of you who don't know her, this is Nimue Pesketaer, one of my former students." Franseza is still standing. She has a troubled look on her face. "Nimue claims to have news of the Asclepius Congregation. Nimue?"

"Yes." My fingers are toying with the glass tube in my pocket. "I already knew the Asclepius Congregation from before Breizh closed its borders. I have been inside their walls. I know the people who work there and I know what they do. That is why I know that Gwennec is no friend of theirs. They called themselves heroes, but did monstrous things – first with our orphans, then with our sick."

No one opposes my statement.

"I know the man who leads them. His name is Cormack Cairn. He has made mistakes that are unforgivable. But he is... he is also a good man."

"A good man?" asks the district official. He leans forward. "Under his regime, the organisation stole our children! They took advantage of the chaos of the tidal wave and the big storm. Despite our efforts, many of those children never came back. How could you claim that he is good?"

Despite my exhaustion, I get up, walking halfway around the round table before I let my gaze rest on Pereg Berthou. "You knew my father. Do you also remember my mother, Rona?"

"Definitely. She wasn't born in the area, but she loved it here. Then she left."

"Why?" the district official asks.

"My mother had a brother," I reply. "He stayed in Central Europe while my mother came to Gwennec. He had a company called Fenix Group. Later, that company became the Asclepius Congregation. Cormack Cairn is his heir."

For a moment, it seems as if all sound is being sucked out of the room. The district official falls dangerously quiet. Finally, it is Franseza who is the first to say something: "You didn't mention that this morning."

"I'm not proud of it," I say quickly. "And I didn't ask to see Cormack again, I swear on Gwenhael's grave. He was looking for *me*. He showed me a medicine that could save us from the Black Influenza. Don't tell me that we're not desperate for it."

"Wasn't it a lie to get access to Free Breizh?" asks one of the doctors. He stands at the window and now takes three steps towards the table. "This man uses the name of Asclepius almost blasphemously. I swore by my office not to kill, never to maim, never to harm. And what has he done with his congregation of snake poison?"

"All that," I have to admit, while my courage sinks a little. "That is true. But Cormack is a misguided man, not a liar."

The doctor shakes his head and resumes his position at the window, arms crossed. "Don't be fooled by him. That group has no solutions to offer."

"They have this." I finally show them the serum, holding the tube between my thumb and forefinger. "This has brought children away from the brink of death. They are still sick, but stable. If the Asclepius Congregation wants to share this with us, how can we refuse? Last night there were four victims. I watched them all die. You walk around the camp too, don't you? You see the cold, the hunger, the fear. Gwennec has no more resources and *The Starry Wind* is not ready yet. The Asclepius Congregation can help us." I can't believe I'm standing here advocating for those Snakes. I feel like a traitor. I gently close my fingers around the serum and lower my hand. "Cormack Cairn is willing to sign a treaty. I think we should encourage it."

The harbour master points to my closed hand. "Has it been tested?"

"It's still under development. And I don't want to lie to you... The results are not very good yet." I speak softly. "But there are results. Please, district official." I turn to him. "If *The Starry Wind* is Gwennec's only plan, then it is doomed to fail. And I love Gwennec. This is my home, my birthplace. I wish I could live here safely and that my grave would be at St Gwenhael's. But the world has changed. Many people will leave Gwennec forever, that's for sure. Even in the north, the disease can strike us. And what is to become of all those who stay behind, without clean water and shelter?"

"You can stop now." He raises his hand and I remain silent. The district official heaves a sigh. "We are desperate enough to take it."

"Wrong," Franseza interrupts unexpectedly. "We must be hopeful enough to accept the offer. But not blindly." She rests her hands on the table and looks around the room. "We will accept this serum and their help on our own terms. No one leaves Gwennec to be absorbed into their institutes; everything they have to offer, *they* come and bring to us. I want to see their serum work. I want to speak to this Cormack Cairn before we put even one name on a document. Do we have an agreement?"

Pereg Berthou takes the floor: "What does this mean for *The Starry Wind*? We can't wait, or sail earlier. My stowage charts and course calculations are too precise to change our plan now."

"You're going to sail *The Starry Wind*?" I ask.

He gives me a smile. "I have been asked to captain the ship, yes."

I feel relief. Not that I know the man well, but I remember Dad's words of praise. Berthou is an experienced sailor and an honest man. He will keep my friends and the pioneers safe for the entirety of the crossing.

"It means nothing to *The Starry Wind*,' says the harbour master. "She will sail as we have calculated, by the next new moon."

"So you agree?" I turn to the district official. "You want to cooperate with the Asclepius Congregation?"

"I want to talk to that man. And I cannot deny that I want his medicine."

"Don't give them too much power," says the doctor at the window softly. "Once you hold the reins, you determine the horse's course. Let them help, let them advise us if they must, but remember that we are now *Free* Breizh."

"Fine, sounds good to me," I say. "Let the Snakes work for you. They have enough to make up for."

The district official gives me a stiff nod. "How do we arrange a conversation with them?"

"With this." I take Cormack's second gift out of my pocket. He gave it to me just before he got into the car. "It's a device that lets people speak to each other. A voice transmitter..."

"A telephone," he smiles.

"That, yes." The device is a mystery to me. I have seen the computers in the Asclepius Congregation. I sort of assumed they were big electronic boxes. I can't quite grasp how such a small, flat device can make my voice travel across half of Central Europe.

"And the number?"

"He said that was not necessary. He said it was already in there and you just have to press this button."

He nods. "I'm not promising anything. Let's first wait and see what he has to say and whether it's convincing. Then let's see what Brevalaer thinks, and after that..."

There is a loud knock at the door. A moment later, Yannick rushes in, white-faced and her eyes as wild as those of a startled rabbit.

"I have bad news," she says. "More people were brought in, and they all have a fever. Most of them have the black lumps, others are coughing blood. They are from the camp. There are babies among them."

"Gwenhael save us." Franseza steps forward. "How many?"

"I don't know. Fifty... Maybe more. They say the newcomers from Brevalaer brought it and that it won't be long before it spreads through the whole camp. Panic is about to break out." Yannick licks her lips. She looks as if she is struggling to control her own panic. "We must evacuate the school and quarantine the sick there. Anyone who comes into contact with them will be in danger."

"Cordon off the area around the school. Clear the camp to a mile around the vicinity." The district official slams the phone down on the table and heads for the window. He stares out at the market, which is coming to an end. "And seal off the city. Anyone from outside Gwennec should stay away."

"The people can hardly support themselves," says one of the men I did not recognise. Now I suspect it's a city guard. "Sir, we can't just *close* the market."

"We are forced to do so. Make it happen."

The man nods, albeit unwillingly.

"Those patients need a hospital, not a cold school," says the doctor at the window. "Brevalaer wants to be the leader so badly, then let them take responsibility!"

"Brevalaer won't take them," says the district official grimly. "And it is too late to transport the sick. Get the school ready."

"Yes, sir," Yannick confirms in a muffled voice. She looks at me. I look back, with despair and terror like cold water in my heart.

Wolf, I think. He has to stay away. I don't want him to be in any danger. Oh Gwenhael, and Yannick...

"Let me help," I say. "Let me do what I can."

Franseza shakes her head. "What can you do for them? Stay away."

"We have some quarantine suits," says the doctor. "Yannick, do you have access to one?"

"No," she says.

"I'll get you one. From now on, entering the building without a suit is prohibited." He looks at the district official, who nods in response.

Yannick nods again, then turns and disappears as fast as she came. She's scared, I know it. More scared than she was after the tidal wave.

My conscience is pounding like a painful headache on the inside of my skull. I can save all these people... I find myself clenching my hands into fists and trying to relax. Forcing my body to work even harder, to become stronger. I can banish the Hunter and prevent disaster in Gwennec. All I have to do is run after Yannick...

The phone catches my eye. I snatch it from the table and press the button Cormack showed me.

"Nimue?" Cormack's voice sounds raw. "What is it?"

"Come back to Gwennec and bring the whole supply of your medicine," I beg. "Please, come and help me. I can't do this alone."

***

The chaos in the camp is frightening, and organising the quarantine location is a bit difficult and messy. People are chased out of their tents and barely get a chance to gather their already meagre possessions. The school is emptied. The medical supplies, the checkpoint, the infirmary; they are all put up in draughty tents as far away from the new quarantine area as possible. The beach road and the surrounding areas will be empty once more, as they always used to be. But this time, the emptiness is ominous and oppressive.

At the beginning of the night, patients are lying row by row in our old classroom. Most of them are so sick that they do not realise what is happening around them. It's only for the best, I think, because the conditions are so poor that even the Asclepius Congregation could offer better care.

We do what we can. Only a handful of doctors are allowed into the building, all dressed from head to toe in white insulation suits. Yannick is also wearing one. I hardly recognise her. She hands one of the suits to me and insists that I dress according to the standards. So I do. Not because I could be infected, but because I don't want to let all of Gwennec know what I am.

The sight of the sick is making me nauseous. I kneel down next to a man lying on an uncomfortable straw mattress, which is barely thick enough to soften the concrete floor. Not that it bothers him. His eyes are rolled way up. His lips are wet with blood and saliva. But him coughing up blood is not the worst thing. No, the worst part is his flesh, which has large soft and dark patches, as if he were a dead animal that has been rotting by the side of the road for several days. The stench rising from these patches is not masked by my insulating headgear.

It is clear that his body has decided that it is dead even before he has actually died.

It takes a lot of effort to touch him. When I finally put my gloved fingers on his chest, my hairs stand up in horror. Everything about him is just *wrong*. I can feel the brokenness penetrating my senses deeply and I recognise it: this feeling, this *smell*, is just like the Hunter. I remember his body, his shark teeth, his claws, and his shining eyes, of which he had far too many.

Don't think about him, I tell myself. And to my relief, I manage to concentrate only on the problem at hand. Very slowly, a glimmer of life is returning to the man. His breathing calms down, his eyes roll down. For a moment, we look at each other, then he falls asleep again. It is an exhausted kind of sleep, but hopefully one that helps the healing process.

But I'm not satisfied yet, because the rotting patches do not disappear. By Gwenhael, I hope that they won't spread, now that I have eliminated the source of the disease. Such a cure demands a lot from his body. I know I have tapped into energy sources and reserves that would normally take weeks to restore a body, all in a matter of minutes. I look at his sunken face and wonder if I haven't given him an extra problem to deal with.

When I get up, dizziness overtakes me. I steady myself against the nearest wall. It wasn't just his body reserves I drew on. I used mine too.

"Nim?"

I blink. Through the dancing dots before my eyes, I see Yannick.

"What's wrong?" she asks.

"Nothing," I say. "A brief fainting spell. It's normal after a cure... This man needs more help."

"You're trembling on your legs, Nim. I don't like it."

"I used to be better at this." But then again, I wasn't pregnant before. I let out a sigh. My vision clears and I can let go of the wall.

"Nim, go home."

"Not yet. I must save who I can."

The night creeps by. The patients groan, spit blood or fall silent. My work is as slow as the hours that pass. Every time I lay my hands on someone's body and force my mind to make contact with their bodies, the process gets off to a slower start. It feels like climbing a mountain in a nightmare: driven by great haste and yet with legs as heavy as lead.

When the darkest of nights fades, Yannick guides me outside. I have no choice but to lean heavily on her. When Wolf sees me, he doesn't say a word. He takes me in his arms and carries me to bed, where I immediately fall asleep.

The next morning, Wolf does not let me go back to the school. He cradles my cold face in his hands and says: "You need rest. You don't have an order of life and death, Nimue. Not today."

"I should have done more last night," I mutter.

"No." He kisses me. "You have worked miracles."

"I wish I was stronger."

"Nimue, you give all your strength to our child. That does not make you weak."

And he is right about that. I do not protest against his decision to not go back to the school and do not go near it that day or that night. From the hill of Saint Gwenhael, we watch how the camp is forced to move further back. I know that the beach down there is muddier. The salt water will flow into the camps during high tide. The sea will force its way into those poorly insulated tents. Another problem for Gwennec to solve. At night, we watch from the hill again, seeing fire cut through the darkness like knives. That is how we bid farewell to the dead: by burning their bodies until only the ashes of their bones remain.

For the first time, I look forward to the day that *The Starry Wind* will set sail. I track the moon, visible through the haze and clouds, and calculate the days before departure: nine more. It is too soon for me to say goodbye to Yannick, but if it means she and a few hundred others will be far away from the Black Influenza, it cannot come soon enough.

Every evening, I light a candle in the windowsill of the barn that Wolf and I have made our home. As long as I can keep my eyes open, I watch the dancing flame and say my prayers to Gwenhael. I pray for the safe passage of the gigantic ship. And I pray that Cormack will come soon. The days go by without a word from him, or from Sini.

Gwennec yearns for him. Gwennec is dying without him. I never thought I would look forward to his arrival, as if he were our saviour.

But that is what I do.

14

KNIGHTS WITHOUT IRON

Again, my dream begins with a fragment of a story. Again, I cannot make out who or what is talking, although the sound is penetrating and almost desperate:

The sea kept still and could not move. Darkness enveloped her. For centuries they were like that, undisturbed... "Oh," sighed the Sea. "Oh, where have all the stars gone that the sailors used to navigate by? Where are the fish and plants in my belly? And where is the moon, which could draw my tides? It used to be different!"

The Darkness heard this, and he rejoiced.

"It's no use complaining," he whispered. "Long have I waited for the light to disappear from below and above: centuries and centuries and longer. Now I have won, and I am everywhere."

"Who's talking to me?" I whisper. "Who's there?"

There's no reply. The only voices getting through to me are those of Goldilocks and Arthur. A moment later, I'm back, standing behind my brother near yet another campfire, this time in a quarry.

"...Even if I manage to find my way back in one go," I hear Goldilocks mutter.

Arthur nods. I silently listen as they go through their plan, suspecting that they have repeated these words out loud many times before, as a spell to encourage themselves.

Goldilocks tells him what the Hunter's territory looks like: deader than the plain, a place where every grain of sand is permeated with the brokenness that the Hunter carries around like a death trap. His nest lies high on a mountain, encased by rock walls.

137

"They keep anything from going out or coming in," she says. Only through the luck of finding a single, narrow slit could she escape herself. "You and Lance certainly won't fit through it."

"We'll figure it out when we get there," he reassures her. "And after that...

He does not say what should happen next. His friends already know. I can guess: after that, they must fight the Hunter. The Grail must be stolen from under his watchful eye, and his blood must flow into the chalice. It sounds easy when you sum it up like that.

"Do you also feel like it's getting colder?"

"I think so," confirms Goldilocks. She sits cross-legged on a boulder, polishing the crown of the Fisher King with her sleeve. The gold was so dull before it seemed almost black, but now its former glory is beginning to shine through again. "I remember the cold in the nest. The wind pierced through my clothing. The only place to find shelter was by the rack..."

Morgana looks up. She's on the other side, warming up some water in a primitively carved wooden bowl. "A rack?"

"The Hunter loves trophies. Sometimes he decides to put them on display, flayed and opened like rabbits..." She shivers.

"Who does he flay?" asks Morgana sharply. "His victims? Is he going to do that to Olwen?"

"I don't know. He chooses at random. I remember that we waited, that nobody dared to make a sound when he came back..."

When Morgana takes the bowl from the fire, she spills half the water.

"So we know that we can expect more cold," Lance says. "The better we prepare ourselves, the more chance we have of succeeding. By the way, I'm hungry."

"We're all out of tubers," Arthur says. "Give me your knife, Lance."

"I'll go with you," says Goldilocks. She puts the crown aside.

"And me," I whisper, though I know by now that it is useless. Arthur waits until Goldilocks has grabbed a torch, then leads the way. Both of them shiver when I sneak up behind them. Do they feel my eyes in their backs, or do they think I am just one of those chilly patches of mist?

Every now and then, they stop, as if to avoid a large boulder or a protruding branch. I worry about the poor visibility – what if we come face to face with a monster? Goldilocks and Arthur seem less worried. Perhaps they are used to the danger by now.

"Tuberous plants," says Goldilocks. They stop and begin to pry the tough roots from the soil.

"You were very brave when you escaped from the Hunter," Arthur remarks after a while.

Goldilocks looks up at him. "I didn't run because I was brave. I fled because I was afraid. It felt as if my body would shatter."

"You made it all the way to the Fisher King's tower. And now you are coming back to the nest."

If only I could tell her that he was right. Katell used to be so scared, so small and alone. So different from the brave girl who now looks thoughtfully at my brother.

"What is it?" he asks.

She shakes her head. Her blonde hair sways with the movement. "Nothing. I thought I remembered something about you, Sire."

"Arthur."

"Yes... Like, I know you." She keeps staring at him.

I hold my breath. Could she be...?

Goldilocks shakes her head. "No. I don't see how that's possible."

Disappointed, I let out my breath.

"We all have strange memories," says Arthur. "Maybe I'm one of those things that you used to take for granted."

She smiles and pulls out two tubers at a time. "It doesn't matter now. And whether I'm afraid or brave doesn't matter either. How will you kill the Hunter after we manage to steal the Grail?"

Arthur lets out a sigh. "I think I'll try to outmanoeuvre him. First, we lay a trap and then I'll strike quickly with the lance..."

She shakes her head. "He said that stone alone could not harm him."

"Then we must find a weapon before we enter the nest."

"Like what? If stone doesn't do anything to him, brambles will only tickle him."

"I have no intention of attacking the source of evil with a bramble bush," murmurs Arthur. "We'll have to get a knife. A dagger. A fishhook, if need be."

This gets him a shocked look coming from Goldilocks. "You would use *iron*?"

Arthur seems as confused as I am by her reaction. "Gladly, even. Even Lance's knife is already crumbling."

"I can't even think about iron without feeling sick," she says hesitantly. "I don't think Lance can do it either."

"It is a tool, Goldilocks, not poison. What is so terrible about iron?"

"It doesn't belong here." She says it slowly, as if she has to think hard about it. "Holding iron or... or steel, that would be like... like hanging your guts out. It's wrong and... perverted."

Somewhere, from the depths of my memories, I conjure up grandma's voice. Weren't the fairies and spirits in her fairy tales also scared of iron?

Suddenly, Goldilocks jumps up. "Someone is here."

She can see me! Excited, I step forward, but then I hear the quarrelling voices of boys. Goldilocks picks up her torch and creeps forward, Arthur following in her wake.

Not very far away, the quarry slips into a valley, where the fog lifts a little. I smell the smoke before I see the two boys standing around a poor excuse for a fire. A third boy is kneeling by it and is poking the sputtering firewood with a branch, obviously hoping to keep it alive.

"I told you not to use those branches," one of them says. He is the taller one of the three. His shoulders are covered by a green cloak, which looks as if pieces from other garments have been sewn together. A piece of old coat, a bit of what might once have been a jumper or a vest. The whole thing is held in place by a leather cord.

"What do you want me to use? Nothing else grows in this cursed place!" The other boy is shorter, but stronger and more agile. He is wearing nothing more than trousers, ripped at the knees, and a grey vest with a large hood. He pulls the hood over his head now, in an attempt to keep the chilly mist away from his neck.

"If those beasts attack us now, all we have is a little smoke. You will be the death of us," growls the first.

"Yes, yes, everything is my fault. All you do is complain."

Arthur coughs quietly, then steps forward with his torch raised. The boys shut their mouths at once and stare at him.

"Hello. You're making a lot of noise out here."

Goldilocks, who has followed him, points to the failed fire. "You have to build it up like a tent, not just throw branches on top of each other."

"Don't come any closer!" The boy with the green cloak has something in his hand: a sharp piece of stone. Not as good a knife as Lance's dagger, but hard and sharp enough to disfigure anyone's face with.

"You're drawing too much attention to yourselves," Arthur says. "You have no torches or shelter or proper layout for your camp. If I were a monster, I would have gotten to you before you could do anything to me with that stone."

"We know enough to know that monsters can look like humans," says the shorter one with the grey jumper.

"We carry fire." Goldilocks points to her torch.

"She's right, don't be silly," says the boy with the green cloak, before saying apologetically to Goldilocks and Arthur: "We're just being careful, that's all."

Goldilocks shrugs. "We have a camp, fire and food. Come and sit with us."

The boys exchange glances. "How many are you?"

"There's two others," says Arthur. "One of us has bigger weapons than you."

The boy with the green cloak lets out a laugh that sounds like a snort. "We could sure use that. My friend here was attacked by a monster last night. He almost got dragged out of the camp."

The broad-shouldered boy shows the bloody gashes on his arm.

"We're stronger when we are together," says Arthur. "I'm Arthur, this is Goldilocks."

"My name is Val."

Surprised, he looks at the broad-shouldered guy. "You remember your name too?"

"Not entirely. Only the last part of it: Val. I've forgotten the rest."

"And what about you?" Goldilocks asks the other two.

The green cloak puts the sharp stone in an inner pocket of his remarkable garment. "I couldn't tell you."

"I call him Green," says the boy in the grey jumper with a laugh. "I remember a few sounds of my name. Something with a G, or a W or an N..." He grins briefly. "Maybe my name was George William Nicholas. Green calls me GWN."

Goldilocks casts a glance at their camp. "Your fire is almost out. We shouldn't stay here too long. Green, Val... and, uh, GWN. Come with us. We can share what we have."

"We don't have much to share," says GWN. "A little bit of food and some flints."

"That's enough," says Arthur. "You are most welcome."

Because together, they are stronger than alone... Staying dead silent, I hover behind my brother. *Together, or not at all.* Is there still a small part of him that remembers those words?

15

The Undreamed

"**Y**ou must wake up. Now."

I resist. I want to stay inside my dream, close to Arthur. The hands shaking me won't leave me alone, though. Yannick pulls me halfway up as I try to open my eyes. My sleep was deep from all the exhaustion, and still I don't feel well-rested.

"It's nighttime," I mutter. "Let me sleep."

She throws my clothes onto the footboard, followed by my medical clothes. "Get dressed. I'm sorry, Nim. This can't wait."

She takes me to the school, a dark block of stone where the faint glow of oil lamps comes through the windows. It is the only light in the area. Now that the surrounding tent camp has been cleared, the candles and lamps that people left burning at night are also gone.

My work here is far from finished. Yannick knows that. I don't have the strength to save lives when I can barely take two steps forward. Yannick knows that too, and yet she says: "You have to help. It's too important."

"Why?" My irritation turns to concern. "Who is it?"

"Pereg Berthou."

He's on a mat under the window. The sparse light from the oil lamp on the windowsill illuminates the blood clinging to his lips. There is also blood on the front of his beautiful, white shirt. I can already hear him struggling for air before I approach.

"Gwenhael's grave." When I crouch down by his side, I watch as more blood flows from his lips. It bubbles. I feel the familiar, wry revulsion I always feel when

143

confronted with blood. My sleepiness fades into the background, drowned out by a sharp fear. "How long has he been like this?"

"He was brought in an hour ago."

"Has he been to the camp? Where did he get infected?"

"Probably in the eastern part of the camp. That's where the others came from as well. He had no business being there, but Franseza says he insisted on helping." Yannick heaves a sigh. "Foolish man."

I slowly open the buttons of his sodden shirt. "Shine some light, will you?"

Yannick picks up the oil lamp and holds it closer.

His skin seems undamaged. He is hot with fever, but without the hideous black bumps or the rotting patches that other victims often have.

"I think it's just in his lungs," I say. I move my hands further up his body and lift his head a little.

"I cleared his airways before I came to get you. I can do it again."

"It doesn't matter. His lungs are disintegrating." In the lamplight, I see her face twist in disbelief and prefer not to ponder it too much. I have no choice. "I can feel it, Yannick. I can feel the way his body is breaking down. And it's happening fast."

I don't know if I have it in me to repair this damage. Yannick looks at me with tightly pressed lips. She doesn't say it, but I know what she's thinking: *The Starry Wind* must leave now – it's sail or perish for the pioneers hoping to escape Gwennec. If Pereg Berthou dies, there will be no captain to sail them safely across the uncharted sea.

I no longer hesitate. I squeeze my eyes shut and, hoping for the best, plunge my mind deep into a trance, as if diving into dark, cold water.

His body is broken into a hundred pieces. Something black is slithering through him, gnawing at his guts like a poison. It is alive, but not living; it belongs to the Hunter as if the Hunter himself were here to put his claws into Pereg's body.

I'm trying to find a starting point to heal him. A piece of tissue in his lungs to recover. It works. I draw some courage from it. Some more tissue, a pulmonary alveolar that is slowly closing and taking up its function again. I close the holes and mend the fray as if I were darning a sock, as if I were sewing buttons onto a coat. The Hunter's tentacles fight my spirit, but I push them away. Every time they come too close, I put up a shield around my mind. I try to hum a melody, as Wolf always does for me. I hold on to that delicate strand of music, so I can find my way out of my trance, back up, once my work is done.

Little by little. I go ever so slowly. Somewhere far away, I'm aware that my body is losing energy like a leaking bucket. I know that I'm collapsing across Pereg Berthou's body. I lose my grip on the work I'm doing and for a moment, I'm somewhere else.

I see Arthur. He is sitting by the fire, his legs stretched out in front of him. Someone says something and they laugh, Arthur the loudest of all. They have fire, they have weapons, they have enough company to relieve each other in taking watch. They almost seem like a normal group of friends out camping. Almost. The danger seems far away...

I'm back. The left lung is almost done. The blood is looking for a way out, but I trust Yannick to remove it. His heart, I think vaguely. His heart also has a problem. Something is nestling behind the heart valves and it needs to be exorcised....

"I think I'm going to taste your child on my tongue."

I stiffen. Where am I?

"How weak you are. Your mind wanders through the Two Worlds like a drunk man." The Hunter is in front of me, looming out of a landscape of mist. He is so big when he is close by. His stench fills all my pores. I remember his weight on top of me, his teeth in my flesh.

I stumble backwards. "Go away!"

"I will never go away again. Don't you get it? I'm inside you. I'm inside every creature of flesh and blood that is infected by me. You think you can stop it, child of the sea? I thought so too, once, but it's a lie. No one can beat the emptiness. No one can beat the cold and death. Everything that is whole, will break. And you will give me your magic, whether you like it or not. Then I'll never leave, I'll be as eternal as the darkness..."

"Nimue!"

Yannick pinches my cheeks. Her hands are covered in blood. I gasp for breath. The darkness before my eyes disappears and I feel my mind slipping back into my body. I stare at Yannick. She stares back, at least as frightened and confused as I am.

"I can't do it," I pant. "He will catch me and my child! I can't."

"Please," she begs. "Do it one more time."

I sit up straight and rub the blood from my face. I don't know if it helps, or if I'm just spreading it out more. "I can't."

"But..." She doesn't understand. Her eyes can only see this world. She doesn't know how real the Hunter is, how dangerous.

I struggle to maintain all the defensive walls around my mind so that he cannot reach me. "Is he still breathing?"

"Yes," Yannick whispers. "He's breathing better than before. What you did helped. There is less blood."

I turn back to Pereg Berthou and very carefully lay a hand on his neck. I feel his heartbeat beating irregularly. The disease still lingers within him, under his ribs.

While I have my fingers there, I feel his heartbeat fade. "He's slipping away," I say softly. "I don't have the strength, Yannick."

But I have the serum. I didn't want to use it, I wanted to save it for another loved one if needed.... I reach for it, but the protective clothing is in my way. I curse and struggle out of the white suit. The tube feels almost lighter than before.

"Prepare an IV drip. If anything can save his life, it is this. Hurry up!"

Yannick doesn't waste any time on asking questions. She prepares the drip and we watch in silence as the serum disappears through a tube into his vein.

Berthou starts to groan. He sounds like an animal in pain, squirming on the mat. Yannick grabs the drip to make sure he doesn't pull the tube out of his arm.

"I's working," she says. "His body is responding to it!"

I feel his pulse again and know that his heart is fighting against the invader that I could not chase away. Very carefully, I dare to lower my defences a little, just enough to connect my spirit and his. I'm startled by what I feel: Pereg Berthou has withdrawn far into his body, into a remote alley of his consciousness, where he flickers and dances like a dying flame. The only thing that remains in his body is the corruption. Too late, it dawns on me that I should have started with his heart. His heart is pumping the disease to every corner of his body. The lungs I have cured cannot save him.

Pereg Berthou slips into a coma, as Cormack also noticed with his other patients. If Gwennec had the resources available to the Asclepius Congregation, we could keep him in that deep sleep for a long time. But this is a fishing village, not a hospital. We have no money and no energy to keep one man alive on a machine. Not if he can no longer do anything for his people.

What I'm doing feels like a nightmare slowly unravelling. I know it is the only way, and Yannick will never do it. She has sworn an oath to always heal and not to harm. I have never promised anything like that. With a heavy heart, I grab his arm and pull the needle with the drip out of his vein. It takes a few moments, then Pereg stills.

Yannick stares at me uncomprehendingly. "What is going on?"

I don't look at her. "His heart gave out. Too much was wrong with him for me to save him. His mind was already gone."

She looks from his arm to the needle in my hand. "The serum...?"

"It didn't work. There was only a small chance anyway."

She kneels by his head, feels his artery, tries to feel for his breath near his nose before she looks up again. "You decided this on your own."

"Yes," I admit hoarsely. At last, I risk looking up, straight into her startled eyes. "I have ended his life. Let them stoke the fires high."

She gets up and all her movements are stiff. By that alone, I can feel her anger. "I did not bring you here to end a life!"

"I tried to save him... I'm so sorry. He was your captain..."

"Yes, he was our captain! *The Starry Wind* needs him! Now our mission will fail before it can even begin! Gwenhael's blood on you, Nimue! You had no right."

"Yannick, he was already gone! His body could have kept breathing for a while, but he was broken inside. It would have been cruel..."

She turns her back to me. "Take your rest. I will take care of the body. And tomorrow I will spread the news."

"I'm sorry," I say again. I struggle to get up. My back protests and my stomach feels heavy. My knees buckle under the movement.

She doesn't respond and I leave the building on my own. It's not my fault, I tell myself gloomily. I did my best and it wasn't enough; Gwenhael knows it wasn't up to me to save the man. I hope Yannick will understand that too... but right ow, she doesn't come running after me. She's letting me step out into the dark night all by myself. I didn't even bring a lamp.

She may know it is not my fault, but the captain is still dead. Tomorrow morning, *The Starry Wind* will no longer be a beacon of hope, but a painful sign of a failed opportunity. If I had started with Pereg's heart, would things have turned out differently? And if I had been stronger, if the Hunter had not distracted me?

It's no use worrying about it, I tell myself. I stumble through the night until I find my way back home.

Early in the morning, I watch as the flames creep up the shoreline. That's where Pereg Berthou gets his last salute, before his body is delivered to the flames. Wolf and I are standing on the edge of the group of silent spectators. The crowd is so dejected. They always are when yet another dead person is delivered to the fire. This time, besides sadness, there is also hopelessness. The feeling seizes me along with the smoke and the stench.

I listen to Franseza and the district official saying a few words, their voices almost drowned out by the hissing of the funeral pyre. They are trying to console us, but have nothing to say that can make *The Starry Wind* set sail.

I wait for them to fall silent again. Then I kiss Wolf, causing him to look surprised before I step forward until I'm standing inside the circle of spectators.

"I have something to say." The fire burns hot in my back. "Pereg Berthou died in my arms last night. I had a medicine that could have saved him, but it was too late. Maybe he would have survived if I had acted faster. And for that, I am sorry."

I'm aware that my words shake people out of their numb trance. Franseza looks at me in bewilderment. She knows exactly what medicine I mean. Do I see a glimmer of anger in her eyes? My gaze falls on Yannick. Her face is tight. No smile, no tears.

I clear my throat. "*The Starry Wind* leaves in two days and you need a helmsman." Wolf pushes forward past the people and stops when I gently shake my head at him. "I can navigate by the stars, I know how to sail on uncharted waters. I've done it before. Give me Pereg's star charts and his calculations, and I'll sail *The Starry Wind* to the north. On Gwenhael's bones and blood, I promise."

Yannick is the first to break the stunned silence. "Why? What about your family?"

I swallow. "Yesterday, I suddenly understood something. Where he is now, Arthur doesn't need my help. He is following his own path, so I choose mine." I look at her. "Together with you."

"Can you really do it?" Mart asks. "Can you send *The Starry Wind* that long way into uncharted waters?"

"I promise." I look around, at all the faces with a mixture of relief and confusion on them, and I find Wolf's eyes. He didn't know yet. I hadn't told him anything last night. I walk up to him and he takes my hand. We don't say a word, but as we walk away from the fire, people make room for us.

I take him to the broken remains of the sarcophagus of St Gwenhael. My fellow villagers rescued him from the church before all the stones were torn down. After many years, maybe even centuries, he has come down from his hill. Now his head and torso are inside the mill, no longer solemnly laid out, just there on the ground. The door groans on its hinges as we enter and Wolf leaves it open, probably to allow as much light as possible into the dimly lit room.

The ground is covered with a layer of fine flour. Far above our heads, the wings are still. The mill used to turn every day, now it only works a few hours a week. Today, we are its only visitors.

I stand next to the sarcophagus and look down at its serene face. Wolf looks at me instead; I feel his eyes on me and wait for him to say something.

"You cannot promise them this and then just change your mind. You know that."

I nod. "I know what I promised."

"I need to be sure that you know that." He moves closer and I feel his warmth in my back. "You won't be back in Avalon in time to give birth there. And the north is a hard midwife."

"That is true." I find his arms and pull them around my waist, so that he embraces me. "But I'm not the only one who ever had a child there. And *you* have been a child there."

"I was a child there, but I was surrounded by my family."

"I have you."

"You have me, wherever you decide to go."

I smile. "And it is your home, Wolf. Cruel people took you away from it. You deserve to return."

"So you're sure about this?" His fingers rub small circles into my belly. The bulge is now visible under my jumper. "What about your mother? Arthur?"

"I want to come back one day. That is why I have come here, to take an oath." I show him the small knife I have brought with me and slowly run its point across my open palm, just deep enough for a little blood to well up. Spreading my fingers, I press that hand to my patron's cold stone chest. "I swear that I will see my family again. No storm and no darkness will separate us. Wherever I go, my path will also return to them." I'm silent for a moment when Wolf lays his own hand on top of mine. The space around Saint Gwenhael's stone heart slowly warms up thanks to our combined body heat. If he ever listened to the people of Gwennec, I hope he can hear me now. I feel a lump in my throat. "Saint Gwenhael, keep this promise for me. Help me to keep it. Guard us, fixed star. Have mercy on those who stay behind, on those who go out to sea. We are your people. We cannot be separated, like brine cannot be separated from the sea."

When I withdraw my hand, I discover that a shard has come off. A drop of my blood has turned it dark red. An unexpected answer from Gwenhael, perhaps? A new talisman, now that I have left the seal pendant with Arthur. I slip it into my pocket and resolve to drill a hole in it later to wear it around my neck before I begin this long and dangerous journey. I know that it's only a piece of stone, that I'm incredibly superstitious to think that it can protect me and my loved ones. Nevertheless, I feel a lot better.

"Can you be ready in two days?" Wolf asks.

"I have to be. I will study Pereg's charts and notes and take them out to sea. *The Starry Wind* is a big ship, so it will be different from the fishing boats I used to sail. There is also one advantage; such cargo ships are partly computer-controlled. I just have to learn how to work the wheelhouse."

"Nimue, it's not that easy."

"Trust me," I say. "I trust you to lead us when we step ashore. So trust me when I say I know how to get there."

He lets out a sigh, and I can feel his warm breath on my neck. "When it comes to the sea, I trust you blindly. Let's not waste time. We have a lot to prepare."

That is undeniably true. In my head, I make lists of things that need to be done. I wonder if I can pass on a message to Mum. But to whom? To Cormack perhaps – if I'm willing to tell him about Avalon, if I trust him enough to even reveal the location of the island to him... If he comes with his help and the serum, I think. Maybe I'll trust him then. So far, the phone I always carry has been silent. But he can't wait much longer. He should have been back by now... we should have heard something from the Asclepius Congregation.

As if these thoughts were a prelude, the cars of the Asclepius Congregation arrive in the village the next afternoon. I have asked Franseza for Pereg Berthou's notes and preparations and am sitting at the kitchen table of Yannick's home, bent over the papers. I'm so absorbed in them that at first I don't notice the commotion outside. It is only when I get up for a moment and glance outside that I see the thronging people on the beach road. People wearing the Asclepius Congregation uniform are unloading boxes. I don't know what is inside, but every time a box is taken by one of the bystanders, a short cheer rises up.

I step outside and run towards them. Where is my cousin? No doubt he is somewhere among the people.

"Nimue."

It is not Cormack's voice, but Sini's. She is standing by the only car with its doors closed. She has her dark brown hair pinned up in a braid on her head. Her clothes look newer and more expensive than I remember them to be.

"I'm sorry I didn't call. We had some problems with the connection," she says.

"You are here now, that's what matters." Again, I look around. "I was hoping Cormack would come himself."

There is something in Sini's gaze – a restlessness that I cannot place. "Cormack is here. In the car." Before I can ask more confused questions, she says: "Get in. We need to talk somewhere less crowded."

My skin starts to tingle. "What's the matter, Sini?"

"Please," she says softly. "Use the passenger seat."

I look at Yannick, who is taking two boxes at a time. I see Will, who apparently arrived at the camp last night, taking a girl on his shoulders so that she is tall enough to see above the crowd. My gaze goes back to Sini, and at the same time I feel the knife that is still in my pocket.

"I see that you don't trust me," Sini says. She crosses her arms in front of her chest. "You don't *have* to get in, Nimue. But I can't talk to you here."

I try to see Cormack through the tinted windows. Now I remember how strange his behaviour was, last time we spoke. Whatever was wrong then will have something to do with this whole pomp and circumstance. I let out a sigh, walk around the car and get in.

Cormack is sitting in the back seat. He looks relaxed, his legs stretched forward as far as the car seats will let him. He looks at me with a languid smile, but I miss the focus in his eyes.

"What's wrong with you?" I ask.

Sini pulls the door shut and starts the engine.

"Hello, Nimue," Cormack replies.

"You still don't look good."

"There is nothing wrong with me."

We drive further down the beach road, then Sini gets off the paved road and the car jolts and bounces across the dunes. I hold on to my seat, not used to sitting in a car. For a moment, I'm even afraid that we might topple over. Before that happens, Sini switches off the engine and we are suddenly parked between two medium-high dunes. The village is hidden behind the last bend in the beach road.

I turn back to Cormack. "We are alone now. You can talk freely."

Cormack looks at me disinterestedly and pretends not to have heard me.

"Nimue, he's not himself anymore." Sini's regret is evident in her voice.

Then, the realisation hits me full in the face, like a storm wind: Cormack's eyes, his posture, the emptiness behind that strange smile of his...

"No." I say it out loud, hoping that this denial will work like a magic spell. "Tell me you didn't do it. Cormack, tell me this is just some lame joke!"

"A joke?" Slowly his head bobs back and forth. "I can't imagine myself liking jokes."

I suddenly feel like I'm suffocating. I open the door and let the chilly, misty air stream in.

"He took the serum," Sini explains softly. "We all hoped it would work, but his hopes were mostly set on you. When he came back from Gwennec, he wouldn't let anyone into his office for hours. When he came out, he was in worse shape. The serum was clearly not working."

I stare at her, then at Cormack. "After what I told you about the Undreaming... Cormack, how could you do that to yourself?"

"We tried to stop him. But his order stood." Sini looks uncomfortable. "There was a conflict. In the end, some of the staff proved unable to disobey an order. Cormack Cairn remained their employer."

On the back seat, he raises his hands and I hear the rattling of an iron chain. Only now do I see that he is wearing handcuffs.

"Now they have taken my Asclepius Congregation from me," he says. He doesn't sound like he cares. He can't anymore – everything that drove him to passion and inspiration has been cut out of him.

"You look like you're going to faint," Sini tells me. "Get out and take some fresh air."

I do as she says. I clamber out of the car and lean on my knees to gasp for breath. Cormack, split in two, skinned like a trapped rabbit and stripped of his soul. Sini gets out too and drags my cousin off the back seat. It is as if she is letting a prisoner out for a breath of fresh air. That is exactly how she sees it, I realise at once. I wouldn't be surprised if it was she herself who put him in irons.

I take a look at him. The afternoon light, filtered through the mist, makes him as pale as a ghost. Now I know it's not just the light and the mist that are doing that to him. Oh, I should have known! I *could* have known.

"I'm terribly sorry," I say. "You came to me seeking help, and I didn't provide any. I was blind. And you refused to ask me after you found out I was pregnant. Right, Cormack?"

"Don't feel too guilty about it," he says in his new, bored tone. "It's better this way."

"No. It's not better for anyone. Maybe only for the monster that did this. Your soul has become prey to the Hunter, Cormack. You knew that when you did this, didn't you?"

"But what do you know? About how approaching death feels? This plague has no hold on you."

"Everyone dies eventually, Cormack!"

"At least now I won't die of this disease."

I groan in anger and frustration. "Don't you feel it? Don't you feel how your soul is lost in the Other World?"

His smile is without friendship or warmth. "I feel only calmness."

Emptiness is a better word for it, I think. I saw it in all the people who had been Undreamed: although some were able to hold a conversation, most were left with nothing more than a body looking like a hushed husk. Cormack is strong – he keeps his thoughts collected and takes the trouble to string a sentence together. What he says infuriates me: "The serum offers false hope. Undreaming is the only real method. The Asclepius Congregation has one task, and that is to eradicate the disease from humanity by its very roots."

"Not that we'll allow it," says Sini quickly. "We came here with goods and people have come to provide assistance. Some profound changes are about to take place in the policy of the Asclepius Congregation." Despite the situation, there is a note of satisfaction in her words. When she looks at Cormack, I see that glimmer of triumph in her eyes again. This is her victory. Maybe she can already see herself sitting at Cormack's wide, oak desk. Maybe she's even sitting there already. I don't care. I just got used to the idea of Cormack being my ally, and now I have to deal with his shocking decision.

I shake my head. "I can't stay. There is so much to do and the days are too short. Sini, promise me that the Asclepius Congregation will stay on this course."

"On my honour," she says seriously.

"And Cormack..." He looks at me silently and I can't hold back the tears burning in my eyes. He could have achieved so much. He could have been so much more. I surprise Sini, and actually myself, by gently wrapping my arms around him. I expect him to push me away, but he gives no reaction at all. I'll get more warmth and intimacy from a bag of potatoes. Still, I kiss him on the cheek, where the stubble rubs against my face. He will look like a wild man in a few weeks if he doesn't regain an interest in shaving. I hope Sini will save some of his dignity and not let that happen.

"I'm so sorry," I say again. "I wish I could turn it around. I wish you had told me what you were afraid of."

Suddenly he speaks. "You wouldn't have saved me, Nimue. Benji knew all along where the problem was – with Rona, and now with you. I refuse to be your victim. Nimue, let go of me."

My arms slip away from him and I take a step back. I try not to feel hurt.

For a moment, his eyes flicker and I feel like there's real awareness in them. Then, that brightness fades again and his face becomes as smooth as before. I noticed these changes before in Katell. Sometimes she seemed almost like herself, other times she floated away from me like a flake of sea foam.

"It's time I take him back," Sini says. No doubt she has also noticed the change, because this time she is not as heavy-handed as before, gently ushering Cormack to the car.

"I'll walk," I say.

"I'm sorry, Nimue. I really am." She hesitates for a moment. "Should I not have brought him along?"

"I don't know," I admit. "He's not the first Undreamed I've seen. I know what it's like."

"I thought you had to see him like that, to understand that what we are doing with the Asclepius Congregation now is necessary."

"I really don't care," I say, and that's quite true. "As long as you are doing good. Are you taking good care of him?"

"We will."

"Sini..." Now I remember why they came. "The medicine? Cormack promised us more."

"It's all in there," she reassures me. "But you know it doesn't always work. We'll keep working on improving it."

"Good luck," I say softly, knowing that I won't be here to see if they'll manage to improve the serum. "Cormack wanted to be the light in this world. Work hard on that."

"The light in this world?" She obviously likes that sentiment, because she smiles. "I will do my best. Good luck, Nimue. I have his phone. You know how to call me."

I do, but I won't. Sini pulls the door shut, turns on the engine and drives the car away from the dunes, bouncing and hopping as she goes. It can't be easy for Cormack, with his hands cuffed like that.

I watch as it reaches the road. Then the car is enveloped by mist, becoming a mere blurred contour for a while before it completely disappears from view.

In two days I will take the helm of *The Starry Wind*. In doing so, I'll leave behind a world where the only choice seems to be to die or break.

My thoughts turn to Arthur and that makes my hope soar like a bird. As long as he goes on, not everything is lost. In the meantime, I must learn to be strong. I may not be able to prevent deaths, but there must be a way for me to let my strength shine through. By Gwenhael's bones, if my little brother can be a king, surely I can be more than just the daughter of a fisherman?

16

EXODUS

Lanterns and candles have been placed in rows along the vast beach. They reflect the stars that must be shining somewhere in the sky, although they are obscured by a veil of mist and clouds. Large bonfires do their best to break through this hazy enchantment. In some places, they succeed. Everything becomes colourful and warm by the circle of light that they're spreading.

I'm wearing my finest clothes, the ones I brought from Avalon: a blue tunic with embroidered sleeves, which freely shows my growing belly. The shard of Saint Gwenhael is around my neck strung on a leather cord. I have even made an effort to scrub my hands clean and to brush the sand from under my nails.

It's a night for celebration and mourning. We don't have time to distinguish between those two feelings, so we do both at the same time: a celebration for the people who will board *The Starry Wind* tomorrow, and a time of mourning for those we have lost – villagers and refugees alike. After all, we are all brothers and sisters as soon as our bones decompose on the funeral pyres.

In a way, there is not so much difference between the way we are sent off with flames and candles and the way we bid the dead farewell. We expect that our journey out of Gwennec will eventually come to an end, as inevitable as death itself.

Together with Wolf, I zigzag along the clusters of people who have gathered, looking for Yannick. Her family is standing by the fire in the centre, which is blazing high. But they don't know where she is.

I find her on the far end of the beach, away from the light and the sound and the singing. She is sitting on the rocks and lets the surf wash over her bare feet.

"Wolf," I say softly. "Will you give us a moment in private?"

He takes off, disappearing into the shadows.

I take off my boots one by one, carefully place them out of the water's reach and sit down next to Yannick.

"You have one more night, you know. You'll regret it if you don't say good-bye."

"I know. But I had to have a moment alone." She looks up from her feet and says: "I've never set a foot outside Breizh."

"You'll get used to it," I say.

"Really?"

I think for a moment. "No. Eventually you just grow accustomed to the sting of loss. Part of you will always long for home. Only... what you really want is to go back to your home as *you* remember it."

"And the world is changing very fast," Yannick sighs.

We are silent for a long time. Then Yannick smiles. "This isn't good either. We are about to embark on the adventure of a lifetime, and here we sit alone, isolated from the others. Where is your lover?"

"Somewhere behind us."

"Well, call him."

I don't even have to. As if on cue, he comes towards us. I shift so that he can sit behind me and lean against him as he wraps an arm around my waist.

"Tell me about the north," Yannick says. "Not about the hard things. I've already worried enough about the hard things."

"You will see that it is different from Breizh," Wolf warns her. "There are other plants, other animals. In the valleys it mostly rains, while snow covers the highest peaks. I remember the lakes acting as mirrors of the sky. The water rushing down from the mountains was cold as ice. My grandmother warned me not to drink it too greedily or it would give me brain freeze." He smiles vaguely. "I remember the smoke of fires as I lay dozing between hides and furs, and the sound of caribou outside our tents. The winters were eternally dark; that made the *jerv* come close to our herds. Sometimes, even lone wolves came, if they were hungry enough to defy our dogs."

"*Jerv*?" I repeat.

He thinks for a moment. "A hunting animal. Like a wolf or a small bear."

"What kind of flocks? Sheep?"

"No, caribou. Reindeer. They were the heart of our people, our livelihood. We drank their milk and ate their meat and made clothes from their hides, everything else from their antlers and hooves. It was a way of life that had existed for centuries, long before the Impact changed the world. It was not difficult for my people to continue in that way after the civilisations of the South fell apart."

"Are they still there?" I ask. "Those people in the north?"

"I'm sure of that. But not my people the Hura. Not my family. They have all been slaughtered."

I remember that story, of course. I take his hand between mine and Yannick closes her eyes again.

"You asked for happy stories," Wolf says a little later. "Winters may be dark and desolate, but magic does happen in the air. You will never have seen anything like it. My grandfather used to tell me stories about how the spirits danced through the sky and escorted the dead into the Other World. That was just a fairy tale for the people who lived in the cities. They had long since discovered that this sudden light in the sky was not magic, just particles of the sun moving through the atmosphere." Wolf smiled. "If you ever see those lights, I'm sure you'll feel the same magic we did. I just don't know if it will be visible. Maybe this fog will spread to all corners of the world."

"Maybe the fog won't be so bad there," I say. I'm not sure how to picture the dancing lights in the sky. "Does it look like moving stars? Like the moon?"

Wolf laughs, the sound rumbling through his chest against me. "When winter sets in, you'll see."

"Winter will be a long way off when we arrive."

"Winter never strays far enough to be forgotten about," says Wolf. "You have to learn to think about the cold while summer is at its height."

"Like we have to think of Storm Season when the sea is still like a mirror," Yannick says.

Wolf nods. "And the summer brings the land back to life. The forests are much denser, much deeper than I have seen here in Breizh. High up in the mountains are pine trees that stretch endlessly in all directions. You could travel for days and never see an open plain. Down in the valleys, aspen and birch grow. You will like the coast, Nimue. The beaches there are not as wide as they are here, but the land stretches out into the sea like giant fingers. The people of the coast called them fjords." He pauses. "I lived far away from the fjords. My people had nestled themselves deep among endless miles of lakes and forests and mountains and long, foaming rivers, full of salmon."

"That sounds like we'll have more than enough to eat," Yannick jokes.

"If you know where to find them." Wolf's fingers intertwine with my hair and begin to play with the strands. "But there are plenty of other creatures who have the same meal in mind. It was my grandfather who taught me to hunt."

"How old were you then?" I ask, trying to imagine what he looked like when he was young.

"Oh, I was a child. I was maybe five years old when he took me on my first trip. We went to the Heemu River, as we called it, which had long stretches of land on both sides of the water. On the west bank, he'd laid a trail of wild traps. It was a long walk. I only managed to keep up with him because I knew it was important. He showed me his snares, how the threads were tied. They killed martens and hares, even foxes. Occasionally a *jerv* as well, which we needed for their furs. I remember dragging two hares all the way along the Heemu back to our camp. I can still remember how they smelled when they were cooked."

I haven't often heard him talk for this long. As if he has heard my thoughts, his voice trails off and Wolf slips back into his usual silence.

"That sounds like you had a good life there," I say quietly.

His hand caresses my neck, a lovely, warm feeling. "They were good days."

"We're going to make it. Aren't we? We're not going to die there," Yannick says hesitantly.

"You could die anywhere," Wolf replies. "Yet even there it is possible to live a good life. You will need a few seasons to adapt. It won't be easy, but I can teach you."

Yannick nods with a serious look on her face, as if she is memorizing every word. I wonder how scared she really was and for how long she walked around with that fear kept within her without showing me.

Finally, she smiles. "I'd better get back. This is not a night to let pass quietly."

She dries her feet with her sleeves, puts her shoes on and disappears in the direction of the biggest fire. When Wolf and I catch up with her much later, someone has picked up a flute, another the hurdy-gurdy, and people are clapping their hands as the music begins. Yannick is dragged into a dance by her father.

I grab Wolf. "Let's dance."

"I can't dance."

"Tonight you can." I pull him into the space created for the dancers and don't let go of him. It takes two quick dances, during which my hair gets messy and I'm out of breath, before he smiles. As I spin around in his arms, he laughs out loud. I join in.

"Don't exhaust yourself," he says.

"It's good for a baby to dance and to hear music," I say. "It will make him happy."

"Then I'll dance with you every day."

"I'll hold you to that." We are not the only ones who have exhausted ourselves with this burst of energy, so the musicians are now playing a calmer tune. Although our feet barely move, we still dance together.

"Those herds of yours that you used to have... did you keep them on pasture, behind fences?"

Wolf smiles as he shakes his head. "Caribou migrate. Each year they make the journey from their summer pastures to their winter resting place down in the valleys and forests, where it is less cold. We followed our animals, not the other way around."

"We won't have the furs, or the flesh, or the bones, or the antlers, then..."

"It would not be a bad idea to gather a herd after a few seasons. We could start with a mother with a calf, and one bull."

"Is it that simple? To catch a wild animal and tame it as if it were a dog or a donkey?"

"They are not dogs or donkeys, and most of them will never be tamed. But you can teach them the advantages of being with us. The first calves that will be born after they join us will grow up being used to that new life."

I smile. "Like our child."

"I will teach him everything I learned from my grandfather. Or her." Wolf smiles. "And you will learn it too. You are clever and brave."

I hope by Gwenhael that he is right. I can't imagine a world so far north. The winters in Breizh are cold, but the days are never so short that the sunlight is completely swallowed by darkness. But if I can milk cows, surely I can milk female reindeers; if I can sew clothes from the hard leather we produce Gwennec, I can do the same with marten fur. I can skin, disembowel, cut needles from bones and make cord from intestines. It will be different from Gwennec, but I can adapt.

"Nimue," says a voice behind me. "I have been looking for you."

When I look behind me, I see Will. I tear myself away from Wolf and say: "I saw you were back. Sorry I didn't have time to talk before. Where's Mirna?"

"Devouring the food, what else?" He grins and points towards the fire. "On the road, we have little variation in our rations. I thought we were going to take you across the border? Here I am trying my best to get the safest path clear and now I hear you're getting on that boat?" He tilts his head. "Why the change of plans?"

I shrug. "I now know where I am really needed."

"Oh, I see." His obvious curiosity hangs between us for a moment, but when I make no move to explain further, he seems to shake it off. "Well, yes. Then I guess this is our goodbye."

"I'll miss you, Will. You and Mirna."

He smiles. "I have a feeling we've said our last goodbyes before. I think we parted on pretty good terms back then, didn't we?"

I laugh. "That's true."

"Well then, let's not start messing about with something that was already perfect. All I ask for is this one dance."

Wolf reluctantly lets go of me, though I think I see a hint of relief on his face now that he can escape from the next dance.

Will is keeping things decent, though I suspect that is mostly down to the fact that Mirna comes over and keeps looking at us with two sweet buns in her hands. He puts his hands in my sides. When the music starts, he spins me around. "And I have one last request: take care of yourself, Nimue. Do your best not to die," he says.

I let out a laugh. "Don't die yourself. And don't let anything happen to Mirna. She's a gem, Will."

"Oh, like I didn't already know that. No other girl would want me."

I chuckle, then get serious. "That's why it's not a bad idea to take care of yourself. If you want a future together, as Wolf and I do… don't be too afraid to pursue it. You've already done so much for others. For the Undreamed."

Will shows me that faint smile of his. "But there is still so much we can do for the living. You taught me that."

"Keep it in mind anyway. One day you may tire of your endless fight against injustice. Mirna might want something else. If that happens, don't let your generosity get in the way of what you can have for yourself, Will. Promise me that – for Mirna's sake too."

He smiles and spins me around again. "I will remember that."

"Is that a promise?"

"Who knows? It's in the back of my mind, as you wished."

And I'll have to make do with that. As the night progresses, the fires burn brighter. We dance, we drink, we sing ditties that gradually seem less like songs and more like cries to the sea. I think about Arthur more than once and wish he were beside me to face the uncertain day that comes next.

Just hours before dawn, Wolf and I leave the party to crawl into bed in our barn. I fall sleep immediately, surrounded by the smell of burning wood. Or is it Wolf, who has carried the smoke with him in his clothes? Before I tumble over the edge of sleep, I fantasise about a tent close to the tree line of a deep forest, where wolves howl at each other in the distance, the dogs nearby howl more quietly, and the scraping sound of the hooves and the low growl of the caribou will lull my baby to sleep.

The sea kept still and could not move. Darkness enveloped her. For centuries they were like that, undisturbed... "Oh," sighed the Sea. "Oh, where have all the stars gone that the sailors used to navigate by? Where are the fish and plants in my belly? And where is the moon, which could draw my tides? It used to be different!"

The Darkness heard this, and he rejoiced.

"It's no use complaining," he whispered. "Long have I waited for the light to disappear from below to above: centuries and centuries and longer. Now I have won, and I am everywhere."

"Why do you want it so badly? I remember a time when light and dark had their own place. Light was in charge of life, which danced and grew and dreamed and worked, and Darkness was in charge of death and silence and the Longest Watch."

The Starry Wind is ready to embark. I hold on to Wolf's hand as we step onto the gangway, because my knees feel rubbery. The railing is higher than two grown men standing on each other's shoulders. I can see everywhere that this ship is old: the metal shows rusty spots, the paint is peeling away. The money for the repairs has clearly not gone towards a fresh new exterior.

Wolf grabs the ladder, climbs on deck and then helps me make the final ascent. My back protests for a moment before I flex my muscles and end up on the deck of the ship that will take me far from my birthplace for the second time in my life. This ship, which will have to cleave unknown currents and cross long distances, which will sail the course that I will have to maintain with my own hands.

We walk to the foredeck, where the captain's cabin is. It feels as if we are standing on a tower with the sea far below us. This is also the largest living space on the ship, if you don't take the hold into account. My offer to replace Berthou has given me the only bit of real privacy on this ship.

The beach is packed with people. Several hundred embrace their loved ones – if they still have them – before climbing aboard. Everyone else stares after them. Towels are raised like pennants; as greetings, as goodbyes. If nothing goes wrong, the pioneers will never see this coast again.

The thought depresses me and I calm myself by remembering that *The Starry Wind* must make at least one return journey, to bring news of the arrival in the north and to bring new travellers. But not before our child has come into the world, like a little stranger in a strange land.

No. I will be the stranger; not my child. And neither will his father. I have to keep encouraging myself with that.

Slowly, *The Starry Wind* fills up with passengers. Some of the faces I see in passing are familiar to me: Anouel and Marie, Taran, Judikael and Marci; Mart and his family, Nanicka with her husband and son. Besides the residents of Gwennec, there are hundreds more whom I have never seen or spoken to. Some have the dark features of Central Europeans, others clearly come from the other regions of the Periphery.

Finally, when the last person is on board and the gangway has almost collapsed beneath the weight of passengers boarding, and the foredeck and aft are filled with people wanting to catch one last glimpse of the coastline, I have to give the order. I put my hands to my mouth. "Get the plank up!"

Marci and Judikael have been waiting for the command. A dejected silence envelops the people on deck as the gangway is being pulled up. The connection between us and the land is falling away. Behind me, Wolf takes a deep breath.

"Lift the anchor," I command.

The rattling of the chains is heavy and loud, but not as loud and deep as the rumbling of engines in the belly of the ship when I switch on the steering programme. No sails or oars for me this time – *The Starry Wind* sails by digital coordinates and requires almost no touching of the rudder. Nevertheless, I put my hands around the steering wheel. We are moving like a giant iron animal, which has been in a deep sleep and is now waking up. From my window, I can see the hull of the ship and the sea foaming white against the underside of the railing. Cheers rise up from the deck.

"Eyes forward," I say softly to myself. "Legs wide. Chin up."

Wolf's hand lands on my shoulder. "Are you scared?"

With my hands around the wheel, I feel the ship move beneath me. "I'm not afraid," I say. "The ship is speaking to me. Come – feel it too."

Hesitantly, he puts his hands around the steering wheel. His jaw tightens. "That's a lot of power."

"Nothing to fear," I say. "It is the power we need. That power will sail us straight into the arms of the north."

I take the helm from him again and stare out the window above the heavy ship's wheel. The fog lights are drilling holes in the mist in front of us. Very slowly, we make a turn. I steer her with a feathery light touch. The flank of *The Starry Wind* turns towards the beach, then the bow is turning towards the unknown. Gwennec is still visible behind us, but I choose not to look back. Gwennec, the end of the world, turns out to be nothing more than the harbour belonging to the last known city. *We* are the people of the end of the earth, and we set sail into a world larger than we could ever imagine.

17

LESSONS

During our first night at sea, everyone is restless. Gwennec has disappeared from view, as has the sun. That leaves us with only the fog lights on deck and the few lights allowed down in the hold.

With a ship's light in my hand, I make a tour of the ship. Yannick is decorating her own cabin. Apart from the captain's cabin, this is the only room with a bed and a small working space that can be locked. Her crates are stacked together on the floor. It almost seems as if she has packed the contents of an entire hospital to take with her.

An iron hatch leads me below decks, into the engine room, where the floor trembles and the noise fills my ears. Next to it is the pantry, also locked with a simple lock. All our preserved food has been neatly stored there for days, along with a huge tank of purified drinking water. Everything else – tents, tools, weapons, even a few torches with batteries for emergencies – is stored in the back.

I run into Nanicka in the pantry. She shows me a long list of everything we brought with us. "I'm leading the first group, taking care of the rations," she says. "We work three-day shifts. Have you seen Hannus anywhere?"

"I saw him on the middle deck with Mart, that tall boy."

"Ah, good. I asked him to check the hatch. I nearly broke my neck tripping on an open crack when it got dark. They swore that everything about the ship was in good condition!"

I let out a sigh. "It's an old ship; there are bound to be holes and cracks." When I see her face fall in the light of my lamp, I quickly add: "No real holes, of course. *The Starry Wind* is as seaworthy as any good ship I know, Nanicka. You can sleep peacefully."

"Well," she says. "I don't think anyone is going to sleep well tonight."

I return to my cabin thinking that the same will be true for me, although I'm used to the sound of the sea. The thought of the deep, wet darkness beneath us doesn't frighten me, but Wolf thinks otherwise. He's on a chair in my tiny workspace, as far away from the window as possible.

"You haven't lit a light," I say in surprise. I put my lamp in its niche and turn on the oil lamps on the desk by the window.

"I was planning to, but I wanted to wait until I felt better."

"Are you nauseous?"

He growls something in reply, not really giving an answer.

I can't help but chuckle. "I can't believe that I, of all people, had to fall in love with a man who can't stand the sea."

"You did make a very strange choice," he mutters.

"Well, it's too late to go looking for a handsome fisherboy." I take off my boots and carefully put them in the wooden cabinet opposite the desk. That's the only place to store our meagre personal possessions. In practice, that means only the clothes we wear on board. The rest – the padded fabrics and boots with snow soles – is stuffed into one of the bedstead's drawers. The tip of one of Wolf's boots is bulging out and I try to avoid tripping over it when I open the shutters of the box bed.

"Shark blood." I kick the boot back into the drawer. It's as if I'm trying to push a bubble of air underwater: immediately, a folded jacket pops out next. I shake my head, step over the coat and drop down on the mattress, which is also not particularly wide. We had more room in our shed. Oh well. At least we have this space to ourselves, without a single thin, wooden bulkhead separating us from another couple. I don't envy the passengers downstairs in the hold, although I also feel slightly guilty. There's no reason I should have this luxury, besides the fact that I let the life of their former captain slip through my hands.

A little later, I hear the creaking of his chair and his footsteps on the floor as he comes over to lie down with me. The mattress squeaks and sags deeply.

"I prefer the hay."

"Me too," I smile with my eyes closed. "Although I'm looking forward to waking up without hay in my hair."

"I enjoyed plucking that out of your hair."

I laugh softly. "We shouldn't complain. It's a privilege to have this."

"You think so?"

"Of course." I open my eyes and look at him. "The only room I ever had to myself was in the Asclepius Congregation."

"I prefer the forest to this oppressive space."

I kiss him, then crawl deeper under the covers. Despite Wolf's discomfort, I notice that he falls asleep quickly. I lie awake a while longer and let myself be rocked by the swell of the ship. There are still layers of iron and wood between me and the sea, yet I feel the water tugging at my blood. I hear the engines louder than the waves, and yet in between them I hear that enticing voice: *Nimue, swim, and come to us...*

I know I have fallen asleep when I suddenly find myself on a beach. It is enclosed by cliffs whose pointy edges are shrouded in a thick layer of mist. The tide is coming in. There is no sound except the roar of the surf. Confused, I look around.

Then, as if gliding on air, she emerges from the fog: my grandmother Sela. She looks younger than my mother is now; a strange sensation. The last time I saw her was on the beach at Gulls Island. I didn't think she would ever show herself to me again.

I wait silently until she is standing in front of me. Her skin is as white as the mist around us and she wears her seal skin like a loose cloak over her shoulders.

"Is this real?" I ask.

"As real as any dream." Sela touches my cheek with her cool fingertips. "I have come to teach you."

"To teach me what?"

"Many things. We will start at the beginning. Come with me." She takes my hand and guides me to the edge of the sea. When my feet are deep in the cold water, I hesitate.

"Do you want me to swim?"

"Indeed," she smiles. "But not in your present form. Change."

"Sela, I'm not a selkie. I can't do what you can do."

"You are a shaman. In this world, you can turn yourself into whatever you want. Come now, you must learn this."

"How?" I look down at my feet and legs in the water. Undeniably human feet and human legs. I try to imagine them as fins and a tail. Nothing happens.

"You have to implore your mind to change you into a creature of the wilderness. A seal would be your natural state, but if you prefer a whale, or a shark..."

"You think I'm a shark type?"

Sela laughs softly. "Close your eyes," she then says. "Don't look at your body. Your eyes only see what they *think* your body should look like. This is not the First World. Here, you can be anything you want."

I try. The water starts to get deeper and less cold at the same time. It is only when I'm up to my mouth in the sea and gasping for breath that I realise I'm no longer Nimue. I am a small, grey seal. Every swell of the waves lifts me up and gracefully lowers me again. Moving through the water has become as easy as breathing.

"Well done," says Sela. "Now swim with me."

She takes her coat from her shoulders and wraps it around her body. I don't know where exactly the change takes place, but in less than a heartbeat, she is by my side like a shiny, jet-black seal. I follow her through the sea and when the shallows give way to a dark, deep rough, I let myself slide into the depths with her.

I'm not sure how long we keep swimming. I only know that at long last, there is light ahead of us. When I reach the surface, I am human again. I'm soaked and shivering from the wind that now sharply bites my skin.

Sela stands beside me. Silently, she wraps her seal coat around her shoulders again. If her wet hair is bothering her, she doesn't let it show.

I look around me. To my astonishment, we are not on the coastline, but in a riverbed. My feet are planted on mud and cracked earth. All the water has disappeared and dried up. A few reeds have turned an unhealthy, brown colour.

Above me is a sky without a sun. Around me is only a dry valley, surrounding the river. Further away are mountains – even a forest, that is still green. You'd have to climb a steep and winding ledge to get there.

"I recognise this place," I say. "This is where Arthur passed by."

"He is not far from here."

Hope flares up in my heart. I look around. "Where is he? He can never see me, but if he can see you..." A movement in the corner of my eye makes me go silent. Someone comes shuffling towards us, one foot tucked into a shoe and the other bare and caked in mud. He limps as though he's injured, and when I come closer, I indeed see traces of old blood on his trousers. He walks with hunched shoulders, occasionally pulling small things from between the cracks in the riverbed. Sometimes he puts them in his mouth, sometimes in his pocket.

As he approaches us, my mouth becomes drier. I knew what would happen to Cormack after he Undreamed himself, but to see him here like a half-damaged animal is worse than seeing his hollow stare in my own world. Instinctively, I take a step backwards.

His gaze shoots upwards. There is no recognition in his eyes, only distrust. His fingers clench around the small crab he's holding, as if he is afraid that I will try to take it away from him.

"Cormack." I swallow. "Can he see me?" I ask Sela.

Sela's voice is soft. "Hardly. He sees a patch of fog, hears an echo of a voice."

"Why? If I can travel to the Other World, why can't I make myself known?"

"You have to practise that. That's why I brought you here. But don't practice it with him." She looks at Cormack. "He doesn't remember his own name. He hasn't gotten a new name yet."

I don't want to look. It's like staring at a terrible accident that I can't help but look at.

"His mind is completely gone, isn't it? He is broken."

"It is sad," Sela says. "He loved my son like a father."

"Why has he become like this? Arthur is not like that. Katell is not like that. The others who are with him are brave and clever and... human."

"The shock of the mind being expelled from its body, the Second World atmosphere it lands in... all these things influence how a person reacts. Most are not made for that transition. Most souls become nothing more than a shadow, an echo of what they were. The Hunter feeds on them, but he prefers to feed on the strong souls. He thrives on their light and strength. That's why the finest and strongest spirits were the first to fall prey to corruption in this land. That's why it is no longer safe for those of us who remain. I cannot stay with you long, Nimue."

I look from Cormack to her. "So where does that leave you?"

"We hide. In the grey areas between the Two Worlds, in the cracks that have appeared. Not quite here, not quite there." She heaves a sigh. "It's a cold existence."

"Can Arthur solve this?"

"I hope so. He needs help – more than just his brave knights."

"Knights? They are only boys and girls."

"It is what we do that elevates us above our birth, Nimue." Sela holds out her hand. "Come. Let me take you to Arthur."

I want nothing more, but a glance at Cormack stops me. "Isn't there anything we can do for him?"

"Very little. But nothing comes without the risk of drawing the Hunter's attention."

"But there is a chance?"

"There is... a way to lift the veil from his clouded mind. It is a simple healing spell. But it's dangerous, Nimue. Every spark of magic is like a bell ringing across the land. The Hunter can hear it. Nimue, you must know what the Hunter wants from you."

"He wants me dead." I shrug. "Just like he wants you and Arthur dead."

Fear and pain shimmer in Sela's dark eyes. "He wants more than our death, dear child. It is the magic he wants from us, which he chases like a thirsty animal hunts for water. His body is dead mass, sustained only by the life force of others. That's why he hunts and destroys every trace of goodness and life force in his victims. In each spirit, he puts a spark of his own black magic – to sustain him, to make that spirit hunt too... For each spirit that finds a victim and in turn feeds on life, gives part of that life back to the Hunter. He is like a spider in his great web; he is the heart of one great organism. But there is a downside to his victory." Sela turns away from me and her voice softens, as if she fears that even her whispers may draw danger to us. "The Hunter knows that he will soon be the king of the realm of the dead. Where will he get his life force from then? How will he sustain himself when all life has been consumed by him? That's why I'm hiding, Nimue. That's why he's looking for you. Our magic comes from the sea, which eternally renews and always transforms itself. With our magic in his possession, he can sustain that dying body of his forever."

Unsettling words to let sink in. The White Wolf had already given me a warning, but I hadn't listened.

I look at Cormack. My poor, foolish cousin. He scurries on, agonisingly slow and with painful steps, oblivious to our presence. "The Hunter's not here yet, is he?"

"We never know where he is," Sela says.

Even the Hunter cannot be in more than one place at a time. He may want my magic for himself, but he will have to catch me first.

"I can't keep hiding," I say slowly. "And Cormack needs me. Sela, I want to try. Do you think I have the power?"

Sela hesitates. "I believe so."

I lick my lips. "I owe it to him. If he had asked me, I would have cured him. He didn't believe I would do that for him, he thought I shouldn't risk it because of my child. By Gwenhael's bones, I can't leave him like this."

She casts a searching look around her – the landscape is deserted. Finally, she nods. "Then try and be quick about it. Remember that your magic is powerful as long as you allow it to be. The spell is simple: you chant a few words." She chants the sounds to me. They are not words with meaning; at least, not to me. "It is our oldest language," Sela adds. "Older than the mountains. It came into being with the rising of the primordial sea, and with the first souls that were born from it. Be careful, Nimue."

I nod and approach my cousin. This magic carries a depth that is stronger than I have ever felt before. It flows through my body like a swirling river, almost painful, and my hands seem to know more than my head. When I get close enough, I touch Cormack. He is noticeably startled. His eyes are bloodshot, the pupils unhealthily widened. He looks around as if he's expecting a spirit somewhere. And that's exactly what I am to him, of course. I wonder if he experiences me the same as I once did the first fragments of the Fisher King: not as a creature of flesh and blood, but as a nebulous string, one moment almost real, the next a fragment of my uncontrolled imagination.

"Don't be afraid," I say, in case he hears something of my voice. "I won't hurt you." Again, I put my hands against his face, which causes him to shiver violently. Miraculously, he doesn't move. I take a deep breath and gently let the air escape from my body. I push my fear of the Hunter aside, then let the magic flow from my hands. The words sound awkward as they come from my mouth, not as fluent and natural as when Sela sang them, but they seem to work. The longer I stand like this, weaving the spell around Cormack, the more the feral look disappears from his eyes. That fear gives way to a different kind of bewilderment – not like that of a wounded animal, but of a lost man. He looks around with his mouth open, his pupils returning to normal. I let go of him and take a step back. Cormack raises his hands. For a moment I think he has seen me and is looking for support, but when I extend my arms, he steps back. He stares at his dirty hands as if wondering what he did, digging in the mud. Then he looks at the blood on his trousers and at his one bare foot.

"Oh, Cormack," I whisper.

"Come." Sela's hand on my shoulder is stronger this time. "The Hunter surely will have noticed this. We can't just stand here."

"Cormack will be vulnerable!"

"Not as vulnerable as you and me if the Hunter gets on our trail. Benji's son must learn to use his wits in his new country."

I don't want to leave him here all by himself, but I'm even less eager to meet the Hunter, so I allow Sela to pull me away from the dried-up riverbed and my stunned cousin. We trek up the hill and disappear among the trees of the forest that seemed so far away a moment ago. I don't think we are really walking; sliding is a better word.

In the shade of the trees, the daylight seems less strange. The sky is blocked by protruding branches. There are fewer leaves growing on the trees than I first thought: up close, the green haze I saw is a moss that covers all the trunks and branches.

We go deep into the forest. There are no paths, but that doesn't seem to be a problem. Eventually, Sela stops at a small quarry and I smell the scent of a campfire.

"Your brother will need your help to succeed in his mission," Sela says. "So go to him. Help him remember who you are."

"I don't know how," I complain. "He can't see or hear me. I am a ghost to him, as I was to Cormack."

Sela smiles. She extends a long, white index finger and momentarily touches the shard of Saint Gwenhael around my neck. "You brought your own magic, I see."

"This? This is nothing more than a little superstition." Strangely enough, it has come with me and stayed on my neck during my transformation, although my body is asleep next to Wolf in our rocking cabin.

"But it is so much more than superstition. Look, you bled on it."

I frown, but just as the significance of those words begins to take shape in my mind. Sela steps back into the mist. "The way back is easy. You just need to wake up."

"Wait!" I shout. "Sela, don't leave me alone!"

"Who's there?"

Arthur calls out the question like a command. I turn around with a jolt and moments later he emerges from the tree pit with a torch in his hand. The flames almost hit my face when he waves it around.

"Shark blood, Arthur!" I jump backwards.

"Monster or human?" he snarls.

I burst out laughing. "Can you see me?"

He raises his eyebrows. "Were you trying to stay invisible?"

"Just the opposite!" Relief overwhelms me and I come forward to take Arthur in my arms. He waves the torch menacingly and I quickly stay in my place. "Arthur, you must recognise my face. I am Nimue, you fool. Your sister!"

My words do not have the desired effect. He takes a step back and lowers his other hand to a stone blade on his belt. "You know my name?"

"Of course!"

"I don't remember any sister."

"Do your best, by Gwenhael!"

He blinks his eyes. "Gwenhael... I know that name. I *use* that name."

I try not to get closer again, but show him my smile. "I've been watching over you, Arthur. Ever since you woke up. Katell found you, didn't she? I mean... Goldilocks. All this time, you couldn't hear or see me, no matter how loudly I called out your name. I'm sorry. You have to know how sorry I am." Suddenly, tears squeeze through my eyes. "About the bullet. How I couldn't save you. How I arrived in Avalon too late. How you never got to see Mum again..."

"Stop!" Arthur turns paler and stares at me as if I was suddenly caught on fire. "I don't know what you're talking about! And what is that?" He points at my necklace. "A strange force s coming from it. What is this... Magic?"

I curl my fingers around the stone. "It's something from home."

His gaze takes in my face and observes my clothes. Very slowly, something dawns in his eyes.

"I think you have something similar," I say cautiously. "Under your jumper. A... a seal necklace?"

His hand disappears from his weapon and he very slowly pulls out the pendant. "How did you know?" he asks hoarsely.

"Because it belonged to Mum. Because I hung it around your neck when you were... lying in bed in Avalon... on the day I left." I, too, am beginning to sound hoarse. My euphoria about finally talking to Arthur makes way for sadness. "I didn't want to leave you. I know you don't realise it, Arthur, but your body, your real body, is sleeping on an island far away, where Mum is at your bedside every day."

He lapses into deeper silence. His fingers play with the chain. I know how it feels: how many times have I nervously run my fingers over the smooth stone?

"I hope it protects you," I say. "I think I understand... This is what binds us together... my stone, with my blood on it. You say you remember Gwenhael - this is a piece of Gwenhael, a piece of the statue that was in the old church."

"A church?" he asks.

"Yes, Arthur. In our birthplace, in Gwennec. And you wear her talisman – the necklace of the woman who bore us. And my blood on this stone." I laugh despite my tears. "This is blood magic. As the Fisher King said to me: Blood remembers and connects."

"The Fisher King!" Arthur's confusion turns to interest. "You spoke to him? He also spoke to us about blood magic, to..." Arthur shuts his mouth and suddenly stands alert. His nostrils flare, as if he smells a scent warning him of danger. He lets go of the pendant and draws his knife. "Did you lure him?" he asks in a muffled voice. His anger is back. "Were you lying?"

"What? Arthur, no! Who?" I don't need to ask who he's noticed. I slowly turn around and look straight into the face of the Hunter. He is standing at the edge of the quarry, almost as tall as the trees. Very slowly, like a stealthy cat, he bends his knees and lowers himself, ready to leap out.

"Run!" Arthur says. "Run! Get fire!"

"I can't leave you alone!" My legs suddenly seem to be made of concrete. I want to run, but the Hunter's eyes root me to the spot. His claw-like hands come up, palms turned outwards, and the eyeballs in them roll towards me.

"What a surprise," he murmurs, each word slowly stretched out. "The sea witch's two children set eyes on each other's faces." He applauds us. I cringe at the sound, only realising a beat later that he's mocking us. "And I thought the child-king was deaf and blind, like a worm."

"You won't get us, Hunter," Arthur growls, his voice shockingly low.

"Arthur!" The others come running from the camp. Lance is heading the troupe, his great spear thrust forward. Behind him comes Morgana with torches flying, and next to her are Val, Green, GWN, and Katell. I finally manage to break free from the Hunter's gaze and stumble backwards until I'm standing behind a shield of fire.

And then, to my frustration, I feel my sleeping body starting to wake up. My mind is drawn back to it as if I were tied to it with a string. I resist fiercely, but it is no use. While being able to shout a warning to Arthur, I wake up. I feel as if I've had a blow that has knocked the air out of my body.

With my fists clenched in my lap, I sit up straight and close my eyes tightly. My breathing falters. I must go back. Now! I don't know what I can do against the Hunter, but I know I have to protect my little brother.

Go back, I tell myself feverishly. My consciousness seems to cling to my waking body. No matter how desperately I search for a way to reach the Other World, I cannot find it. I start panting.

A hand grabs my shoulder and my eyes fly open in fright. Wolf sits upright, frowning at me in the darkness of the hut. "What's wrong?" I try to tell him, but he stops me almost immediately. "Catch your breath first. Calm down."

I force myself to breathe in and out. The air flows a little easier through my lungs. Finally I say: "The Hunter was ready to attack Arthur. Because of me – I lured him by using magic. I have to go back and help Arthur!"

It's a very succinct summary, but surely Wolf can understand the despair on my face? Still, he shakes his head briefly. "Not as long as you are so upset. It takes energy to travel, Nimue. You need time between trips to recover."

"I don't have time for that! The Hunter is with them right now and I can't get into that stupid trance anymore!"

His voice remains steady as a rock: "If you go into a trance with such a high heart rate, or with such accelerated breathing, you will only fall. You might get completely lost and then you wouldn't be so different from those poor Undreamed."

I stare at him, torn between impatience and fear caused by what he's telling me. "Something like that can actually happen?"

"You wouldn't be the first shaman it happened to. But all those shamans were stupid. Nimue, listen to me carefully. If you want to travel back, I will be your guide." He puts his flat hand just above my belly button. "And you must promise to follow my instructions, to wake up when I tell you to. Is that clear?"

"Yes," I whisper. "I promise."

"Good. First, you rest."

"But…"

"A few minutes," Wolf says decidedly. "Close your eyes again, and don't squeeze them so hard this time. And breathe in. Breathe out when you feel my hand pushing down."

I do it, and after a few minutes I feel calmness taking over my body.

Wolf begins to drum softly against the wooden headboard of our box bed. At first, I wonder why he is doing it, but he says: "Just listen. Just listen to this. Let this be the only sound that matters, then make it a ladder to climb to the Other World. When I stop, Nimue, when you hear the drumming stop, you must wake up."

I nod as a signal of understanding. For a while, the drumming of his fingers against the wood is nothing more than that: drumming against wood, rhythmic and uninterrupted, before my body and mind start to tune into that sound. The rhythm becomes part of me – or is it my mind that starts to wrap itself around the rhythm?

I find the place in my mind where I started before: the beach where Sela met me. This time she isn't there. Without wasting time, I walk into the cold sea, transform my body into the small, grey seal and dive into the water.

I come up, not to the riverbed but closer to the forest. It is as if my wish to find Arthur has summoned the place before me. Having become human again, I run to the trees. My eyes search left, right, everywhere, for a sign of my brother and his friends.

The signs are there: charred remnants of wood on the forest floor, deep footprints in the mud that suggest a chaotic run away from something. My heart grows cold.

When I find their camp, it is deserted. It has clearly rained, so again my timeline has diverged from theirs. *But not by much*, I pray hopefully. *Let it not have been too much time*. It looks like it hasn't, because the fire hasn't been out long and the coals are still partly glowing in their hot nest.

"Where are you?" I whisper. Did he manage to escape, or was he taken? There are footprints everywhere, but they have become an indecipherable track for me, obscured by the rain. If Wolf had come with me, he might have been able to make sense of it.

I suck in a breath and shout Arthur's name. After that, I wait, feeling goose-bumps rise all over my body, terrified that my noise will attract unwanted spirits and monsters. There is no reply – neither from my brother nor from any other creature.

"Gwenhael's blood on it!" I curse Sela for leaving me with this, I curse Cormack for him needing me so much, and most of all I curse myself for practising the magic that drew the Hunter to us.

Just as I'm about to give up, my eyes are drawn to large, black spots on the trees and on the ground further away from the campfire. The smell of fire is unmistakable as soon as I get closer. I crouch down and discover a strand of golden blonde hair left on a bare branch. It is Katell's, there is no doubt about it.

When I look more closely, I notice the deep imprints in the moss. They are not as visible as footprints in mud, but clear enough to identify.

They ran, I think, and I smile cautiously. I see no traces of the great feet of a pursuing Hunter, though that does not necessarily mean that he wasn't following them closely. In any case, they were running for quite some time, because the tracks lead me far away into the pervading mist. And the lock of hair is scorched at the ends. Someone has set fire to the trees, blocking this path.

They have escaped, I think with relief. I hope to Gwenhael that they have found a place to hide.

I get up, intending to follow the trail deeper into the forest, when my ears pick up something. I freeze. No, that's it – I hear *no* sound, and that attracts my attention. The rhythm has fallen away. I wasn't aware of it before, but now that it suddenly stops, I realise that it has been in the background all this time, keeping my mind balanced.

I hesitate. I want to find Arthur so desperately and make sure he is unharmed, but I made Wolf a promise. He won't thank me if I break it. And he has told me in no uncertain terms that it is not good for me to travel so soon after having done it before... I must think of my baby.

Unwillingly, I admit that I will have to content myself with the idea that Arthur and his friends have probably escaped from the Hunter. *Probably*. What if they were caught just beyond this camp?

A voice from afar reaches me; a voice that speaks to me insistently.

Well, Arthur is no longer here, and he's clever, and his friends are strong. If anyone can escape the Hunter, it's them. I cling to that bit of confidence as I give in to the gravity of my body.

When I slowly open my eyes, Wolf is holding me up by my shoulders.

"You have been away for too long."

I'm stunned at how weak I suddenly feel.

"You have exhausted yourself. Stay still."

I find it hard to even sit up straight, so I can assure him that I feel no need to move. Wolf leaves me alone for a moment and I hear him rummaging around in our poor excuse for a living room. When he returns, he thrusts a hot cup of something into my trembling hands. Steam rises from it and the smell is bitter.

"Drink up. All of it."

"It smells disgusting."

"Yes." He offers me no further comfort.

I blow on it and take a sip. The bitter taste fills my mouth all the way to the back of my throat. I pull a face and have to force myself to swallow it. "Stinging jellyfish, what's in it?"

"*Huldrevot*," says Wolf.

"You have made it so bitter."

"I made it strong. Drink more, or you will faint from the exertion of the journey."

Fainting is almost worth it, that's how dirty this brew is. I obediently drink it all up, until there is only some black sludge left at the bottom of the cup.

"In our language, it meant *chase away the devil*," Wolf says.

Despite everything, I laugh. "No devil would want this."

"How are you feeling now?"

"Better, I think." I carefully roll my shoulders. "Not so dizzy anymore. But I am tired."

He nods. "That is to be expected. Nimue, promise me one thing." He grabs my chin and gently lifts my face. "Don't do this again. No matter how worried you are, you're not strong enough to go on journeys this intense that follow each other up in such quick succession. It's not good for you, and it's not good for our baby."

I lower my gaze and hug my own belly and the child inside with it. "I'm sorry. I panicked…"

"I know. Did you find Arthur?"

"No. I found their tracks and I hope they escaped." I can't be sure. I don't need to tell Wolf that; he should be able to read it all from my face.

"Don't you think you would know it if he was dead?" he asks me tenderly. "Do you really believe that he can slip away from you unnoticed?"

"I don't know," I mutter. "How can I?"

"Perhaps in the same way that you always knew your mother was still alive somewhere."

That is true. Against all odds, there was always a soft voice in my heart that kept insisting Rona wasn't dead. Gone, changed, yes… but not dead. I feel a little better, and not because of the *huldrevot*.

"Thank you," I say to Wolf. I lean forward to kiss him on his mouth, long and hard. "I wouldn't know what to do without you."

"You would make it, Nimue. You know that as well as I do." He is silent for a moment. "You taste like that brew."

"Very strong, isn't it?"

He chuckles for a moment, then pulls the blanket up. "Come, go to sleep. Tomorrow is a new day full of our own challenges."

I allow him to cover me and I feel my droopy eyelids close. When I fall asleep this time around, there is nothing but ordinary darkness.

18

THE GREAT, WILD NORTH

The mountains are the first signs of change. They are giants and their heads are shrouded in veils of mist and clouds. At first, I think they are just waves. Only when we keep moving forward in a continuous northerly course and the shapes do not move from their position do I realise what we are really approaching.

"Wolf!" I shout. I point to the horizon. "Land!"

I hand him the binoculars. He peers through them for a long time, before swallowing and lowering them again. "Adjust the course slightly to the north-west. There are more beaches over there, where you can drop anchor more easily."

I let my fingers dance across the keyboard of the computer system, which I now know as well as I once knew the ropes and lines of *The Ragdoll*. I glance at the built-in compass on my left and adjust the coordinates. "Like this?"

"Better." He is silent for a moment. "Just when I was getting sea legs."

I start to laugh, but we are interrupted by running footsteps on the stairs. Yannick barges into the wheelhouse the next moment. "Did you see it?"

"Our course has been adjusted." I smile.

Her face beams with excitement. She takes the binoculars from me, sucks in her breath and smiles. "We made it! Sometimes I didn't dare hope for it anymore."

I know what she means. The days on the ship soon became long and monotonous. The only excitement came from the weather, but not in a pleasant way. The stormy nights terrified the passengers The water supply soon dwindled. The only way I have been able to wash myself for the past few weeks has been with icy, salty seawater. That made my curls stand out like a fluffy explosion around my face. Most of the men on board have stopped shaving, including Wolf. He looks like the man I rescued from Platform Zero again.

We are all exhausted from the wind relentlessly pounding against us, from the taste of salt that has seeped into pretty much everything. Even I long for solid ground under my feet. And now my belly has undeniably grown heavier. The season has changed as we have crossed the wide sea. We are now in the middle of spring. May, I think. Only four months to go before it's my time to give birth. And only four more months of good weather, because according to Wolf, winter arrives early in the north. My uneasy feeling always peaks whenever I dwell too long on these two facts.

Yannick rescues me from my gloomy train of thought. "How long until we can dock?"

"A day and a half, perhaps." I look out the window. "It depends on the coastline. We won't be able to sail in the shallows. Let Mart know he should ready the rowboats."

Yannick beams. "Yes, Captain!"

I flash her a grin too. "On your feet, land swab."

Yannick leaves the cabin. Moments later, a unanimous cheer coming from the deck penetrates the walls of the cabin. Wolf comes and stands behind me, his hands on my shoulders. In silence, we watch the looming landmass. No doubt his heart is beating as fast as mine. I wonder what he is thinking now. His fingers, squeezing my skin quite hard, betray a mixture of hope and fear within him.

"You have been away from your homeland for a long time," I say softly.

"Too long."

"Are you afraid that you don't belong there anymore?"

I can hear from his breath hitching that I'm hitting a nerve. "I'm afraid I'll have lost the ability to survive there."

"I doubt that," I say. "I see it in your eyes every day. I saw it during our first meeting. This life is a part of you, Wolf, as the sea is in my blood. This north is your haven."

He bends down and presses a kiss to the crown of my hair.

A deep waterway, three times the width of our ship, leads *The Starry Wind* inland. To our left and right are mountains, so high that they pierce the mist and fade into the sky. Breizh doesn't have such high peaks anywhere. I feel very small standing in the wheelhouse of our big-bellied ship, and even smaller when I remember that no villages or towns await us in this wilderness.

The water is as smooth as glass, except along the sides of the ship. Wolf says we're not sailing on a river. This is a fjord, a tall crack in the coastline, and if we follow it, it will eventually bring us to a beach where we can drop anchor. I desperately long to leave the ship's deck, to feel stable, hard earth under my feet again. We move forward at a glacial pace. I keep the engine running at half speed, wary of protruding rocks beneath the surface, of unexpected constrictions in the waterway ahead, of anything I can't foresee on this unfamiliar terrain.

Around noon, we have left the open sea far behind us. That is when I notice a flattening of the land in front of us. The ship's computer gives a sudden warning signal: we are rapidly losing depth in the water. I switch off the engine and we drift a few hundred yards towards a small beach, after which we come to a gentle stop.

"Drop anchor!" I order.

The command is picked up by Judikael and Taran. Wolf and I leave the wheelhouse and together we listen to the heavy thunk of the anchor securing *The Starry Wind* in place. There is a good mile between us and the beach.

The rowing boats are lowered into the water. I watch how people are throwing out rope ladders, how Judikael resolutely barks orders and allows a group of strong boys and girls to be the first to pick up the oars. The second rowboat is for the parents with young children. I put my hands on my belly and Wolf wraps his arms around me from behind. Anouel has to lift Marie off the last part of the rope ladder, because the girl is too scared to jump into the boat.

The oars creak, the rowboats dance on the waves, and then we all witness the first pioneers feeling new land under their feet. Even from the deck I can see how brown and stony this patch of beach is. A rockface rises up again behind it, although the rocks seem less impassable than along the fjord. As I peer at it, my vision blurred by the salt that stings my eyes, I see dark tree peaks and the mist clouding everything. The cries of the children blow away on the wind.

With a lot of splashing, the rowing boats return. Wolf helps me get down the rope ladder. He catches me when I have to let go of the last part. I haven't been this close to the water in a long time. I keep my eyes on the approaching land and hear Wolf's breathing quicken. As the bow rubs against the sand, he slowly lets out a sigh. In that sigh, I hear everything he isn't saying. I think I understand him. Just as my body reacts to the proximity of the sea, he feels the great, wide north pulling at him.

The forest I saw from *The Starry Wind* is suddenly so close by, its tree trunks as high as the walls of St Gwenhael once were. Perhaps even higher. Along with the sea air, I can smell their needles and the resin clinging to their bark.

"I need two scouts to come with me," Wolf says. "The route goes up, and to the northwest."

"I'll come," Mart says. He's already rowed to and from the ship twice, but he flashes a grin. "I'm curious."

"I'll join you," says the man who I think is called Rodin.

Wolf nods. "We will go up and see what awaits us there." He casts a glance at the sky. "The heat of the day won't linger much longer. We should make sure we're back in two hours."

"Take care," I say softly, as he leans in to kiss me.

"I will." His beard rubs against my cheek for a moment before he straightens his shoulders. "Make sure some supplies are offloaded, but keep the rest on board until we know where we're going. If we're not back before dark..."

"You better be back before dark!"

He smiles. "It would mean we are being held up and must camp out somewhere. If that happens, you should return to *The Starry Wind*."

"I know," I say. "We all know what to do, Wolf. Just go and find us a path."

"It will be a good way to get my land legs back," he chuckles. "Just when I was getting used to that wretched ship."

I grab his shoulders and press a last quick kiss to his mouth. "Be the landlubber you always were."

Despite my own reassurances, I find it hard to relax as long as he's away with his scouts in tow. Together with Judikael, I coordinate the unloading of our luggage. No more than the bare necessities – tents, blankets, just enough rations to get us through the night. The youngest children are constantly getting in the way. I don't know whether it is because of the hint of cold in the air or because they feel liberated after their weeks of confinement on the ship, but they're tumbling over each other like seagulls swooping and diving, and unfortunately they're making just as much noise.

"They are wasting their energy," Judikael grumbles. "If we still have a long journey ahead of us, they'll be tired before we can find a place for the night."

"Try and stop them."

Even shy Alma hobbles after her brother, zigzagging across the small beach. When they threaten to get too far away from the tree line, a shout from Anouel is enough to make them turn back.

I say out loud what I'm hoping for: "This land will make them strong."

"It'll have to. And it will make them brave too."

Wolf hasn't returned when the mist dissipates and I'm able to stare at the high sun. Only when noon has long passed do the three of them emerge from the forest again. They look elated and unharmed.

"An old road runs through the forest, straight up the mountain," Wolf says. "Some parts are bad, but we can always follow the trail next to it."

"Where does it lead?" Anouel asks.

"We had to turn back before we lost the light, but every road eventually leads to a place where people once lived."

"Can we make it before sunset?"

He shakes his head. "We'll go at dawn."

And so we get ready for our first night in unknown teritory. We put up our tents on the gnarly beach. Wrapped in a sleeping bag and a blanket, it's not so bad to sleep on the ground. Wolf finds us a place in the lee of the cliffs. The wind scrapes along the beach, blowing sand through the cracks in the tent, right into my face until I pull up my hood. That makes me feel surprisingly comfortable: the sand beneath me slowly turns into a snug hollow where I fit perfectly, the wind is kept out a little, and Wolf's warmth radiates down on me. And although I don't immediately miss the constant lapping of the sea, I longingly think of the creaking bed in the captain's cabin. I don't think Wolf shares my longing... The iron around us, the dark, and the little space to move around all reminded him too much of his cell in the Asclepius Congregation. I hope we'll find real shelter tomorrow before nightfall. My hands rest on my swelling belly. Before I fall asleep, I think I hear Wolf humming the night song: a soft hum above the murmur of the sea and the whistling wind around the cliffs of the fjord.

I see Cormack – his Undreamed self – wandering as a ragged vagabond in the harsh, open landscape of the Other World. A cold wind rubs against him.

Cormack is not alone. I wish I had the courage to shout a warning at him, but instead I cower like a frightened mouse: I make myself small, inconspicuous, almost invisible.

The Hunter takes his time. He stalks Cormack, his back arched and his lips pulled back in a wolfish grin. I know he's picked up Cormack's scent. All those eyes in his palms are rolling. He reaches out with one hand and gently scrapes his claws across Cormack's face. My cousin stands as if frozen, keeping silent. I remember how hard it is to make your muscles obey when faced with the Hunter. He holds sway over his victims as if they were flies in his sticky web.

I want to look away and yet remain an unwilling spectator. The Hunter speaks: "I name you. And the name I give you is Pain, in our oldest language: Mordred."

"Cormack, run away," I whisper. "Run for your life."

Only, Cormack seems to be hypnotised by the words of the Hunter. He continues to stare at him, his wide eyes unwavering.

The Hunter laughs. The sound is like nails across stone. "You will forget that you have seen me. Now go and wander. Go and find the Child-King."

"Leave Arthur alone!" I wonder if I can do anything. Just like smoke slowly taking shape, I begin to create a body for myself. It is a pale version of me, transparent as a sheet of mist. I push and pull the magic I feel surging through me and form my hands, my arms, so that I can touch Cormack. Maybe my magic can bring him out of his trance. Maybe...

But then, the Hunter comes towards me. He moves as fast as a spear flying through the air. His stench hits me in the face and penetrates my whole being, Dream body and soul. Before I can think rationally, I feel a tug at the place behind my belly button. My Dream body is sent in another direction, without me being able to control it. The Hunter's snarl abruptly fades away.

I'm standing in front of a tall man. His face is indistinct in the bright light that seems to shine from within. The antlers sticking up from his head are as wide as a small rowing boat. I have seen him before, I realise. His voice is soft and familiar. He speaks to me, though he doesn't move a step closer.

"The sea kept still and could not move. Darkness enveloped her..."

"Wait!" I interrupted him. "It's you! You keep telling me the same story. Was it you who saved me from the Hunter?"

For a moment, he is silent. His head with the huge antlers slowly bobs up and down. "Nimue of the Sea, I have called you for a long time. Yes, I pulled you away from the Hunter, but I don't think I have the strength to do so again. Listen to me, Nimue, listen to this story."

I take a deep breath. My Dream body feels thin and restless. I know that I'm about to wake up.

The man with the antlers speaks again: "For centuries they were like that, undisturbed... "Oh," sighed the Sea. "Oh, where have all the stars gone that the sailors used to navigate by? Where are the fish and plants in my belly? And where is the moon, which could draw my tides? It used to be different!"

The Darkness heard this, and he rejoiced.

'It's no use complaining,' he whispered. 'Long have I waited for the light to disappear from below to above: centuries and centuries, and even longer. Now I have won, and I am everywhere.'

"Why do you want it so badly? I remember a time when light and dark had their own place. Light was in charge of life, which danced and grew and dreamed and worked, and Darkness was in charge of death and silence and the Longest Watch."

'And now I have The Longest Watch of All!' spoke the Darkness triumphantly. 'And the silence, the death, the dreams and the stories all belong to me.'"

My Dream body gives me a tug which I have to follow. Though I try to speak, my voice fades away as I sink back into my real, warm body, asleep in Wolf's arms.

At the next dawn, the clear weather has disappeared. The sky is full of a mist so dense that I can hardly see more than ten steps ahead of me. I'm wearing an extra shirt and a second jumper against the cold, but all my clothes stay very damp during the first hours of our trek.

In the forest, daylight is becoming scarce. We put up lights to avoid losing each other. If we are indeed heading northwest, Wolf has a better sense of direction than I do. I myself am only aware of the uphill climb, the nagging pain in my ankles and in my back. The pavement of the road we found the day before is so bad at times that I wonder if we haven't wandered off it, but Wolf leads us forward without hesitation. He has the landscape in his blood and in his bones; something pulls him unerringly in the right direction.

I don't know how long we have been trudging on for. At least a few hours. As the day passes and the mist increases, the children grow tired and sleepy. Wolf seems restless.

"We won't rest anymore," he informs us. "We have already lost most of the day."

"We can set up camp," Rodin says irritably. He's carrying two full bags on his back and is clearly weighed down. "There are so many of us that we can surely keep the wild animals at bay."

"We might," Wolf admits, then shakes his head. I am close enough to him to see his black eyes taking in the forest. "This is not a good place. We keep walking."

Struggling, I push myself away from the tree I was leaning against. I shift my weight to a thick walking stick I have found for myself. Every muscle in my body is stiff and aching and I'm cold underneath all my clothes. Yannick has urged me not to carry any luggage, so instead of bags and baskets, I keep Alma and Pedre with me. They don't complain, although Alma's face is full of scratches from low-hanging branches and Pedre is holding his shoes in his hand because they pinch.

With a few steps, I catch up with Wolf and softly say: "Maybe spending the night here is not such a bad plan. We are tired and no one knows if we can get out of the forest before dark. This road could go on for hours."

He looks at me for a moment, then bends down and pulls something off a low-hanging branch. "Bear hair."

I startle and whisper: "Are you sure?"

He comes to a halt, touching the bark of a pine tree. Only now do I notice that there are wood splinters underneath it and deep grooves in the tree bark. Something with huge paws has made those. "The track is quite new," Wolf says. "His territory stretches out for miles and bears move faster than we do. If we spend the night, he'll come after our food. We keep walking."

So we walk, occasionally rest for a moment, then walk even more. It is quickly getting colder and the ground is muddy, sometimes soaking wet. My boots protect me from getting my feet wet, but not everyone has enough clothing, let alone proper gear to protect them from the climate of the north. I feel sorry for the refugees who have been travelling for so long. Will their journey ever end? For now, the forest stretches in all directions and the night announces itself heartlessly. The cold, the threat of bears and other wild animals, the pain and fatigue are beginning to discourage me.

Suddenly, I notice that I no longer have to make any effort to climb up. The ground is leveling out and begins to slope downwards further on.

And then, someone utters a loud cry. Alma stiffens in my arms and I feel the hairs in my neck stand on end. Who is screaming? What has he seen? A wolf, a bear? The darkness and mist make it impossible to see any danger coming.

"There are walls!" someone shouts. I think I recognise Nanicka's voice. "And stone pavement! There's a square here!"

Wolf roughly puts an arm around me to help me forward. Further on, the lights of torches dance up and down because the people holding then are walking excitedly back and forth. When Wolf and I are approached the square they found, there are already dozens of people crowding around it. I look at my feet. Underneath the moss and accumulated needles, the ground is hard. I wipe a spot clean with my foot, point my torch down and discover grey, flat stone.

"Look," Yannick whispers, appearing right behind me. "Oh, look at that."

In the light we have gathered by standing so close together, we stare in amazement at the houses that loom among the trees. The walls and windows are dark and mostly broken, but even with the moss and climbing plants covering the walls and roofs, it is clear that this little town was once perfectly habitable. The square we have arrived at leads us to a street branching off into narrower paths leading to all the buildings. The longer I look, the more houses and sheds I discover.

"Sweet Gwenhael be praised," Yannick mutters.

With a groan, I put Alma down. "Stay close to me," I warn her. Yannick switches on her torch and steps onto the veranda of a house. It's impossible to contain my curiosity, so I follow her. The outside walls are covered with moss, but in some places the light beam reveals that the house was once painted red.

Glass and branches snap under my boots as we slowly walk to the door. It's hanging off rusty hinges, ready to clatter to the floor with a single push.

"Careful," I mutter.

Yannick shines some light in through the cracks. I see a glimpse of a room, an old cupboard, a floor covered with leaves, earth, and other traces of the forest. When I gently put my hand against the door and try to push it aside, something on the other side clatters to the floor. Immediately something flutters up to the roof. Birds, or bats?

Pedre has come up behind me and grabs my sleeve as he peers in. "Look at all the tracks," he says.

Only now do I see them: animal tracks in the mud criss-cross the veranda. Some are small, others ... much bigger. My apprehension returns. I look around and notice a tree next to the house.

"Wolf," I call softly. I point at the bark, which seems to have been roughly sanded away. I imagine giant bear claws smashing into the wood. "We are not safe."

Wolf studies the violated tree and shakes his head. "This isn't the work of a bear, but a moose. They rub against the trees to shed their antlers." He gives me a brief smile. "It's a good sign. The animals feel the warm weather approaching."

For the first time, I fully realise how harsh the winter must be in the north. I cannot imagine how we would have survived if we had found this forest under a layer of snow. How cold and how dark and how deserted we would have felt.

It's as though Wolf can tell what I'm feeling just by looking at my face, because he continues: "It has become dark and cold. It's time we found shelter to explore what this town has to offer once it is light again."

"We should stay here," Yannick agrees. She lets her torch light dance across the square next to the neglected house. "Rebuild everything. There's more than enough material."

"This isn't a town anymore, it's part of the forest," I mutter. "A refuge, like the Ark."

"We can cut down the trees and make room for life." Wolf slips his arm around my painfully stiff shoulders. "Now don't worry about the days that haven't arrived yet. You are tired, we have walked far. It's time for you and the little one to rest, be warm and dry."

"Warm and dry," I moan, putting my hands lovingly on my belly. "We've earned that, haven't we, my little fish?"

Some houses, like the one with the veranda, are in such bad shape that it is dangerous to enter. Further on, we discover buildings made of stone and cement. After walking down three neglected streets, we come to another square, bigger than the previous one. There are iron poles – old streetlamps that have been extinguished for decades. In the middle of the square is an old fountain, its deep basin full of leaves. At the edge of the square, a building rises up that must once have been stately, with a white marble façade and two staircases on either side leading to the entrance. It is sheltered by towering conifers. We walk towards the entrance across a deck covered with fallen needles. Here too, the windows are cracked and draughty, and here too, the door is rotten and easily pushed off its hinges. Inside, it is spacious and dry. The smell of the forest pervades the space, along with the smell of animal droppings. Perhaps this spacious hall we have found was once a council house, but now it seems to primarily be a shelter for small creatures of the forest. As soon as we set foot inside, something scurries away around the corner. A moment later, I see a red flash pass us by.

"We have to share it with foxes," Wolf smiles.

Nanicka, Cezar and Hannus are not far behind us. Anouel huddles against a pillar with Marie, blankets wrapped around their legs. I see Mart going along the walls and windows to see how safe they are, together with his father. Taran and Marci are standing to our left. Taran pulls out a blanket, puts his head on the bag he's using for a pillow and is asleep within three minutes.

Yannick and I make more of an effort to make ourselves comfortable. She spreads out three blankets on the cold floor and insists I use that as my bed. Wolf helps me take off my boots and when I let out a sigh of relief, he takes my aching feet between his hands and gently rubs them to warm them up again.

A few people manage to get a fire going. Some of the smoke can get out through the cracked windowpanes, but most of it lingers in the room. Soon, the smell of burning pine needles and leaves overpowers the smell of the fox family that we have now undoubtedly scared away.

Here and there, pots and pans are brought out. Our supplies have dwindled over the past few weeks. Nobody has had fresh, warm food since we boarded *The Starry Wind*. Even the obscure stew that Yannick manages to prepare goes down my throat like a veritable treat.

Once we are fed and warmed up, we go to sleep. I can hear in Wolf's breathing that it doesn't take him long to find his deep rest, and Yannick, Alma and Pedre don't waste time tossing and turning either.

I lie there with my eyes open, however, staring up at a ceiling I cannot see. Our little fire has shrunk and is sputtering in its pit. Like the flames, I don't want to surrender to sleep just yet. I want to know what will happen to us now that we have irrevocably arrived in a strange world. Can we rebuild these houses to live in them safely? Our fate is frighteningly similar to the neglected houses of the town: in order to build a new life, we have to demolish, rearrange and rebuild our lives from scratch with the materials the forest provides.

"And then there's you, little fish," I whisper, with my hands on the swelling of my stomach. "It won't be long now before we finally see your face. I do hope you'll be willing to come out of Mummy's tummy quickly, when the time comes." I let out a sigh. "Quickly out, straight into Daddy's arms, I think that would be best. Will you do that?"

I think I feel a movement. A gentle reaction from my baby. It is not the first time, yet it still surprises me. I smile and finally close my eyes. "Agreed."

I turn on my side, make my breathing deep and regular and then let my mind dive down to that mysterious place – the beach with its eternal surf that Sela showed me.

19

THE HUNTER'S NEST

As soon as I sink below the surface of the water, I notice my shy companion. The little fish is a skittish white flash in the corner of my eye, gone as soon as I turn around in the water to glide along on my back in a swift current. I turn around again and continue towards the trough that will lead me to the Other World. The fish returns as a glimmer by my side. Every time I turn my seal head in its direction, it flits away. I slow down and deliberately look straight ahead. Now that I'm no longer trying to catch it with my gaze, it keeps swimming beside me.

Its fins and scales are a translucent white, like thin ice or moonlight on a lake. When I turn on my back, it follows my movement; when I slowly turn the other way, it does the same. We do this slow dance until darkness gives way to light.

I mould my Dream body the same way I would mould something made of clay. My companion has disappeared. Who was it? A curious little spirit from the depths? I thought that most of the friendly spirits had disappeared by now, or that, like my selkie grandmother, they hide in the slits and cracks of this reality.

I'm standing at the foot of a mountain range, with my feet deep in mud. The scarce light is no more than a dull glow. There is mist here too, veils floating slowly above the black, rocky ground. I start walking and soon pass more muddy pools of water between the cracks in the desert earth. To my left and right, the ground slopes slightly upwards so that I'm walking in a shallow trench. I think I'm in the imprint of a riverbed, possibly the same dried-up river I found last time. I wonder if it ever flowed through the entirety of the Fisher King's domain. If I followed this bed long enough, it might lead back to the tower.

The mountains are approaching fast. A fierce wind begins to blow, making howling sounds around the peaks. I stumble upon a winding path weaving its way through the stones and rocks. I follow it upwards.

Suddenly, something moves in the corner of my eye. I quickly turn around, immediately on my guard. I don't want to cross paths with the many malevolent spirits roaming around here, but my deepest fear is of the Hunter himself. I only have my selkie magic to defend myself, and I have barely tested those powers. Besides, my previous failed attempt is still fresh in my memory.

Despite my fright, I don't see anything moving. Slowly, I continue my way. Then there is another flash of movement, this time on my other side. I feel something rubbing against my leg and almost jump in the air out of fright.

At my feet is a small, fox-like creature. He is white, like freshly fallen snow. Not a hair of his coat is stained with mud or dust. He looks up at me with round eyes – eyes that take my breath away, eyes like two silver pools of starlight.

"You shouldn't be here," I say. "It's dangerous."

The little fox doesn't seem to understand me. He keeps looking up at me. When I crouch down slowly and hold out my hand, he flinches before he circles back, his neck stretched out to extend his nose towards my fingertips. He seems too skittish to be touched, but when I get back up and keep walking, he effortlessly keeps up. He dances around my legs, left, right, in front of me, then behind me again. I catch myself smiling as I look at him, a smile that widens as soon as I notice the glow of a fire ahead.

They have gathered around their shields of fire: Katell, Lance, Morgana, GWN, Green, and my brother, and they stand up as soon as they see me, their hands tighten around their weapons. Arthur stares at me.

"Who are you?" he asks. "Spirit or human?"

Technically, I am both, for my Dream body is merely a vessel to carry me through the Other World. I let out a sigh. I half expected this to happen, but I still feel a little betrayed. "Human. And by Gwenhael's grave, Arthur, don't keep forgetting me."

He looks confused. "Have we met?"

I show him the shard of St Gwenhael around my neck – one of the few objects capable of crossing the veil between my world and the Other World. "Do you recognise this?"

Morgana lets out a hissing sound as Arthur steps forward. She makes a movement as if to stop him, but he ignores her and stands right in front of me, studying the stone. "I feel a certain energy. A power coming off it."

"There *is* power in it," I say. "You said that last time."

He is so close that I can see the many cuts and bruises on his face. His golden curls are tangled from the fierce wind.

"You could use a bath, little brother."

He lifts his blue gaze to meet mine. "Brother?"

I nervously remain silent. If the memory doesn't resurface for him, there's little I can do about it. He must know me – he simply must!

And as if my fervent hope were some kind of magic spell, his face suddenly lights up in recognition. "Nim!"

I make a sound, something between joy and relief, and put my arms around him. He feels so real. Not at all like a dream or a spirit. He is warm, firm, and he stinks.

"I can't believe I forgot about you!" he gasps. "You have been here before! But then the Hunter came and you were gone. I should have looked for you... I should have been sick with worry!" He sounds embarrassed and confused.

"I don't think it's your fault," I say soothingly. "It's this place. It's like a clock that keeps changing time."

"That's right," Arthur agrees, obviously baffled that he didn't realise it sooner. "It feels like I'm swimming in a current that is pushing me in every direction."

"I don't get it," Val says. He steps around the fire with a crude flint dagger in his hand. "Arthur, we don't know her, do we?"

"I do know her. She is my sister."

They all stare at him, mouths wide open.

"You never told us you had a sister," GWN says. "Arthur, this could be a trap."

"It's not a trap," my brother says. "I don't know why I keep forgetting... You know how it sometimes feels like we're recalling fragments of another life, like having strange dreams?"

Goldilocks comes and stands beside him. She takes me in with her big, blue eyes. Her face is beautiful in the light of the flames. "I feel like I'm supposed to remember something," she admits. I hold my breath and hold her gaze. She stares back with a serious expression. At last, she says softly: "A song. And candlelight."

"Skipper's Mass," I remind her. Val and Morgana look hostile, but Goldilocks allows me to come closer and gently take her face between my hands. "I know you very well. You've grown since the last time we saw each other."

"How did that song go?" she whispers, as if suddenly nothing in the world is as important as that song from back then.

I sing to her softly: "Gwenhael, lord of the wild sea…" and continue.

When I fall silent, tears stream down her cheeks, which she quickly rubs away. "It sounds like I've heard it a thousand times, but I still don't know when or… why."

"Oh, Katell," I sigh. Her face changes as soon as I say her name, as if she feels the pain of a dagger in her heart. It dawns on me that her memories may not be pleasant ones. She is a soul torn away from her body, she is a concoction of dreams, hopes and fears no longer connected to the identity she once possessed. And that's what they all are, this group of displaced young people. So brave, but so lonely. I suspect that's why they are fighting so hard against reliving the memories of their old lives. Perhaps I would, too, if I had been cruelly torn away from everything I once was.

I turn to my brother and say: "I have come because I want to help you. I know what you are up to and what your mission is."

He gestures to me to sit on a log next to the fire. He sits on my left and Goldilocks takes the spot on my right. She still looks as if she is trying to fit several puzzle pieces together. The others gather around us. I notice their faces, even though I pretend I'm only looking at the flames. Lance wedges his lance between his knees just in case, but he trusts Arthur. I hope he will give me the benefit of the doubt. Morgana seems far less sure of my presence. She no longer gives me angry looks, but her posture is tense and she continues to track all of my movements with her eyes. Val, too, keeps glancing around, wary of anything that might move outside our camp. Perhaps he's wondering if I'm the vanguard of malevolent spirits, or even the Hunter. I can't really blame him… Even if he doesn't remember, I remember very well that it was my magic that lured the Hunter to them last time. I'm determined not to use magic again – at least not as long as I might put my brother in danger by using it.

"Can you help us?" Arthur asks.

"I don't know," I confess. "You were chosen by the Fisher King from the start, not me. I wish I could always be here to protect you." I give him a sad smile. "I can warn you, though. You must watch out for Cormack, Arthur."

He frowns. "Cormack...?"

"Do you remember him?"

"Yes... No. I'm not sure."

"The man who leads the Asclepius Congregation. Benji's son."

As soon as I mention Benji, Arthur stiffens. His expression darkens, as if the light of the flames can no longer warm him. "Oh, yes."

"He did something to himself," I continue softly. "He... he got sick and then he tried to heal himself by doing what he did to hundreds of others. What he did to Katell..."

Goldilocks looks at me with a slightly queasy expression on her face. "Don't say it," she begs.

"I have to. Cormack split himself in two. His body remains on our side. He can still think, but all his feelings are gone. His mind is here somewhere." I gesture to the desolate landscape around us. "Where he wanders aimlessly, like all the lost souls that the Hunter preys on."

Morgana unexpectedly speaks up: "Is that what's wrong with us? Are you saying that we are *split*?"

I turn my eyes to her. "Every one of you and everyone else chased by the Hunter is... broken. You were part of another world and you became terribly ill. There was no salvation for you except to let you die or... mutilate you. My cousin chose to desecrate your entire existence. I'm sorry."

A shocked silence ensues.

"It's worse than I imagined," Morgana finally says. "If it's true."

"It is true," Arthur says. "I remember it too." He slowly looks up at me. "That means I fell ill too, doesn't it? And Cormack also Undreamed me."

"No, Arthur! Your body is safe and in good care. You've never been ill. You... you had an accident, that's true, but not an accident that killed you. Your mind decided to take off on its own." I try to smile, though I don't really succeed. "Mum believes that you chose to obey the Fisher King yourself. Do you remember that?"

"No," he says. "Not in that way. I remember waking up." He seems to be digging deep into his splintered memories. "Before that, it's just darkness.

And... pain. And tiredness. Cold." He shakes his head, as if to shake off the feelings I evoked as well. "Did you find Mum?"

I nod. "Just when I was about to give up all hope, I found her. Arthur, she's with you now, you know? At Avalon."

He processes this information in silence. I don't know if he is trying to hide his sadness from his friends, or if the Other World has made his memory so hazy that he has trouble understanding the full extent of my words. When he says something again, it is to change the subject: "What about Cormack?"

"He ran into the Hunter. I was able to watch the encounter, but I couldn't stop it. The Hunter ordered him to find you. I'm not sure what the consequences will be, but I know they can't be good. He wants to catch you, Arthur. Don't let Cormack get close."

"Okay," my brother says. "That's not so difficult. We won't let him get close, if we meet him anywhere at all. He won't find us so easily."

"I found you too," I say.

A warning shout makes us all jump up. Something flies past Lance's long legs, past GWN, who literally growls, and past the fire. Before I know it, it's hiding behind my legs, small and white and soft. It's the snow-white fox.

"What is that?" Arthur asks.

"I don't know." I bend down to get a clearer view of the little creature. He seems as shy as ever. "I don't know why he keeps wanting to follow me."

"It's a soul," Goldilocks whispers unexpectedly. "Like us... Or almost like us."

We all look at the little creature.

"Are you sure he's not dangerous?" Green asks hesitantly.

Goldilocks shrugs and Lance says: "What can he possibly do? Chew on us? Even his teeth are tiny."

He's right, but that is not the reason why I'm convinced my little companion is harmless. I feel a strange warmth coming from him, almost as strong as the heat coming from the fire.

"Are you sure he was following you and not fleeing from something?" Val asks sharply. "We are in the Hunter's territory, after all."

"Everything is the Hunter's territory."

"This place is different," Arthur says. "Have you looked around? There's nothing left. Nothing alive, not even the roots we ate. When I woke up, there was still a forest, and even as we travelled on, there were some plants and trees left. But then the river dried up and the fog got worse. Now there are only rocks left.”

“And I have committed this place to memory from before,” Goldilocks adds gloomily. “I remember how painful my feet were when I ran across these rocks, and how cold I felt when I couldn’t find shelter on the dry plains. There is no water here, no food. It is all desolate. Just the way the Hunter likes it.”

Arthur puts an arm around her. Goldilocks looks up in surprise, but doesn’t protest. “This isn’t like that time,” he tells her. “This time, we are together.”

“How close are we?” I ask, feeling a shiver running down my spine. Now I understand Val’s restless looks to inspect the area around the camp.

“Very close,” he says, before he shuts up. There is a sudden sound in the air, carried across the camp by the freezing wind. It is like the drawn-out wails of a young child and makes the hairs on my neck stand up. I bend down and try to catch the little fox, who is shivering between my legs. Another wail follows the first. This one is louder, more filled with pain too. It swells to a scream and then suddenly fades away.

“We think it’s the captured souls,” Arthur whispers. The colour has faded from his face. “It started yesterday. We haven’t dared to go on yet.”

“He keeps them in his nest.” Goldilocks’s voice trembles. She seems to be the most out of sorts and leans against my brother as if he’s the only one keeping her from falling off the tree trunk. “Like trophies. Some, he kills. Some, he holds captive to play with. Some, he even lets run away for an hour, just so he can catch them again...”

Before I can put my horror into words, the screaming and shouting starts again.

Suddenly Morgana jumps up. “That’s Olwen! Oh God, I can hear Olwen!”

We listen to the voices overlapping each other.

“How do you know it’s her?” GWN asks hesitantly.

“I can hear it! I...I knew she was alive! He’s holding her captive there, can’t you hear it?”

“Morgana, calm down,” Lance says. “We can all hear them. I’m sorry, but we have to stay calm until the time is right. We agreed to wait for a good time...”

“We can’t!” she shouts, before she appears to collect herself while heaving a deep sigh. “We can’t wait and let them suffer. They need our help *now*.”

"We can explore," Val suggests. "See how close we really are. The wind carries far, maybe we are misjudging the distance."

"I'll go with you," GWN says.

"We should wait for daylight," Goldilocks says.

Morgana snarls: "Who knows when it will be light again? It's been two days since we had any light. It may never come back."

"But we have no weapons," Goldilocks protests.

"We don't even have a plan," Morgana says. "And we're not going to be able to formulate one if we just sit here huddled up. We have to move." She looks around. "Who agrees with me?"

Val and GWN nod.

"You're insane," Goldilocks hisses. "It's practically suicide to go now! We have to use our brains…"

"You need less brains and more backbone," Morgana snaps.

"Morgana, stop. You too, Goldilocks." My brother reaches into his shirt and pulls out something I recognise immediately: the golden crown that once belonged to the Fisher King. Arthur holds it up and lets it reflect the light of the flames. I notice that everyone's eyes remain on it; even Morgana can't look away.

Arthur continues: "We must not allow ourselves to be divided. I have not felt quite myself since we entered this area and I know you feel the same."

"There's something evil in the air," Lance agrees.

"The Hunter is sowing discord, which we must oppose," Arthur says. "For the Fisher King. He trusts us and his hope is on us."

"He wants us to fight," Morgana says. She steps forward, closer to my brother. Her thick, black hair cascades down her shoulders, her dark eyes betraying a storm raging inside. "He said we must defeat the Hunter. How can we do that if we don't actually make a stand? If we just sit here and take no risks, nothing will change!"

"The Fisher King chose Arthur," Goldilocks begins again. "You heard it yourselves! He chose Arthur to be king, and now you talk as if that doesn't matter! Is that how you follow a king?"

"Don't be silly," Morgana says. "If Arthur is a king, I am a worm."

I press my lips together. This is a dispute they'll have to settle among themselves, but it takes a lot of effort not to defend my dear little Katell.

But Katell is not so small and sweet anymore – not in this land. A fire burns in her eyes as she turns to Morgana. "Have you forgotten the words of the Fisher King so quickly? Didn't you see with your own eyes how Arthur handled the crown? What did *you* think the Fisher King meant, then?"

Morgana looks as if she is about to throw a burning branch at Goldilocks.

"Listen to me," Arthur says. "Gather round the flames." He holds up the crown to catch the light once more, then carefully places it on the rocks near the fire. Morgana and Val look displeased, but when the others gather in a circle around the fire, they join in.

Arthur looks at our little circle with satisfaction. "No one is wearing or holding a crown right now. Nobody is king. We must not quarrel. Morgana, if most of us want to go out and explore the Hunter's nest, we will. We will venture there together, or not at all. That, I think, is how it should be done. What do you say?"

"Together," I hear Morgana reply, though hesitantly. "That's how I want it too."

"All right," says GWN. "As long as we don't do anything reckless."

"Lance and Val?" Arthur asks. "Green?"

The other two knights nod and Lance says: "If we are going to explore, I will take the lead. I know about weapons and I know about hunting. I will keep you as safe as possible."

Arthur turns to Katell. "Goldilocks?"

She is clearly terrified at the prospect of walking straight into the Hunter's nest – the place where all her nightmares take place. I admire her courage as she gives a small nod. "If you say so, Arthur, I'll go with you."

Finally, Arthur turns to me. "Nim?"

I hold out my hand to him and he grabs it. "I'm not really here. My body is sleeping somewhere far away. Time passes differently there too; I could wake up at any moment. If I stay here too long, I endanger my own safety."

Arthur looks disappointed. "So you're not coming?"

I squeeze his hand. "I will go with you, for as long as I can."

They collect their knives and daggers of flint. We light torches to dispel the darkness. I have no weapon other than my own selkie magic and I'm not prepared to use it immediately, so I must begin the journey unprotected.

"Don't worry," Arthur murmurs to me. "I won't leave your side for a moment."

"Stay here," I instruct my mysterious white companion. Maybe he doesn't understand me, maybe he is too stubborn. In any case, he follows me as soon as we leave the relative safety of the big campfire.

It is not difficult to find the way. We only have to follow the wail carried by the wind from the highest mountain in the area, a peak that isn't even hidden by those thick veils of fog.

The path is clearly not made for human feet, because it is so narrow and steep that we have to move in tandem and cling to whatever we can get our hands on. I don't know what makes the hairs on my arms rise more: the heart-rending wails of the Hunter's victims, or the silence in between. Perhaps the Hunter is far away, wandering the plains of what was once the realm of the Fisher King, or perhaps he is up there, looking down on us with the deadly silence of a predator... I shudder.

The narrow track ends as soon as we reach the peak, and we clamber up a ridge enclosing a deep crater like the wall around a fortress. Katell gasps quietly. I glance at her and notice how pale she has become, almost as white as my little fox friend, who is trembling against my knees. Instinctively, I reach down to stroke him between the ears.

Our torches shed light on what is inside the Hunter's nest. The first thing I notice are the sticks – chalk white and scattered all over the ground. A moment later, it dawns on me that they are not sticks, of course. No – they are bones. Of people, animals, and the sad remains of creatures that were something else entirely.

Placed in a semi-circle in the heart of the nest are giant racks.

"Hunting frames," Lance whispers. "We use them to hang and skin game."

"There's people on them," GWN mutters. He sounds as if he is going to vomit at any moment.

"They're dead," Goldilocks whispers. She sounds even more upset than GWN, like she's about to break down and fall apart. "He keeps them alive for days, but now they are dead. Their pain is gone. *They* are the ones suffering." She points a trembling finger at the things that I had paid no attention to this far. They are hidden in the shadows, out of reach of our torchlight.

I squint my eyes before I fully realise what I'm seeing: cages made of bones, some as big as a cabin, others as narrow as a trap. It is not difficult to guess where the wailing cries are coming from. Just as I consider it, a voice starts sobbing softly. It is the voice of a child, sounding so abandoned that it tears me to pieces. I feel my Dream body trembling, as if it wants to leave this place of its own accord. I have to do my best to stay where I am. I don't think I'm succeeding very well, because Goldilocks turns her head towards me and stares at me in fear.

"Nim? What's happening?" Arthur whispers close to my ear. "You're fading."

I close my eyes and try to calm my breathing. It's not easy, with the rancid smell coming from the nest. It smells of rotting flesh and dirt and decay.

"It's alright," I whisper. "Worry about the victims down there, not about me."

"Olwen is over there somewhere, in one of those cages," Morgana says. "If she knew I was here..."

"Don't shout out!" Lance growls. "Are you crazy?"

Morgana looks at him and hisses: "She is my *sister*. If the Hunter isn't here, this is our chance!"

"No, it isn't," Arthur says softly. "Look, down there – by the cages."

They flicker at the edge of my vision, camouflaged by the colours of white bones, black rock and old, red blood. Now that I have caught sight of them, they are impossible to miss: they are spirits, but they're nothing like the creatures that visited me on the beach at Gulls Island. Those spirits were powerful and beautiful. These wretched things cling to the area with the cages like sharks circling a lifeboat, waiting for their chance to snatch their prey. Instinctively, I understand that they are the result of the corruption brought into the Other World by the Hunter, and that even the Fisher King fears to end up like this one day.

"We can chase them away," Morgana suggests. "We have plenty of fire."

"Maybe we can chase away three or five of them," Green mutters. "Look how many there are."

"At least twenty, maybe more," Lance says, his breath hitching. "Morgana, even if we chase a few of them away, we'd still have to descend into the heart of the nest, break open those cages, and flee. I don't think we'd make it."

Morgana's face is a whirlwind of conflicting emotions. The evident rage and bitter disappointment eventually give way to dull resignation. "We can come back with more fire."

"Yes, with more fire *and* with a better plan," Lance says. "Now that we know what the nest looks like, we know what to watch out for. I promise you this is not in vain."

She nods stiffly, staring at the bone cages in the crater, where the wailing continues, before abruptly turning around. "I can't listen to it anymore. Not if we can't help anyway."

"Okay." Arthur looks at us. "Time to retreat."

I cradle the little fox spirit close to my chest as we begin our silent evacuation. My Dream body is shuddering again, as if my real, sleeping body is trying to pull me in like a fish on a line. I have no idea how long I have been gone for. It could be morning in our new village by now. Wolf could be waiting for me to open my eyes. He won't be happy if he finds I've overexerted myself again.

Just thinking about my real body makes the trembling more intense. By the time we reach the camp, it takes all my energy to stay where I am. I feel exhausted.

"Who is that?" GWN asks.

Someone is sitting on the tree trunk and warms his hands and feet by the flames. The smoke partly obscures his features, but it cannot disguise how tall he is. When he notices that we are approaching, he stands up and steps into the light.

"Forgive me for the disturbance," Cormack says softly. "I came for the fire. I noticed it was unattended and decided to keep it lit..."

"Who are you?" asks GWN sharply again.

"That's Cormack," I say, before he can answer. "He's here by order of the Hunter. Arthur, send him away!"

"I don't think that's my name," Cormack says. He looks confused rather than offended. "My name is Mordred. Nobody sent me. I've been wandering around, I can't remember for how long, but when I saw the fire, it gave me hope for some warmth and companionship."

"No." Arthur gruffly shakes his head. "You are not welcome here. Go your own way."

Cormack's face becomes drawn. I see despair behind his eyes, fear of the darkness of the Otherworldly night. "I wish you no harm. Let me sit here alone; I won't even speak. I will only seek refuge near the flames until the light returns."

"No," Arthur says again, but Lance asks: "How did you penetrate so deeply into the land of the Hunter? Most souls and spirits know to stay away. Only the Hunter's bloodhounds and their prey are here."

"Which of the two are you?" Cormack asks.

"You don't need to know that," Arthur says.

Cormack raised his hands in a peaceful gesture. "I think I can guess. You have seen that nest on top of the mountain and can no longer bear all the suffering. I, too, am aware of it. That mountain is calling to me. I think I can help you."

"That is a lie," I say heatedly. "The Hunter is deceiving you! By Gwenhael's blood and bones, don't fall for it, Cormack!"

"Mordred," he corrects me gently, shifting his gaze from Arthur to me. "I don't know you. If that is my fault, I am sincerely sorry. I do know that there are many souls trapped up there. I carry strong magic within me, so trust me, I can help."

"The only bit of magic you might have within you is some dark substance the Hunter has put there," I protest. "Arthur, don't listen to it. I know he's family, but he's dangerous, far too dangerous to let us..."

My Dream body pulls at me, strong as the sucking tide. For a brief moment, I'm aware of both worlds at once: the camp by the fire and the cold, stone floor in the nameless town, and Wolf stroking my hair.

"Nim?" Arthur's voice is a dull sound. "You're fading again."

"I'm sorry, Arthur," I whisper, and I know I'm muttering those words out loud in the real world at the same time. "I stayed too long. I have to go."

"Very good, darling," Wolf murmurs at my side. "Come back to me."

"Wait! Are you coming back?"

I open my mouth... and then I'm gone.

My eyelids are sticking to my skin when I try to blink. Morning light blinds me and I feel a heavy, throbbing headache coming on. I groan, my mouth and throat as dry as the lost river of the Other World.

"Just stay still," Wolf says. His hand is reassuring as it rests in my hair. The next moment, I feel the rim of a cup pressing against my lips. It's that damned bitter brew. I down it all in one go.

"Good. Now let it do its work."

It dawns on me that I must still have the little fox spirit pressed against my belly, for I still feel its warm, gentle presence with me. I smile dazedly and open my eyes, but there is no small white creature there. Of course there isn't. I just wrapped my arms around my pregnant belly just now, like I always do when I sleep.

I raise my eyes to Wolf and mumble: "I think I've met our child."

20

A Weapon for the King

The cold, as sharp as a knife, penetrates my clothes. The trees are close together, their intertwined branches forming canopies that still show the remnants of a late snowfall. On the ground, our boots make soft noises in the mud. Wolf leads, I follow, and I'm proud to be able to keep up with him despite my pregnancy.

He draws my attention to our surroundings in a voice that barely rises above the silence of the landscape around us. Can I hear the sound of a river coming down the mountain at great speed, he asks me? There is no need to cross it, he assures me. Can I see the tufts of fur hanging from the lower branches, broken tree bark so that the trees appear to have pale wounds? They are all signs that animals walked there before we entered the trail. Wolf reads the landscape like a storyteller.

"A reindeer was here, a young bull. There was a *jerv*, maybe a quarter of an hour ago. His tracks are clearly visible in the mud – can you see? Over here, two other bulls were fighting over a female. And listen." He smiles, falling silent for a moment. In the distance, between the rustle of the wind and the pine needles, I hear irregular, hard knocks, as if someone were hitting a tree with sticks.

"There they are again, still at it," Wolf says. "They are here early this year."

"Are they dangerous?"

"We'll just let them do their thing. Give me your hand."

He leads me up the mountain and helps me cross a bubbling stream, which is no wider than my arm, despite its sucking current. We continue on, until the trees become less dense and the gradient slowly begins to taper off. Not much later, Wolf slows down, looking for signs that completely elude me, until he shows me a trap. It's a simple piece of rope, wrapped around a tree and hanging down from a branch. It has done its job well, for a motionless bundle of fur is dangling from it.

"A *jerv*," he says softly. He takes a knife and cuts the rope loose. The animal falls to the ground with a dull thud. Wolf's voice is filled with a kind of awe that I don't often hear in him: "He was strong. He must have fought that trap for a long time. Look at those jaws. They could tear a moose to pieces."

As he spreads out the dead animal on the ground, I realise that I have never before seen a creature from this world that looks so strange. He looks like a bear, or maybe a dog? No matter from what angle I look at him, he still has a strange blend of different species in him. His fur is a dull brown, the hairs long and thick. I kneel down and run my hand through it. A dying vestige of warmth touches my skin.

"Is this for the winter supplies?"

"We don't eat predators," Wolf says. "A predator has already ingested the flesh of other animals. That's wrong... At least that's what my grandfather taught me. We take him because of his pelt and coat." He too strokes his hand over the hair, in a tender way. "His fur will be the first bed for our baby."

He ties the *jerv*'s front and hind legs together with a new piece of rope so he can hang it across his shoulders. The animal was not thin, despite the fact that we have just come out of winter, and I imagine that he also had a lot of muscle mass. I don't envy Wolf for having to drag the animal all the way back.

During the few minutes it takes him to reset the trap, I stretch, put my hands on my sore back and let my gaze wander. We are just below the highest point of the mountain and the trees on this side are younger and leaner. Our plateau offers a view of the white tops of the conifers on the slope downward, the green treetops deeper into the valley and, further down, the glistening of a wide lake. The haze today is only a thin mist, giving me the feeling that I'm looking at everything through a finely woven veil. That's why, at first, I think I only see mist when I look at the lake. But no, my eyes do not deceive me.

I point to the distance. "There's smoke coming from there."

Wolf turns to me. "It's too wet for a forest fire."

"There are more plumes of smoke."

"I see them."

I pull my gaze away to study his tense facial expression and say out loud what the only option is: "People."

"Keepers." He breathes out the word slowly. "Who have set up camp by the lake."

This realisation silences us both for a moment. Despite Wolf's stories, I never really believed that we would encounter the small tribes of the vast north, at least not so close to our own town.

"What do we do now?" I ask, just as the wind is transporting the soft howl and barking of dogs into our direction. Perhaps they are wild dogs, which we have sometimes seen around town, but it seems more likely that they are the keepers' dogs, who use them to keep a herd of reindeer at the lake. I'm filled with strong curiosity. "We should visit them."

Wolf shakes his head. He seems to need all his self-control not to drop the *jerv* and run in the direction of the distant campfires, but he holds on tight to the rope. "That will be at least a day's journey. In the meantime, they might move on and we need our attention focused here. Perhaps another time, when we have everything in order and when everyone has moved into a home." I can tell from his voice that his throat is constricted for a moment. "When the baby is born and when I know you are safe and warm. Maybe we can go look for them by then."

"We can send others," I suggest. "Rodin is strong. Mart and Judikael and even Nanicka..."

He silences me with a movement of his head. "Such a long journey requires skills they don't have yet. They don't speak the language of the keepers – I do."

"That's true," I sigh with disappointment. I wrap my arms around my round belly and think back to my earlier fantasies in Gwennec, in which our little child would doze off to the smells of tent furs and cooking fires. "Perhaps they will find us."

"Perhaps."

When we return to the town, Nanicka greets us and walks up to us. "Merciful God, what is that?" she asks, glancing at the dead *jerv*. It has made a trail through the mud leading from the forest to the old paving stones. Its fur is grubby and smeared, its head bent at an unnatural angle. He looks much more dead than when Wolf cut him loose from the snare.

"That's my baby's bed," I chuckle.

Her eyebrows go up. "My husband and a few others have started clearing the southern edge of the town, and they've stumbled across buildings that contain some interesting things. I told him to leave the stuff alone so the hunters can have a look at it."

"What kind of things?" Wolf asks. I'm tired from the trip, sweating under my thick clothes and feeling cold where my skin is uncovered, but Wolf seems as lively as he was this morning.

"Horse harnesses, tools... Rodin already claimed most things, so I thought you'd want to make some haste."

Wolf and I drag the *jerv* to the town square, which by now has become a kind of preparation area for furs and meat. As long as the weather remains good, we prefer to light the fires outside the buildings, so that we don't have to sleep inside, with the smell of smoke and animals. There's even a hunter's rack set up. Wolf's idea, not mine. Whenever I see the rack, I am reminded of the Hunter's Nest.

"You go," I say to Wolf. "I'll finish this job."

"Are you alright? You should rest."

"I'll take a short break," I admit. "I'll be fine after that."

I watch as he takes large strides across the town square, disappearing into the treeline on the southern side of town.

The *jerv*'s skin is hanging loose under the trunk when Wolf comes back. He is dragging something behind him that I recognise as a sledge. In Gwennec, only children would toboggan down the hills after a night of snow. Never have I seen a sledge so big.

"Rodin has claimed all the good stuff for the town guard."

"What *is* the good stuff?" I ask curiously.

He crouches down beside me and studies my progress with the *jerv*. "Hunting rifles. The snow boots he left for us, but I believe we'll be better off when we eventually make them ourselves."

"And that thing?"

He grins. "There are more barns on the southern border than we thought. They have mostly collapsed, but it was stupid not to look there before. I suspect hunters kept their storage there. We have sleds and some snowmobiles with a hundred-year-old fuel in them. I don't expect we'll be able to get those running again. We've also found navigation equipment that might still work on old satellite signals, according to Rodin. Do you know what a satellite is?"

I shrug my shoulders in doubt. "Something people used to have. Like the computers in Central Europe and the phone Cormack gave me."

"I think you're right. There was more: traps, some even seem to be working, weather charts and maps. A lot of knives." He gets up and rummages around in a bag inside the sledge. He shows me his loot: small knives and blades as long as my forearm, some wide and thick as my hand and others narrow and sharp. Some are smooth, others have hooks, or tips sharp like the teeth of a shark.

"Stainless steel," he says with satisfaction. "With proper maintenance, they will still be usable for decades. Except for stone, they can cut through anything – fur, skin, muscle, sinew, bone. They are a hunter's ideal gadget."

"Through everything, you say?" I stare at the large blade in my hands and sense an idea niggling at my mind.

"You're frowning," Wolf points out. "Is that a good sign or a bad one?"

"Let me think."

"At least tell me what you're considering."

The blade reflects the pale sunlight penetrating the mist. As I move it to and fro, it flickers and casts into my eyes. I turn my gaze to Wolf and find myself reaching for the shard of Saint Gwenhael with my other hand – for that piece of stone from my homeland and that drop of blood that holds such power that even the boundary of the Other World is bridged by it.

"I'm thinking of Arthur," I say slowly. "And I'm thinking about magic."

Wolf takes me to a house on the edge of town. "Nobody ever comes here. You can go into a trance and find your grandmother. I will lead you." He drapes a blanket in the corner, away from the broken window that lets cold drafts into the house.

I settle in with my legs crossed.

Wolf is holding a round drum in his hands. He has made it from a piece of cut wood and the skin of a marten he once caught. It is a simple instrument, crudely put together, but as soon as his fingers begin to tap out a rhythm, I feel that I could float away on it.

Soon, I am more acutely aware of the waves washing over my Dream feet than of my real body. The beach is empty and desolate and the grey sea is retreating. I look for signs of life. There are no seagulls darting above the waves; no crabs scuttling away as I wade along the shoreline.

"Sela!" My call is too muted in the vastness of my surroundings. I call out her name again and this time, I feel my magic stirring. "Sela! Come and speak to me!"

A shiny, round head bobs up in the waves. I remain still and wait as the seal struggles against the surf to get to land. She slides her belly across the grey sand, then looks up at me with dark, wet eyes. Those eyes look reproachful.

"I need your advice," I say.

One moment, I see an animal. The next moment, something shifts and she is a woman draping a wet, shiny coat over her naked shoulders. Her hair covers her like strands of seaweed up to her belly button. Her youth and beauty are ethereal, as always.

"Haven't I told you everything already?" she asks softly. "I helped you with my daughter. I helped you with your brother."

"I need you again, Sela. You're the only one who knows how my magic works."

"It is dangerous to be your teacher, dear child," my grandmother says in her soft, melodious voice. "Even here, in the folds between the Worlds, we are not fully protected."

I look around. Apart from the beach and the sea, there is nothing. Not even a sky. "Will the Hunter show up here?"

"I don't know," she admits. "I believe that, in time, he will possess every corner of the Two Worlds. So tell me, while you still can, what help you have come to ask for."

"You told me I had brought my own magic." I hold up the shard of Saint Gwenhael. "Somehow, this stone can make the crossing to the Other World. You said it was because my blood contains my power."

"Yes. Our blood, the heritage of the selkies. That is our strength."

"I want to take something else with me to the Other World."

For a moment she is silent. "What?"

"A knife," I say. "Made of stainless steel. A blade that can cut through fur and skin, muscles, tendons and bones. Something that doesn't break or bend."

Sela, already white as a pearl, becomes even paler. She shakes her head. "I'm afraid that's impossible, dear child. Neither iron nor steel belong in the realm of the Fisher King. My kind cannot bear the touch of it; even being near it makes us uneasy."

"That's why I have to take it to Arthur," I say firmly. "To save the Fisher King, he must bleed the Hunter into the Grail. To make the Hunter bleed, he needs a weapon with extraordinary powers. Isn't that so?"

I can almost hear Sela's thoughts turning as she gives an unwilling nod.

"What could be more powerful than a weapon from another world? You know I'm right, Sela. There is one thing more powerful than the Hunter, and that is something the Hunter himself cannot bear! A stainless steel knife, a big knife... So sharp that it will cut him open before he realises what touches him."

"Even if that is the case," Sela says, "and even if we find a way to achieve the impossible, how is Arthur supposed to hold a knife that is not made for spirits? He is no longer the human boy he once was."

"He wasn't born a spirit either. Arthur remembers his name. He remembers what it is like to be a human being. more so than the others. He will be able to hold the knife. He *has* to."

Sela turns away from me to look out over the boundless, grey sea, which pushes and pulls at us. I know we are both aware of that pull. I can almost hear the sea singing my name, just as I am sure it is calling out to my selkie grandmother. For a long time, Sela doesn't answer and I only hear the waves. It would be easy for her to slip away under the water again and leave me to deal with my problems all by myself. Far away, deep down, where she can hide from the Hunter.

I can hear myself saying: "If you don't help me now, you might have to hide forever."

Sela turns her head towards me and her dark, moist eyes focus on me. "*Seolh uu-la*. Those are the words of transformation. *Seolh uu-la*... If you chant that, you will harness the power of the selkies, and there is almost no stronger magic to be found in the Two Worlds. I can only help you with one thing now, Nimue. If you choose to carry steel into the Other World, you will have to be smart and use your own powers. One drop of blood will not hide the blade. Nor will two, or three, or a whole handful. You will have to cover the entire blade with your strength and risk having no strength left for yourself."

An unsettling feeling starts to gnaw at my gut. "I understand."

"That was not my advice. It is this: you carry more strength in you now than the last time I saw you. When I see you now, it is like looking into the light of a full moon. You are carrying a special child, Nimue. If you must bring steel to the Other World, do it while your magic is still entwined with that of your unborn child. That is my advice."

"Sela, thank you. This will be Arthur's best chance, I'm sure of it. I can feel it." I grab her cold, white hands and notice how she shivers.

"I pray that you're right," she whispers. "I pray that the young king will allow light to return to this land. And I pray that you can lead him."

"I thought there were no gods among the waves?"

She smiles; such a sad and beautiful smile. "Times are changing in your world and in mine. Perhaps it is time for us to change too. And for the Fisher King, I'm willing to do anything... Pray to a god I didn't know before, place my hopes in a king who has yet to accept his crown, and in the unborn child my granddaughter is carrying. Or help her smuggle steel into my world. Go with speed, Nimue, and be safe. And remember: now that you know the words, you are even more vulnerable to the Hunter. Protect the secret of the sea... protect our magic."

On impulse, I kiss the pearly skin of her cheek. "I will find my brother and I will bring him his weapon. Soon the tide will turn. Have faith in that, Sela. Have faith in us."

21

The Lady in the Lake

"**B**leeding on the knife?" Wolf's gaze meets mine, dark and filled with anger. "What are you thinking?"

"I think it's Arthur's only option."

"You are carrying our child!"

"I'm also thinking of our child's future. A world without the Hunter!"

"Think about your child's present, Nimue. No, you are not going to cut yourself open."

"Wolf, I have to..."

"Travel to the Other World, knowing the price you have to pay? Every time, you come back to me weakened, trembling like an orphaned puppy."

I look at him with my lips pressed together. Guilt gnaws at my heart and I'm almost ready to submit to his command. Just then, I feel the child move in my belly, and a warm, tingling feeling of power surges through my veins. A child with a magic woven together with my own power... I take a deep breath and shake my head. "I'm sure I can do this. I think I have the strength, and I know we have no time to lose."

"Nimue, no."

I avert my gaze. "I'm sorry, Wolf. I know what I have to do."

When he remains silent for a long time, I muster the courage to glance at him again. His face is contorted with anger, but when my eyes meet his, I also see his pain. I know I'm not being fair to him, but Sela was right: I feel so strong. "Trust me," I beg. "And help me."

It takes a long time before he moves. During that time, I wonder if he is even breathing. Finally, he drops his head and his shoulders slump forward. I want to pull him in, but he raises his hands to keep me at a distance.

215

"Let me make the preparations. You will follow my instructions carefully." He is silent for a moment. "You will not bleed alone. I will add my blood to yours."

"It only works because it's selkie blood," I protest. "Because it's my magic that can transform the blade and carry it past the boundary."

"You forget that I'm also a shaman. I have my own share of power, even if it's is not as strong as yours."

His sharp look makes me swallow my objections. "If you're sure."

"Very sure," he says gruffly. "Now make sure you get enough rest. I'll come and get you once I've finished preparing."

"Wolf…"

He shakes his head and leaves me alone to ponder my decision.

When he finally comes to get me, he leads me away from the town, along a path that I haven't walked before.

"Where are we going?" I ask. He doesn't answer, just presses his lips together and wraps his arm around my waist to support me. The mud beneath our feet is slippery and the ground slopes upwards. I can feel the tension in his trembling body and decide that silence is the best method to prevent him from changing his mind.

We move forward for a long time. He makes me sit down every now and then to take a rest. At first, it bothers me, but after what feels like hours of walking, I'm grateful for it. By now, we are so far away from the town that I don't think we'll make it back before dark. By Gwenhael, what obscure location has this man chosen?

I find out when the forest finally thins out and the trees make way for a vast body of water. The lake is motionless and grey. Patches of fog hover above the surface like silent ghosts. On the pebbled bank, between the water and the tree line, a small tent made of animal skins offers shelter from the wind. A campfire is ready to be lit. A fresh supply of wood is neatly stacked next to the tent.

"Did you do all this?" I ask.

"If we're going to do it, we do it my way. The way my people taught me."

He lifts the tent flap and I go inside. More furs cover the ground and I breathe in the heavy, sweet smell of unfamiliar spices.

"Sit down," he instructs me.

I do as he says and breathe a sigh of relief. My back hurts terribly and so do my feet. "Where are we?"

"By a lake."

"Wolf..."

He kneels down in front of me and takes a wooden bowl and a pestle, which he uses to crush more herbs. "When I was a boy, we had a lake just like this one near our summer camp. My grandfather called it a holy place. He said that the border between the forest and the water was the place where the spirits passed between the Two Worlds."

"Do you believe it will help me?"

He shrugs.

"What are you making?"

"Something to keep you going. Don't worry about it."

I watch him work. First, he finishes crushing the herbs, then he lights the fire. Heat fills the tent and the furs retain the warmth. Wolf takes his water bottle from his belt and heats up some water over the flames before pouring it on top of the mixture of herbs. He blows on it, then pushes the wooden bowl into my hands.

"Take three sips. The rest is for later."

I sigh and bring the bowl to my lips. I expect the same bitter brew he has given me twice before, but to my surprise, this one is sweet and refreshing. I feel a strange tingle running down my spine.

"Three sips," Wolf warns me again. I try my best to stick to it. He takes the bowl away from me before sitting down in front of me with his legs crossed. He sighs deeply. "Take the knife."

I take it and put it between us. For a few moments, he only stares at it. The flames outside are bright enough to cast a flickering red glow onto the cold steel.

"Tell me you're sure about this. It's not too late to change your mind."

"And abandon Arthur? I won't do that."

"Very well then." Wolf unclasps another knife from his belt – smaller and narrower – and without a word, he draws the blade along the length of his palm. Bright red blood immediately wells up. He holds his hand over the stainless steel knife and smears the blood over the blade. I'm not convinced that his plan will work.

"Now give me your hand."

"It's alright, I'll do it myself."

I use the blade to cut my skin. The pain is sharper than I expected. While holding my breath, I watch my blood run down the blade. Wolf doesn't say a word, but turns the knife around so I can cover the other side as well. By the time there is no longer a glimpse of the bare steel to be seen, pain lances through my entire arm and I feel light-headed.

"That's enough." Wolf grabs my hand and quickly wraps a bandage around it. I look with blinking eyes at our mingled blood on top of the steel.

"Is this going to work?"

"I doubt it," Wolf says.

"We have no other plan." I lick my lips, which have become dry. "It's so hot in here. I... I'm feeling pretty light-headed."

"Here." He offers me the bowl again. "One sip. You'll soon be glad of the warmth."

I'm not so sure about that. My anorak is sticking uncomfortably to my back. I take a large sip and feel the liquid wash through my body. A moment later, my head clears.

"I'm ready."

Wolf picks up his drum. "Take time to breathe. The herbs will facilitate the trance and my drum beats will give you guidance. Remember: you will have to return as soon as you notice that the drumming has stopped."

"I know." I fold my fingers around the handle of the knife, slippery with blood. Is it enough? Will the spell work? I swallow my rising nerves and remember to take three breaths from the depths of my abdomen. When I close my eyes, even my eyelashes are sticking to my sweating face.

Wolf rolls his fingers against the drum. He creates a slow rhythm for me, like the heartbeat of a sleeping child.

"*Seolh uu-la*," I whisper. I grab the knife more tightly. "*Seolh uu-la*."

The words melt in my mind. The drum reveals a path for me and an unknown force in my blood seems to want to push my spirit out. I wonder if that's the effect of the herbal drink. I can already see the beach with its missing sky in front of me, but as soon as I start to shape my Dream body, I discover that my hands remain empty.

I pull back from the dream world, taken aback. I'm clearly doing something wrong, but can't figure out what exactly. Is it the blood – should I have refused Wolf's sacrifice? Did we use the wrong words for the spell? No, I'm sure I'm pronouncing Sela's words correctly. My head begins to spin, caught between the tent and the beach. I can't stay in this state of in-between for long and I have to get the knife to come with me... "*Seolh uu-la*!"

Then it dawns on me that Sela has not instructed me to speak the words... She told me to sing them. I open my mouth and improvise a melody. I'm not singing very on-key, but it will have to do. The words suddenly taste different, like melted honey on my tongue. I turn towards the beach and place myself on the border between water and sand. My gaze stays fixed on my empty hands, held open as if I'm expecting a gift from the empty sky. Time and time again, I chant the spell, weave my magic around the knife, and pull at the steel as if I were the moon pulling the tide.

And just as the sea is drawn in towards the land, so is the knife, pushed into my Dream hands, piece by piece. At first, I see only a faint glint of steel, like cold starlight on a lake. Then, the handle feels tight in my grip, and finally the bloody blade becomes visible.

Very slowly, I let my singing fade to a hum, and then to silence. The knife remains in my hands, as real and firm as when I held it in the tent.

"Ha!" My exclamation disappears into the desolation of this in-between land. There's no time to lose now. I step into the surf and dive down, and when I surface again, I have the thought of Arthur firmly lodged in my mind. As always, that should be enough to track him down.

I let my eyes wander over the new surroundings, grinning at the thought of being able to give this gift to my brother in just a moment. I recognise this place: the encampment, close to the Hunter's nest.

My grin slips from my face when I see that the remains of the fire are cold. There are no footprints in the grit and dust covering the rocky earth. It seems that no one has been here for a while. Have they moved on? Where did they go? Farther from the nest, or – Gwenhael forbid – closer to it? A sharp fear settles in my stomach. Who can say that they are still alive? The Hunter may have overpowered them at last... And even if they are alive, they might be trapped in those awful cages right now.

I stare up at the peak of the black mountain, the knife held out in front of me like a sword. If Arthur's dead, I'd feel it. Right?

A tug at the spot behind my belly button startles me. In the distance, the sound of the drum dies away. I think I hear Wolf sharply calling my name.

The next moment, I'm slumped over, panting and trembling. Wolf is near me, wrapping a blanket around my shoulders.

It takes a while before I understand that I have just fallen back into my real body. A body from which all warmth and strength has been washed away. Even the muscles of my lips and eyes feel weak.

"Open your mouth." Wolf carefully wrenches my jaw open and puts something on my tongue. Salt. I grimace. The taste of it jars my senses and seems to connect my thoughts to my body again.

I raise my gaze to him and ask hoarsely: "What happened?"

"Don't speak. You will soon feel a little warmer and that will help. Just breathe for a while."

That's easier said than done, because my body is as unstable as a paper boat on the waves. I suck in the air and blow it out again, until I notice that the warmth is indeed returning. Then I look at Wolf and repeat my question: "What happened?"

"You slumped forward. And you became white as snow, Nimue. I think we underestimated the price of this ritual."

"No," I groan. "I can still do it."

"Nimue, please. Look at what you're doing to yourself."

Instead, I look at the knife. Somehow I have retained my cramped grip on it. "I can finish it. Let me try again."

"Nimue, you can't go on like this. You are exhausted."

"One more time," I say breathlessly. "I must try to finish it. Please."

Wolf sighs. His face wavers in my field of vision, but I can see clearly enough to know that he's not happy about it. I was too close to victory to give up now, however. I feel his hand come to rest on my shoulder, warm and strong.

"Fine, one more time."

Arthur, I think, *let me find Arthur. Seolh uu-la...* Dizzy as I am, I immediately spin back into the Other World. I feel too disoriented to stick to one direction.

Deep, icy water surrounds me. It happens so suddenly that it overwhelms me. Water is everywhere, even in my mouth and nose. I push myself up, swimming towards a faint glow. As soon as I break through the surface of the water, I suck in fresh air. I still have the knife with me, the blood dripping from the steel.

I don't know where I am. As far as my eye can see, I see rock walls surrounding me. There is a distinct smell of moist sediment, like in the belly of a cave, and I can smell smoke mixed in with it. I see fire.

People are sitting around flickering flames. I think I can count seven or eight. I fill my lungs with air again and call out: "Arthur!"

The people jump up and come towards me. I can make out fragments of their faces by the unreliable light of the fire.

Goldilocks is the first to reach me. "It's her! She's in the water!"

I cough and do my best to keep my head above the surface. My real body is pulling hard at my mind and I know I only have a few minutes left before my strength will have completely burned out. I thrust the knife up, out of the water.

"Take my hand," Goldilocks says, but as soon as she bends forward and catches sight of the steel knife, she flinches.

"Nim?" Arthur pushes Goldilocks to the side and crouches down. "Come, take my hand, come out of the water."

I shake my head, my teeth chattering from a new wave of cold that overwhelms me. "Take it."

His eyes shoot to the knife. He hesitates.

"Take it!" I push it towards him and he grabs the handle. A shudder goes through him. Even in my dizzy state, I notice that he starts to tremble as much as I do. We stare at each other and for one long, bitter moment I'm convinced that I was wrong: that this spirit of Arthur cannot touch steel any more than Sela can, and that this whole mission was a waste of power and energy.

But then his fist tightens around it. Arthur clenches his jaws and pulls the knife towards himself. The water is up to my lips: I'm sinking. "Learn to use it, Arthur. Kill the Hunter!"

His mouth opens and closes; it takes a moment to realise that he's speaking. But he is already fading, along with the cave, the fire, and his pale companions. I catch a last glimpse of Morgana with her raven black hair, clinging to Cormack's arm – no, his name is Mordred now. I turn my eyes to my brother and my lips try to form a final warning about our cousin. But the words do not leave my mouth before the water swallows me up.

22

THE HUNTER'S TRAP

My baby is a white seal cub, dancing around my floating mind. His playfulness and faith in me fill me with warmth. He stays with me as I drift back to reality.

I'm about to open my eyes.

I'm about to sink back into my own body and tell Wolf to put his worries aside. I feel the magnetic pull of my flesh on my mind. Now, daylight will return to my eyes.

Instead, the darkness suddenly deepens. Freezing cold fills every corner of this unknown gap. I try my best to slip away from it, but it's like swimming through a freezing sea. Wherever I am, I'm caught in it.

The smell of decay permeates my senses. Rotting flesh, I think, and immediately after: living, dead flesh.

The cold air becomes a breath, brushing against my back. It's a sickeningly familiar feeling. Before I even turn around, I know who is spying on me from the darkness. Whose dagger-like claws I can feel scraping across my Dream body.

"Go," I whisper to the trembling white seal cub. He has stopped dancing and is pressing himself against my legs. "Escape, little one, quick."

"He can't." The voice reminds me of the sound of shattering bones. The darkness closes in on me. "I told you once, I told you twice, oh, how I warned you, little sea witch. Did I not promise you that I would find you in the depths of darkness? That I would suck your blood and quench your magic?"

The sound swirls around me and I imagine the Hunter stalking me, circling me, spying on his prey from every precious angle. I'm chilled to the bone.

"Now then, little sea witch, you have been eluding me for a while. No more slipping and sliding. I got you." The tips of his claws scratch my cheek. An involuntary moan escapes me, which elicits a laugh from him that sounds like wet blood. "I must admit, I admire your powers. Steel and iron... even I wouldn't have thought that possible. Well done, sea witch, well done."

I squeeze out the words: "Are you saying you're glad I brought Arthur the steel?"

A hiss, followed by a cold stream of rancid breath. "I will put an end to this child-king as soon as I have pulled the last splinter of bone from you with my teeth. How good you will taste! Like a ripe berry, heavy with the juice of magic. I smelt the fragrance of that power from so far away. I heard it resound like a ringing bell."

If only I could summon all that power one last time, I might be able to escape to my real body... I keep very still, convinced that any swift movement might cause the Hunter to lose his patience and pounce on me like a wild dog with sharp teeth and claws. Again, he circles me. I don't know how I manage to breathe.

"Your fear is such a sweet smell."

Excellent, I think. Let him focus on that, let him revel in it. As long as he stretches out the duration of my predicament for his own sadistic pleasure, I have some time to gather my remaining strength. Not that there is much left. The trance has weakened me, and I was exhausted before I even began my search for Arthur. Fresh panic rises up and suffocates me. What if this is the end? What if I'm torn to pieces here, in the middle of a darkness where no one can reach me or even say goodbye? To die alone, in complete isolation, is the worst thing I can think of.

I'm not alone, however. Small and timid, the soul of my unborn child clings to my legs.

"Let me tell you something about that child-king you call your brother," the Hunter whispers. "Sooner or later, that blood tie between you will become frayed and thin. The day will come when you will forget that you love him and he loves you. That's how it goes in the cycle of things, little sea witch."

"What nonsense," I whisper, barely louder than a breath. There are tiny cracks in the darkness above my head. I can only see them if I move my eyes a little, like distant stars always seem to dance out of sight if you try to catch them with your gaze. No matter how dull they are, those cracks let the light through. Perhaps the Hunter has not closed his trap as tightly as he thinks, or perhaps I'm stronger than either of us realised. Either way, I have to make sure he doesn't notice my sudden interest.

"Dare you say that you haven't seen it with your own eyes?" The Hunter is behind me, still invisible. I feel his claws hook into my hair, letting them slide down through the strands. My Dream body trembles and fades, before it is pulled back by that familiar jolt behind my belly button. The Hunter laughs. "No, little fish, you're not getting away from me."

Eyes on the cracks, I tell myself. There must be a way to reach up and slip through them. "What should I have seen? Benji and Rona?"

"Ah yes, Benji. What a perfectly broken heart! I could nestle in it and feast on its sorrow and anger for years."

Carefully, I breathe in a little air. Enough to mutter the transformation spell, soft enough for me to be able to hope the Hunter doesn't hear it... If I can make that spell work again and turn my Dream body into something smaller, I might be able to fit through one of the cracks. I will have to change my baby too. Excruciatingly slowly, I gather the last remnants of my strength.

"What are you mumbling about?" The Hunter moves again, and suddenly I'm staring straight into his yellow eyes. He has to stoop low to bring his face directly in front of mine. It takes all my willpower not to flinch.

"I said that Benji was more than what you made him out to be," I snarl. "He had a righteous side. A good side."

"Well, child, I didn't create Benji Cairn; he created himself. I only had to lead him during the dance." The eyes widen and the pupils become two pitch-black pools. "I once had a brother. Has anyone told you that yet? The child-king, perhaps? He and I chose very different paths. In the end, even blood ties can be cut without much regret."

I prepare to bend down, snatch up my baby as fast as lightning and turn us both into bees, or flies, or fleas...

"Oh, and now you look so worried! I confess I lied a little, dear sea witch. I've been waiting for my chance to sink my teeth into you, but my priorities have changed."

I squeeze my eyes shut and try to block out the Hunter's words. He's only tormenting me, I tell myself, and I must ignore him. I must sing the magic one last time.

The Hunter doesn't give me the chance. He moves so fast that I can actually feel the darkness brush past me. My eyes fly open again. One moment, I'm not sure where he has gone, the next I hear a sound that makes my heart freeze. The white seal cub is letting out a loud, piercing scream.

My baby! He has taken my baby! I scream, and yet I'm too overcome with horror to move. Or maybe I'm just too weak, because I feel my strength draining away like the blood draining out of my unborn baby. Oh, merciful Gwenhael...

The Hunter bares his teeth. "You have been excellent bait, little sea witch. You've delivered this little miracle right into my hands."

"Let go of him!"

"I'm going to devour and digest every fibre of his strength."

"Gwenhael's bones, no! Don't hurt my baby, I beg you...!"

"Begging is useless." He turns my baby over in his claws and squeezes hard. The wail he produces breaks me into a thousand pieces. "Or are you willing to share your secret with me?"

"What... my secret?"

"The song of the sea, witch. The words of your magic."

Stunned, I shake my head. Sela has made me swear never to give the Hunter that secret... even the White Wolf said it would be better if I died instead. But my child?

"You will give me the words, just like your magic," the Hunter whispers. "You know it's the only way to save this monstrosity."

"You are a curse to this world," I whisper, weakened by nausea.

The Hunter laughs. "A trap without bait is not really a trap, is it?"

"You want my magic?" Somewhere inside me, a deep and destructive anger is exploding. I have no control over it; my thoughts are pushed into the background and my Dream body is shaken out of its petrified state. "I shall give you my magic!"

I move like a foaming sea, like a towering wave at the height of a storm. I pounce on the Hunter, drowning him in my true magic, with my last, desperate reserves – I cannot say exactly what state I'm in, and care little for an answer. The Hunter lets out a furious and pained growl. The white seal escapes from his clutches, but plunges into the depths and darkness below, in free fall.

Like a cormorant, I dive after him, catch him and press him against me. Without pausing, I push myself up again and smash the dark eggshell that is holding us prisoner. The black dome breaks open along the cracks and we fall back into the sky, into the light.

When I can see something again, it is Wolf, who's kneeling beside me, his face as pale and cold as a full moon. I open my mouth, choke on the words I want to speak, roll onto my side and violently start to empty my stomach.

23

THE BELLY OF THE BEAST

It is as if my mind is being torn in two. Images flash through my mind: Arthur and his friends near the Hunter's Nest, then Wolf talking desperately to me, stroking me, holding my face between his hands. Morgana and Goldilocks snarling at each other like angry dogs. Yannick pressing a cup of water to my lips as I lie shaking on the ground, spilling the cold water over my chin and chest.

"Nim," she begs. "Drink something."

"Goldilocks is right," Arthur whispers in the Other World, looking at a narrow crack in the rock ahead. "We won't fit through here."

"Nimue, darling, come back to me." That's Wolf. For a moment I see him clearly. His mouth is pressed into a tight line, there's a stubble on his jaws, his hair is a wild mess. I try to cling to him, but I feel like a leaky boat on a turbulent ocean and am being flung in all directions at random. The images jump around like feverish fragments.

"We have already been through this," Morgana says with restrained anger. "We've seen him leave and he often doesn't return for days on end! Don't be such a coward!"

"I'm not a coward," Goldilocks snarls. "The Hunter may be gone, but his nest is never empty! Use your head, Morgana."

"Quiet, you two," Lance scolds them. He peers at the small sliver of light, where the shadows of the lifeless Hunter's land have the upper hand again. "We will look for another entrance, and we will do it quietly. Arthur, I think you and your knife should come with me."

Arthur grabs Goldilocks' hand. "If we don't return, you and Morgana must find the Grail. Whatever happens, that Grail must get to the Fisher King. I trust you."

Her fingers pinch his arm for a moment.

"I'll make sure they stay safe here," Mordred says softly. The tall man towers over Goldilocks.

Lance and Arthur are at the beginning of a tunnel in the mountain.

"Stay here," Lance says. He gets up. "I'll fetch the others."

"Take the torch."

"Keep the torch. I will find the way."

Arthur peers out from a tunnel. His torch has started to smoulder and gives off no more than a faint glow. Arthur lets his eyes wander over the dark contours of objects that rise up here and there inside the deep crater. The pervading silence is thick and unsettling; the shrill cries that pierce it every now and then are even worse.

"Nimue, please wake up. Listen to me!" Wolf shakes at me until Yannick angrily pulls his hands away from me.

After that, the blackness inside my head persists for a long time. I don't remember how we made the long trek home. I don't remember being laid down on coats and blankets, or how someone carefully removed my coat and boots. I vaguely remember watching the fire with feverish fascination. How I watched it burn low, how it briefly went out and how someone stirred it up again.

"By the devil's bones," Green says. It's not difficult to guess what he means: the stench coming from the Hunter's Nest is strong enough to make me gag.

"This is the worst plan yet," he mutters.

A smoky twilight clouds the landscape, making it hard to see anything.

"It's our only plan," Arthur says. "We can slip down and disappear in an hour, without the Hunter even being near."

"Maybe not, maybe so," GWN murmurs softly.

"Keep your cool," Arthur whispers. "And remember, we will not try to fight the Hunter until we find the Grail."

"She has a fever. She needs rest and water."

Yannick's voice seems so far away. Something heavy presses down on me. I open my eyes just slightly and see three blankets draped over me. It feels suffocating. I feel trapped. I try to tell them to take the blankets away. But only a groan escapes my mouth.

The ground is covered with rubble. Arthur raises his flaming torch and the others gather around him. Opposite him is the pale, serious face of Mordred. An uneasy shiver runs down my spine.

Spirits near the bone cages circle Morgana excitedly. Some tower over her, others are only as tall as her waist, but even the smallest ones have withdrawn their lips to show their glaring teeth.

***

"...medicine?"

"Not without putting the baby in danger."

A quiet sob, close to my ear. Wolf?

Morgana is kneeling by a small cage of bones, reaching no higher than her waist. Arthur lowers himself beside her. "Is the Grail in here?"

"Grail? No, it's my sister. It's Olwen."

Olwen's lips are cracked. Blood and dirt have collected under her nails. "Olwen?" Morgana whispers. "It's me, Olwen. Don't you recognise me?"

Slowly, Olwen opens her eyes. Her lips move. Then she briefly shakes her head.
"*Who?*"

"*Your sister.*" *Morgana herself seems barely able to hold back a sob.* "*We'll get you out of here. It's going to be alright.*"

"*Hunter. Go away.*"

"*He is not here now. You are safe.*"

Olwen shakes her head again.

When Morgana raises her eyes, the smouldering anger in her black pupils returns. "*We have to carry her away and get her somewhere where she can rest. Back to that cave, at least there's water there. Or if we can make it as far as the forest, we can...*"

"*Morgana, we can't leave.*" *That's Arthur.* "*Not without the Grail.*"

"*You'll never find that stupid Grail! Do you really think that monster just carelessly leaves his treasures lying around? Mordred! Help me lift her up. We're taking my sister to safety.*"

Mordred kneels down to take Olwen in his arms.

The girl groans and shudders. "*Wait...*"

"*Olwen, it's going to hurt for a while. But we have to carry you,*" *Morgana says.*

Olwen shakes her head. It seems to take her a lot of effort.

"*Grail?*"

"*Don't worry about it now.*"

Olwen starts coughing so hard that her body is shaking. When she calms down again, little drops of blood are clinging to the corners of her mouth. "*I have seen it. I know where he keeps it.*"

"*Where?*" *Arthur breathes in sharply.* "*Olwen, tell us where, please!*"

"*You can't have it...*"

"*Olwen, you could save us all if you tell us where the Hunter has hidden the Grail.*"

Olwen's eyes are bloodshot. Her eyeballs bulge slightly in their sockets. "*Inside,*" *she whispers.* "*He put it inside himself. I saw him... split open his stomach... he put it inside him. Then he seared the flesh together. It stank awfully.*"

Again, the images in my head jump violently, so fast that I feel a new wave of vomiting roll up.

The group is halfway down the tunnel leading out of the nest, but for some reason they are all staring at Mordred.

Mordred says: "I think he is behind me."

From the smoky darkness, the Hunter's slender shape slides forward.

"Well done, Mordred."

Mordred turns deathly pale when the hand with the black, curved claws comes to rest on his shoulder. The man is like a herring next to a shark.

The Hunter bares his teeth. "Those who enter must learn to taste the raw fear."

Everything falls apart, turning into chaos. The Hunter's spirits leap at the group like dogs woken from their sleep. Morgana screams, Val and GWN wave their torches around, Green runs away.

Arthur slips under the Hunter's arms and thrusts the knife into the dirty grey flesh of his belly. The skin is covered with old burns and cuts: marks that speak of the fires and claws and teeth and spears that have tried to harm this king of the wasteland. All those attempts failed. All victories were claimed by this monster.

However, the steel knife doesn't fail. It cuts straight through the leathery outer layer of the skin, sinking deep into the organs. The Hunter's roar is deafening.

Dark, clotted blood drips down the wound. The Hunter is writhing in pain and rage.

Arthur's friends stand back-to-back, their torches raised. Goldilocks holds her left arm at a strange angle, her pale face smeared with blood.

From a great distance, I watch as my brother thrusts his fist into the gaping abdominal wound and then out again, holding a smeared goblet. The claw lashing out at him is so strong that he falls backwards. Arthur rolls further back until Lance pulls him to his feet. The Hunter roars more loudly than he did before, a fury as immense as the beast itself.

"Run," Lance hisses. "As fast as you can!"

There is a layer of blood at the bottom of the Grail. It is dark, almost black. Despite my feverish state, it dawns on me that something is wrong. Is the Grail useless if it isn't filled to the brim? Can the Fisher King be saved with just a few drops of his brother's blood?

The Hunter approaches Arthur and....

"Arthur!" I scream, so loud that Wolf and Yannick are startled. "Run!"

"Shh, my dear, calm down." Wolf leans over me again, kissing my clammy forehead. "Shut it out. Let it all go. Come back to me, Nimue. Come here."

Through a mist of tears and sweat, I meet his gaze. My head is pounding: *Shut it out. Shut it out. Shut out the Hunter, so he will never get me or my child.* I squeeze Wolf's hand hard with mine.

And then I shut everything out.

24

THE ROAD TO THE REINDEER PEOPLE

I'm aware that I'm lying in a secluded room. I also notice that my blankets are regularly aired out before I'm tucked in again. Even in the warmth of this bed, I sometimes shiver from the cold. When I wake up from a deep sleep, I notice that I have been tossing and turning and that my back is soaked with sweat. Even now that I'm awake, I sink into a dull fog that covers all my thoughts. The whispering voices of Wolf and Yannick are just background noises. I know they are worried about me. If I could think a little clearer, maybe I would be worried about myself too, but the fog in my head is holding me captive. I'm overcome by an intense fatigue that I can feel to my bones, and a hollowed-out feeling just below my stomach. As if something were missing from me. I contemplate the thought in a detached way, just as I would a passing thought about an ant that happens to crawl past my bed. Is this how Undreaming feels? Not deprived of my mind, but too numb to connect with the world around me?

There is a window behind me. Someone has repaired the shutters as well as they could, so that I don't suffer from the nightly cold. The cracks and fissures in the wood let the sunlight through, and as soon as the sun is down, I can see strips of the night sky. I don't know how many changes of day and night pass by the room. I'm more aware of Wolf and Yannick, who never leave my side. Sometimes I think I recognise Anouel or Nanicka in the background. I sense the unspoken fear in their whispered words. Nobody raises their voice. Maybe they are afraid to disturb me, or maybe they think they would scare me with what they're saying.

They whisper about fearing for the baby in my belly. Yannick, in particular, is afraid that my son has quietly slipped away.

During one of these nights, when even Yannick has left for a bit, I notice Wolf holding my hand. I notice it because my fingers are squeezed tight in his grip. My eyes are heavy and feel too dry. His head comes to rest on my heavily covered chest and it dawns on me that he's crying.

Wolf cries, sobs racking his body.

Even in my dazed state, I cannot bear it. I manage to lift my free hand. As soon as he feels my touch, he stiffens. Then he straightens.

"Nimue?"

I try to swallow. My throat feels like a dried-up riverbed. I push his hand down with mine until they both rest on my stomach.

Wolf casts his eyes downwards. Then he says hoarsely: "Yannick told me. There's nothing left to save…"

I shake my head, an effort that makes me dizzy. My lips form the words, and a moment later, my cracking, weakened voice joins in. "I can still feel him. Alive."

"Yannick said she hadn't felt any movement. Not for days, Nimue…" Again, a sob bleeds into his hoarse voice.

My fingers curl around his large hand. "He's alive."

Our child is alive, because despite everything, I can feel him. Like a kite, his soul is floating near me. The thread that connects him to me is very thin, however. A heavy gust of wind could blow him away from me forever. I'm not saying that out loud, not even if I'd had the strength to do so.

Wolf talks to me. He doesn't get an answer, because the darkness demands my full attention again.

I sleep. I dream confused dreams, which twist and turn like a ball of yarn. The few times that I see Arthur, his appearances are frustratingly brief. I only seem to be able to look at him from behind a foggy window. Wherever he is – a quarry, a cave, the old forest near the dry river – I cannot reach him and he doesn't see me. Most of my dreams, however, are filled with frightening images of storms and waves as high as the dunes. As soon as I find myself in one of these nightmares, I try to escape from them. When I wake up, I feel such overwhelming tiredness in my body that I immediately want to fall asleep again.

Then comes a night in which the usual fevered dreams stay away. Instead of being in a storm, I find myself on the hill in Gwennec. The ancient walls of St Gwenhael reassuringly rise up around me. The candles burn warmly, no corner or niche is left to darkness. Saint Gwenhael himself lies on his ancient plinth. The fractures he suffered in the great storm have been undone. His hands are folded over his chest and, as always, his eyes are peacefully closed. His stone mouth is curiously folded into a smile. It is as if he wants to give me an encouraging sign. I come closer and run my hands over his face. I'm startled for a moment when his mouth starts to move and I feel his breath against my skin.

"Nimue," his voice whispers. Part of me knows that this cannot be real and that the statue has never spoken. Yet his voice is warm and familiar.

I smile back. "I'm here."

"Nimue." A warm hand with rough fingers strokes my cheek. It's not in my dream. The voice comes to me from outside. I resist it. I don't want to wake up. This is the first dream in days where I feel warm and safe. What is waiting for me outside? Fear and cold, fatigue. I want to stay here, in my church on the hill, where everything is as it should be...

"Nimue, you have to wake up."

Reluctantly, I push myself out of my dream, back to the surface of reality. Wolf is hunched over me. As soon as he sees me lift my eyes, he leans back to give me some space.

"Can you hear me?" he asks.

"Wolf." My voice cracks. I hardly recognise the way I sound. Nevertheless, a hesitant smile appears on his face. The smile doesn't drown out the sadness in his dark eyes. I want to touch and comfort him, but I can't life my hand more than an inch above the covers. I don't have more strength in my muscles left.

Wolf understands my gesture and folds his hands around mine. He is so much warmer. His strength and warmth are reassuring, and at the same time, it shocks me how badly I've weakened.

"Listen, Nimue. I'm going to tell you something. You don't have to talk. Just nod if you understand me."

My eyes are heavy and dry. I struggle to keep them focused on his face. He is so serious. Maybe I can manage to wait a little while before sinking back into my deep sleep. I flex my muscles and nod.

Wolf's thumb strokes my hand. "Do you remember how you got so sick? We did a trance and you used your selkie magic."

The blood and the knife. I remember that. Again, I nod.

"Something happened to you afterwards. You refused to tell me what was wrong."

My eyebrows come together in a pained frown. "I didn't refuse."

"Ssshhh, don't speak. You got very sick, Nimue. I carried you home and called Yannick. By the time we had laid you down here, you seemed to be in a coma. Nothing could wake you. We thought..." He doesn't tell me what they feared. His deep sigh is enough. "You haven't been poisoned and there is no other cause for your sudden illness. Nimue, I think something worse has happened. I think you got stuck halfway through your trance and that something went wrong when you tried to pull yourself loose. Is that possible?"

It takes me a long time to find the right words. Even longer to say them. "The Hunter... lured me. Into a trap."

Wolf nods, as if he already suspected it. Shadows flit across his already serious face. "I suspect the Hunter's shock has driven you to put up a shield around yourself. Maybe *he* can't get to you now, Nimue... But you're holding yourself prisoner too."

He remains silent, perhaps hoping that his words alone will be enough to lower my shield. I remain silent and do not move. Even if I was willing to expose my mind, and that of my unborn child, to all the dangers of the outside world again, I wouldn't know how to do it. My thoughts begin to sink back into the soft cotton wool of my sleep. The dancing flames of the fire next to Wolf turn into moving animals: deer and hares, leaping over each other...

"Listen to me, Nimue. I don't have enough experience or knowledge to help you. If nothing is done, I fear you'll surrender to the darkness."

The deer and the hare are chased by giant cats. They jump up from the flames and disappear from my sight.

"I went out and followed the tracks of the reindeer herders. They are not far; a two day's journey or less. Nimue, please look at me. Nod if you hear me."

I let my breath flow deeply through my chest before exhaling slowly and fixing my eyes on his face. Reluctantly, I nod.

Wolf looks relieved. He leans in closer, as if he believes I won't be able to shut him out that way. "Chances are, there are still shamans among the reindeer herders. *Real* shamans, with more experience and power than I have ever known. I believe they can help you, Nimue. I believe they are the only ones who can help you."

I concentrate on the black, wide circles of his pupils. They serve as an anchor to keep me in place. "Are we leaving?"

"Yes, my love." His other hand caresses my belly. "We are leaving tomorrow."

To do Wolf and Yannick a favour, I try my best to stay awake when the morning light heralds our departure. I'm carried outside on a stretcher. The sudden jolts upset my stomach. Two or three times, I throw up on the floor and everyone stops until I lie down on my back again, exhausted.

It is a long walk. I shiver under my blankets. I see the sun, high above the pointed tops of the firs. Much later, my face is moistened by fine, cool raindrops. The rain soon stops – either that, or I become unconscious, because when I notice my surroundings again, we have stopped and I can hear the loud, rushing sound of running water.

"You're awake." Yannick appears beside me out of nowhere. "Good. I want to help you up."

"I don't think I want you to do that," I mutter.

Her eyes shift from me to a point behind me. "We have to lift you onto the boat. It would be easier if you sat up straight for a while."

So we are near a river. I open my eyes further and discover a riverbed full of pebbles. The ground is coming from an area further down the slope, where the trickle turns into fast-flowing water. A lot of water. It makes my head spin.

"How do we get a boat?" I hear myself asking aloud. This is the first thing resembling a conversation since Wolf spoke to me yesterday. Yannick's eyes widen a little, maybe from surprise that I'm responding so coherently, or maybe because it gives her some new hope.

"Rodin found it near those hunters' sheds. It's an old thing and will probably make some water. Mart and his father looked at it and they said it would be fine. It has to be." She says those last words softly and firmly.

"Is she awake? Let me help you sit up." Wolf crouches down on my other side and strokes my cheek. "You're freezing. Do you need more blankets?"

"I don't want to move," I complain. "And I don't want to get into a boat."

He ignores my words. He gestures to Yannick. As if they have practised this together, they shove their arms into my armpits and knee hollows, and force me up. Now I'm sitting up and awkwardly lean against Wolf to stay upright. All my limbs instantly start trembling. My head is spinning.

"I'm going to puke."

"If you have to, you have to," Yannick says calmly.

Wolf says: "We will lift you into the boat on the count of three. Be prepared for that."

I'm not. I'm sure I'll faint again. Wolf counts down and I'm lifted from my makeshift bed. The sudden lift into the air is enough to make black spots explode before my eyes. I don't throw up. Nor do I completely lose consciousness, because I do remain aware of the wind around my head and the water splashing in my face as Wolf's boots make noise as they trudge down the riverbank. My head is slumped against his chest.

After a few moments, I feel myself being lowered again and I lie on soft fur and blankets. I'm rocked in a familiar way by the water under the hull of the boat.

Slowly, my sight returns. I'm lying on the bottom of a small rowing boat, with my head towards the stern. I can barely see past the thick layers of fur that Yannick is draping over my shivering body. She tucks me in tightly on all sides.

The boat bobs down to the right as Wolf gets in and sits down on the middle rowing seat. He doesn't realise that I'm watching him as he clumsily tries to get the oars into the forks. The man who once avoided open water like the plague now has a determined expression on his somewhat rugged face. He *will* row me across this roaring river, no matter how seasick it will make him.

Yannick notices my eyes being partly open and follows my gaze across her shoulder. She mutters a few instructions to Wolf, and he shifts the oars so that they securely fall into place.

The others – Mart, Taran and Hannus – stay ashore. I think it's Mart who pushes the boat off. The current gets us immediately. The boat shoots forward, rocking to regain her balance. I hear Wolf utter a curse. As the water growls close to my head against the metal frame of the stern, we are pulled with great haste into the forested valleys of the north.

As the day passes, the thick fog slowly thins. As the river widens, the water becomes more peaceful and the boat glides calmly forward. I'm having one of my lucid moments when Yannick rises from her bench to peer through the mist, with eyes half closed.

"Smoke from cooking fires?"

"I see it too," Wolf says. "We're close."

Again, they pick up the oars, making a lot of noise as they splash through the water towards the shore. Unexpectedly, the keel hits a pebbled riverbank and we come to a halt. I'm lifted from my furs. Wolf carefully carries me ashore and lays me down on the ground as comfortably as possible. My head is still spinning as I spit out the last bit of acid mucus I had in me.

"She's burning with fever," he says to Yannick. Maybe he doesn't realise that I'm conscious. To be perfectly honest, I'm not entirely sure that this isn't part of another fever-induced daydream.

Yannick moors the boat by wrapping a rope around the silver-coloured trunk of a birch tree. The boat sways back and forth, making the rope creak and splash in the waves of the shallow water.

"I have some fever medicine. If she wants to drink, we can give it to her."

Wolf's distressed face doesn't escape me my notice, even through my semi-closed, swollen eyelids. "And the child? Earlier you said the pills wouldn't be good for him..."

Yannick shakes her head. "If her fever doesn't come down, her body is going to give out. I'd rather give her the pills, even if the child is... struggling." She has the decency to avoid using the words *dead*.

When she kneels down with the water bag, I close my lips and refuse to drink.

"Come on," Yannick insists, annoyed. "Don't be so stubborn."

But I don't want it. Not if it can harm the fragile life of my unborn child. I try to explain to her how I feel him clinging to me, like a kite to its string, where one rough tug of the winds might separate him from me. I don't think she understands me. She probably thinks I'm delirious. I can see that she's trying her best to be patient with me, but her eyes betray that she is afraid and angry. After a while, she has to give up her efforts and puts the pills back in her pouch with a sigh.

And then, it is time to move again. They have brought a simple stretcher made of branches and furs for this part of the journey. Wolf gently lowers me onto it. I want to ask how long we have to walk like this. Is there a path through the dense spruce, or will they continue to follow the course of the river? Before I can find my voice, Wolf has turned away from me to lift his small bag of necessities.

Smoke stings my nose. The smell of boiled meat triggers my nausea, while at the same time making me acutely aware of my empty stomach. Surprised voices rise up near us, their words as incomprehensible as the barking of dogs further away. No one responds, until Wolf gives a hoarse and uncertain answer. My stretcher shakes and moves and I end up near a roaring, comforting heat. The smell of meat is suddenly overwhelming, as are the smells of animals around me. All this is enough to make me blink and open my eyes.

I see a face. Not Yannick's face, but that of a young woman. She has dark skin and even darker hair, just like Wolf. Her eyebrows are set in a deep frown. She mumbles something and I notice that she is missing two front teeth. When she sees me looking straight at her, one corner of her mouth curls up in a smile. At the same time, she shakes her head. Her hand gently comes down on my eyelids.

Sleep, she probably means. Or maybe not. I don't care what she means, because I've just decided that my curiosity is not worth the price of my exhaustion. The heat – a fire, I now realise – has also lost its charm. Now it only makes me sweat, and the sweat makes my clothes stick to my body in a very uncomfortable way.

I wake up in a tent. It suddenly dawns on me that I have been staring up at a blue tent canvas that I mistook for a sky. My head feels clearer than it has felt in days, although that doesn't stop a throbbing, piercing headache from tormenting me. I let my eyes wander around my new surroundings.

The floor is covered with light brown fur from an unknown species. Out of the corner of my eye, I can just see a sort of nook where an assortment of copper pots and pans is piled up against the tarpaulin. A pair of padded gloves has been casually left at the tent entrance, where a heavy layer of extra tarpaulin protects me from cold draughts coming in.

A fire burns low in a stone circle, right in the middle of the round tent. The smoke curls upwards in an almost straight column and escapes through a hole in the pointed roof. The pungent smell of peppermint is everywhere.

As for me, I am loosely covered by a woven blanket. My back cramps painfully, although the furs on which I am now lying are thicker and softer than those on which I was carried during the journey.

My clothes have been taken off. I'm only wearing a long white shirt that is definitely not mine. Now that I'm inspecting myself a bit more closely, I can smell the sour odour of my own sweat.

The tent flap is lifted and the same young woman I've seen before enters, followed closely by Wolf. As soon as he sees that I'm awake, he kneels down next to my head to put a hand against my cheek. For some reason, his skin against mine feels so intense that I almost hiss in pain.

"I'm sorry." His hand is quickly withdrawn. "Nánná said you could be sensitive to touch."

My eyes go from Wolf to her. She has turned her back to us and is busy stoking the fire. I groan.

"You have to sweat," Wolf clarifies. "They say it's good for you."

"And who are they?" I manage to ask in a cracked voice.

To my surprise, that elicits a broad smile from Wolf. "You *are* better."

"Seems like it." I push the blanket off my upper body, but it's no use. The newly lit flames fill the small round tent with their searing heat. "The reindeer herders? We found them?"

"Actually, they found us." Wolf looks a little embarrassed. "We were following the trail I had laid out earlier, but a rainstorm had obliterated my clues. We were wandering around for a good few hours before we heard dogs. A hunter brought us back to camp."

"I remember the smell of meat…"

Wolf smiles. "Are you hungry?"

"I don't know what I'm feeling."

"You will have to fast. Nánná has a plan for your healing, but she has imposed strict rules on all of us. You are not better yet, Nimue. Not by a long shot." His hand gently goes to my stomach and comes to rest there. "I believed the child had died, but Nánná detected a faint sign of life."

I'd already told him that. I stay silent, though.

Wolf lets out a sigh. "Nánná has come to talk to you. I will translate for you."

When she hears her name, Nánná turns towards me. She smiles, revealing her two missing teeth, and smoothly lowers herself onto the ground beside me. Her shiny hair is pinned to the sides of her head in two braids. She is wearing a dark blue tunic with simple brown trousers underneath. A yellow, woven sash is around her waist. When she speaks, she only uses practical, short words.

"She says she feels a lot of turmoil in your mind," Wolf says. "A lot of anger and fear. She says you've closed yourself off." He is silent for a moment, listening to her words. "Like a mouse in its nest, deep among the tree roots. A human being cannot live like that. You have to break free from the depths."

"Or I won't be able to reach Arthur anymore?" I mutter. It's amazing how little that thought does to me. The loss of Arthur should scrape my soul like the point of a knife, but I seem numb to it.

Wolf falls silent, his expression solemn. I look at him questioningly. "More than that," he finally admits. "You'll spend the rest of your life as one of the Undreamed, Nimue."

Like Katell. And Cormack. In the past year, I have seen more Undreamed people up close than any other in Central Europe. And I know only too well how broken they are. Only I was safe from the knives of the Asclepius Congregation. No one has ever dared to maim my spirit. It's hard to believe that one terrifying encounter with the Hunter could have the same effect. A raw, eerie sound fills the tent. It takes a moment before I recognise my own laughter. I laugh because it is so ridiculous, and so unfair, and because I feel none of the horror that should be racing through my body right now.

Wolf seems upset. Even Nánná no longer looks very calm.

"I'm not really Undreamed," I say finally. "Right?"

"No," Wolf admits uncomfortably. "You've closed yourself off. And you're not my Nimue anymore."

That stops my laughter like a cold gag in my throat.

Nánná starts talking again. Wolf translates: "There is a way to break through the barrier, but it won't be easy. Nánná says that you can feel pain, both outside and inside. She says you have to make the journey into the darkness to face what has made you so fearful. You will need extraordinary courage to face that challenge. Although she says that this is ultimately the path of enlightenment."

He falls silent for a moment, and Nánná mutters a final piece of advice. "We will begin when your body has sweated out these evils. Rest while you still can."

25

TO THE DEPTHS

They wake me up when the fire burns low. I taste the bitter taste of herbs in my mouth, which makes me suspect that my sleep was induced by something Wolf and Nánná gave me.

Wolf is kneeling beside me on a thick brown fur. I notice that he's doing his best to look relaxed, but the lines around his mouth and between his eyebrows give him away.

"Would you like some water?" he asks, as soon as he realises I'm awake. I nod and he helps me drink. After only a few sips, I fall back onto my blankets, tired.

"It's time," he tells me. I have no idea what he means. "Nánná has prepared everything carefully. I know you're scared, Nimue. But you have to do this. For all of us."

I give him a confused look before I see Yannick sitting in a corner of the tent, near the entrance. She looks at me and is clearly worried.

"Why are you afraid?" I ask her. My words drag a little. If I didn't know better, I'd think I was drunk. "Nothing serious is going to happen, right?"

Her eyes widen a little. "Of course not. Nothing serious."

"Nimue," Wolf says, "don't you remember what you said?"

I try to remember, but my head is like a black hole. "What did I say?"

"Nánná said that you should prepare for a journey to the Other World. She'll guide your mind to make the journey beyond, because you're not able to do that by yourself. To heal, you must face your fears."

"I don't remember any of that," I mutter.

"You said no to it. You said you couldn't do it. You were shaking like a leaf and you were crying." He is silent for a moment, clearly uncomfortable. "We put you back to sleep to give you a bit more rest. Nánná says we can't wait any longer. The time has come."

"I don't want to do it. I already know what I'm going to see. Wolf, I never want to see the Hunter again! He'll hurt the baby. He almost killed us already."

My words upset him – I see the pain in his dark eyes before he seems to pull himself together. Wolf leans into me and wipes the tangled curls off my sweaty forehead. "I'll tell you something my *nani* taught me, after I discovered I was a shaman. Maybe you remember how shocked I was when I found out."

"You were sick for days," I remember.

"That's right. And my *nani* said: 'Boy, remember. You can always ask for help in the Other World. A guide will always come, if you dare ask for it'."

I remain silent. Not because I don't want to answer, but because thinking takes up all my energy. I remember the first time my mind slipped behind the veil of the Other World. I tripped and fell in the middle of it, like a child falling into the deep, dark sea. That uncontrolled journey took me to the arid plains of the Fisher King, and it wasn't long before I felt the hot breath of the Hunter on my neck. When I cried out for help, all I saw was a creature flashing past me in the undergrowth. The second time, I was swallowed by a huge killer whale. Not every rescuer showed me his face, but there was one guide I knew better than all those other spirits: my grandmother Sela.

"Nimue?" Wolf's voice brings me back to the present.

"I heard you," I say hoarsely. "There are no good spirits left in the Other World. They have all been felled or they fled. I can't do it, Wolf. No one can protect me from the Hunter."

"It is that fear that you must defeat. Not the Hunter himself."

Yannick speaks up unexpectedly. "Your mother always told you to be strong and brave. Do you remember?"

"That's different," I say plaintively. "I'm not that strong and brave anymore."

My best friend looks very pale, as if she has been with me all night. Despite her tired face, she rolls her eyes. "Shark blood, Nim. Don't be a coward."

I don't know what to respond to that. Fortunately, at that moment, the tent flap is lifted and Nánná enters. She's carrying a bag with colourful stitching on it. The woman nods in satisfaction when she notices my open eyes, then frowns when she sees Yannick sitting there and says something in her native language.

"She says you have to get out to give us space," Wolf translates.

"Forget it," Yannick says. "You're going to perform that hocus-pocus on my pregnant best friend. I'm staying right where I am."

"It can be upsetting for you," Wolf says softly.

She folds her arms, as if challenging him. "I'll sit quietly in a corner. Don't mind me."

Nánná looks at Yannick. My best friend's posture should be enough to convey the meaning of her words. With a brusque shrug, the woman turns away from her to face me.

"She will give you something to drink," Wolf translates. "A very powerful herbal drink. Even if you resist, it will push your mind into the Other World. You may find yourself in a confined space, or in a dark place. You must not be frightened. If you find a path, follow it."

"I can't," I say, gasping for breath. "I can't!" If anything scares me, it is the darkness on the other side. In that darkness, the Hunter will be waiting for me. I can almost feel him already, his rancid breath on my skin, and his many eyes staring at my body like I'm nothing but meat.

"You are strong." The words reach me through Wolf's mouth, but are spoken by Nánná. "You are powerful. You have magic in you that I have never seen before. What is broken, you can heal with one touch. What is lost, you can bring home with one touch. What you fear, you can understand. That is all you have to do, Nimue. This is not meant to take on the Hunter. Leave that to Arthur; that is his job. All you need to do now is go beyond the darkness and discover what is at the heart of your fears. If at any time the darkness causes you to panic, remember this: darkness is never alone."

Nánná stops talking. I want to ask what in Gwenhael's name she means by that: darkness is never alone? Does she mean that it will bring the Hunter with it? She can save herself the trouble; I already know that sickening truth.

"Are you ready?" Wolf asks.

"No. I don't want to do it."

"Yet you will do it. For our child."

My body is on fire and my baby's life is on the brink. He will not live long if I don't get better. To heal, I must find my own strength again, or at least try my best to do so. Slowly, unwillingly, I let my breath escape and I inhale deeply. "Alright then."

Nánná takes her attributes out of the decorated bag: a cloak and headdress of woven fabric and brown feathers, an oil burner giving off a pleasantly sweet smell, a sort of wand with bells attached to it that make a jingling sound with every movement, and a flat round drum. With these, she will put me in a trance. I don't know what the other objects are for. Wolf points them out one by one.

"The rattle is to scare away evil spirits. The burner contains oils that will help relax your body. The cloak and headdress have been in Nánná's family for generations; they will guide your mind through the Other World like an antenna."

"Nonsense," I mutter, glancing at the worn fabric. The feathers are old and dull.

"Nonsense for anyone who is not born with the ability to make the transition. But not for you."

I never needed such things. A deep breath, a long sleep, a little guidance from Wolf, and I was in the Other World. But back then, I didn't feel this sickening resistance that I now sense in every cell of my body.

"Go ahead," I hear myself say. "Before I change my mind."

Wolf translates my words to Nánná. She nods approvingly. In the next moments, I'm covered in the old cloak and headdress, which sinks halfway down to the back of my head. The wide feathered collar is like a yoke on my shoulders. To my relief, they don't let me sit up. As soon as I have put on Nánná's old family paraphernalia and have downed the bitter drink, I may lie on my back. The oil burner sends sweet scents towards me and my eyes close automatically. I feel fine. Much better than I expected. Even when the soft drumbeats start, I don't lose it.

Nánná talks. Her words are probably not meant for me, as Wolf doesn't bother to translate them. She speaks in a lilting tone that strings all her words together like an incessant chain of rising and falling sounds. I let myself be carried along by that stream, into a silence inside me that I have not felt for a long time.

It is only when I feel my spirit slowly slipping out of my body that I begin to resist. I start sweating and gasping for breath. Far away, at the outer limit of my consciousness, I can hear the sound of waves. We are too far away from the shore for me to hear the sea, but the sound is continuous and grows louder with each moment. My senses become overwhelmed with the sweet smell of oil, mixed with the Otherworldly smell of salty and wet sand.

I don't want to. I don't want to! I don't want to go to that place!

I start to sweat even more. Pain lances through my body, like red hot lava flowing from the core of my stomach to my arms. My cheeks are soaking wet – from tears, or sweat, or both.

It is as if Nánná's drumbeats fill my head. Each beat thumps inside my skull like a heavy headache. Each beat pushes my mind in a direction I don't want to go in. Then the dizziness sets in. It comes in spirals and subsides for a moment, but like waves washing further and further up onto the beach, I'm increasingly overwhelmed by the feeling that I'm like a whirling boat knocked loose from its anchor. Somewhere in the back of my mind, I know that I'm lying on my side, that I have solid ground beneath me that I cannot sink through. My mind and my senses tell a different story, however. I'm spinning in all directions. No matter how hard I try to stay away from the abyss, there comes a moment when I lose my grip. I scream and fall over the edge.

Into the depths.

26

THE FIRST STORY EVER TOLD

The darkness is so dense that I feel like I have died. I'm a thought floating in nothingness, unable to find my body or to distinguish bottom from top. It is frightening, but not as frightening as what will undoubtedly happen next: the Hunter's claws will sink into my back. Maybe he hasn't smelt or seen me yet. I curl up, make myself as small as possible and keep very still.

For a long time, nothing changes in the darkness around me. Time seems to have solidified. There is nothing to indicate that the Hunter is near: I hear no rattling breath, no claws scraping across a surface, no tongue licking lips turned up in a snarl. Maybe it is a trap. Or maybe I really am alone.

It slowly dawns on me that I'm waiting for something that will never come. Very carefully, I feel around me. I don't have a Dream body – I'm not brave enough to create one. Yet I'm vaguely aware of an uneasy feeling, a nagging pain that disappears as soon as I concentrate on it. I reach out to the empty space with the feelers of my mind. When it feels safe, I begin to explore more bravely. Suddenly, I remember Nánná's instructions: if there is an exit, I must take it. I don't know where I am; my feeling tells me it's somewhere underground. So I stretch upwards. The higher I get, the less intense the darkness seems to become. The black becomes greyish, and I see a streak of greenish-blue light ahead.

I break through the barrier surprisingly fast and am immediately surrounded by water. Not the clear water of a river, or the turbulent water of the sea, but dirty, stagnant water. I hurry through it and finally reach the open air.

The water from which I have freed myself is a large pool. It mirrors the sky above me and is completely still. It's not a peaceful silence, but a motionlessness reminiscent of death. Around me I can't see anything besides desolate salt flats. A pale sun illuminates the white ground. There's not a tree in sight, not even a blade of grass. If this is supposed to represent my greatest fear, it seems that I'm mostly afraid of boredom.

After making sure that I'm the only living soul in the whole area, I give myself my familiar Dream body. I walk around the pool. I crouch down and run my fingers over the rock, bringing my fingertips to my lips and tasting the salt. There is no path, no end to the horizon; no sign telling me what to do next.

I sit down in a cross-legged position and wait.

I wait a long time.

I scratch drawings in the salt surface until hours must have passed. Only then do I realise that nothing is going to happen. Unless I *make* something happen.

I sigh deeply and close my eyes. My deepest fear. There is no point in wondering what it is, but how do I face the Hunter without being swallowed up? I can't make sense of it.

I need help.

Again, I take a deep breath. I feel slightly foolish as I speak aloud into the void: "By Gwenhael's broken grave, I ask for a guide. Please come and help."

For a few moments, I hold my breath in anticipation. When nothing happens, I feel disappointed. The salt stings my eyes and my patience is beginning to run out. I rub away the stinging feeling. When I take my hand away, a jolt goes through me when I see something.

A figure has appeared on the horizon. It's an elongated figure, a shadow against the shimmering plain. I squint my burning eyes and intently gaze at him, how he moves in my direction.

When he gets closer, another shock runs through me. It is the horned man. He towers over me, his antlers casting a shadow on the ground. Somehow, he radiates more light than the dappled sun.

I catch myself staring at him with my mouth hanging open.

He bows his massive head and I catch a glimpse of his face. He has the eyes of a human, sharp and intelligent. The rest of his face is covered with soft fur – his nose and mouth remind me of that of a deer.

"Who are you?" I ask.

I had expected a heavy, booming voice to belong to him, but he speaks softly, almost in a whisper: "I am the Hunting Lord. You called me, daughter of the sea."

"Are you my guide?" I do my best not to be intimidated by his height and huge antlers. "I have seen you before. I have seen you many times and I dreamed that you spoke to me."

Again, he inclines his head, almost like taking a bow. "I also tried to call you, but you pushed me away each time."

"Not on purpose." I think for a moment. "I'm very ill and the life of my child depends on me. I'm meant to overcome my deepest fear, but I don't think I'm doing a very good job..."

"You found it."

I look at him, not understanding, and then let my eyes wander over the deserted plain. "Where?"

"Where is the wrong question. Who?"

My anxiety begins to return. I automatically take a step back. "The Hunter."

"That's me." He must see my startled look, because he continues: "I am what the Hunter once was. You look frightened, daughter of the sea. Rest assured, I will not harm you. I'm nothing more than a grain of sand in an oyster, a locked-up memory. So fear me not."

That's easier said than done. I wrap my arms stiffly around my own waist and take another step backwards. I don't know where to turn my eyes to: to him, or around us. The Hunter has tricked me before; who's to say this isn't his second attempt?

The Hunting Lord, if that really is his name, spreads his arms, palms turned upwards. "You seem confused."

"I know what the Hunter looks like," I say slowly. "You are not like him."

"I am no longer that which is the Hunter. I am what is left, buried deep beneath layers of darkness and hunger and hatred. It was not easy to reach out, to call you. I fade away as my brother faded away in his tower."

"What do you want from me?" I whisper.

"I have called you, daughter of the sea, to pass on my wisdom to you before I'm completely gone. I can help you with your fear."

Again, far away, I feel a few waves of pain washing over my consciousness. Whatever it is – probably a side effect of Nánná's drink – it distracts me and I push it away, annoyed.

I consider my options: I can stay, or I can turn right around and hope to find my way back to my body. The Hunting Lord doesn't give me the impression that he wants to stop me if I want to escape. But I have come in order to get better. I lick my Dream lips and slowly lower myself onto the ground of the salt flat before saying: "I'm listening."

He smiles. A strange sight in a man with a deer head.

"You say that you have come to conquer your fear. What you fear, you must learn to understand. Therefore listen to my first lesson.

Once, there were two brothers: the Fisher King reigned in the west and the Hunting Lord in the east. One day, the ground shook for a long time. Poisonous substances poured up from the earth, deadly acid rained down from the sky. In the First World, the lights went out one by one. Seas rose up and swallowed continents. Poison, manufactured by human hands and released by falling rocks, seeped through rivers and forests and hills until it reached us. After that came a time when a disease swept across the land. Hungry as a wolf, it prowled, and no one was spared. There was darkness in it. My brother and I wandered through our lands, and we heard our beloved spirits groaning and decaying. Then, I travelled to the source of the darkness, armed with bows and arrows. But shadows cannot be fought with weapons. So I threw myself upon the source of the disease and swallowed it whole. I believed I had the power to keep that curse inside. I believed I could be a prison and a fortress at once. But I was slowly eaten from within, until finally, I lost myself. My life seeped out of me and my heart came to a stop. And in that silence, my conscience fell silent, until there was only room for a single desire: to consume and digest. Destroy and burn. I became a Hunter."

I don't know what to say. It's hard to believe that something of this gentle creature still remains inside the Hunter.

The Hunting Lord seems to be able to read my thoughts from my expression alone. "You have never come close enough to suspect that the Hunter is meticulously guarding the last vestige of his soul. I assure you: I have lost my heart, not my mind. As sure as the smell of blood means prey, I'm sure you and Arthur can harm me. I fear you. The Hunter fears you."

That's even harder to believe. I want to go away, back to the safe tent and Wolf's arms. "Even if that's true, I don't want to see the Hunter again. I've gotten too close once already."

The Hunting Lord takes a step towards me. The shadow of his antlers is cast upon me and when I look up, I stare straight into his gold-speckled eyes. "I give you this second lesson: to face the darkness, you must want to smell it, taste it, swallow it. And then you must find the deepest power within you, that source which bends all darkness to light."

"I don't have that kind of magic! My magic is unpredictable and it makes me weak..."

"You are a child with selkie blood. You carry hope in your womb." The Hunting Lord speaks patiently and kindly. "Have you never realised what your true magic is?"

"Healing," I reply, somewhat annoyed. "I know I can cure the disease, but that..."

"You heal because you transform. *Seolh uu-la*, aren't those the words that give you strength? Words of transformation. Like the sea erasing all traces on the beach, like a selkie shedding its fur and taking on a different appearance, you change the world with one touch. *That* is your magic, child of the sea."

They are beautiful words, but I'm not convinced. "I don't believe it. If it was so easy to transform the Hunter with a trick, Sela would have told me a long time ago. I would have done it already!"

"A trick? Nimue of the sea, what I ask of you is nothing less than mastering the oldest magic, the deepest magic, the magic that shaped the beginning of creation, that underpins every kind of renewal and liberation. I didn't say it would be easy for you. But nothing is impossible. Since the beginning, darkness has swallowed up light. Since the beginning, the light has deceived the darkness. Since the beginning, I have hunted my prey to feed myself, yet life continues to be reborn. So, no – nothing is impossible."

I have to take deep breaths to process all this. Because if the Hunting Lord is right – worse, if he can somehow force me to confront the real Hunter – I don't think I will get a peaceful and safe birth for my baby. "My brother is also still here. He still has a chance. I have faith in him."

"Your brother," the old spirit whispers thoughtfully. "I caught a glimpse of him. He shines with the light of the bright moon. But you have the power of the sea. Together, you may be able to push and pull and turn the tide. The time of fog and emptiness has almost won. Even now, I can feel the change coming. What will remain is the monster I have become – a Hunter with an insatiable hunger, who cares nothing for balance, only for the swallowing of flesh. He will swallow it all: the land, the sea, the spirits and the animals. So you see, you have a choice: fall as all creation falls, or find a way to let the light in again. If you hurry, you can still make it in time. You might be strong enough together, if you try."

I turn away from him and stare at the dead water. "Is there no one else who can do this? Goldilocks, or Lance?"

"Nobody."

"I'm heavily pregnant."

"I feel your child, I feel his warmth and his strength. You will see him sooner than you think. Daughter of the sea." Something in his voice forces me to turn to him. "At least take my words into consideration, I beg of you. I'm a mere phantom, a memory of a better time. My brother is chained in his tower; he can do little more than dream of the light. I myself remember less of the sun every day. If you no longer wish to hear my pleas, listen to my last gift. Consider it a gift to your child, a message for the future."

I swallow. "What kind of gift?"

"There is one last lesson I can teach you. This is the message I have been trying to bring you all this time. It's... a wise and foolish story, I admit. It's the first story ever told." He is silent for a moment and I'm silent too, tense and expectant. "The sea kept still..."

"The darkness and the sea!" I gasp. "Yes, I remember this!"

"I'm glad you heard me sometimes, but I doubt that you remember the whole thing. This is the oldest story, and not many spirits existed to hear this first tale. I was there, as was my brother. It's not much, just a saga from the very first days. I have called to you because this is the last gift I can give to the Two Worlds. So listen well, child of the sea, and take my last lesson to heart."

He starts to narrate.

"The sea kept still and could not move. Darkness enveloped her. For centuries they had lain like that, undisturbed.

"Oh," sighed the Sea. "Oh, where have all the stars gone that the sailors used to navigate by? Where are the fish and plants in my belly? And where is the moon, which could draw my tides? It used to be different!

The Darkness heard this, and he rejoiced. "It's no use complaining," he whispered. "Long have I waited for the light to disappear from below to above: centuries and centuries and longer. Now I have won, and I am everywhere."

"Why do you want it so badly? I remember a time when light and dark had their own place. Light was in charge of life, which danced and grew and dreamed and worked, and Darkness was in charge of death and silence and the Longest Watch."

"And now I have The Longest Watch of All!" spoke the Darkness triumphantly. "And the silence, the death, the dreams and the stories all belong to me."

"How did it come to this?" asked the Sea, defeated.

"Ah, Sea," said the Darkness. "The first people lived alone on a mountain. They were weak and fearful. The cold killed their sons. The fire killed their daughters. The wilderness shut them in on all sides. Then the first man came down from the mountain. He spoke to Eagle and said: *"The darkness blinds us and we cannot see the danger coming. Eagle, if you are a friend, will you not help us?"*

Eagle took pity on the weak man, and said: *"From this day forward, I share my keen eyes with you, Man. For I live in the sky and you live on the ground; we shall not get in each other's way."*

Then the man went to Bear. *"Predators are killing our children. Bear, if you are a friend, won't you protect us?"*

Bear thought for a long time, but then said: *"You will be strong like me, good friend, for the forest is full of fat prey. We will not get in each other's way."*

Satisfied, the man went back to his family, and they prospered. Soon, however, they became frightened again. The man descended the mountain again and wandered through the wilderness. He cried out: *"Who will tell me the secrets of the earth? We see danger coming and we catch fat prey, yet we die without knowing why! We walk but on the crust of the earth and we know not where we came from or where we go when we die!"*

This time, it was Snake who heard him. He felt sorry for the yelling man and said: *"Where we come from and where we are going, we do not know either. But I will show you all the secrets of the earth, so that you can fathom its secrets."*

Even once people knew the secret of the earth, they were not happy. They had children, and their children had children. The mountain became full and the people became thirsty and hungry. The man went to see Deer and begged him: *"Let us share in the good watering places that you always know how to find!"*

Deer said: *"Good friend, water is abundant for everyone. I gladly share my watering places with every thirsty creature. One thing you must promise me: when we quench our thirst at the pond, you must not hunt us."*

The man promised. But as soon as the people quenched their thirst at Deer's watering places, they saw that Deer and his family were not paying attention when they drank. And because the people were always hungry, they aimed their spears and arrows and shot Deer.

Deer lay bleeding on the ground. The man bent over him and said: *"If you are a friend, Deer, give us your flesh and give us your blood too. Thus we shall grow in strength and number."*

With his last breath, the dying Deer shouted a warning to all the animals in the forest: *"There is a hunger in man that never stills! He will continue to take and take, until the day everything is gone. Then the Darkness will come and devour us all!"*

"Yes," sighed the Sea, after the story had ended. "Yes, you are very strong, Darkness. But I know deeper secrets that you will never know."

"Oh, really?" said the Darkness. "Prove it. What is deeper than the secret of silence?"

"The secret to break that silence."

"And what is deeper than the secret of death?"

"That is the secret of what happens after death, Darkness."

"And you know that for sure?" sneered the Darkness. "You, a mass of empty water!"

"Everything was born from me and everything spawned from me," replied the Sea. "Why do you think I am still alive, now that you have devoured everything?"

"Then tell me: what is deeper than the secret of the Longest Watch?"

"That, Darkness," said the Sea, "is the secret of the Last Tale Ever Told."

"What is that?" snarled the Darkness. "Didn't *I* just tell you the very last story?"

"You told me the story of how it began," the Sea whispered, so softly that the Darkness had to prick up its ears to understand her. "This is the story of how it ends... The end was near; the Darkness was everywhere. And the Darkness sighed and came to rest."

The Sea was silent for a moment, and a long drawn-out sigh resounded, as if the Darkness had finally fallen asleep after millennia of restless nights.

"That's not the end of the story," said the Sea, and she continued: "The Sea lay enclosed by darkness and felt empty. Slowly, something stirred; deep, deep in her belly. And from her belly rose the First Sun – and look, Darkness, here he comes already! – And the First Sun settled in the sky. The light travelled to all points of the compass, far beyond the boundaries of the water. The hunters leaped forward, newly born. And where they set their feet, vast plains and wild forests grew out of the shadows, and in the distance, the wild beasts leaped forth: Roe and Deer and Aurochs and Wolf and Bear and Boar, and all beasts great and small."

Everything the Sea said happened, exactly as she said it.

"And the First People learned to dream, and out of dreams came imagination, and out of imagination grew stories. And a young storyteller sang a song: the Very First Story Ever Told. And at last there emerged a Man, his hair and skin white as milk and his eyes deep as two pools in which starlight reflected. The Prophet, he was called, and he stood surrounded by a circle of animals: Owl and Serpent and Eagle and Bear and the others.

"Now that I can do so much and know so much, I will be careful not to abuse what you have given me," said Man. *"For your gifts are a good servant, but a bad master. Though now I have knowledge of all the secrets of the earth, and have the sight like Eagle, the strength of Bear, and all other gifts, I would still be lonely if you had not come to my aid."*

And so Man and Beast lived together, as it had been at the beginning of time. And the Light ruled over life, and all that danced and dreamed and worked. And the Darkness guarded death, and silence, and the Longest Watch. And that," said the Sea, "is how it ends."

The Hunting Lord may be weakened, but his soft voice flows like honey. I can almost taste his words on my lips. I feel them enter me, like a balm for my frightened heart. As I bring my hands to my Dream face, I'm shocked to find that my cheeks are soaking wet with tears. I wonder if my real face is also wet with tears, if Wolf and Yannick are worried right now about what's wrong.

The truth is that I am feeling better than I have in a long time. It is as if my lungs have opened up and I'm getting fresh air for the first time in days.

"Is it really possible that it is like that?" I ask.

"That's how it has always been," the Hunting Lord says, even more quietly than he spoke before. I get the impression that he's radiating less warmth, as if the conversation has exhausted him. "When darkness remains in its own do-main, when the Two Worlds recognise their harmony again, the White Prophet will come to usher in a new time of peace and healing. That time is now, Nimue of the Sea. That time begins with The Coming King, with you, and with the child you carry. I hear the bells ringing. Listen to their call and do not be discouraged by that one trap that the Hunter set for you. Listen and be brave. Listen and be strong."

I think I have been listening well and, more importantly, I got the message. "I carry the power of the sea in me."

"Yes, Nimue. You do."

"And the sea carries all life. And the sea transforms."

"As she has always done."

"And you are him." The words escape my lips like a whispered breath, for the true meaning only now dawns on me. "*You* are the hidden sun in the middle of the darkness."

"I'm weaker than a sun. But I am the rumour of a new dawn."

"And the sea..." Deep in my belly, I feel the familiar push and pull of the tide, the force I have always felt, but not always recognised. A shadow of an idea is revealing itself to me. Something so absurd that it balances on the edge of madness... "The sea will give birth to you again."

The Hunting Lord looks at me with his gold-speckled eyes without replying. I don't even need an answer anymore, because I feel as if fresh morning light is shining down on my sleepy head. "I think I'm ready to find Arthur."

"I've been waiting for the moment you would say that." The soft voice comes from behind me and is not coming from the Hunting Lord. The woman has emerged from the water and looks at me with her familiar, black eyes. She smiles.

"Sela," I say in surprise.

"I'm glad you were able to find us again." Sela extends both her hands to me and I take them automatically. "Come, dear. I will take you to your brother now."

27

THE FALLING WORLD

When the clammy mist presses against us, Sela lets go of my hand. At first, I think we've gone in the wrong direction, but then it hits me that the fog in the Other World is so dense that you can't see an arm's length ahead.

"Where is Arthur?" I ask.

Sela gestures with her pale arm. "He is close by. Keep walking forward and you will find him."

"Aren't you coming with me?" The idea that I have to make my way through this fog alone makes me uneasy.

"It's not safe for me here," my grandmother says softly. "I'm one of the last spirits who managed to escape from the Hunter, Nimue. He cannot find me, because if he does, all the selkies will have vanished after that. But you don't need me anymore." She smiles her familiar, sad smile. "Remember your strength. You and Arthur are the north star in the dark night. Now go."

"Be safe, Sela," I whisper. My grandmother nods slowly, then simply seems to dissolve into the grey, wet mist.

I take a deep breath, shivering as the uncomfortable pain briefly overwhelms me before subsiding. I tighten my grip on my trembling Dream body and take the first few steps forward. To my relief, it's not long before the glow of torches becomes visible.

A little later I hear voices. I recognise Arthur's voice, quickly followed by the clearly angry voice of Morgana. I hurriedly bridge the last few yards, until I'm suddenly standing within their circle of light. On the ground, in the middle, sits a pale girl I haven't seen before. Her black hair and face with sharp angles make her look like Morgana. Unlike this girl, who looks stunned and exhausted, Morgana has the glow of a raging fire about her.

260

"Nimue!" Arthur blinks hard, as always when he recognises me after a long time of absence. And then, as always, his eyes begin to shine. "I thought you wouldn't come! And sometimes, I thought…"

I pull him towards me and into an embrace.

Arthur starts to grin. "Nim, you feel weird. Like fog."

"This is a Dream body," I remind him, wiping tears from my cheeks.

"You're crying." He seems surprised. "Is something wrong?"

"Not anymore. I was very ill and I thought I might never see you again."

"Touching," Morgana snorts. "Can I have some attention now? We were talking about my sister, not some piece of burdensome luggage!"

"I know that," Arthur replies impatiently. Have they discussed this matter before? My gaze takes in the circle. The dozens of torches illuminate tense, almost frightened faces. Goldilocks has her chin thrust forward and her jaws clenched tight. She's crossed her arms in front of her chest. "Morgana, no-one is voting to leave Olwen behind. We are voting to determine if we should seek a safe shelter for her, where she can wait until we reach the Fisher King."

"There *are* no safe places," Morgana snarls.

"We know the caves that once sheltered us are," Lance says. "Think about it, Morgana. Olwen cannot keep up with us and she continues to lose strength. Every hour counts. We must consider…"

"Leaving her behind." Morgana sounds as vicious as ever. "I'll bet the only safe place is the Fisher King's tower. Olwen can rest once we get there, and then the Fisher King can help her. You know this as well as I do! Yet you propose to leave my sister behind in some cave, all alone!"

"Not alone," Goldilocks says.

"Oh, that's right. In the company of the man you all just voted *out of the group*!"

My gaze darts outside the circle and suddenly I see him, retreated so far away that the light of the fire almost doesn't touch him. Mordred is standing there with his legs wide, his arms crossed. Shadows and mist have claimed him, obscuring his face. Yet he radiates a kind of calm – something I have rarely seen in Cormack.

"Is he *still* with you?" I groan.

"He won't be for long," Val says. "As soon as we leave here, he can go his own way. We don't have room for the Hunter's dogs."

"I was tricked and played," Mordred speaks softly from his secluded spot. "Nevertheless, I'm sorry that I have put you in danger. I will leave peacefully, but keep the girl with you. Morgana is right: there are no safe places."

"You have magic. If you really had good intentions, you would offer to protect her."

"This magic is not my own," Mordred says. "I fear it's only something the Hunter has put in me. It is better if I never use it again.'" He bends down and pulls one torch out of the ground. His face is pale and serious, his eyes bloodshot. "Take Olwen with you and keep walking. You know you cannot rest in the same place for long."

"It's decided then," Morgana says, before anyone else can say anything. She hooks her arms under Olwen's elbows and pulls her up.

"Where are we going?" I ask. "How far away are we from the Fisher King?"

"It's not too far," Arthur says. "But the journey is getting harder. The fog is getting thicker by the hour. We have to climb down, and the dry riverbed will get deeper further on, according to Lance. There is an old bridge across it. After that, there is this plain..." His facial expression becomes more solemn.

"The plain with the fire and the vapours?" I guess. "I've been there."

"It won't be easy to cross that with limited vision."

"But the tower is just behind it." My optimism slowly begins to return a little. "Once we've crossed the plain, we'll have made it!"

"With a small amount of blood from the Hunter." Arthur fumbles for something at his side. Only now do I see the copper goblet he has tucked into his belt.

I open my eyes wider. "You got it!"

"I just hope it will be enough." Arthur turns away from me to give the group directions. Quickly and silently, the improvised camp is packed up and an orderly group has been formed. Lance and Arthur take the vanguard, armed with spear and knife. I'm pleased to recognise the stainless steel knife in Arthur's right hand. Morgana and GWN are in the middle, with Olwen between them. Goldilocks, Val and Green close the ranks.

I stay a bit behind to approach the tall man, who has been waiting silently all this time. The only torch he has kept for himself casts a flickering light on his face.

"Why are you so calm?" I ask.

Mordred looks at me with a surprisingly mild expression. "What else should I feel?"

"Anger," I say after a short pause. "Or fear."

He shows me a tired smile. "I'm often anxious or angry. It doesn't help."

I want to say something to him. I don't know what exactly – something that can bridge the distance between us, perhaps? Something that makes me feel that we are still connected somewhere, somehow. But nothing comes to mind. Only his name, and I utter it like a sigh: "Cormack."

He looks at me and I have no idea if he remembers anything of his old life. "Go with your brother," is all he says.

Then he's turning around, and before the torchlight of my brother's group has been gobbled up by the mist, his flame has already disappeared.

****

The bridge is a weathered contraption made of planks and ropes. The wind swings it from side to side across the dried-out riverbed. The other side is invisible in the mist. Below us, the riverbed has become a veritable abyss. Lance is clutching the rope to his left and has taken two steps onto the bridge. With his other hand, he's holding up a torch. The flame dances in the air. He tests the wooden surface by kicking it, shifting his weight and taking another step forward.

"The planks aren't that bad," Lance calls over his shoulder. "We can take our chances, if we cross them quickly. No more than three of us at a time."

One after the other, we venture onto the planks. The bridge creaks and shudders with every step we take. When I'm almost on the other side, a loud screeching cuts through the fog. It is enough to make my Dream body tremble and fade.

"Morgana!" Arthur shouts. "Morgana, what's wrong?"

Morgana's answer is a more drawn-out, even louder scream. Lance, who is just ahead of me, grabs his spear, Arthur seizes his knife and before I can say anything, they disappear across the bridge.

Goldilocks and I exchange a glance before Goldilocks pulls a torch from the ground and sprints after my brother. I'm not far behind.

Arthur and Lance are there, with their weapons in front of them. Morgana stands nearby, her shoulders shaking with every hysterical breath she takes.

A few yards away, with its giant front legs on the bridge and its rear body on the mainland, is an evil spirit. It has the maw of a dog and the size of a bear. Blood is dripping from its teeth. For a moment, I think either Lance or Arthur have succeeded in wounding and frightening it. But then the beast lowers its head and snaps at something lying on the ground. Someone. Olwen.

To my surprise, it is Goldilocks who moves first. She screams a curse and thrusts the flame of the torch forward. I grab Morgana and hold her to prevent her from throwing herself at the spirit as well. Morgana struggles and scratches at me, her curses raining down upon me, but her only weapon is a short flint knife; all she would achieve is she'll end up bleeding out on the ground, just like her sister.

The spirit jumps off the bridge and Lance sprints after him. The creature raises a giant paw and thumps it to the ground. Lance' spear flies out of his hand. Before I can check whether Lance is still moving, the beast turns around. Olwen is dangling like a limp rag doll from its jaws as it disappears into the mist with lightning speed.

"Let go of me! Let me *go*!" Morgana twists and turns in my grip, then punches me in the stomach. I groan, overcome with pain and dizziness, and have to let go of her. She uses that moment to run away from me.

"Nimue, what is it?" Arthur asks.

"Nothing – it's already gone." I slowly get up.

"Morgana, it's no use," Goldilocks says.

"She is alive! Didn't you see her eyes? He didn't bite her to death, she is alive!"

Lance groans. I crouch down by his side and am shocked by the state of his face. Half of it is scratched open and bloody. His left eye is swollen shut, his lips bruised and split.

"Hold still," I instruct him. I touch his face with quick, careful fingers. When I look up, Goldilocks and Arthur are staring at us. "We need something cold to stop his eye from swelling," I say. "I'm afraid something may have been damaged."

"Damaged?" Lance moans, through cracked lips. "Will I go blind?"

"Maybe not," I reassure him. "It's too early to tell. Goldilocks, the river is dry. Is there any other water nearby?"

She shakes her head. "The plain is completely barren. I only have this leftover drinking water." She unties a drinking bag from her side and kneels down beside me. Slowly, she lets the trickle of water seep over Lance' wounds. He groans again, but the coolness seems to do him good, because when the water runs out, he lets out a deep sigh.

"We must reach the tower as quick as possible," Arthur says softly.

Morgana whips around. "What's the point in hiding anymore? Once we're in the tower, we'll be trapped!" she snaps.

"We have the Grail, we have the blood," Arthur replies. "We must go on, Morgana. If Olwen isn't dead, she'll have been brought to the Hunter's nest. He is too clever. He's trying to drive us apart. We have only one goal, and that is the Fisher King's tower. That's where we are going." He is silent for a moment and looks at Morgana guiltily before he adds: "With or without you."

Something seems to change in Morgana. Something cold replaces the smouldering fire in her eyes, her shoulders become a little stiffer, her face a little paler. But when Arthur and I help Lance up, and cross the bridge with him and Goldilocks, she does come after us.

≫≫≫ ≪≪≪

As always in this spirit land, night falls early, as dark as death. No moon, no stars, nothing to guide us. The torches mark the boundaries of our small, somewhat safe bubble. I sit next to Arthur with my knees pulled up and stare into the vast darkness of the plain.

"The sea can sometimes be dark like this for a while."

I'm startled by Arthur's voice.

"What do you remember about the sea?" I ask.

His clothes rustle as he shrugs. "Bits and pieces. How green she was on a hot summer day. How grey the water looked when the sky was overcast. The sound of the surf in Whale Bay. You know that one time a whale washed up on the beach?"

"I remember." I smile. "Do you remember how Dad used to paint the boat every year?"

"When I'm with you, images come to mind. But they fade away as soon as you disappear. I remember the smell of new paint. I remember the... No. I don't remember the name."

265

"The Ragdoll."

He repeats the word softly, each syllable separately, as if to make sure it will stick in his memory. Then he says: "I also remember another boat. It was night, pitch black, like here. I remember your voice, how you screamed. How wildly we bobbed up and down..." He looks at me. "I remember so much pain, but I can't place it. All I know is that this can't have been on *The Ragdoll*. This memory doesn't fit anywhere in that life as I remember it. Nimue, something like this never happened, right? It's just a dream."

"Oh, Arthur," I sigh. I wish he didn't have to be reminded of that night. "It happened on *The Herring Gull*, near Camlann. That was the last time we were together... That you were still in one piece, I mean."

He needs time to process that. I listen to the crackling of the flames and the muffled conversation between Val and GWN, a little further down. These sounds don't seem to take away the immense silence surrounding us, but rather emphasise it.

"You told me before that I'm in Avalon," Arthur says at last. "My body is there, you mean. And I'm not whole. My leg was taken off." He sounds surprised, as if he doesn't really believe me. No, I think, it's not that he doesn't *want* to believe me – he just doesn't seem to feel it. Here, in this world, he only suffers from scratches and bruises he got during the journey. "Do you think I will ever be able to go back?" he asks.

"I hope so," I say. "By Gwenhael, I hope so. You haven't been Undreamed, no one has cut the spirit away from your body... You've left your body behind yourself. Ana said you had... withdrawn. Why wouldn't you be able to choose to go back?"

Arthur thinks for a moment. "Not as long as the Fisher King needs my help."

"But after that, you can try to come back," I say hopefully.

"In that world – in your world... we are not near each other. Or are we?"

"A sea and a continent apart," I admit.

"And when I wake up, I won't be able to get off the island with just one leg."

"I can come to you."

His eyes bore into mine. "You'd make that long journey?"

"Eventually," I promise him softly.

Arthur focuses on the fire again and seems to see something there that I don't. "What kind of life would I have if I can't walk, Nim? Think about it. We are fishermen. I can't jump into a boat, I can't drag that boat ashore through the surf. I can't brace myself to bring in the nets. What can I do with one leg?"

"You don't have to fish, do you?"

He lets his breath escape through his nose and closes his eyes. "I don't know any other life."

"Arthur." I reach for his hand. "We'd manage. We are no longer alone – Wolf is there, and Mum and Ana and Yannick... Arthur, please. We're not complete without you."

"I know." He allows a short silence to hang between us. "As soon as the Fisher King no longer needs my help."

We stop talking and again, I listen to the deathly silence shrouding the plain. My eyes take in the dark contours of Arthur's friends and linger on Goldilocks, her bunch of fine curls like a golden halo around her face. Suddenly I wonder if *she* is the reason Arthur isn't sure about returning. Even if he can return to his body unharmed, she probably never will. Katell has been Undreamed, cut off and mutilated. I even wonder if Goldilocks is still really Katell. Goldilocks is stronger, sharper and faster than I remember the shy Katell to be. And GWN, Val, Green, and Lance? They too are doomed to wander the Other World. I wonder what will happen to them when their bodies start failing. Will they continue to exist, or will they disappear like the sparks from these torches: one bright flash before they are extinguished forever?

Suddenly, I sit up straighter. My eyes go back and forth over the small camp, taking in the familiar faces. "Wait. Where's Morgana?"

"Morgana?" Arthur looks around. "When did she disappear?"

"Perhaps she went somewhere to pee?"

Arthur doesn't look convinced. We wait for a while, but when Morgana doesn't reappear, he gets up and takes a torch. "GWN, come and search with us. The rest stays at the camp. You too, Lance."

The night prevents us from walking quickly. We need the light from the torch for every step we take. I narrow my eyes and force them to see as much as possible. Far away, a reddish glow catches my eye.

"I think it will be morning soon."

"That's not the morning glory," GWN says. "What you see are the flows of lava just below the earth's crust."

We circle around the camp, further and further away from the safety of the torches.

"Morgana!" Arthur calls out, but his call goes unanswered.

"I don't think she went for a pee," I say uneasily. "Arthur, she was furious when we left Olwen…"

"We didn't leave her *behind*! You saw what it was like. We had no chance of…"

"I know, but imagine how she must be feeling. If it were me, Arthur, what would *you* have done?"

He stops to look at me and licks his lips. "I would have gone after you. To the bottom with all dangers!"

"Footprints," GWN warns us at that moment. He takes the torch from Arthur and lowers it to the ground. With difficulty, I can make out a dusty footprint someone left behind.

GWN points ahead. "That way."

We are almost back at the bridge when we finally find Morgana. She's not alone. My cousin has wrapped his arms around her and is holding her close as she presses her face to his shoulder. Arthur, GWN and I come to a stop as if on command. For a moment I think Mordred has grabbed her to drag her back to the nest as well. A moment later, I realise how stupid that thought is. Morgana would scream and fight, not lift her face to him and nod in response to something he's murmuring in her ear. She raises a hand to wipe her cheeks. After a few parting words, she turns around. She doesn't spot us until Mordred has disappeared into the mist and shadow. Shock and anger are brimming in her eyes. "What are you doing here?"

"That's what we'd like to ask *you*," GWN replied. "Morgana, have you lost your mind?"

"I wanted to be alone."

"You were not alone," I say. "Morgana, you cannot seek comfort from Mordred. He can't be trusted."

"He didn't do anything to me," Morgana says. She briskly walks past us, in the direction of the camp.

"Listen," I begin. "I know him, Morgana, I knew him before he came here…"

"You knew a man of flesh and blood. Be honest, none of us are made of flesh and blood anymore."

Morgana gives me a fierce look and doesn't slow down. I have to make a real effort to keep up. "I know he's charming and clever. But it's not safe to trust him."

"Nobody is safe! Not Arthur, not you, not Lance! Nor my sister, was she? No one could protect her!"

"We tried."

"And we all fell short." The sob in her throat is suddenly clearly audible. Looking at her in the light of the flickering torch, I see that her cheeks are glistening with tears. "All you guys talk about is the Fisher King and that cursed Grail and that damned blood. Olwen was an inconvenience to you. You say you're sorry she's gone, but all you think about is the mission. Mordred listened to me, at least. That's all." She swallows. "He wanted to *listen*."

"Morgana, I understand what you're feeling..."

"No, you don't."

"More than you think. Arthur is my brother and his body is half-dead on a distant island somewhere. He forgets me whenever I'm not here. Believe me when I say I understand your pain."

She looks at me, but doesn't say a word.

I sigh. "If you want to be angry about Olwen, you can. But at least take it from me that Mordred is not the friend you need right now."

"I wanted to know if he could help me. He refused to use his magic." Morgana clenches her fists, but then the expression on her face softens. "He's lonely, just like me. In any case, he understood me better than you."

I nod in agreement. "He *is* lonely. But he chose his own path. Believe me, there were many crossroads where he could have chosen a different path. It could have all gone very differently."

"You are very cold," Morgana says. "We can't all be as pious as King Arthur and Saint Goldilocks."

"You have us," I say, as if I haven't heard her last remark. "You don't have to be lonely. You don't have to make the same mistake as Mordred."

"What do you know of his mistakes?" she snarls.

"Much more than you."

Morgana shakes her head in exasperation. "I don't want to talk about this anymore. I want my sister, that's all. That's the only thing I want."

"I don't think Arthur has given up on her yet, you know. He doesn't just leave people behind. Give him time to think of a new plan. He won't forget Olwen."

"Let's hope it's not too late by then," Morgana says bitterly.

The rest of the night, she sits silently by the fire, staring at the plain beyond the glow of light. When darkness, as always, gives way to a grey day, we get up and walk on. The aching feeling tugging at the edges of my consciousness becomes harder and harder to ignore.

"Nim?"

Arthur's worried voice makes me look up. Inadvertently, I slow down.

"Is something wrong?"

"I don't know." As if by themselves, my hands go to my stomach. "Nánná said I could experience pain..."

"Look!" Val points to the sky. A snow-white swan is circling above us. Its wings cast a shadow onto my face. I gasp when it suddenly lands at my feet. Up close, its beak is bigger and sharper than I thought possible. Its eyes look straight into mine. Bright eyes, like pools of water full of starlight. I stand frozen. And then the swan's long neck shoots out and sticks its beak into my belly like a dagger.

My breath falters. The pain flares up like a sudden flame and I'm carried away by it. My body – my real body – is pulling my mind back as if I'm suddenly seized by gravity.

28

THE WHITE CHILD

"There she is again. She's back! Take a deep breath, Nimue. Deeply exhale."

Yannick leans over me. I see her face through a haze because I'm dizzy from the sudden change. I feel like a meteorite that has crashed to earth. Never before has the landing been such a heavy blow.

When my vision clears, I become aware of Wolf stoking the fire and Nánná being busy with rags and water. They have undressed me from below and pulled my legs wide apart.

"What is happening?" I groan. I peek past my swollen belly to my drawn-up knees and feel the pain go through my lower body like shivers. "What's going on?"

"He's coming, it's happening now," Yannick says, dipping a white cloth into a bowl of steaming water. "You're going to have your baby, Nim."

I shake my head and let out an involuntary cry as another contraction passes through me. "It can't happen yet," I puff. "Arthur and... the tower... and... I'm not ready!"

"Ready or not, he's coming," Yannick says. "You're going as fast as lightning now."

"They say I should breathe with you." Wolf presses his hand against my cheek for a moment. "A deep breath in, then pant..."

"Shark blood, get lost," I groan. "I know how to breathe!"

"It's important that you pay attention to..."

"Shut up," I snarl. "No, wait. Sing..."

"What?"

"Sing that song." I gasp and then try to exhale while panting as best I can. As Wolf hesitantly begins to hum the lullaby, I press my fingers hard into his hand. I think of Gwennec, I think of my own birth in the waves. I squeeze my eyes shut, wishing I could be home again in a flash, and that Mum was with me.

Suddenly, the soft baritone of Wolf's voice falters. I hear Yannick's breath halt too. "Sweet bones of Gwenhael."

"What?" I ask hoarsely, forcing my eyes open. Frightened, I forget to properly breathe out at the next contraction that overwhelms my body. White shreds of mist have entered the tent, almost suffocating the fire. Nánná pushes the tent flap aside. A quick glance outside tells me that something unexpected has happened. Things have changed. There is a new kind of cold in the air. The pine trees have faded, as have the other tents. All I can see is a sea of grey mist. Throughout the camp, dogs start barking. Something is coming out of the mist.

"Gwenhael's bones," Yannick mutters again, startled by the creatures that are making their way to our tent. Most of them are small: hares and rabbits, a few skinny foxes. They move without making a sound and their shapes are almost transparent.

"What *is* this?" Yannick whispers. "Where did they come from?"

"Spirits," Wolf says softly. Next to the tent flap, Nánná starts muttering something between words and song. She recoils as soon as a crow with dull feathers enters the warmth of the tent, followed by a creature that momentarily makes me forget the pain of the contraction. She's still as white as ever, her coat as pure as freshly fallen snow, but her eyes look more tired. The wolf boldly strides past the struggling flames of the fire and stops only when she's right next to me. Up close, her head is bigger than I first thought.

I stare at her. Suddenly I know why they are here. The cold from outside creeps up on me. "You can't have him!"

"It was promised to us." The wolf doesn't move her mouth, only her lips tremble slightly. Yet I can hear her voice as clearly as Yannick's harsh, agitated breathing and Nánná's continuous, low chanting. "A life for a life. You entered into that agreement yourself. We have not forgotten it."

"You're not getting my baby!" I shout, at the same time that the next contraction thunders through me. "Over my dead body!"

"You bear us a holy child," the crow croaks. His voice scrapes over stone like a knife. "Your love for him pales in comparison to the light of his destiny..."

"By Gwenhael's sacred blood and bones," I pant. "If you don't get out of here, I *swear* I'll drag you to the bone cages of the Hunter's Nest, where you'll never see daylight again!"

I don't know how I could ever follow through on that threat, but I do know that somewhere inside me is a hidden vestige of power that is now swelling to a towering wave spurred on by my anger and my pain. Perhaps the two spirits notice this, because they're backing away.

I have no time for a second angry outburst. It feels like my body is trying to push out a whole sea and I have no choice but to surrender to it. My head falls back and one moan after another leaves my mouth.

Suddenly, Yannick and Wolf are at my side again. "Keep breathing," my friend instructs me. "He's coming fast. He's so fast! Push, Nimue!"

I'm breathing and pushing. I'm completely wrapped up in the pain and the rapture of the moment.

Wolf lets out a cry and Yannick gasps. "I've got him, he's coming out! Don't stop now, push him out!"

She doesn't need to tell me that. I push like the rising tide. There is blood. I utter a wordless cry. Something comes out of me.

So abruptly that it is shocking, I feel the baby leave me. I feel something warm and wet between my legs, followed by the sudden decrease of pain. Silence ensues. I gasp. Where is that first cry? Why does nobody say anything?

I open my eyes and see Wolf's deathly frightened face. Yannick is holding my baby. The baby is as small as a cat. He shouldn't be this small, an exhausted part of my brain realises. And he shouldn't be so quiet. Also, I have never seen a baby with the skin colour of white seashells and pearl.

"Oh, Gwenhael," I groan. "He's dead."

My world is falling apart so fast that I think it will turn black before my eyes. I start shivering violently. Nánná has finally stopped her invocations, pulls my shirt down and draws a blanket up to my chest. It doesn't help me at all.

"He's not dead." The white wolf speaks in the silence, a reminder that she and her companion are watching me. "Let him cry and he will begin to breathe life."

Yannick jerks herself out of her startled silence and slaps the child on the back. And to my wordless relief, the child suddenly starts to move. He opens his mouth and lets out a plaintive cry.

Wolf begins to laugh, as sweat and tears drip from his face. He dips a piece of cloth into a bowl of warm water and gently pats the baby clean.

I can't stop shivering, but that's no longer important. There he is – a very pale boy. Naked and small, but breathing and crying. Despite my exhaustion, I try to sit up. When Nánná stops me with a clucking tongue, I stretch out my arms longingly.

"You'll get to hold him in a minute, love," Yannick says. Her sideways glance at the spirits sitting like sentries at the entrance to the tent doesn't escape me. She wraps my son in soft white cloths, which make him look even paler. With an expression bordering on awe, she then kneels beside me to surrender the child to my breast. "Your son."

The moment I am holding that small, warm creature in my arms, something awakens inside me that I have never felt before. While the outside world may be dying in mist and fog in this moment, the sun inside me is born again. My son has a little bit of hair, thin and soft like dandelion fluff. His lips are minuscule and perfectly formed, and a deep instinct already guides him to make gentle sucking movements.

"Is he healthy?" I whisper.

"He... he seems..." Yannick doesn't seem to know what to say.

"He is... white," Wolf says. He bends down and strokes his child's soft cheek with a calloused finger. "As the messengers of the spirits have always been. The little boy is healthy and well, dear."

I shudder and press my face against that warm bundle. "He is beautiful. He is ours alone."

"The White Prophet belongs to no one." The white wolf stiffly rises to her feet and approaches silently from the other side of the fire. "He is a creature of the in-between-world and swears his allegiance as much to this world as to ours. We need him now, daughter of the sea. You too know how much we need him. The Coming King didn't complete his task as well as we had hoped..."

"Have faith in Arthur," I growl. "He's almost there."

"Look at the world outside this tent," the crow says. He jumps onto the back of the wolf. "The mist has won. We all feel it: the Two Worlds have been torn apart. Give us the child, let us teach him, so that the White Prophet can once again be the bridge between the worlds. If you refuse, we will be separated forever. The mist will drive us apart. You will never see your brother again."

"What about the Fisher King?" I whisper, with a sick feeling in my stomach. "Once he is resurrected…"

"The Fisher King is dead." That is the wolf speaking. "He has breathed his last. If you want proof, look at the mist. It's done, child of the sea. Your brother is late, he has failed. Our king is dead." She bows her big, white head. The gesture is as sad as it is human. "So believe us when we say there is only one way to save our common future: the White Prophet could finally be the balm on the wounds the Hunter has inflicted on us. Yes, if times were better, there would have been two – a Fisher King and a White Prophet – to keep the Two Worlds in balance. King and Prophet, one to rule, one to mediate. Now one has been taken from us; so do not refuse us the other."

"Spirits." Somehow, Wolf has managed to subtly position himself between me and the two creatures. Although his voice is soft, the words he speaks are hard. "I mourn with you. But I would rather see the Other World crumble than give you my son."

"Who says we're giving you a choice?" growls the White Wolf. Her lips pull up to reveal her gleaming teeth. "We have come to take the child. That is how it was promised."

"You have no power to negotiate or to threaten," Wolf says. "You are already fading away."

With a speed I had not expected from her stiff limbs, the wolf leaps past him. She stands over me and opens her jaws. Her teeth snap at the cloth wrapped around my baby.

I act from instinct. The magic in my blood fizzes when my fingers dig into the white fur on her head. With that power, I force her heart to skip a beat, and another. I demand that her lungs cramp, that her blood congeals in her veins. The wolf whimpers and shrinks back. My hand feels limp and falls back on the blankets. That was transformation in the most gruesome and cruel way. But it has worked. The wolf trembles, shakes, becomes duller. I recognise the process: this is how my Dream body wavers whenever I struggle to stay in the Other World. The crow doesn't have the strength or courage to approach me. Within a single sigh and one blink of my tired eyes, all the spirits have disappeared.

Gone for good. The thought hits me right away. I have defeated the little strength they had left. They have faded away, and I doubt that even Gwenhael knows what their fate will be.

Yannick pushes the tent flap aside and looks out. She has turned three shades paler. I can see past her shoulder and look at what she sees: a world covered by impenetrable fog, which is cold and grey and envelopes us all.

"I don't think the sun will penetrate that," Yannick says solemnly. "Everything will wither away."

"It's never impossible for the light to return," I murmur, my eyes fixed on the sleepy face of my newborn son. Again, it hits me how tiny he is, how his skin seems to be made of perfect white porcelain. No wonder Wolf and Yannick were horrified when he came out. And I have to admit that the boy looks strange – more spirit than man, perhaps. At the same time, he's the most beautiful creature I have ever seen.

"I'm afraid Yannick is right," Wolf says quietly. "The gates have closed. The worlds have separated. I doubt you will even dream of Arthur again." He looks tired and sad. "My dear, I'm afraid the story is over. The song is over. And you need to…"

I seek his hand with mine. "When the song is finished, we will start a new one."

He sighs and shakes his head. "You need to rest. You and our little son both need sleep and peace."

"We can rest when the world is safe." I don't really know where I'll get my strength from, nor what I can actually do, if it is true that the Fisher King has died. I just can't accept a defeat that would cost me my brother and my future, both on the same day, so I insist: "I don't want it to be too late, Wolf. What good is it going to do our son if we give up now? The trees will shed their leaves, the animals will die. The Hunter wins everything and leaves nothing for us – only darkness!"

He is silent. Next to him, Yannick has wrapped her arms around herself and is slowly rocking back and forth by the fire.

One last try. I clear my throat, but my raw, abrasive voice remains. "For the sake of everything we love. For Gwenhael's blood and bones, don't we owe it to everyone we left behind in the town? And for the refugees in Brevalaer. For the victims of the Black Influenza, all over Central Europe. For your family in Gwennec, Yannick, and for mine on Avalon. For my brother." My words linger for a moment. My son lets out a soft cry, his mouth searching for something to suck on. Instinctively, I put him to my breast. I don't have to think about it. We both know exactly what to do – I give him the milk that will nourish him, he will drink and grow. My gaze stays on my child as I continue: "When Nánná forced me into that first trance, I learned a lesson: the sun can rise from the depths, life can return to dead soil. I have seen the true heart of the Hunter. I know there is still a way to move forward... I'm sure I can find a path, just a little while longer, while the gate hasn't quite closed.... I can't let the worlds drift apart, Wolf. And... I can't leave Arthur alone."

"Nimue." A bit of desperation is evident behind Wolf's tender gaze as he kneels down beside me and cups my cheek with his hand. "You are a young mother, my love. There is nothing you can do for the outside world and the spirits. Let this burden be taken away from you. It's time you went to sleep."

I caress the back of his hand and smile at him. My Wolf – the first voice I heard on the other side of the cell wall, the man who turned my life upside down. How I will miss him. "You're right," I tell him softly. "I will sleep and you will watch our baby."

"Of course," he mumbles. "Of course I'll look after you. Now rest. You are safe."

It is a relief to be able to lower my heavy eyelids. I let Wolf gently cover me with blankets and furs. The warmth of my child on my chest is comforting. His life, that has sprung from my life. His life, that I have cradled with my own body for nine moons. His life, which is short, is already a thousand times dearer to me than my own. For him, I will make this last journey. The gap between the worlds, which I feel somewhere in the depths of my mind, is growing as narrow as the cut made by a sharpened knife. If I don't go now, the gate will truly be closed.

So there it is; suddenly and without a farewell or one last kiss, I must go. I make myself small, breathe deeply and let go of my body.

Most of all, I wish I could say some last words, something my son would remember me by when he's older. But how could I explain my love? How do I explain that I'm leaving him with the purpose of giving him every opportunity in life? That I'm voluntarily leaving him in order to complete a mission that will almost certainly take me the rest of my life?

As my mind slips through that final opening, the words suddenly come to mind: *Know that my devotion has never wavered, that the love I have for you is as true as the north star and as steady as the tides of the sea. Never in my life have*

I loved anything as deeply as you, and I cling to the knowledge that nothing, no storm and no darkness, can ever take that away from me.

Be strong and brave, my little star. And above all, be safe in a world at peace.

I wish I could whisper them in his ear, but my mind is already far away, close to the tower of the Fisher King; a tower besieged on all sides by suffocating mist, and by the bloodthirsty creations of the Hunter.

29

THE BROTHER

The Hunter has gathered an army. With flashing teeth and snarling lips, they attack the tower.

"The Fisher King is dead!" It is a fierce cry of triumph, rising again and again above the din. "The throne is empty! The crown has fallen! Bring down the tower!"

The spirits arch their backs, saliva dripping from their blood-red tongues. Some of them look like huge bloodhounds, while others are so distorted that it's impossible to tell what animal they once resembled. I see horns and pointed tails that shatter the stones. I see beasts with their entire ribcages exposed, as if their bodies begun to rot after the Hunter destroyed their souls. They attack the tower in an insane frenzy and all this violence makes the ancient walls groan and tremble. On the south side, the roof has collapsed and part of the wall below has fallen away, revealing the stairwell.

Above the noise of falling stones, I hear someone shouting an order. However hoarse he sounds, I would recognise that voice anywhere: Arthur.

I can't see him, but at least he's alive. I take a moment to gather strength and courage. Until now, I have managed to stay unnoticed but that changes as soon as I force myself forward. Immediately, the hunter's dogs are on top of me, their saliva gleaming on their lips.

"Stop!" I shout. "Don't touch me! I want to see the Hunter!"

I put my hands in the air to show that I'm unarmed. The spirits lock me in, push against me. I feel teeth clenching around my legs. I breathe deeply to stay calm and their rotting breath instantly enters my senses.

"I have come for your master," I say, half gagging. "I have what he wants: my magic."

A humanoid creature pushes forward past the bloodhounds. His skin is black as a shadow, only his eyes are light. As he approaches, the sickening smell of sulphur seeps into my nose.

"You are his enemy," he says in a voice that reminds me of the crackling of flames in a hearth. "Why would you bring him your magic?"

"Because I want to live," I reply. I don't have to pretend to be trembling with fear. I force my eyes to stay on the shadow man, not to avert my gaze. The spirits growl low near my legs. They must be able to smell my fear like blood. I know they will catch me if I try to run away. "And I want to save my brother. I have come to trade my magic for our lives."

The shadow man hisses slowly. "The witch is a coward."

"Yes!" I agree breathlessly. The stench starts to give me a headache. "I am a coward, but I have what the Hunter wants."

The hissing turns into something that might be meant as laughter. "He will come."

"Let me through." I take a step forward and notice that they don't grab me. My hand accidentally rubs against one of the spirits. I feel his dead flesh under the fingertips of my Dream body and shudder. The Hunter's slaves are nothing more than moving carcasses, fed by the flames of his hatred. But my words have an effect: where I walk, a narrow passage is being created. As long as I still have the magic, they dare not harm me. I wonder if the Hunter is inside the tower. Does he know I'm coming? It doesn't matter. The Hunter and his spirits are one big organism – now that I have shown myself, it won't be long before the Hunter finds me. By the bones of Saint Gwenhael, let him come.

I'm almost at the tower when I hear Arthur again. His voice is not coming from inside, but from further away on the north side. The spirits have driven them into a corner, behind a meagre shelter of fallen stones. GWN and Green do their best with their spears and torches, Lance hitting creatures from left to right, dealing a blow with his weapon here, then letting the stone blade fly through the air next. My brother manages to squeeze himself between two huge fragments of stone and thrusts his knife forward. The steel sinks into the flesh of the bloodhound coming at him as easily as a knife cutting through the soft underbelly of a fish. The spirit stumbles and Arthur pulls back with a shudder, but not in time to avoid a second spirit from hitting him. The creature has the build of a bull, its horns sticking out like two spears. I shout a warning and run forward, ducking under the trampling forelegs of a bear-like spirit and feeling the tips of its claws hook themselves into my hair. I thank Gwenhael that I'm faster than he is, and reach the bull at full speed.

"*Seolh uu-la!*" It's more of a shout than a chant, but I feel my transforming magic pouring over him like a wave. As Arthur drops, the huge beast shrinks to the size of a hare. I hook my arms under Arthur's armpits and pull him away, back behind the piled-up stones.

"You're back?" Arthur asks, dazed. He rubs his damaged leg.

"Are you hurt?" I ask. "Is it deep? Let me see."

He pushes my hands away from him. "It's just scratches. Shark blood, Nim, I can't keep track of when you're there or not."

"Don't break your head over it," I say. "From now on I will stay with you. Is everyone unharmed?"

Goldilocks crouches down with her back against the stone wall and rubs shiny sweat and mud from her forehead. She looks as battered as my little brother.

"We can't keep this up," she pants. "There are too many of them."

"The tower has collapsed," I say. "The opening is too small for the spirits, but you would fit through it."

"We tried to get to the hole." Goldilocks shakes her head. "There are too many of them. I've already lost my weapons and so has Morgana."

"We're stuck," Arthur sighs. He stares at his blood-stained knife.

"Get up," I say. "Stay close to me. Keep your weapons ready, but don't attack unless you have to. I will get you into the tower."

"How?" Morgana asks, who until now has been watching in silence, from behind a piece of stone not much higher than herself. Her normally dark skin has turned white and her eyes have lost their fire. Even her usual snarl doesn't sound convincing. "This is the end. And they're screaming that the Fisher King is dead, so what are we doing it all for?"

"Come and stand behind me." I take a deep breath, raise my hands and start chanting my short spell again. The bloodhounds and shadow creatures blocking the way to the tower let out deep sounds from their throats. If I didn't know better, I'd think they were afraid of my power.

It doesn't matter. Afraid or not, intelligent beings or dumb soldiers, they have to make way for me.

"Why don't they attack you?" Arthur breathes in my ear.

"They know I have come for the Hunter." I keep my gaze fixed on the hole in the tower. When we make it behind the protective walls, I dare to breathe again. "Hurry up. To the opening, to the stairwell! I'll follow."

Arthur's eyes remain wide open as he grabs Goldilocks' hand and pulls her through the hole, followed by the boys.

Morgana slips past me last, but she stops as soon as she reaches the other side of the wall. She whispers: "You *called* for the Hunter?"

"Go upstairs," I hiss back.

The stairwell is long and narrow. By the time we reach the last step, I have to lean against the wall to catch my breath.

"Nim?" Arthur asks.

"Don't worry." It's only recently that my real body has had a very different kind of struggle, I remind myself. I don't have the energy I would like to have for my plan. With a soft groan, I straighten again. The good news is that we have a head start, although the clamouring coming from below continues unabated. The floor beneath my feet trembles with every jolt that passes through the tower.

The bad news is that the roof has come down over our heads. The landing leads to only one place, and that is a solid wooden door, now blocked by stones and gravel. A little light comes in through the broken roof, and at the same time, fog patches meander down the stones. It's as if the mist has come to life and is now seeking out the weak spots in the rock.

Arthur starts pushing stones aside. I see how he tries to keep the weight off his leg, even though he doesn't complain about the pain that the horned spirit must have caused. Val and Green put their weight against a piece of stone that reaches up to their shoulders. No matter how hard they push, they can't get it to move.

"The stones are blocked by something." Lance leans against the wall and rubs his left eye. His eyelid is still thick, swollen and dark, and he has scratches across his forehead and cheek that look inflamed. "We have to dig from the other side."

Arthur stops pushing. "You're right. If we can get the door open, the heaviest stones might roll in. Goldilocks, will you fit through the gap?"

Goldilocks studies the narrow opening through which the light is coming. "I think so."

She brushes her messy strands away from her face and crawls under the heavy stones. I hear her cursing before she exclaims: "I need help pushing!"

"I'm coming," I say. "Morgana?"

Morgana nods.

"Nim, wait." Arthur thrusts something into my hands: a knife, like the ones Morgana and Goldilocks have – not made of steel. but carved out of stone. "Just in case."

"Give us the Grail," Morgana says unexpectedly. She's silent for a moment, and in that silence we hear the triumphal cries of the spirits approaching. Their cries echo from within the walls of the tower. "We don't have much time."

If Arthur hesitates at all, he doesn't take long. He pulls the copper goblet from his belt, his hand on top of the chalice to protect the splash of blood in it. Morgana yanks it out of his hands. "We'll be quick."

Lance aims his spear at the dark opening of the stairwell. I see no movement, but the sounds are getting louder.

Without wasting time, Morgana and I push ourselves through the narrow gap between the stones. Goldilocks throws her entire weight against the door. I push her aside, place my hands on the wood and whisper the words of transformation. A deep groan comes from the wood and a moment later, the door pops open. Like a small avalanche, stones come tumbling down, but two massive blocks remain in place.

Inside, the tower is as I remember it from my earliest journey to the Other World: the round room, the bare stones, the cold wind coming in through a single window and yet manages to chill the whole room. The stone throne, with its back to us and facing the window, so that the king could look out over a once flowering plain. The iron chains attached to the base of the throne are also exactly as I remember them. The fact that my cousin is standing in front of the throne, flanked by three of the Hunter's bloodhounds, is something I didn't expect, however.

He stands with spread hands wide beside the throne of the Fisher King. Flames come to life in his palms, licking along his fingers. His face doesn't betray any pain. I doubt if he feels the heat. I wonder if he feels anything at all.

"How did you get in?" I say.

"I was there before the stones came down."

"You are a traitor!" Goldilocks says furiously.

"I didn't want to be here."

I spit on the ground. "Then go! I promise we won't stop you."

"I can't do that, Nimue. Not until my job is done."

At the door, Goldilocks unexpectedly lets out a shout. "Nimue, they are fighting!"

I turn around and become aware of the noise behind the blocked door. Arthur's voice rings out above the clatter of stone weapons: "Save the Fisher King!"

Morgana takes three steps towards the throne, her fist clasped around the Grail. In the pale light coming through the tower window, I see the blood glistening. Mordred spreads his fingers and suddenly he is the centre of a sea of flames. His clothes bulge in the heat, the same heat that hits me in the face and forces Morgana backwards.

"Don't be a fool, Morgana," he warns. "You know what will happen."

Morgana stands frozen, the Grail in her trembling hand. She must feel the fire searing her skin.

Someone is screaming in pain. Lance?

"They are blocked from reaching the door," Goldilocks says in a trembling voice. She stares at the stones that are still standing. "They are being pushed back. The spirits are coming..." Suddenly, she slams the door shut.

"Goldilocks!" I shout. "You need to keep them out!"

Guilt and fear are visibly warring for precedence on her face, but she remains, her back pressed against the door to keep it shut. "You heard what Arthur said. Save the Fisher King."

"Morgana!" Mordred's warning draws my attention. Morgana has taken another step closer to the throne and the flames seem to be creeping in her direction.

"Mordred, get out of the way!" I cross the hall, and the heat from Mordred's flames strike my face. I narrow my eyes. "Please."

"You can't match my magic," Mordred says softly. "You can't walk through fire, Nimue."

No, I cannot. But I have some magic of my own. I start to sing the transformational words, so softly that Mordred can't hear it above the roaring fire. I raise my hands to the licking flames. With each word I sing, the magic flows forth like a cooling stream, but my breaths become heavier with each word. My clothes are sticking to my body drenched in sweat – not just from the heat, but from the exertion. It is as if I'm imposing my will onto a mountain. No transformation has ever been this difficult for me, not even the most complicated cure for the Black Influenza... What is wrong with me?

Mordred growls. I open my eyes and notice that the bright glow has become duller. The heat no longer scorches me as I leap forward and thrust the knife at him. For a moment I feel the resistance of flesh and muscle, then Mordred slumps down. I let go of the knife and get ahold of him.

"Morgana, now!"

A heavy, pounding sound stops her. It's like a thunderstorm right above our heads, or an earthquake shaking the tower.

"Gwenhael save us," I hear Goldilocks whisper. "He's coming."

Mordred pushes me off with surprising force. The pillar of flame around him has died down to smouldering embers. He's bleeding from his abdomen and the sleeves of his already dirty shirt are red and soaked. I half expect him to try to run, but when he moves, it is to walk towards Morgana, with difficulty.

Morgana stares at him before her eyes dart to the door. The Hunter's heavy, sluggish footsteps on the stairs are growing louder, complemented by the clinking sound of iron against stone.

Morgana looks as if she can't breathe. The Grail trembles in her hands.

"Do it, Morgana!" Goldilocks is still pressing herself against the door. She is as white as the dead Fisher King, and she shudders together with the door, that shakes with every step the Hunter takes.

Morgana's eyes go from Mordred to the throne. Why doesn't she move? Is the imminent arrival of the Hunter too much for her frayed nerves? She raises the Grail.

"You still have time," I whisper, clasping my hands around my cousin's arms to contain him. Once, I used my magic to give him back some of his sanity. Maybe I can do it again, maybe I have enough power to pull the thoughts influenced by the Hunter out of him, turn them into the memories that actually belong to himself. The heat of his fire stings my eyes and makes my mouth dry. I continue to stare straight into his eyes and wrap my magic around his entire being, like a giant spider wrapping its web around a fly. I push, I knead, I force him to change shape from inside, as if I were trying my best to shape a hard piece of clay. I push into him and discover that there is indeed still something there –

thin threads of memories, buried under layers of thoughts and feelings that the Hunter has smeared him with.

"Mor... gana..." Mordred grabs his head and sinks to his knees.

The heavy footsteps fade away. Suddenly, it is silent on the other side of the door. And then, with a look as if someone were twisting a dagger in her belly, Morgana throws the Grail to the ground.

The goblet makes a clattering noise against the stones. It leaves a trail of dark red blood as it rolls away and comes to rest against the iron chain of the Fisher King.

A stain of dark red blood on a grey floor. I stare at it in horror, all of my magic forgotten.

Goldilocks begins to scream. Her curses rain down on us. Then the noise of a terrible explosion fills the room and large chunks of stone whizz through the air. Goldilocks is flung backwards, crashing into the floor with a loud thud. I feel a hard blow against my stomach that knocks the air out of my lungs and my eyes instantly go black.

New sounds come to me as I crack my eyes open. My Dream body pulses with pain. A dirty hand presses against my mouth, muffling my moan.

"Sssh." Goldilocks' mouth is close to my ear.

I roll from my back onto my side and open my eyes wide. I'm looking at the feet of the dead Fisher King. Somehow, I ended up behind the tall, stone throne. Perhaps Goldilocks dragged me here. The girl has bleeding scratches all over her face, but she doesn't seem to have suffered anything else. My gaze travels up the poor excuse for cover that is the throne.

The Hunter stands as a hunched figure in the middle of the room, accompanied by three bloodhounds and three shadow creatures, and a small figure bound in heavy chains. Where there used to be a door is now only a large hole leading to the stairwell, and all the stones that blocked the passage have been hurled effortlessly through the entire throne room. I hear the scraping of footsteps, and a moment later, my brother, Lance, GWN, and Val are spilling into the room. Arthur has his arm pressed to his side, but the knife is still in his other hand. Lance aims his spear at the Hunter. The Hunter rises to his full height. His grin stretches from ear to ear, the rows of teeth so much sharper than the stone knives my friends are carrying. His tongue slowly licks his lips, ready to taste blood.

His spirits position themselves at the door like guards. No way out, unless we want to throw ourselves out of the window.

I scramble halfway up, ready to come out from behind the throne. Goldilocks grabs hold of me.

"Are you crazy?" she hisses. "Stay down!"

"This is my fight," I whisper. "Let go of me."

She clasps her hands around my wrists and holds me with unexpected strength.

The Hunter's voice easily reaches every corner of the room. "Where is the sea witch? She wanted to see me and I have come. Where is she?"

Before I can do anything, Morgana suddenly screams. Her scream pierces the bone: "I did what you said! Give Olwen back to me!"

The Hunter turns to her. He lets out a barking laugh.

A feverish fire burns in Morgana's eyes, as if she is delirious. She raises a trembling finger. "I have broken the Grail. Now you will give me Olwen back. That was the deal!"

I feel Goldilocks pressing against me, her frail body as tense as the string of a bow.

"But of course," the Hunter says. "You've earned her."

He gives a tug on the chain. The small figure stumbles forward. Olwen looks worse than the last time I saw her. Her face is so sunken that I can see the outlines of her skull, her hair is a matted tangle full of dirt and snags, and her hands, now groping the stone floor in an attempt to push herself up, are caked with dirt. A few fingers look broken.

I watch as Morgana's face changes from hope to horror as the Hunter drags the girl up and flings her into the air. Olwen lets out a scream that fills the whole room. The Hunter's claws snatch her out of the air, he yanks her head back and wraps his jaws around her throat.

The scream stops immediately.

A moment later, the limp body falls back to the floor with a dull thud. Her blood glistens on the stones. It's dripping from the Hunter's lips.

I can't bring myself to look at the body, so I stare at Morgana. She's rooted to the spot and has turned the colour of ash. I want to shake her. Did she *really* think she could make a deal with this monster? The Hunter takes pleasure in death. I could have told her that weeks ago. She should've known. She should have...

Morgana opens her mouth and starts screaming. It's the scream of a wild animal in a desperate rage. She flies forward so fast that it catches me off guard. Not towards Olwen's body, but towards the Hunter.

Her body slams into his and she attacks him with her nails, her teeth, her fists. The Hunter laughs and throws her to the ground. She lands hard on her back, but pushes herself up again and launches a second attack, apparently oblivious to the blood running down her face. She is like a bird fighting a bear.

When Morgana is thrown backwards for the third time, I hear something snapping inside her body. This time, she doesn't get up. The Hunter grins and takes a step towards her.

"Enough!" My brother lets out a furious cry and rushes at the Hunter, his knife thrust forward. He's followed on his heels by Lance, GWN, and Val.

"Goldilocks, you have to let go of me." I pry at her fingers around my wrist.

"He'll kill us all," Goldilocks hisses. "Unless Arthur wins."

"He won't kill me as long as I have what he wants." I begin to pick at the fingers of her other hand. It's as if Goldilocks' hands are frozen solid. "But he'll kill Arthur if you don't let me go."

I push Goldilocks to the ground, against the legs of the Fisher King, and press my finger against her lips. She looks scared and confused. I take a deep breath, grab the armrest of the throne and pull myself upright. For a moment, the whole throne room trembles before my eyes as I try to take in the situation. Val, GWN, and Green are fighting for their lives against the shadow creatures. Arthur and Lance circle the Hunter in a dizzying dance, Val is thrown backwards, hitting the floor with a smack...

Mordred staggers towards me, blocking my view of Arthur and grabbing me hard. "What have you done? What witchcraft have you unleashed on me?"

I can easily pull his hands off me. He falls to his knees again and I step past him. He must have known that Morgana made a deal with the Hunter, it occurs to me. He helped her... That rotten fish. First he was Benji's puppet and now the Hunter is tugging at his strings. Meanwhile, my brother has landed on the floor, groaning. His arms and head are covered in blood. For a moment I'm filled with cold horror, then I feel a hot rage boiling in my stomach. I fill my lungs with air. "Hunter!"

The Hunter turns to me. His back and shoulders are hunched, like a cat about to pounce on its prey. I raise my hands in the air and step over Arthur's legs. My Dream body has become pale, I notice when I see my own hands. I'm tired, exhausted. But I must keep up my strength. My brother raises his face to me and mumbles something.

"Here I am!" I say. "Stop the fight. Negotiate with me." With my arms spread wide, I'm a laughable obstacle between the Hunter and his prey. It's no wonder that he laughs out loud and holds out a long, pointed finger at me.

"The sea witch has come to beg for her life?"

"Not for my own life," I growl.

"Give up. You have already wasted all of your strength."

"Not everything." I raise my hands slightly higher. "You want my magic? I'm willing to give you what you want."

"And why would you give me that?" the Hunter growls. With his back hunched, he slinks closer. All his eyes are fixed on my raised hands, palms facing forwards.

"Because you will let my brother live." It takes all of my willpower not to shuffle backwards. My Dream body pulls at me, as if it wants nothing more than to hurl me back into my own reality before something can happen to me. But the portal between the worlds has closed. I breathe in and out. "You let my brother and all his friends live."

"Spare the vermin?" The Hunter's lips curl up into a grin. "Why not? I give you all their lives, except that of the Coming King."

He shoots past me faster than a spear and snatches Arthur off the ground. My brother lets out a cry that penetrates my very bones. Arthur is in the Hunter's clutches, his feet dangling helplessly above the floor.

"Let him go!" I try to grab Arthur's feet. "My brother stays alive, or our deal is off! Think what you are doing, Hunter! I'll give you what you want, everyone else stays out of this. That's my final offer. Let Arthur go!"

The Hunter runs the tip of his tongue across his lips. For a moment he stands motionless, his head tilted. His claws dig into Arthur's belly and I hear a deep groan come out him. The Hunter lifts him even higher and then throws him down hard. My little brother rolls like a limp doll across the stone floor and only comes to a stop when he hits the broken stones in one corner of the hall.

For a moment, I'm weighed down by a heavy, oppressive feeling as I look around me. Lance is on his knees, his weapon broken in two. He has his arms clasped to his chest and is breathing heavily. Val is lying on his side with his face turned away from me. GWN is leaning on the broken half of Lance' spear in an attempt to keep himself upright and fends off a bloodhound with his other arm. Goldilocks is still kneeling before the Fisher King, her head close to his chest. Her fingers are fidgeting with the Grail.

"Now then." The Hunter lowers himself until I can almost look him straight in the eyes. "Show me your magic. Witch."

By Gwenhael, he will see more of my magic than he would have ever liked. I turn my palms towards him again. "Remember, before you eat me, you must know the words."

"Say the spell," he growls.

I spread my fingers and point them in his direction. If I take one more step, I might be able to touch him. Despite my exhaustion, my magic flows through me like a bubbling river. I can feel it pressing against my skin, ready to submerge the Hunter and myself completely. I wasn't lying when I said that the Hunter could have my life: what I'm planning to do could very well take my very last bits of energy.

"Not yet," I say. "I have one last wish."

A shudder goes through me as his face presses against mine. "A wish, you say? What could be so urgent on death's doorstep?"

"I want to tell you a story," I whisper, without hiding my disgust. "It's called The Darkness and the Sea..."

The Hunter freezes. I see something cross his distorted face: shock, and something that looks like momentary fear. Then his face contorts with rage. "Say the spell, *witch*!"

I laugh, loud and hoarse. Slowly, almost tauntingly, I let the spell roll from my lips: "*Seolh uu-la...*"

He dives at me like an eagle. I brace myself to throw my magic into him like a spear. Sharp claws hook into my back and the back of my head. Hot pain shoots through me as I feel myself being pulled up and for a moment, everything goes black before my eyes.

Someone close to me lets out a loud roar. The heat of the fire hits me and a moment later, I am crashing to the floor. The Hunter's weight on me has disappeared. His furious sounds pound against my eardrums. I recognise Mordred's voice. If he is shouting words at all, they are lost in the roar of the flames he has poured out over us. I roll backwards, towards Arthur in the far corner.

"Nim!" He has regained consciousness and shakes my shoulder.

I groan. The magic churns through my body without an outlet. It seems to be mashing my bones and muscles together. I should have caught the Hunter with it... I was ready for it... What happened?

"Look at the Hunter," Arthur whispers.

I roll over onto my side and scramble to my feet. Flames rise up from the Hunter's body. For a brief moment I think this is his latest, hideous trick. But then his pained cries become evident and I realise that the Hunter, like all his creations, detests fire.

Like a vengeful god, Mordred stands before him, bathing in a sea of flickering flames. They lick at his clothes, at his skin, at his hair. He hasn't only set the Hunter on fire – he has conjured a shield of flames between our corner and our enemies.

The Hunter staggers. I behold it in bewilderment. What Arthur and Lance and even I have not managed to do, our nephew has finally done: the Hunter goes down.

Mordred begins to laugh triumphantly. Even as his clothes turn to ashes and the smell of searing flesh fills the room, he's still laughing.

The Hunter shakes his head. His whole body is moving. He shakes off the flames like a dog shakes off water from its fur. Mordred's laughter fades when the Hunter grabs him, sinks his teeth into his unprotected belly and bites through it. When Mordred hit the floor bleeding, the fire around the Hunter extinguishes. Only the protective flames around our corner are still burning.

"He's dead." I hear myself say it, though I barely register it. I feel dazed and confused, and the magic is painfully rushing through my blood vessels. "Arthur," I hiss, when I see him moving forward on his hands and knees. "What are you doing? Sit still!"

Mordred fell down a short distance away from us. Arthur grabs him by the smouldering fray of his shirt and pulls him towards us through the flames. He hisses in pain as the fire scorches him. He kneels down at Mordred's side. There's little left of his handsome face: his eyebrows and eyelashes are singed away, his lips cracked by the heat, his skin cracked by the heat. His skin is bruised and swollen, tinged red. Where Arthur dragged him across the ground, a trail of thick blood followed in his wake.

I look from him to the flames, then to the Hunter behind them, trying to guess why Mordred wasted his last moments when that barricade can only temporarily keep the Hunter off our backs. As soon as the flames die down, I have to be ready to work my magic on him again. It's frustrating that Mordred interrupted my plan, but at the same time, I feel an exhausted sense of relief that I now have at least a few moments to catch my breath.

The last embers die away in Mordred's hands. His fingers are blackened and curl inward.

"He's dead," I say again.

"No, Nim. Look at his mouth."

Mordred's lips move, and a low, broken sound comes from his mouth. His chest trembles and suddenly, he sucks in a gulp of air.

"Sweet Gwenhael," I whisper. "Mordred?"

"Cormack," he groans. "Cormack Cairn."

A bittersweet taste fills my mouth. My magic has worked. It looks as if he's trying to open his eyes. His whole face turns into a painful grimace and eventually, he gives up.

"Why did you do this?" I ask hoarsely.

"You saved me..."

The frayed edges of his shirt are soaked with his own blood. For a while, he breathes in slowly and heavily. Each breath rattles softly. I know that at this moment, blood is rushing into his lungs. I carefully lift his head into my lap and place my hands on his chest. "I can heal you."

Cormack shakes his head. He licks his lips, a movement that seems to cost him a lot of energy. After a while he says: "You have wasted enough of your powers on me."

He is right. My brief respite is rapidly coming to an end. Behind the fire, the Hunter bellows out my name.

"And another thing..." Cormack coughs for a moment. "When you get back, don't look for my body. If I die here, my body will die as well..."

"Oh, Cormack," I mutter. "This is not how it should have gone for us."

His burnt lips part – I don't know if it's a grimace or an attempt at a smile. "Listen, Arthur... Nimue... you have done well. My memories... That I could choose to give my blood for you... I understand my father's words now." A long pause. I lean into him. "We have no choice but to be each other's salvation, he wrote. This should have happened much sooner. Benji should have stood beside his sister. Rona should have stood beside her brother. They should have remained as one, instead of two..." Another pained grimace and a rattling breath. "...bantams. Let my blood take the place of Benji's, so we can repair the breach."

"Cormack," Arthur says. "None of us are coming back. If these flames go out, we go out too."

"No." It is almost a growl. "Be brave. Be smart. Why haven't the two of you thought of this yet..."

"We *were* brave and it wasn't enough," Arthur snarled. "We had the Grail, we had the blood, but you and Morgana betrayed us! How dare you speak of continuing?"

"Arthur," I say softly. "He's right. I had a plan..."

"Listen." Cormack swallows with difficulty. "Brother's blood. Yes? Who is the brother?"

"You know it was the Hunter's blood," Arthur barks. "Only *his* blood could heal the Fisher King..."

Again, Cormack shakes his head. "You don't understand... When there are two brothers, who is the brother of the other?"

Arthur looks annoyed, but I feel as if the wind has finally filled my sails. "Gwenhael's bones! Cormack is right. The Hunter isn't the only brother!"

Arthur looks up. In the ruddy light of the fire, the blood sticking to his face is glistening. "You mean the Fisher King?"

We cannot help but be of help to each other... "Arthur, it may be too late to save the life of the Fisher King, but he has given us the key to defeat his brother."

"The blood of the Fisher King..." Arthur suddenly raises himself higher, his blue eyes wide and round. "If one can exist, the other must perish. He called it blood magic."

I grope around me, find the stainless steel knife smeared with ash and blood on the stone floor, and push it into Arthur's hands. "Before the flames go out, we run through them. The Hunter won't be expecting it. Instead of attacking him, run to the throne. The Grail is still there and Goldilocks can help you. Whatever happens, don't let it stop you. Take his blood, Arthur. Take the last gift of the Fisher King."

"And you?" It's as if it's only now that he realises what I shouted at the Hunter before. He grabs my wrist. "You were going to sacrifice yourself! Nim, you can't mean that. I can't do this without you!"

I look down at Cormack's face. His mouth is half open, as if he wanted to say something. When I hold out my hand, I don't feel his breath. I carefully lay his head on the floor. "If the brother's blood can weaken the Hunter, this may not be my last day."

"Nim..."

"We have to rely on each other. We have to do this together, Arthur."

"We'll do it together." His hand squeezes my cold fingers. "Do I count to three?"

"We need protection," I mutter. If the Hunter sees what Arthur is about to do, he can pounce on him and tear him to pieces before he can plunge his blade into the Fisher King's heart. I look around and my eyes linger on the chunks of fallen stone that the Hunter has thrown around the room. I press my hands flat against them. The transforming words pass my lips more like a deep sigh than a melody, but the material is willing and easy to change. I recall the stone statues of kings in St Gwenhael, the effigies carved into the niches. For a moment, my sight goes black and I don't know what is above or below before my vision becomes clear again. Instead of shapeless boulders, two grey kings stand beside me, armed with shields and swords. I feel a shred of my own awareness nestling in their stone bodies. For a moment it seems as if I'm three people at once – as if I'm looking at the throne room with three different pairs of eyes.

From behind the diminishing flames, I can hear the Hunter laughing mockingly. "What power you have! So much stronger than when I first saw you."

"Count to three," I whisper to Arthur.

He lets go of my hand and stands up. I see the fear in his eyes, but also his determination.

"One," he says.

I, too, scramble to my feet and straighten my aching back. Mordreds flames dance in front of me and the heat gives me strength.

"Two..."

"Hunter!" I shout. "I'm coming."
"Three," Arthur whispers, and leaps the fire.

30

The Last Blood

A wall of hungry flames burn my clothes the moment we leap forward. Blisters appear on the burns I already had, but I can't let that distract me now. It only takes us two leaps before we're out of the heat and away from our last safe haven.

Val's body lies sprawled on the ground. I try not to look at him. Lance and GWN are in the other corner, clearly still alive, but they're hardly moving. I don't have time for them either. Later, I promise myself, when this nightmare is over...

I raise my hands as if I were a magician and let the fire blaze. Despite my instructions, Arthur continues to stare at me as if riveted to the ground. Perhaps he remembers a much younger sister who was barely able to heal herself from the burns of the rain. I'm no longer that old Nimue; I'm a witch, my red curls fluttering in the heat of the fire, along the flames I am forcing to become a closed circle around the Hunter.

The Hunter lets out a hoarse cry and throws himself against the bars of fire. I react by stoking the fire even more, making the flames so high that for a moment, I'm afraid I'll set myself ablaze too. "Arthur!" I call, all the while keeping my focus on what I'm doing. "Keep walking!"

I can tell from his stumbling footsteps that he's running, despite his injured leg.

One of the stone kings remains at my side; I feel his presence like a burning flame of consciousness, as if he's attached to my mind by invisible thread. Without looking, I feel that the other stone king is positioning himself like a guard in front of the throne.

As long as I keep the fire burning high, the Hunter is powerless, but with every second that passes, the flames seem to become more erratic and furious. One false move and I lose control. It doesn't help that my concentration is just as erratic: one moment I'm Nimue, a beat later I'm looking through the eyes of my stone king, another heartbeat later I'm aware of everything that is happening behind the stone guard at the throne.

Arthur has reached the throne and his leg caves beneath him. With a groan and a curse, he drops to the ground.

"Arthur?" Her voice is a soft whisper.

"Goldilocks. Are you hurt?"

She has hidden herself in the lee of the throne, huddled up like a little bird. Her pretty face is covered in bright red scratches.

"A little, not very much. I was lucky." Her blue eyes are wide open. "I saw it all. I heard everything." Her hands are trembling as she presents the Grail to him. It's even dirtier than she is. "You cut open his heart, and I will collect his blood."

"I don't know if he can bleed enough. He has been dead for days."

"Not quite dead," Goldilocks whispers. "I was able to save some of the blood. When Morgana threw the Grail on the floor, a few drops remained. I rubbed them over his heart. He breathed again, Arthur. A few breaths."

Concentrate, Nimue. The fire! I momentarily regain control of myself and notice that the flames are lower. The Hunter motionlessly stares at me, his eyes narrowed. He's waiting for his chance – but so far, I've held him with my power. I dare to loosen my grip a little, to see through the stone guard's eyes what is happening behind me.

The flesh of the Fisher King seems to have turned to stone from his legs up. A deep crack runs from his heart down his chest. The pale eyelids tremble in the ruddy light of the flames that set the throne room ablaze.

"Only a few drops?" Arthur asks. "Was that really enough?"

"Not to bring him back to life," Goldilocks says. "Just to make his heart beat a few times. To make his blood flow." She grabs his hand. "You must do it now, Arthur."

My brother shifts his weight onto his good leg and gets up. The crack running across the Fisher King's chest is deep. Arthur sticks the point of his knife in, right above the heart. His hand trembles slightly and Goldilocks looks a little nauseous as she holds up the goblet.

Arthur thrusts down the blade. The crack splits wide open and blood gushes out. Goldilocks rushes to catch it all. It's only a small cupful. She has barely caught the last drop with the Grail when the petrified body of the Fisher King falls to the ground and shatters into pieces. From my spot by the raging fire, I also hear the sound of stone breaking.

Goldilocks hands the Grail to Arthur.

"It's done," he says hoarsely. "We did what had to be done."

"What had to be done," Goldilocks repeats in a tight voice.

Arthur turns around. "Nimue!"

His voice wakes me from the dreamlike state in which I was looking at him. The flames wrestle themselves out of my grip.

As the fire finally goes out, my strength seems to give out too. The Hunter straightens and comes at me like a giant ablaze. Instinctively, I stumble backwards. His opened maw comes too close; I'm feeling sickened by his rotten breath, and the residual blood of Olwen clinging to it makes me even more nauseous.

"Your tricks are impressive, little witch," he growls. "But you are fragile, and I'm persistent. No matter how strong you are, your strength is nothing more than a spark in the night. And do you know what, little witch? I *am* the night."

Sweet Gwenhael, even the spinning eyeballs in his hands are staring at me. I desperately try to raise the shield of flames again. For a moment they flare up, but I'm too tired and the fire is running wild.

The Hunter is free. With every step he takes forward, he leaves a trail of smouldering embers. My back hits a wall. If only I could catch my breath, gather my strength again...

"Are you struggling, little witch?" the Hunter asks in a sneering tone. "I'm not surprised. Transforming fire must feel like twisting your soul into a thousand knots. You know why, don't you? After all, you get your power from the sea."

Water and fire. I should have known.

Behind the Hunter, half hidden by the smoke, I catch a glimpse of Arthur stealthily moving forward, step by step.

Too late. I'm driven into a corner. My heart begins to beat painfully loud, a last panicked attempt to stay alive. The Hunter is now standing close enough to kill me with a single stroke of his claws.

I want to be brave. I want to defy him with my gaze until the last moment.

The Hunter laughs loudly and curls his claws.

A flash in the corner of my eye – it's the stone king who stayed with me. I had almost forgotten about him. With one jerky movement, he raises his shield and sword and the Hunter's claws and teeth sink into the hard rock instead of my soft Dream body. His rough laughter turns into a furious snarl.

Arthur has almost reached the Hunter's back. The crackling flames make his footsteps inaudible and the stinging smoke probably conceal his smell. He presses a finger to his lips.

Keep still. I must try, for his sake, though every cell in my Dream body is screaming at me to take advantage of this moment and just run.

"How long can you keep this up?" Another step ensures that he's no more than a hand's breadth away from me. My back presses hard against the unyielding wall. "One more minute? Maybe two, if you're prepared to exhaust yourself to death. You are, aren't you? Don't worry, death is coming for you – I'm his missionary. I'll be patient..."

"Death comes to us all," I hear Arthur say.

The Hunter's surprise lasts long enough to make me crouch down and roll away from him. A few feet away, I stand up, panting while I stare at my brother as he pours the contents of the Grail down the Hunter's bent back. The red blood splashes across the sickly grey flesh and sticks to it like thick oil.

The Hunter lets out a startled, low sound. He twists his arm and grabs at his back, as if he suddenly feels an insect biting him. A shudder goes through his whole body. The Hunter clutches at his flesh, scratching and tearing at the red spot, but only ends up pushing the Fisher King's blood deeper into his own flesh.

The sound coming from his throat becomes a scream that rattles my eardrums. Yet I can't immediately tear my eyes away from the scene unfolding before me. I can't run away like Arthur. It's only when the Hunter staggers and falls to the ground like a giant, felled oak that I become aware of my own muscles again. And of Goldilocks, yelling hoarsely, telling us what to do: "All the blood! Use *all* the blood!"

Arthur dips his fingers inside the Grail, runs forward and smears it on the back of the Hunter's head. The Hunter twists his neck like a rabid dog. From here I can see the sharpened teeth sinking into Arthur's sleeve, but the Hunter seems to lack half his strength. When Arthur pulls away his arm and hastily joins me, the Hunter remains where he fell. The blood does what the flames couldn't: the huge body twists and turns in pain and rage.

I know what has to be done now. This is exactly what I have prepared for.

I fix my eyes on our fallen enemy. I feverishly begin to mutter the words that have become familiar to me: *Seolh uu-la....Change.*

"What are you saying?" Arthur whispers.

I ignore him. Again and again, I repeat the spell, lilting and quiet enough for the Hunter not to realise what I'm about to do to him. Fine as silk threads, my selkie magic wraps itself around him. A while longer... A little more... I stop singing, take a deep breath and raise my voice to rise above the Hunter's growling: "If you are the night, I am the voice that summons the sun back into the sky! I am the voice that calls back the light from the deep. You are the darkness, Hunter, but I am the sea that knows a secret which even *you* have forgotten, and it has hidden itself in the deepest part of you."

Merciful Gwenhael and all the good spirits of the sea, I am so tired. I tremble as I speak. I cannot collapse, not yet. I raise my hand and point a finger in the direction of the Hunter.

"Can you hear me?" I shout more loudly. "Because you are dying. I have wrapped you in my magic, Hunter. It's too late to fight me! So listen to me while you die! I'm going to bring you back to life."

31

THE CROWNED FISHERMAN

I hear Arthur's breath hitch. He stares at me, but I have no time or energy to give him an explanation. I take two careful steps towards the writhing Hunter. Even now that he's lying on the ground, he is huge. My magic flows into him. I feel the dark pulse keeping him alive. It's a familiar feeling: these are the tendrils of darkness that wrapped themselves around my mind when I was healing someone. These are the shadows that have tried to poison me for so long. And it is that same poison that is currently battling against the blood of the Fisher King. I don't know what the blood does to him, although I can take a pretty good guess – I know better than anyone how powerful blood magic can be. If my own blood was already able to lift the seal magic spell from my mother, how much more powerful must the blood of the Fisher King be? This is what the old king wanted me to do. In any case, I think I understood, the moment Mordred muttered his last words: the Fisher King has sacrificed his last blood, but someone must still be here to summon the magic.

That someone is me. And I summon it. I reach inside the Hunter, deeper than I ever dared to go and deeper than I thought possible. For a long time, I find nothing except the suffocating darkness that he carries within him. If I hadn't had that one-time encounter with the Hunting Lord, I would have called myself delusional for daring to hope for anything. For daring to believe. And even now, I almost think I've lost my sanity.

From a distance, I'm aware of Arthur calling my name, and a moment later, his leg dragging on the ground as he comes forward and supports me with one strong arm, just as I did for him before. And he's not the only one. I startle when Goldilocks appears at my other side and wraps her arm around my waist as well.

"Go on," she whispers. "We will guard you. We won't let you fall."

301

I fully focus on the Hunter again. And then I discover it – *there*! Like a ray of sunlight breaking through the depths of the water, I catch a glimpse of the Hunter's repressed soul. Like a sculptor, I scrape away the ugly around him and draw out that small core of the Hunter from before.

"Wipe the darkness from your soul," I whisper. "Come back and claim the body that was once yours."

That wafer-thin memory of the Hunter isn't in any hurry to obey me. Just as the Hunter twists and turns on the ground and scratches himself open, so he fights and twists inside himself. But the blood has weakened him. It has sunk deep beneath his skin and penetrates blood vessels that had long ceased to carry blood. It forces the dead heart to remember how to beat. And each beat is long-simmering, intensely painful. I feel that pain as an echo blending with my own senses and take a deep breath. I'm the voice calling the light. I'm the sea that gives birth to new life. I'm the shaman with the gift of the selkies, and my will be done.

My will, not that of the Hunter. Everything he put into me, I give back to him: the attacks of dizziness, the fevers, the dark voices whispering in my head. *Take it all and take it to your grave*, I tell him viciously. *Your power over me has shrunk. It means nothing anymore, and I am free.*

He screams out loud when that knowledge penetrates him too. Shivers run down his grey, rotting skin. On the inside, his heart continues its painful beating because I do not allow it to stop.

"Remember," I command. "You were a gentleman instead of a beast. Break your chains and remember yourself."

Goldilocks gasps for breath. I open my eyes and look at the scene before me. I have finally stumbled upon something that is coming out, something that is now rising to the surface. A creature I recognise, because I've met him before.

First the Hunter's face changes. It twists and melts. Thick, velvety antlers emerge from the Hunter's head like growing branches, until they are almost as long as oars. His whole body contracts, and then briefly catches fire as it comes into contact with the last, dying flames. It looks painful. And because I feel the echoes of that pain, I pull myself back, safe within my own body. My legs are like two reeds in a storm. If it weren't for Arthur and Goldilocks, I would never have lasted this long without keeling over.

Slowly, as he tests the control of his muscles and joints, the large body on the floor rises to its full height. The strange face twitches convulsively, as if every movement hurts him. He lets his golden eyes wander through the throne room, past our friends in various corners of the room, across Mordred's cramped body next to the chunks of stone and Morgana's huddled figure. past the empty throne and the now useless chains. Finally, he looks at the broken Fisher King on the floor.

At last, the Hunting Lord turns towards us. I can read the sadness on his face. "It seems that my brother is no longer with us."

Goldilocks finds her voice before we can: "Who are you?"

"Once, I was known as the Hunting Lord, Prince of the East. Brother to the Fisher King."

"I heard that there was a spirit once," Goldilocks whispers. "Someone who got cursed and lost his mind."

"You were not far off."

Goldilocks looks from him to the broken Fisher King. "Can't you do anything at all to save him?"

The Hunting Lord slowly shakes his head. "No power in the Two Worlds is capable of fixing broken stone."

"Nimue has magic. Can't you try...?"

I, too, shake my head. "Katell, my magic doesn't bring back life when that life is already gone."

Goldilocks takes a step towards the empty throne and sinks to her knees. She seems as exhausted as she is sad. "He saved my life and I promised him we would save his."

"We did what we could," Arthur says softly. "Goldilocks, you didn't let him down. I think the Fisher King knew what he was sacrificing. He was a wise king, and very gentle. He wouldn't have been angry with us."

Goldilocks touches a piece of stone bearing the image of the head of the Fisher King. Stone splinters have come away from the face, especially around the nose, lips and forehead. In that sense, he suddenly looks very much like the weather-beaten effigies of kings and saints of St Gwenhael. They too are nothing more than memories entrusted to stone, so that we may remember their courage and wisdom.

Goldilocks interrupts my thoughts with her own. "This world needs the Fisher King. He's the one who protected the land and kept everything healthy. Without him, nothing will change… the world will still be dead." She looks up at the Hunting Lord. "That's right, isn't it?"

"No need to despair, little soul," he says softly. "Have you forgotten that there's another king with you? A king who has been tested for his loyalty, his courage and compassion. In his wisdom, my brother had already lent him his crown. Now it's time for him to wear it as his own."

I had almost forgotten all that. I notice that I'm not sure of what I feel exactly when I turn around and look at my brother. It could be due to the gloomy light in the tower, but he seems to have gone grey.

"The Coming King," the Hunting Lord says, apparently unaware of the effect of his words. "Now your time has come."

Arthur swallows. His eyes have taken on the colour of dark berries; I sense that the stony expression on his face conceals a storm of worry in this moment. In another corner of the throne room, Lance scrambles to his feet and limps towards us, clutching one of his arms tightly to his chest. As soon as he's standing next to Arthur, he heavily drops his uninjured hand on Arthur's shoulder. It seems as much a reassurance as an attempt to keep himself balanced.

"Arthur?" Goldilocks whispers, as my brother's silence grows uncomfortably long.

Arthur looks at me.

"My brother doesn't belong here," I say. "None of these people really belong here. They have all been robbed of their homes, of their own bodies…"

"And that was a cruel act, a mockery of the balance of the Worlds," the Hunting Lord responds. "There aren't many who have survived that process. Those who did, have learned to adapt. They're not so different from my own kind anymore.'

"Goldilocks," Arthur says hoarsely. "Give me the crown."

Goldilocks reaches into the dingy bag she wears around her waist and pulls out the golden crown. Arthur takes it, but holds it out almost imploringly. No one makes an attempt to take it. Arthur clears his throat.

"I swore to do my best for the Fisher King. Only I failed and couldn't save his life. If I have to pay a price for that, I will. But I have never been a king." He looks at us one by one. "I never dreamed of putting this crown on my own head,

I never thought of sitting on that throne. The more I remember of my old life, the more I know what I'm not." He pauses. "My sister is the one who was given all the gifts. She's powerful, full of magic. I'm just a fisherboy."

"You're not a boy anymore," the Hunting Lord says. "A fisherman? Yes. And now you are a king."

"There must be someone else who can do it!" Arthur looks at Lance, then at Goldilocks. "Maybe one of you."

The Hunting Lord lets out a sigh. He takes the crown from Arthur's hands. "My brother chose you as his successor many months ago. You may oppose it if you wish. But if you do, consider the consequences of refusing. We have two worlds – one for my kind, and one for yours. Like you and your sister, like me and my brother, our worlds are related. None could live if the other were to perish. When my brother was Fisher King, he ensured the fertility and safety of this land; he was the pillar on which the world rested. Without the Fisher King, the land will remain as it is now and everything will slowly wither away. You ask: are there no others who can take up this task? I tell you now, young man: our worlds have known much discord in the past centuries. They even began to forget each other. I believe my brother saw the advantage of a king who comes from a line of both spirits and men. That's a new way to do things – but new ways are exactly what we need. My brother chose you, and he never chose unwisely."

"Nimue has the same blood as me," Arthur says, shooting me a guilty look. "She can take the crown. She could, if she wanted to."

"No," I whisper. "I love you, Arthur. But... I love my child more."

Arthur is silent for a moment. "Is this what you want for me? Do you think I should do this?"

In all honesty, I don't have an answer for him. I simply don't know what to think at this moment.

"I want it for you." Goldilocks' voice is clear and powerful. She walks forward and turns Arthur away from me so that he must look at her. "From the moment I found you, I have believed the Fish King's promise: that you were king as long as he was locked in the tower. I still believe him."

"Take the crown, Arthur," Lance says. "I didn't meet any other person along the way who would be better suited better for the job. In the name of everything that is good and fair, take it! No one will object."

"Bravo," a faint voice pipes up from the floor. I didn't see Val regain consciousness, but now he makes an attempt to sit up. "Just put the cursed thing on your head, alright? And then see if you can use that royal power of yours to get rid of this fog. I'd like to see the sun again."

"You took an oath for me," Goldilocks says. She moves closer to Arthur and grabs at something resting on his chest. It's the seal pendant. She clenches her fist around it. "You swore it on something that really matters, remember? Does this talisman mean enough to you?"

It's hard to see what's going through Arthur's mind. For a long, silent minute he stands in our midst. I feel a tight knot in my stomach when he nods slowly. The words that follow seal his fate: "It means everything to me. And you're right – I did take an oath on it." Arthur takes an audible, deep breath. "I accept the crown, and the task that comes with it. If that's what you all want from me, then I'll do it... I will be the Fisher King."

I don't want this for him, but Arthur doesn't pay attention to me. He only pays attention to Goldilocks. A smile softens the strange countenance of the Hunting Lord. "In my old brother's halls I will crown and anoint you. Kneel on the floor."

I watch as my brother staggers for a moment. I watch as he kneels, his knees on the dirty tiles, where a few spilled drops of blood from the Fisher King remain, and have left a faint stain. I hold my breath as long as he sits kneeled like that, his head slumping forward, his golden curls hiding the emotions on his face, while the heavy crown comes down on his head. The crown is a little too big for him, causing him to slightly tilt forward.

"Lift up your head," the Hunting Lord instructs. My brother looks up obediently. A single drop of blood glistens on the Hunting Lord's fingers. I can't tell if it's from the old Fisher King or from his reborn brother. In a movement that seems far too careless, he rubs the blood onto Arthur's forehead.

"In the name of my brother, and for the salvation of the Worlds, I bestow upon you the title of Fisher King. And I grant you the right to claim the crown and throne for yourself, as long as the sun rises in the east and sets in the west. In the name of all the people and spirits, I command you to be guided by wisdom and compassion." He falls silent and my little brother does not move. "Stand up now, King Arthur, Fisher King. It is done."

Arthur stands up. He looks at all of us and my heart painfully squeezes when I see how lost he looks. His curls fall into his eyes. Arthur blinks and brushes them aside. In the same movement, he pushes the crown a bit straighter.

I rush to him and wrap my arms around him. "Are you alright?"

"I'm fine." He meets my embrace, but then gently pushes me aside. "I feel different."

"Different? How so?"

"I don't know." His eyes look dreamy as he lets his gaze wander through the throne room. "Like there's more air than before. Like the ground is firmer. It's like I've found something again, something I lost, without knowing it." His gaze returns to me. "You are sad."

"I don't want to let you go," I say.

"I don't want to lose you either, Nim. But I think I need to be here. Right now, anyway."

"That may be true." I wipe my eyes dry and try to smile. "Long live the king."

"Be joyful, not sad," the Hunting Lord says. "You both have a job to do. The king must build up this world. And you, my dear sea child, I think you know where you belong."

"Yes," I agree.

"And what about you?" Arthur asks the Hunting Lord.

"My task is not yet complete either," he replies. "In my madness I have ruthlessly taken what did not belong to me. Some lives have been so thoroughly destroyed that there's nothing left to heal." He looks at Cormack's dead body. "I hope to atone for some of the damage by giving back what I have taken. Bring all the souls to me; I will return them to their bodies."

"Can you do that?" Goldilocks asks. "After all this time we can still be saved? Sweet Gwenhael." Those last words come out as a sob.

"I will start here, in the tower. Then I will look for the souls that are still wandering around elsewhere. I give you my word on that."

Goldilocks turns to the window. "Look, the fog is lifting! Arthur, I see spirits gathering under the tower. All sorts of spirits."

Arthur just smiles.

32

KING AND PROPHET

Fresh blood clings to Val's forehead. This time it's not coming from his own scratches and wounds, of which he has plenty. The Hunter Lord has cut open his own palm with Arthur's knife; the steel sizzles against his skin and the blood wells up like water from a spring. The blood on Val's face is a mark.

I feel sorry for him. He's completely exhausted, as if the end of the fight has consumed his strength. Every breath he takes seems to hurt him. And he looks scared.

"Can I change my mind?" he asks. "You are my friends, at least. I don't know where I'll be when I wake up. Or with whom."

"You'll wake up in a place where people can take care of you," I reassure him. "Ask for Sini. Explain to her what happened. Mention my name and she'll believe your story."

"You won't be alone," says GWN softly. "If I understand correctly, we'll all wake up in the same building."

Arthur gingerly embraces Val and GWN. "I have no words to thank you."

"Good luck, my friend," GWN says. "I don't envy you."

Arthur lets out a hollow laugh. "You deserve a chance at your own life. Maybe we'll see each other again one day."

"Until that day, perhaps." Val slowly exhales. If he wanted to say something else, he no longer has the strength to do so.

The Hunting Lord nods at him. "Blood connects, blood remembers. Let your soul set out to find your body again." With his blood, he draws the same mark on GWN's forehead, and the boy smiles. The Hunting Lord crouches down and gently blows into their ears. Is he whispering a word? I can't hear it. Val and GWN close their eyes and suddenly turn pale. Their bodies slowly fade away and become transparent. Next to me, Goldilocks lets out an irrepressible sob, and Arthur gasps. I understand exactly what's happening, because I have experienced it myself dozens of times: the spirits of the lost boys are finally returning to the place they came from.

A few moments later, there's nothing to remind us of their presence in the tower.

"Can you imagine what they're feeling now?" Goldilocks asks. Her voice gives me the impression that she, for one, can't imagine it at all. "Now they will open their eyes and..."

"They will be safe," I reassure her. "The Asclepius Congregation is not as it was when we were in it."

She looks at me without saying anything in return. Arthur has walked over to Morgana and is trying to convince her to get up by quietly speaking to her. When she doesn't react, he grabs her gently. Like a doll, she lets herself be pulled up and led to the Hunting Lord.

"Are you hurt?" I ask. Her face is covered with scratches and dried blood crusts, her eyes are swollen and red-rimmed. When I touch her arms, she doesn't flinch. No, the pain on the outside doesn't bother her. It's the pain on the inside that has broken her.

"It's going to be alright again," Goldilocks says hesitantly.

"No." Even Morgana's voice is dull. "It isn't."

The Hunting Lord lifts her chin and applies the seal made of his own blood to her. When he breathes his silent breath into her ear, a brief shiver goes through her body. Then she's gone, like a patch of mist falling apart.

Arthur turns to Goldilocks and takes her hand in his. For a moment he seems to be lost for words. When he speaks, his voice is remarkably thick. "Your turn. Remember: you'll wake up on an island. My family can help you get back to Gwennec. I think you should go at the same time as Lance, and you should find each other again as soon as possible."

Goldilocks shakes her head. "Let Lance go first. I... I'd rather wait, until everyone has had their turn."

"You and Lance are the last," Arthur says. "Green didn't make it. Nimue doesn't need help and I'm staying here."

Lance clears his throat. "I was actually thinking of staying here. I think Goldilocks feels the same way."

"What?" Arthur says. "No, Lance. You still have a whole life to lead on the other side. You deserve to be where you really belong, and I want you to stay together. To look out for each other."

"And who will stay with you?" Goldilocks asks. "Do you think I will abandon you here while I sit on some distant island, mourning your lifeless body?"

Arthur looks down at her in bewilderment.

"Katell, think about this carefully," I warn her. "We don't know what will happen to you if something goes wrong with your body. That goes for Lance too."

"I'm not Katell anymore," the girl says. She keeps her eyes fixed on Arthur. "I don't remember Katell. The things I remember from that other life are all about fear and cold and pain. I know where I want to be."

"Goldilocks, you might regret this. I don't want to be the reason you have regrets..."

"Sire, you're a fool," she says. "You have a good heart, but you're not very bright. That's why you need me."

"But..."

"Be quiet," she instructs him. She grabs his shirt, pulls him towards her and presses her lips to his. I awkwardly look away when her kiss turns deeper. Lance has focused all his attention on a few faded murals around the throne.

Finally, I clear my throat. That jolts Arthur out of his stupor. I have to admit that Goldilocks has a point, because he does look pretty foolish with that silly look in his eyes and that sheepish grin on his face.

"I'm convinced," he declares. "If she can live with it, so can I."

"You be careful," I say. "If you are so easily persuaded, she'll be wearing your crown in no time."

Arthur shrugs his shoulders, grinning. Then he turns to Lance. "What about you? Are you really sure?"

"If I don't have to kiss you for it."

"I'm glad I have some friends left," Arthur admits. "And relieved that I don't have to bury Green on my own."

Goldilocks slips her hand into his. "We'll do it together."

I myself am more than a little relieved that I don't have to leave my little brother behind on his own. And it's clear that he doesn't need me for everything anymore. I ignore the sharp sting of jealousy and embrace him.

"I have not given up hope that you'll return one day. Until then, you'll be a good king, I'm sure."

He holds me tightly. "I wish you could stay."

"You know very well that I can't."

"I know that, Nim. Our lives have grown apart."

I sigh deeply and press a kiss to his cheek before breaking free from the embrace. "Wolf must be terribly worried."

"Wait, Nim." I don't know what Arthur is going to say, because he is interrupted by a noise behind the smashed door. All my muscles automatically tighten again, a reflex I also notice in Goldilocks and Lance.

A white wolf steps into the room from around the corner. The crow sits between her shoulder blades. A small procession of other creatures shaped like wild animals follows behind. I think I recognise the giant bear I once saw at the beach on Gulls' Island. Arthur, realising that these are no longer unexpected foot soldiers belonging to the Hunter, relaxes, but I flinch.

The wolf bows her head. "Hail, young Fisher King."

"Greetings," Arthur replies after a short hesitation.

"Forgive us for the unannounced visit," the bear says. "We have sensed the death of the old king, and the resurrection of the new one. All the Second World is buzzing with rumours. The fog is receding, and our people are returning through the openings that are forming. We are the vanguard. We have come to welcome you."

Arthur bows his head in acknowledgement.

"We have also come to ask about the White Prophet."

"No," I say, before Arthur can say anything. "The answer is still no! My child stays with me."

"We have not come to ask you again," says the wolf with a snarl that can only be interpreted as hostile. "We are here to appeal to the king. This is a matter that concerns our world, child of the sea. The White Prophet is a matter of our people, and therefore, of our king."

"Don't forget your place, wolf," the Hunting Lord says. He doesn't have to raise his voice to be heard. "Your king is part of the tribe of man and the White Prophet has always been there for the Two Worlds."

"Mighty Lord," the wolf murmurs. She bends by lowering her paws and pressing her belly to the ground. "That's true. And yet, we were promised the new White Prophet as soon as he was born. The shaman has already given birth to the child. Yet she refuses to give it to us."

"The baby stays with my sister," Arthur says unexpectedly. All heads turn towards him. For a moment my brother looks surprised, not yet used to his new status. He quickly recovers, raises his chin and lets his gaze roam over all the spirits present. "The child stays with his mother. A child shouldn't grow up alone, should it? Nimue and I know what happens when family falls apart... I won't let that happen to my newborn nephew."

"But sire, Fisher King," murmured the white wolf. "A White Prophet is needed. The Two Worlds are still unbalanced and the damage that is done is almost irreversible. If people and spirits are to make progress, we need a guide who will tread the right path before us, who will mediate between our two species. In times of great peace, a White Prophet has always be our leader."

"Is that so? Will a White Prophet help both worlds to come together again in harmony?"

"Yes, Sire. This is how it should be."

"Then *I* shall be your White Prophet," Arthur declared. "I have come from the other side. I know that world, I love it, as I am beginning to love your world also."

"Sire, you are only half a spirit." The white wolf seems uncomfortable. "A part of you lies on an island, your spirit is still bound to the body of flesh and bone. A body that will decay in time. When that happens, you will perish too."

Arthur frowns. "Does that make it impossible to be the White Prophet?"

"Yes, Sire. To walk between the Two Worlds, you must be one. Complete in spirit or complete in flesh."

Arthur is silent for a moment, his brows wrinkling from deep thought. "I believe I could go back to that body, if the Hunting Lord would help me."

The wolf flexes her head. "Perhaps, sire. Only then you could no longer be our Fisher King. You would live there, and perhaps visit us occasionally, if you learned to be a shaman like your sister..."

"Well," Arthur says. He takes a deep breath and looks at me. "Then there's another choice: to break the connection and become fully spirit."

Those words hit me like a hammer against my chest. "Arthur – no."

"Tell me honestly, Nim. How will I find my body after months of unnatural starvation? Is there anything left of me at all?"

"Of course there is! Your body can heal. You're missing a leg, but you could learn to walk again just fine..."

"Then I will be a cripple for life." He smiles as brightly as the morning sun. "I think I'd rather be a king in this world."

"But king and White Prophet are two different jobs!" the bear protests. "One wears the crown of our country, the other reigns over the Two Worlds. That's how it has always been: the Fisher King and the White Prophet."

"I'll do both," Arthur says. "It's that simple."

"It's unheard of! There have always been two!"

"It's a new tradition – nothing more, nothing less. Like everything was new once. I will be king and prophet, while my sister's child can grow up in peace. Once he is old enough to understand, he will have a choice to make. He still has many lessons to learn before he's ready to decide his own fate, though." My brother's blue eyes are full of warmth. I no longer see a boy standing before me, but a man in the prime of his power. A king about to rise. "I promise you this, Nimue. I will keep the land of the Second World safe. As long as I live, no second Hunter will be able to rise. And you will raise your child with love and wisdom, so that Benji's chains are finally broken."

"I will," I whisper, overwhelmed by a mixture of sadness and love for him. "Wolf and I will. And I swear that you and I will never be apart for long."

"Of course not," my brother says, laughing. He takes the seal pendant from around his neck and puts it around mine. "I wanted to give this to you."

My fingers touch the cool stone as they have done hundreds of times before. "And you take my talisman, so you won't forget me." I give him the shard of the statue of Saint Gwenhael.

He puts it around his neck and seems satisfied. "I won't forget you again. And if I do, the necklace will always remind me that the task ahead is a task that we do together."

33

THE GENEROUS SKY

The smoky smell of the cooking stove wakes me up. I am lying on my bed of pelts and my body feels warm and relaxed. There's no trace of the pain I felt after the fight in the tower.

Wolf is close to me, his back to the tent opening and his arm circling my waist. And we're not alone, for between us, wrapped in a bundle of clean cloth, is our pale-skinned baby.

The moment I stir, Wolf opens his eyes and smiles at me. "Your cheeks are like roses."

"Wolf," I say hoarsely. "You must be angry. I'm so sorry; I couldn't think of another way..."

"Shhh. What are you talking about?"

I rub the sleep from my eyes and stare at his face. He looks back with a silent smile and his eyes are mild. He doesn't know, I realise. He hasn't noticed that I left my body. "How long did I sleep for?"

"Two hours, I think. You slept very deeply. Fortunately the baby slept as soundly as you; I didn't want to have to wake you to feed him."

I look at my sleeping baby. His silvery white eyelids are moving rapidly. I wonder if he has noticed anything of the events in the tower. I hope he's just dreaming his simple baby dreams. "Only two hours?"

"Maybe a little longer. Why?"

"Never mind," I mutter, pressing my face against the small bundle. "I think I was just having vivid dreams."

"I'm not surprised. You should go back to sleep, Nimue. Nánná said she can give the baby some goat's milk if you are too exhausted to feed him today."

"No," I say sleepily. "I'll feed him myself when he wakes up. After all, I am his mother."

Wolf smiles and weaves his fingers through my messy hair. "Are you feeling all right?"

"Hm-hm. Everything is fine. And it will only get better from now on."

"We have to give our son a name."

"Yes, a name," I agree, and yawn. "Soon."

Not much later I doze off again. This time it's a sound sleep, without interruptions.

The next two days are determined by my son's rhythm. I feed him when he's hungry; and when he sleeps, I rest too. Apart from the cries he emits when he wants to eat, he's a quiet child, perfectly content with being rocked in my arms and lulled to sleep by Wolf's gruff voice. Yannick patiently helps me with all the new chores. As soon as I'm awake longer and more often, she gives me the reins. I discover that even changing dirty diapers can't take away my delighted grin.

It's the end of the second afternoon when I can sit up straight. Wolf helps me get dressed, although I can do most of it myself. He presses a kiss to my lips.

"I'll send Yannick to you. I need to talk to the herders about our return to town. I hope they can lend us a better boat."

"The baby is sleeping, and I can manage," I say.

"I hate to lose sight of him for even a moment."

I chuckle and push him towards the tent flap. He disappears and I poke at the cooking stove to stoke the smouldering flames.

The tent flap is pushed aside again. Sunlight meets me eye-to-eye. Yannick enters with a steaming bowl in her hands, from which rises a sweet odour. "I thought you'd be hungry."

"Shark blood! I'm starving."

"Eat it while it's still hot." She takes the baby from me and cradles him in her arms, smiling, while I take hold of the bowl. It contains a thick, sweet porridge, which I start to devour greedily.

Yannick strokes my child's cheek with one finger. "He sleeps like a log, doesn't he?"

"He seems healthy," I say, swallowing a bite of porridge. "Nánná also said that he's completely fine. Despite his skin colour."

"He might still recover. Many babies are born too small, or with strange traits that they might outgrow later."

"Maybe he will, maybe he won't. I don't care if he stays white like this all his life." I look at the little creature in her arms. "He's perfect."

"I have another bit of news," Yannick says. "Did you see the sun shining? The mist is clearing."

"I'm glad to hear it," I say, scraping the last bits of porridge from my bowl. "I feel stronger. If you help me up, I can set foot outside the tent, maybe."

"Huh. I thought you'd be more surprised."

"I'm rather preoccupied with my child," I say, evading the question in her voice.

"Right, Nimue. Somehow you don't seem so worried about the spirits anymore.'

"Well. Maybe Arthur has won." Yannick looks at me as if she can draw the truth from my mouth. I smile at her. "Shall we go outside for a while?"

Yannick helps me fold a sling and ties it tightly. My child's cheek rests against my breastbone and I feel the warm air as he exhales. I'm surprised that he doesn't wake up as Yannick hooks her arm around mine and we get out of the tent.

I suck the fresh air deep into my lungs. So far, the summer has featured only a few warm days, but now the sun is pleasant on my face. The mist has become a translucent haze filtering the sunlight. The smell of pine needles is everywhere, mixed with the scent of smoky fires and meat being roasted. We walk without haste along a stony track winding between the tents. This is the only path in the area, clearly created by many feet walking back and forth, not because anyone deliberately wanted to build a road. The tents are very different from those in Gwennec's refugee camp. Those were small and leaky. These are made to house a full family, to cook, work, play and sleep in. Children in brightly coloured clothes trail us, pointing and shouting at each other as soon as we slow down and look back.

They're not the only ones who are unapologetically curious about us. A woman with a dog openly stares at us. I feel uncomfortable, but smile back when she flashes me a toothy grin.

"It's not surprising that they want to see who you are," Yannick remarks.

"I understand that. You pulled me into their camp half-dead and delirious."

"And don't forget that their shaman was working with you for hours. They can feel in their bones that you have something to do with the fog lifting."

I laugh out loud for the first time in days. "I can't take all the credit for that."

"Hm. Arthur again, surely?"

King Arthur, the boy who will never return to his old life. "Let's not talk about this anymore. Look... Are those the caribou?"

We have come to a field where many hooves have churned up the sparse grass. I count quickly: there are about fifteen deer-like animals, most of them without a rope around their necks. They are gnawing at the trunks of birch trees. A few calves have stuck their heads under their mothers' bellies to suckle.

"It's getting cloudy," Yannick says, glancing up at the sky. "Maybe you should go back inside before you and your little boy get wet."

"Nimue!" Wolf emerges from one of the tents together with an older man. "Should you be walking already?"

"I wanted to feel the sun," I say. "And I'm fine. My legs aren't broken."

"I can see that." He bends down and kisses his son first, and then me. "And it does me good to see you so alive. I have spoken to Arrajuoksa." The old man flashes a grin that reveals his gums. Most of the teeth in his mouth are missing. "He has promised us one of his boats. It'll bring us back a lot quicker and safer than that old raft we had to use. As soon as the salmon fishermen return, we can prepare for the trip. Arrajuoksa and his son have also promised to accompany us to the town."

"Are we leaving already?" I ask, startled. I feel strengthened indeed, but the thought of that turbulent river turns my stomach. As if my son senses something of my agitation, he chooses this very moment to open his eyes and start crying.

"We won't leave until you say we can," Wolf reassures me. "There's no rush."

"I'm sure I'll be able to travel again soon. Thank Arra... juoksa for me." The old man chuckles at the way his name awkwardly rolls off my tongue. I gently rock my baby, but his cries won't subside. "Such a hungry little boy. Yes, yes, I'm going to feed you, darling."

Wolf walks us back to the tent. Yannick leaves us alone to wash the pile of dirty rags. I settle back on my soft furs and put my baby to my breast. Immediately, his eyes close and he starts drinking eagerly. I flinch.

"Is something wrong?" Wolf asks.

"Stinging jellyfish," I sigh. "I love him, but my breasts hurt from all the suckling."

Wolf squats behind me and rests his hands on my bare shoulders. With his fingers, he gently kneads the tense muscles. "I'm sure we can find a solution to that. What's this?" He touches the leather cord around my neck. "Your seal pendant."

I'm startled, and Wolf sees it.

"I thought you had lost it. I thought Arthur had it." When I don't answer, his voice becomes more insistent. "Nimue?"

"I got it back."

"How?" he asks sharply. "When?"

"Everything is fine, our child is safe, that's what matters, isn't it?"

"You lied to me. Is that what you want to say?"

I sigh. "I was afraid you'd get angry..."

"So you just decided to not tell me anything?" Wolf lets go of me and gets up in a flash. "Nimue, you know exactly how much was at stake. You put your life at risk – worse, you put our child's life at risk!"

"No, I protected him! It's all over, Wolf! It's done. Arthur has won, the fog is lifting, the world is right again. We can live in peace, and..."

"You should have told me what you were going to do." Wolf's voice is hoarse; he sounds like he has a lump in his throat. "You always keep secrets. When are you going to trust me, Nimue?"

I stare at him in shock. "I do trust you."

He is silent for a moment. "I don't think so. You didn't trust my judgement enough to let me tell you when you reached the limit."

"If I could trust you to know when to stop, we wouldn't be sitting here," I snap. "Because you would never have come with me to Gwennec. You never meant to find me again, remember?"

Wolf opens his mouth, but doesn't say a word. He turns away from me, but not before I see the guilt in his eyes.

I silently wait until my son has finished drinking, then wrap him up in his sling and get out of the tent.

The pleasant sunlight has completely disappeared and the sky is grey as lead. As I walk down the path, small raindrops begin to fall from the clouds.

"Great," I sigh. I pull up the fabric of the sling to protect my son's head and regret not wearing a protective hood myself. I decide to find Yannick. Maybe she knows another tent in which to take refuge.

As if someone were opening the gates of a dam at that precise moment, the sky breaks open and the rain suddenly pours down in a thick curtain. My baby starts to wail.

I groan and turn around to run back to the tent. There I go again, I think guiltily, almost making another stupid decision that will end badly for my baby. This time, I prefer to swallow my pride.

The path has turned into a mudslide, forcing me to slow down before slipping. My hair is sticking to my skull and my clothes to my body. It's cold and unpleasant, yet something seems different. It takes a moment before I understand what I feel: nothing. My skin doesn't sting, there's no uncomfortable burning sensation. Carefully, I hold up my hands. The water drops roll down from my fingers, that's how wet I am. I start to shiver a little. There are no fresh burn marks on my hands, nor do I feel any on my face. Very carefully, I lift one corner of the sling. My child's head is still as white and uninjured as before.

The rain is clean. Pure. I stand between the streams of mud and stare up at the sky, my mouth open in silent amazement. Drops fall straight onto my tongue: a gift of clear drinking water, without the intervention of purification plants and plastic bottles. The world gives me what I need – for free. Just like that.

"Wolf!" I shout.

He comes out of the tent immediately and is visibly shocked when he sees me.

I laugh, no longer interested in our argument. "Look, taste it!"

"Are you crazy?" He shakes off his anorak and covers me with it. "You shouldn't be standing here. The baby…"

"No, look." I grab his wrist and turn his palm up to let him catch the rain. "Feel it. Feel how it rolls off your skin."

"I think you still have a fever…" Then, Wolf stops talking, and I see the same shock run through him that I felt before.

"What do you feel?" I whisper.

"It's… wet."

"It's just wet. There's no more poison."

"I don't understand." He, too, stares at the sky, Droplets clinging to his black hair and beard. "What's happening?"

I pull his anorak towards me and wrap its ends around my baby to protect him. "The world is healing. There is a new Fisher King, Wolf... Arthur has accepted the crown. Our world and the Other World are brother and sister. When one regains its balance, the other will soon follow. I told you. Everything will be better from now on."

He puts his hands on my shoulders again, and I hardly recognise him when I look at him. He seems years younger, as if all his burdens were being washed away by the rain in this moment. "Come back inside before you both catch a cold," he says, gently pushing me into the warm tent. "And tell me the whole story. I promise I won't get angry."

And so I tell him everything. When I'm done talking, he is silent for quite a while, but it's a pleasant kind of silence.

"I'm sorry about your cousin," he says at last. "He made bad choices, but I can finally admit that underneath all the misery, he had a good heart."

"He won't be missed greatly in the Asclepius Congregation," I sigh. "Sini is sailing a tight course."

"That means the story of your uncle is over."

"Not entirely. A lot of damage still needs to be repaired, and that will take time. I know Sini will do well."

"And... you want to help, don't you?" It's as if he can look straight into my heart. "You can say it if you want, Nimue. When *The Starry Wind* sails out again, you want to be on board."

"Let's discuss that some other time," I suggest. "I need time to think about what I want to do to clean up Benji's mess."

"I've been thinking a lot about him lately."

"About Benji?" I ask in surprise. "Why?"

"Since you told me how the disease of the Fisher King spread to everything around him, I have come to believe that your uncle was not very different. He was injured, and because of that, everything around him was also destroyed."

"That's how it is," I sigh. "He had plenty of reasons to feel that pain. He didn't deserve his father's blows, nor the death of his wife and child. I wish I could've met him." I surprise myself by saying that, but know that it's true. "I wish I could have talked to him before it was too late."

"What would you have said?" Wolf asks softly.

I shrug and shift the weight of my baby to my other arm. He has fallen asleep again, content now that he is dry and warm. "Maybe I would have told him that he had to snap out of his misery. That it wasn't too late. That new children would be born into his family. That life could recover."

Wolf leans into me and strokes his son's cheek. "That family members might love each other without getting caught up in bitter feelings?"

"Yes, all that." I let out a sigh. "I think he knew that in the end. I think he tried to fix it. But he couldn't reach Mum... She was already gone."

"Maybe there's something we can do to put things right in his name," Wolf suggests softly. "I think I know a name for our son."

"Benji?"

"I was thinking of Benjamin. Would you like that?"

I look at our child's face, pure as newly fallen snow. One day, he will have to make huge decisions about his destiny in life; decisions that can change the world.

"Benjamin." I start to smile. "Yes, I do like that."

34

THE BENEVOLENT SEA

I come to a stop at the peak of the hill to catch my breath and look down. Benjamin is sleeping in his sling. He slept through almost the entire hike while I collected berries in my basket. He's a lot heavier, but just as pale as the day he was born. The summer days are almost over and during those long days, all the aches and pains in my body started to heal. Most days were cool and cloudy, a few were hot and humid. Now autumn announces itself by giving the trees a golden sheen. The forest animals changed their routes, just as I was beginning to familiarise myself with their habits. Dark red and purple berries hang from the bushes, ripening. Our little community has spent the last few days weaving dozens of baskets from willow branches to collect as many as possible before the animals steal them. I enjoy these short walks alone with my son. It gives me the opportunity to let my thoughts run free. Today, the air is crisp and the sky is clear. The coniferous trees are close together and their canopy completely covers the sky in some places. Where the branches permit it, sunlight falls down in broad bands onto the forest floor.

I look down on our cosy town in the middle of the wilderness. Little people are moving like ants from house to house and I feel a deep sense of pride for those people – how proud I am of all of us, because we created a new home from the remnants of a forgotten world.

I raise my eyes, this time to peer at the horizon. Not so far beyond the forest and the hills, *The Starry Wind* is waiting for us in the harbour.

As I make my way down, Benjamin wakes up. He whimpers a little, but lets himself be soothed by the sway of my steps, taking in the surroundings with his exceptionally bright eyes. When I enter the storage shed, Yannick greets me in her usual cheerful way.

"Where is Wolf?" I ask as I put the basket down. The berries will be preserved in the large glass jars we brought from Gwennec.

"He has gone down to work in the harbour. I heard Nanicka say that the ship is almost loaded and Mart says she's all fixed up for the trip."

Mart will make the journey there and back. On the way there, I will teach him all the tricks of the trade to navigate *The Starry Wind* safely across the sea so that he can take over my duties when Wolf and I disembark with our son.

"We have all learned a lot about life here," Yannick says. "Judikael has become an excellent hunter. She is quiet and fast and she now knows all the tracks within a twenty kilometre radius around town."

"I know. They will do well here. I don't think we'll have much to worry about when we set sail."

Yannick turns her gaze downwards. "I'd better tell you. I've decided to stay here."

For a moment I don't know what to say. "I thought... that you would come with me."

"My plan was clear when I left," Yannick says. "I planned to help and I'm the only doctor in the area. Besides, I like it here. The north is full of new opportunities."

"You could all come back with me, you know. The Hunter is gone; the Black Influenza will disappear on its own. It'll be safe back home."

"You won't be able to convince these people of that. Besides, where would they go? Most of them have lost everything and left everything behind. They might as well start a new life here."

"That's right," I admit unwillingly. "This is a good place with good people. But it's so far away."

"Maybe far away is exactly what we need," Yannick says. "Far away from Central Europe. The world has changed. We need time and space to change with it. To reinvent ourselves. But..." She looks at me and the corners of her mouth drop a little. "Nimue... You're not planning to come back again, are you?"

"I don't think so," I say softly. "There are people I need to track down – Arthur's friends. They will feel abandoned and disoriented. I know a girl who's going to desperately need my help, who needs to find a place where she can find peace again. Maybe Avalon is the right place for her. I'll be busy enough without sailing back and forth between two continents."

Yannick bites her nails, something I haven't seen her do since we were kids. "This could be our last day together. Forever?"

"For a long time," I mutter. "Unless one of us ever decides to make the crossing again."

"I'm sure," Yannick says. "Probably, perhaps... Maybe."

"Probably, perhaps, maybe." I force myself to smile. "I think we know the right way for ourselves. Oh, Yannick, I wish things were different."

She comes to me and hugs me as though she doesn't want to let go.

The crew set to sail *The Starry Wind* back to Gwennec is significantly smaller than the crew on the outward journey. The ship's holds are empty, apart from the supplies we need on the way, along with a few souvenirs and letters from the people in the town to their relatives across the sea. When *The Starry Wind* docks again in the bay by the fjord, many new people will set foot here, ready for their new lives in the great, wide north. Despite the impending cold season, they will receive a warm welcome.

The sun sinks below the endless line of the horizon, leaving only a fading glow on the water. The wind is strong on the aft deck and hits my face. The taste of salt lingers on my lips. Most of the crew have retired belowdecks. The ship's course is programmed into the computer and on a quiet evening like this, *The Starry Wind* doesn't need a guiding hand on the rudder. The fog lights cast wide beams in front of us, although it is hardly necessary. There's only a slight evening mist hovering above the still water.

Benjamin has been fast asleep for hours, safe and warm in the captain's cabin. I wonder what he thinks of the ship's swaying.

Wolf emerges from the twilight and comes to stand beside me. "Deep in thought?"

I smile. "A little."

"What are you thinking about?"

"I'm thinking about Yannick. I cannot imagine that I will never see her again. There are so many people I have had to say goodbye to already... Arthur, my mother, and now my people, my friends..."

"Never is a very long time," Wolf says softly. "Who can say where life will take you both?"

It is a thin sliver of hope, but I put it away in my heart to keep anyway. "I was also thinking about the sea. What a strange creature she is. For a long time after the tidal wave happened, I felt as though she had taken everything from me... my home, my safe life, even my mother. I never thought the sea could betray me like that." I shake my head. "I know that's silly. The sea doesn't think. She doesn't take or give because someone deserves it. She pushes and pulls, but feels nothing."

Wolf laughed. "You only realise this now?"

"Of course not. I realise something else now; that it doesn't matter how far I travel or what I do, she's always in my blood. I always hear her singing somewhere inside me. The sea has taken my father away, Wolf. She took my home, my grandmother, my village. I should hate the waves. I should fear her power. But despite everything she took from me, she also gave me my strength. My way of life. My inheritance."

Wolf lets his hand rest warmly on my lower back. "That's just life," he says. "We win and we lose. Even if we fight to the death to keep what we love."

"I will always fight for you and Benjamin," I say.

"I know that. Though I hope you've fought your last fight for the time being. Sometimes life also grants us... how do you say?" He laughs again. "A favourable wind and calm waters to sail home in."

I lean my elbows on the railing and feel cold water drops, splashing against my face. Above, the sky shows me a breathtaking spectacle: stars populate the sky and are as great in numbers as there are fish swimming below us. The moon's full silver circle hangs between them like a mother amongst her millions of children.

"Full moon," I say. "By the next full moon, we'll be home."

EPILOGUE

TOGETHER

I stand barefoot in the foaming surf. My skin is wet, cold, and sticky from the sand. I'm close to where our house once stood. My son is splashing in the waves in front of me, delighted to kick the thick, white foam flakes and make them fly. He grows so fast – my strange, beautiful boy.

Wolf said he and Rona would wait for us at the edge of the dunes, where the people of Gwennec have rebuilt a small church. Despite all our travels, he can never really feel at ease by the sea, but he knows I have to come here from time to time, just to wade through the water and bring our son to the place where I was born.

Behind us, the bells of St Gwenhael are ringing out. Last night, they called us to Skippers' Mass, and their sound led us through the deepest valleys of the night. No longer do we expect destructive storms every day, but we still pray for the fishermen who go far out to sea with their boats. And I prayed for that one fisher boy, who ventured out further than all the others, to come to me. I have prayed and waited for a while now.

Presently, a thin mist rises up from the sea. I hold my breath in anticipation. The wisps of mist seem to move of their own accord, almost dancing, until at last I see them transform into the shape of a person. He comes towards me like the old Fisher King before him once did. It seems as if he's walking on water, behind the surf, where the water is deep and freezing cold. But he's not on my side of the world; he never will be.

The mist finally lets him pass and he takes on a clearer shape. As before, I'm sharply reminded of the fact how differently time passes in his world. He now towers over me – a man in the prime of maturity. The gold of his curly hair glimmers beneath the brighter gold of his crown. But haven't I grown up too?

Once, we were running side by side along this same beach, chasing our kite. Now I am on this beach with my son. During these long, strange years, life has taken away so much from us. And life has given us even stranger things in return. In the end, I have enough to be thankful for, just like my brother.

He kisses me on the cheek. In turn, I embrace him. His touch is different from before. I can feel him, and at the same time he doesn't feel quite human. Behind us, the sound of the bells suddenly stops. The sun has risen from behind the edge of the world; a fresh, new morning has dawned. I call my son and he rushes towards me through the surf on his short legs. Just before he reaches us, he slips and falls face first into the mud. His cries instantly join those of the seagulls diving and flying in circles above our heads.

"Let me," Arthur says, lifting the little white boy. Benjamin immediately stops crying and chuckles in delight when he recognises his uncle. It's still strange to see him in Arthur's arms. Sometimes I catch myself being afraid that Arthur will suddenly fade away and accidentally take Benjamin with him. Of course, that never happens. And one day, Benjamin himself will walk from this world to the Other World. Perhaps, I think, a combination of concern and amusement crossing my mind, he will even accidentally stumble across that boundary and upset the delicate balance between the Two Worlds. But even then, I know that my brother will be there for him, and teach him the things that neither I nor Wolf can about the Other World.

For the time being, it is enough for me that we can share exuberant laughter. That Arthur can hook his almost transparent arm through mine – that we can take a slow walk along this coastline that is so familiar to us both. We lift Benjamin between us and let him fly. He laughs out loud. Arthur and I exchange quiet smiles and lift the boy up high again.

We do it together.

www.ingramcontent.com/pod-product-compliance
Lightning Source LLC
Chambersburg PA
CBHW021806130726
47987CB00010B/3035

9789493265929